To Ms. Michelle Anton & family -

Best wishes!

Sara Samarasinghe

April 26th, 2008

iTeenBooks
P.O. Box 171
Middletown, NJ 07748

First published by iTeenBooks 8/28/2007.

ISBN: 978-0-9798997-0-6 *(sc)*
ISBN: 978-0-9798997-1-3 *(hc)*

Library of Congress Control Number: 2007934926

Printed in the United States of America

This book is printed on acid-free paper.

Cover design and illustrations by Sara Samarasinghe

Gotta Love High School by Sara Samarasinghe

Summary: Four high school juniors meet and befriend one another, bonding to deal with athletic and social issues.

iTeenBooks

Acknowledgments:

My heartfelt thanks go out to my parents, sister, entire extended family in both Sri Lanka and Australia, to Bob, and to all of my friends for their never-ending support.

To Sam, who will always have the best sense of humor around, no matter what we'd say. Otherwise, there would be no 'point.'

Table of Contents:

Prologue

"Mom, I'm going out back," sixteen-year-old Brooke called as the door swung shut.

"All right, but don't stay out too late." Mrs. Dawson watched as her daughter gracefully cut through the thin layer of snow, leaving light footprints behind. Blades of browning grass peeked through the whiteness. "Dinner will be ready soon, and you didn't finish all of your homework."

"I know, Mom, don't worry. I'm just going to the shed for a little while. I'll be back soon."

"Okay, honey, but don't forget."

Brooke nodded back as she flew through the yard, happy and carefree. She was always glad to be home from high school each afternoon. It wasn't that she disliked learning. She always tried to maintain a positive attitude about academics, and usually did very well. However, Brooke was a very shy person who tended to avoid her classmates, and so they left her alone with the exception of Trevor Stevenson, her best friend. He was very nice, but sometimes he would obsess over his dream of becoming the star of the basketball team a little too much. It was lonely from time to time when Trevor wasn't available, but she always managed to pull through by keeping herself company.

She visited the large shed which stood in solitude in the midst of the yard. There Brooke would do whatever came to mind and claimed her attention. The main reason she spent most of her time in the building was to practice gymnastics, but sometimes she would also imagine various things, of what she could become, what she could be if she would just open up.

Brooke wanted what many other girls wanted but could not have: to be a cheerleader just like Sophia Garrison and her posse.

Sophia Garrison was the tall, thin captain of Saffrondale High School's varsity cheerleading squad, and she had the best looks in the entire class. She had the thin, naturally pin-straight, shining blonde hair that flew back behind her shoulders when she walked down the hall. Her sparkling blue eyes and smile only complemented her cheerleading uniform. She was extremely friendly, not to mention intelligent.

But since Brooke was quite the anti-social girl, and worried about baring her soul, Sophia hadn't noticed her, since Sophia was always so busy with popularity, cheerleading, and doing well in school. Brooke, on the other hand, had a personality that was very similar to Sophia's, but it was hidden within her. Brooke was a pretty girl, with long locks of auburn hair that curled loosely past her shoulders, and her blue-green eyes. She had a good sense of fashion and was just as tall and thin as Sophia.

Sophia didn't mind being popular – in fact, she rather enjoyed it – but secretly wished for a real best friend, and not just the kindly superficial 'friends' that practically worshipped her. Those girls just wanted to *be* Sophia – or be super close to her for show. Oh, and to snag a totally hot guy.

But it wasn't as if Sophia could look towards a male best friend, although Brett Evans, star of the basketball team, was a great guy who didn't have a romantic interest in her; and since the feeling was mutual, they were pretty good friends. But with the exception of Brett, almost all of the guys around Sophia were equally obsessed as the girls were, but they didn't want to be Sophia. They wanted to be *with* Sophia. She couldn't tell which was worse. Among all of those mercurial and totally confusing people, Sophia didn't really know anyone that she could really be friends with other than Brett, let alone anyone she could fall in love with. Of course, there was Trevor, that cute guy who sat next to her in English class, but he was probably only nice to her because of who she was. Besides, he was very close with some other girl, and to Sophia, they seemed to be pretty into each other. The mysterious girl who Trevor was friends with was Brooke, of course. Sophia was mistaken when she thought that he liked Brooke as more than a friend.

So there really was nothing to stop Brooke from becoming the best of friends with Sophia, but only time could create a bond.

Chapter 1:

The First Night

Brooke

I always spend my free time in my shed.

Trevor's always busy practicing basketball. He says it's for when he gets with Sophia. I personally think it's as impossible as me becoming a cheerleader and Sophia's best friend. But oh, no, Trevor says we should be ready.

So maybe I should practice cheerleading.

But what do I do?

I don't exactly know any cheers, although I do think that I can yell pretty loudly.

I mean, sure, Trevor and I have been to a few basketball games. He's always obsessing over learning new moves, and so he begged me to come because he didn't want to go alone. But after he said that the squad would be cheering, I went to see what they really did.

Their stunts looked snazzy (don't ask where that came from), but difficult. I'm flexible, and I'm a pretty good gymnast, but that's about it. Besides, I wasn't exactly paying much attention to them.

I was kind of watching Brett Evans, *the* star of the basketball team. He's been nice to me, I guess, during the occasions that in math class he asks to borrow a pencil. At least I can prove he's noticed me.

But I am *so* getting distracted by the memory of his face.

That pair of sparkling blue eyes.

His sandy light brown hair.

Streaked with highlights of natural brownish-blond, golden as the sun.

Sitting there in math class, just watching the back of his head and being so happily surprised every time he talks to me? It's just as relaxing as lounging on the beach with your sunglasses on, tanning and sipping an ice cold lemonade. The sun beaming down on you. No worries in the world. Can't you hear the waves crashing against the rocks? Feel the warmth of the golden rays and the spray of the ocean mist?

Well, okay. So maybe I can't exactly kick back and relax during pre-calc. And it's not like if I snuck out of school, I'd be able to get to a beach within an hour. But whatever.

It's really *his* fault that I'm digressing.

Ha, ha.

Who am I kidding?

It's not his fault he's so hot and every single girl at Saffrondale

High has a crush on him. Guess he just got the good genes.

Lucky guy.

But anyway.

I've been saving up my allowance at intervals to buy gymnastic equipment that would help me learn some more techniques. When I found this place in our backyard, I saw some hooks hanging from a rafter. There were all kinds of little pieces of junk in the corners. A little cleaning up, a little shopping here and there, and voila! I'd pretty easily managed to get a lot of equipment necessary to build a miniature area for gymnastics. So from seventh grade till now – or almost four times that I've chickened out of auditioning for cheerleading – I've built up a few of the bare necessities for gymnastics.

For example, Trevor helped me out a little with using some of the leftover wood that I cleaned off.

We built a balance beam and used some of his dad's stuff (my dad isn't exactly a huge fan of other people – especially his teenage daughter and her best friend – touching his expensive tools that he, like, never uses except, like when my mom is like, 'Okay, you absolutely have to fix this *now*,' but Trevor's dad is totally cool with it – he actually begs Trevor to use his carpentry things) wood polish and an electric sander and some other stuff that I can't really name from lack of common knowledge, to add the finishing touches to everything.

The chains that I found worked fine with some heavy-duty plastic rings for me to swing around on.

Add in the mat and the costs of some gymnastic books and outfits, and I had the perfect place and equipment necessary for practicing my stunts.

But I had to pay Trevor back by playing basketball with him

for weeks on end. It was still worth it, though, because now I can spend time on practicing all my stunts.

Sometimes I wonder if cheerleading is the right thing for me.

But I can never bring it up with Trevor.

He'll always say, "Brooke, of course it is. Then you can do gymnastics *and* cheer for me at the same time."

I think in response, 'But then who will cheer for *me*?' Every single time. I'd never say that aloud to him, though. Trevor's helped me enough. I really have got to be grateful for that.

I love gymnastics so much, but cheerleading *is* kind of gymnastics, not to mention it's my way to really shine in school, so I'd definitely go with it.

That is, I would if I had the chance.

But after what just happened, I guess now I'm really going to be practicing a lot. Or at least, I'll be pretending to practice.

The exciting event that I mentioned a second ago was beyond fate. It started with the aerials.

One of my best stunts is the aerial, and it isn't really even a stunt. It's not much, either, and even though I can do the back handspring, it's kind of wobbly. I've spent so much time practicing all these different types of cartwheels and stuff, and lately I've been touching up my front handspring.

So imagine this.

I'm right in the middle of a running start, and just as soon as I'm starting to dive down, my cell phone starts ringing and someone starts pounding wildly and forcefully on the door of the shed.

I almost had a spaz attack.

I mean, seriously.

I need to have concentration when I'm practicing my

gymnastics, right? Otherwise I could pull a muscle or break a bone.

That being a solid fact…

Who would dare to bother me?

My parents think they understand that as a teenager, I need some alone time. So they wouldn't come near me. Besides, it wasn't that late, so it wasn't like they were going to have to call me into the house for dinner or something.

And I totally have a clock rigged up here. So I'm beyond good.

No, even now, hours and hours later, I'm putting away my textbooks and homework up in my bedroom and it's a quarter to twelve. It could never have been late then. I've been up here working for *hours* on end.

So anyway.

Then I thought that I might as well answer my phone.

"Hello?"

"Brooke!" It was Trevor.

"Oh, hey, Trevor. Wait, hang on, someone's outside the shed. Let me just open the door," I stalled for a second.

"Oh, my God, Brooke, it's me!"

I froze. "Wait…what?"

"I'm outside the door. Hurry up," Trevor demanded impatiently. "I've got major news for you!"

"Um. Okay. I'm coming."

I dragged myself up off the mat and practically flew to the door because of the anxiety in his voice. Swinging the door open, I stepped out of the way to let Trevor into the shed.

He slipped in and dried his feet off, leaving a puddle of slushy snow on my scruffy little rug.

~ Chapter One ~

"*What* is *that*?" I asked curiously, catching a glimpse of a piece of wrinkled paper in Trevor's hand.

"Oh, this. *This* is merely our ticket to stardom."

"Excuse me?" I closed the door.

"Read," Trevor commanded dramatically, thrusting the paper right into the personal space of my face.

I scanned the printout of a school sports article quickly.

Saffrondale High School….Scouts…Wednesday… December…Time…Article…Posted: 8:10 P.M…Staff Writer…

And then?

I saw it.

My heart began to beat faster and louder.

"Oh, my God. Are you serious?"

Trevor nodded triumphantly.

I was suddenly speechless.

Well, almost.

"Oh, my God. That's, like, so coincidental. But what do you expect us to do? Attempt to try out?" I asked skeptically.

His ears turned a little redder, and this time I knew for sure that it wasn't because of the biting cold.

Actually, I've always got a portable heater working, tiny or huge depending on its availability, so the ice is always thawing around the shed.

But that's beside the point.

Trevor grabbed me by the shoulders and gave me a little shake. Desperate much? "Look at it this way, Brooke. All the 'good' people tried out already, and most of them made it. So there's nobody left anyway but us."

"So? The people that didn't make it are bound to try out again, and even if you might make it on the team, I won't make the squad. The 'bad' people would dwarf me!" Needless to say, I was not consoled any more or less by those words. Who would be?

"It's never going to kill you to try, Brooke," he said softly, looking me straight in the eye and his voice sounding promising. "Trust me, even I can tell that you've improved a lot over time, and now I think you're good enough. Besides, everyone knows that what doesn't kill us makes us stronger."

Then I made the connections behind the scenes.

Somehow I knew that he just wanted me to try out the same time he did. This wasn't about me making the squad. It was about him wanting my support. And for some odd reason, I guess he thought that this was the only way. That poor child.

That's really the only reason I agreed to it.

Maybe I thought it would give him the courage to make the team, and I did want the best for my closest friend (and only, but I like to look at that as a small and therefore unimportant detail).

But I'll admit that even if I did want Trevor to be happy, I also wanted him to just shut up about everything.

Besides, I had plans for skipping out of the tryouts.

Guilty as I'd feel, I knew that he'd never ever be able to figure it out. He'd just think I didn't make it onto the squad. Plus I'd earn his sympathy.

Ooh, I can be such a bad girl sometimes.

But I guess that maybe the thought of finding a way out later made me say to Trevor, "Okay, I'll do it."

Sophia

I can't believe how tired I get from cheering!

~ Chapter One ~

I'm finally back in my room after the longest game I can remember where the score was actually really close.

But I kind of wish I didn't have to scream all these chants all the time. My voice gets so hoarse.

And wearing that micro-mini?

Yeah, not the best when I'm walking home in the winter. There's snow on the ground, for God's sake. At least for gymnastics I can wear clothes outside according to the weather – over whatever costume I have to wear. Or at least I can change.

But that's beside the point. I shouldn't complain when I'm the squad's captain. If I complain, the rest of the girls might start quitting or something.

I mean, I create the trends, so I might even start a quitting trend without even quitting. How weird would that be?

Oh my God, something totally worth gossiping about happened right before the game, though.

The second lead guy, Jackson Everett, got kicked off the team for some reason. I'm not sure why, but I'll definitely find out tomorrow. It'll be all over the school within a few hours, I can assume.

The team is holding try-outs for a replacement player. Coincidentally, we also have an opening, since Isabelle moved to New Jersey. That poor girl. She had to leave Saffrondale.

No one tried out yet, so we have to use really awkward cheers, since we don't have the right amount of people. It's just too bad that Isabelle just had to be practically the most important cheerleader after me.

Now we need someone who's really good.

I don't have that many ideas about any girls with the possible potential to be the second best cheerleader on the squad.

But I think I have an idea for the basketball team.

I was walking around the area the other day, and I went by Trevor's place – yeah, accidentally-on-purpose. I have to say, it's a really nice house.

And I saw him practicing all these basketball moves on his court.

The really good news about it? He was amazingly good.

I'm going to talk to him tomorrow (during English, duh, I mean, that's where we met!) about tryouts and subtly hint that he should try out. This is totally not based on the fact that he's so nice. I really do think that he would be a good choice for the team.

Last time we had a game, Trevor was there. I swear I saw him somewhere mixed in with the crowd, high up on the bleachers. But I also know that he was with that girl that I still don't know. I have to find out who she is, even if Trevor is totally out of my league. He's probably the nicest guy that doesn't seem shallow.

Maybe I can find out a little more about the other girl. She seems to be pretty nice, too, and she was practically doing back flips right next to Trevor's basketball court. I could find out if she's interested in trying out for the cheerleading squad.

Hey, you never know. She could be that really great best friend that I never had. She might be getting sick of just being friends with Trevor (her boyfriend, maybe?).

Not that I ever would.

Of being his best friend, plain friend, or girlfriend.

Take your pick.

Even though I do know which one *I* would pick.

Ha, ha.

But I really do hope that Trevor decides to try out for the team upon my attempt to convince him, if need be. I'm sure he would make it, and Brett Evans seems to like me enough as a person to do anything for me. Maybe I could ask him for a little help with getting Trevor on the team without revealing anything else about Trevor.

Okay.

Gotta get this straight.

Even though Brett's the star of the basketball team, and I'm the captain of the cheerleading squad, and that means we would totally go together perfectly, I still wouldn't want to be with him.

I also know it would go against a few social rules if I dated a guy that no one knew – a.k.a. Trevor. But since it's me, maybe they'd all make an exception. I am pretty loved, you know. It can totally come in handy.

Plus I could just…make Trevor well-known in school. You know. Popular. Then I'd be able to go out with him in a heartbeat. And I would. It's just that…he really should ask *me* out. I can't ask *him* out. That could be a bit of a problem, considering what *my* social status is.

Oh, my cell phone's ringing. Wait a second…It's Brett!

It's amazing how he practically read my mind and called me up!

Trevor had better thank me tomorrow morning right after I make this conversation go totally well.

"Hello?"

"Hey, Sophia, what's up?"

"Nothing really. Just relaxing. You?"

"Same. I still can't get over what happened before the game though. It's totally crazy, right?"

Oh, my God, he brought up the subject of the game!

All I have to do was maneuver around the basketball stuff and ask if he was looking for someone to try out to be a replacement team member.

"Yeah, I know!" I respond. "So you guys have to find someone to replace Jackson, right?"

"Yeah. I don't know anyone who could, though. That's why I called. Got any suggestions?"

Perfect! Now all I have to do is play it cool.

"Um, I don't know. I know there's a guy who I've seen playing basketball. He seems really good."

"Really? Who?"

"I think his name is Trevor," I say nonchalantly.

I'm not *really* entirely sure what his last name is, though. It *sounds* like it's Stevenson. It *looks* like it's Stevenson. But then again, his handwriting isn't the neatest I've ever seen. Then it's also true that no guy's is.

"Trevor…" Brett trails off in thought. "Hmm. You know what his last name is, by any chance?"

"Stevenson, I think."

Oh, well, it can't kill if I get his last name wrong by a little bit. It might even work for the better.

"Yeah, Trevor Stevenson."

Oh, come on. Who am I kidding? His last name *is* Stevenson. And I *know* it.

"Oh. Do I, um, know him?"

"I don't know. But I really think you should include him in the tryouts. Whenever you have them, that is."

In my head I'm hoping that Brett would agree.

"Sure. Since you seem to really think that he's that good, we might just test his skills and then automatically add him to the team."

Oh, yes! I so second that motion! Go, Brett! Go, Brett! Go, go, go, Brett!

"Brett, that would be awesome! I'm sure he'd love it! Is there anyone else that you're going to evaluate?"

"I don't know. I'll ask Coach Davidson tomorrow. Talk to Trevor and find out exactly how interested he is."

"Sure. I'm almost positive that he'll be willing to try out for the team. He's really, really nice."

Seconds after those words fly out of my mouth, I wish with all my heart that I could take them back.

The last thing I need to kill my reputation is Brett Evans thinking that I like Trevor Stevenson.

But thankfully, Brett doesn't even react. He's probably so excited about getting the perfect addition to his team.

This, of course, will most definitely be Trevor.

I have total confidence in the future.

But oh, my God. How stupid am I going to get? I mean, what does Trevor's being really nice have anything to do with him trying out for the basketball team? I seriously want to scream at myself.

"Great, then. Thanks, Sophia. I guess I'll see you tomorrow at school, then. But one more favor?"

"Um, okay. What is it?" I ask him tentatively.

"Don't mention anything about Trevor and basketball stuff to anyone else, okay? I want to keep the entire situation down low if it doesn't work out with the team," he mutters to me in a really low and quiet tone.

I'm silent for a moment, realizing how right he is and that it might not work out with everyone.

I mean, what if Trevor really doesn't want to be on the team?

Uh oh. Tragedy!

"Sophia? You still there?"

"What? Oh, yeah, sure. Don't worry about it."

"What's the matter with you? You zoned out."

"Sorry. Just thinking," I try to salvage the situation.

But yet again, Brett doesn't really notice.

Or maybe he just forgot. The poor guy has been through way too much stress for one night – for a few hours, even.

I'll give him a rest in *just* a minute.

"That's cool. So, see you tomorrow?"

"Yeah. Thanks for calling."

"Sure. Thank *you* for the advice. I hope everything works out with the cheerleading and basketball stuff."

"Me, too." At least this time I don't have to say it silently.
"Oh, my God!"

"What?"

"The cheerleading! I have to find someone for the squad. Do you by any chance know that girl with reddish-brown shoulder-length hair? She's kind of tall and thin, and she seems really quiet."

"Oh, yeah, yeah. Brooke."

"Excuse me?"

"That's her name. Brooke Dawson. She's in my math class and she sits behind me. She's really, really nice."

"Oh, really?"

"Yeah." He sounds kind of embarrassed.

I think I've caught something here. I mean, I said the exact same thing about Trevor like, two minutes ago. And I definitely didn't mean that he's just 'nice.' I meant that I liked him a little more than just that.

"Interested?"

"Did I ever say that?"

I can practically see his face turning red.

"No…but anyway. I know she's friends with Trevor," I hint.

"Oh, so Trevor's the guy she hangs out with."

"Yeah."

"But anyway, do you think Brooke would be a good cheerleader? I've seen her doing back flips and stuff. She's flexible."

"I think that'd be great. Give her a good chance."

"Of course, *Brett*," I say with the intention of teasing him. "Do you think she and Trevor are, um…?"

Okay, I am clearly at a loss for any sensible words whatsoever. But it has absolutely *nothing* to do with the trivial fact that I was talking partly about Trevor. Okay, so it's not trivial. But do I get tongue-tied when I'm talking *to* Trevor? No. I don't *think* so. So now you get it. Hopefully.

"No. Definitely not."

"Quick response," I observe.

"Oh, shut up, Sophia."

"All right, all right. Well, thanks for the advice."

"Yeah, yeah, you too. We went through this already."

I laugh. "And not a word of this to anyone until it all works out, right?"

"Sure."

"Cool. 'Bye!"

"'Bye, Sophia."

I snap my phone shut and lean back in my chair, feeling quite good about how well I made everything go.

And with the slightest bit of good luck, I have this wonderful premonition that everything is going to work out just fine, and I also know that we're all going to find out how right I am tomorrow.

Trevor

I've always wanted to try out for the basketball team. Always. But I guess I've never managed to summon the courage.

Well, really. What if I got rejected? Well, actually, there really is no 'if,' even though Brooke always tells me that there is. What would happen *when* I got rejected? I hate thinking about that, but sometimes I think that being on the team would complete my life at school.

Actually, maybe my dad would be happier, too. He says grades aren't really good enough, and that I need a real sport to get into a good college. He really wants me to go to an Ivy League school. And I'll try my best, but if I don't get in, I don't get in. It's not going to be the end of the world. I'll still get a good education, and I'll still live a great life. But to tell the truth, I'm not really thinking that much about how I'm going to get into a good college. It's junior year. I'm worried about all the work.

I can't believe how Brooke can study and get her work done all in a matter of a few hours and then have the rest of her time to do her gymnastics.

I personally think it would be better if she had a coach. But no one around here's really a gymnastics coach. So I guess that's that.

Brooke always has had the same problem as I do. We both want to be on a varsity team, but no one knows us, and we're scared of rejection.

I guess that's part of the reason why we've been best friends since practically before kindergarten.

I've always been able to talk to her. She's basically my confidante, and I always listen to her. I figured out that she kind of likes Brett Evans. But shh, that's a secret.

Brooke knows so much stuff about me, even about my secret crush on Sophia Garrison, that incredibly gorgeous captain of the cheerleading squad.

Sophia sits next to me in English class, and I can barely concentrate because of it. Really, just imagine sitting next to the prettiest, most popular girl in the grade.

For forty-one minutes. Every day.

Wow.

And she's much nicer than I thought.

In fact, I would have gone to the game today to see her cheer and pick up some new moves for my futile and totally fruitless basketball attempts, but I have so much to study, not to mention homework. I wonder how they all pull that off.

About basketball…boring news comes first. I didn't get to practice at all today. I really wasn't in the mood for cleaning off the court. I know we only got an inch of snow, but once I scrape it off, the water that's left over gets all icy. That makes it way too slippery and cold to play outside, even if it is my favorite sport.

But that's not all that I've got to say about basketball today.

Earlier this evening, I wondered if our school's team had won the game. I mean, they usually do. Since I was up in my room, I thought that I might as well check the school website to see if the scores had been posted yet. I can only describe my reaction to what I saw on the screen as a forever repeated "Oh, my God." I knew that this was definitely going to be classified as breaking news for some of the people around this area of upstate New York.

There are two official openings. These two chances could be mine and Brooke's.

I also knew that I just had to get in touch with Brooke. This is going to be one of the opportunities of our high school careers.

I forgot completely about the snow. As soon as I printed out the webpage, and I ate a quick microwave dinner since my parents were out, I was on my way to Brooke's place to pay a visit to that little backyard shed of hers.

Oh, and now? I got her to agree to try out.

I hope she won't chicken out on me. I know I would give anything to not have to try out, but I know that this time I can't give up.

This may be my best chance. Oh, and Brooke's, obviously.

All I've got to do is stop it from slipping away.

Brett

Oh, my God.

I can't believe what happened before the game. I don't know how we survived that game without our second star.

Jackson got kicked off the team for some unknown reason.

Coach Davidson was yelling at him in the office right before practice and then the next thing we know is that Jackson's walking out of the locker room without so much as an apologetic glance.

Coach didn't come out of his office for a few minutes, and then when he did, it was only to bark, "Lay-ups! Move it! Now!"

What choice did we have? By the time Coach decided that we

could stop with all of the warming up, he had cooled down a bit. Well, all right, a lot.

But then we got into practice, and after that we had the big game.

Coach said that it was the best that we had ever done. I personally think that he was just really happy to see Jackson gone. I really have no idea why, though. Something just had to have been going on that none of the rest of us knew about. I really want to know what it was, but I guess I'll find out one day.

Eventually.

But back to the info about the game.

We had been up to twenty-one points in the second half, and the other team had twenty-seven.

It seemed totally hopeless, since we were missing our second-best player. There had obviously been no time to hold try-outs, and there was nobody to fill in. So we played with what we had, and we pulled through, beating the other team thirty-six to thirty.

Even though it was a close game, the victory was enough to put Coach Davidson in the best mood we've seen him in for weeks.

As good as it is that we won, we still have to get a replacement player. And he's got to be good. I mean really good.

Since I'm the star player of the team, Coach is definitely expecting me to recruit the greatest basketball guys who aren't on the team so they can try out and we can pick the best one of all.

I don't really know any other guys that play basketball well but aren't on the team, though.

Yet I have to find a few.

Fast.

I thought there wasn't anyone I could ask for help on this,

either.

Or was there?

None of the guys on the team would have been able to help. No, scratch that. They probably wouldn't have helped even if they could.

And out of the girls that I hang out with, most of the cheerleaders are with one of the guys on the team, and they're seeing their boyfriends completely exclusively. Well, except for the ones that might be cheating, but they aren't supposed to admit that, so why would I bother wasting my own time?

This meant that only Sophia Garrison was available, and even though I don't like her that way, I guess we're pretty much almost the best of friends.

I had hoped she would know someone who could play really well. The only way for me to have possibly found out was for me to give her a ring and ask her myself. It could never have hurt to do that, since she's really nice and totally the coolest girl in school. Well, after someone else, of course. And now I'm slowly slipping away from the topic.

Not that I like Sophia that way. I think I've mentioned that before. She's one of my best friends.

Since all of my homework was done by then and I had definitely studied enough, I had the perfect time to do so.

I talked to Sophia for a while on the phone, and she gave me the best advice that anyone could have possibly given me.

She recommended Trevor Stevenson to me.

Not that I know exactly who he is, or anything.

But still.

I think it's all going to work out.

Plus she figured out that I might be a tiny bit interested in

Brooke Dawson. Which can be good and bad in a way.

I don't want to start any huge social problems, so I've been trying my best to keep that to myself. And now I just admitted it.

Oh, well, I'm sure everything will work out. It usually does around here. Except for that whole basketball issue.

But I will be off to solve that problem tomorrow.

So… I think it's safe to say that all's well that is going to end well here in Saffrondale.

Seriously.

I'm on the case.

What could be better than that?

Chapter 2:

Decision Day

Trevor

Everything's going to be amazing – thanks to Brooke, who finally agreed last night to go out for cheerleading, I really think I'm going to have a shot at being on the team. I guess it'll make me feel much better if I know that Brooke's going through the same stuff, trying out for a sport.

I mean, after I slept on it, I feel even better about the whole thing. But somehow I'm worried that this miracle might not last. It's okay, though. That's not really what matters now.

What matters most now is that I can't wait to talk to Sophia in fourth period English today! In less than five minutes, I'll be next to her! Hopefully we'll end up talking about the basketball issues, and maybe that will lead to cheerleading. Who knows? I might even be able to pick up a couple of extra details for Brooke about the tryouts.

Speaking of cheerleading, math can get so complicated and boring, especially pre-calc. But don't get me wrong. It's not that pre-calc is really that hard. It's just that Ms. Sanders, coach of the cheerleading squad, isn't exactly the most exciting teacher. No offense meant there. I know that she's Sophia's coach, and might even be Brooke's future coach. And I've only seen the top of her head from the stands, directing all the cheers and making sure everything goes smoothly. So even if she might be a kind of boring teacher, she's probably a good coach.

There was only one more minute till the bell was scheduled to ring when I thought I was going to die of boredom. Seriously. I was practically begging Ms. Sanders in my head to let us go. And finally, she did.

Now I'm just walking the distance between math class and English class. It was a long math class, and science and history were both just before that. I've got lunch with Brooke after English. Now that I think of it, I have the same lunch period as Sophia and Brett – fifth period. In fact, we all have gym together, but we never all associate during seventh period.

"Trevor!"

Whose voice is that hissing at me?

"Brooke? What's up?"

"Oh, please, Trevor, you can cut the coolness with me. You're not even in English class yet."

Please allow me to just get my point across that I do not exactly appreciate how her voice is so strongly tinged with sarcasm.

"Brooke," I repeat, confused. "What's the matter with you?"

"Look, Trevor, I don't think I want to try out for the squad. It's really not going to turn out to be a good idea after all."

"Are you kidding? Look, I'm going to talk to Sophia. Everything's going to be fine. Just relax and go to class."

"You're going to talk to Sophia? About what?"

"Oh, you know, basketball, cheerleading, that stuff."

She glares at me. Hostile. "Trevor, don't turn into a jock just yet. That position on the team isn't guaranteed for you."

Why is she being so pessimistic?

"Brooke, don't be so negative. I *know* that the place isn't reserved for me. But I've got to prove that it *should* be mine. You have to prove it to Sophia that you are what the squad needs. I have the self confidence that I need. I'm not being selfish or arrogant. You need to find your own confidence. I know that you have got it inside you, but it's up to you to find it and use it."

Brooke doesn't really look too happy, and I can't say that I blame her. After all, I just verbally slapped her in the face. That couldn't have been too pleasant.

"How do I prove it to Sophia? When?" she asks, swinging her tote bag around so she can fold her arms across her chest.

"At the tryouts."

I do understand that that's not very consoling, but what else could I possibly have said to her?

"Trevor!"

I shrug.

"Great help," she snaps sardonically. "I guess I'll have to turn to Brett. Maybe he'll be a little more considerate."

Ouch.

That stings.

"Oh, come on, Brooke. I'm not trying to make you do anything you don't want to do. I just think that this is your chance."

She softens. "I know. I'm sorry. I guess I'm a little nervous because of the sports stuff."

"No problem. Just don't be so sarcastic when you're around Brett. You might ruin both of our chances."

Brooke laughs. "I won't. Thanks, Trevor." She punches me lightly on the shoulder and heads down the hall to math.

Now I can finally get to English.

Wait…

That's definitely not my teacher's voice screaming, "I'm warning you, I have a seating chart and I know how to use it!"

I slip into the room and vaguely recognize the sub as that weird lady who the ever-famous Jackson Everett (the guy that got kicked off the basketball team) once tripped in the hallway.

Don't ask me what her name is.

No one can understand her, so we barely know. Anyway, it's not as if we'd even care, either.

One thing I can do is describe her extremely well.

Her image is one of those types that you can't erase, no matter how much you want to. She's kind of short and stout with thinning gray hair. She wears the most random clothes and can't seem to say anyone's name right.

Not only that, but she has these huge tortoise shell glasses that are about two inches thick and keep sliding down her nose every five seconds.

Plus she can't pronounce many people's names. For example, take the incident involving Asha DeSilva.

It's a classic one that *everyone* around this place knows about.

Jackson's sub had her in English class one day, or so the story goes, and it's pretty clear that Asha's name is phonetic. Easy to say.

But no, Jackson's sub couldn't say it.

I guess that the basic outline of the conversation was the following.

Jackson's sub totally mispronounces Asha's name.

Asha finally tries to help. "Um, it's Asha."

Another mispronunciation, only this time it's even worse.

"Asha."

"Asia?"

No, really, I *am* serious. Apparently, according to this commonly-told tale, that's really how she said it.

"Asha."

"Look, Asia, does it really matter how I say your name?"

And then, over a year later, she changes it to some other variant of Asia. As if that would even make sense.

But now Asha's at some Ivy League or another (great, more pressure on me – I might as well follow in her footsteps), so the name changes can't be made anymore. Yet it's still an epic story.

Get the picture?

Not that I'm judging any books by their covers, or anything.

I'm usually a pretty nice guy. That's something you've really got to know, especially if you're just meeting me.

But this lady? Believe me, she is *weird.*

So you can imagine how I felt when I found *her* in charge of our English class, which is usually taught by an almost equally boring but generally much better and younger teacher, Miss

Halitelli. It wasn't a great improvement or anything, but it would give me a better chance to talk in depth with Sophia.

Normally, my one and only concern about a substitute teacher would be that he or she would let us sit wherever we wanted to, and that would naturally raise my worries that Sophia wouldn't want to sit next to me.

But thanks to this sub, we'd be sitting in our assigned seats. And that would put me right next to Sophia, just like I've always wanted.

You can only imagine a fraction of how happy I was when Miss Halitelli assigned our seats and put me next to Sophia way in the row that's the farthest away from the front of the room. This all happened way back when at the beginning of the school year. Of course, it took a few months to break the ice, but we're still really good friends.

But I'm straying from the subject.

It's been about a couple minutes since the last bell rang, signifying the start of class. Of course, this means absolutely nothing to half the people in this crazy class...even less than the fact that we have *the* sub in the classroom. They just keep talking until the sub decides to attempt to shriek, "*Sit down!*" at the top of her voice. Maybe I forgot to mention that the top of her voice isn't exactly the loudest thing ever.

But really. Even *I'm* getting the slightest bit irritated at the noise level, which just keeps on rising endlessly.

Oh, and also, then there's Sophia, who's so admirable. She strides purposefully to the front of the room, cups her hands around her mouth and calls out, "You guys!" It gets a little quieter as everyone turns to see what *the* Sophia Garrison is up to now. "Hey!" Sophia calls irritably. "People!"

Her obnoxiousness works. The entire class is almost silent.

"Look, you guys, the bell rang a while ago. Just sit down and shut up before one of the administrators comes in here and gets us all in trouble."

Everyone stares, and Sophia stares them back down.

"You heard the girl," the sub squeaks, taking advantage of the sudden silence. "Sit down and be quiet!"

Everyone rolls their eyes and sighs, but they do sit down. This is going to be a long class.

Brooke

It looks like I've got no way out of trying out for the squad.

I tried to explain myself and my thoughts to Trevor, since guilt overrode my need to lie. Trevor's words weren't exactly the best to help me slouch into math class. I know he meant well, but even the fact that Brett was in class didn't help.

I guess I really do look kind of depressed.

But, oh, my God, I can only hope that I won't make a fool of myself once I do try out for the cheerleading squad. I have this gut feeling that I will, though. With some luck, maybe I'll be dead wrong.

"Brooke!"

Oh, my God.

Why is Brett Evans talking to me again?

"Oh, hey, Brett," I manage to say nonchalantly as I sit down at my regular desk right behind him.

"Listen, Brooke, I was just wondering if you wanted to–"

The second bell rings.

Before Brett can finish whatever he was going to say (oh,

help!), Ms. Sanders calls out loudly, "Class, settle down. We have a lot of work to do and so little time."

Thanks, Ms. Sanders. Thanks a lot.

I mean, who knows what Brett was right about to ask me?

No, don't answer that one. I don't really want to know.

The only way to pass the time along would be to do the class work and follow along as Ms. Sanders jumps around the front of the room with all of these equations chalked up on the board. How utterly *un*interesting.

Wait…What is this paper scrap Brett just slipped in with the worksheets he passed back?

I guess you know that there's an opening on the cheerleading squad. I was talking to Sophia Garrison (squad captain) and she told me that she's seen you doing flips and stuff and she thinks that you're really good. She wanted me to ask you if you would try out. Let me know.

Wow.

How does Sophia know that I'm an amateur gymnast?

The only place she could have seen me at is the shed, which is totally impossible, or…Trevor's house.

Oh, my God.

That is so not good.

I really do *not* do that well outside in the cold.

I wonder when she saw me. I definitely never saw *her*.

But I can do *so* much better when I'm in the shed. I personally don't enjoy flipping around on the asphalt. It wouldn't be a pleasant fall, so I'm careful not to do anything extreme. So I really don't even do anything good out there.

I don't know what *she's* so impressed about.

Oh, well.

I always take what I get, and this actually seems pretty good. She thinks I'm really good at this cheerleading business, and I wasn't even doing my best, not to mention that the only time I cheered was when Trevor made a tough (looking?) shot. So I think I have a pretty good chance at that opening.

Maybe Trevor was right all along. What a first.

I guess I really should respond to that note. Brett's probably awaiting an answer from me. That poor child. But I think I'll slip in a little something about Trevor and the whole basketball situation.

> *I'd absolutely love to try out for the squad! Let me know when the tryouts are! I already heard about the basketball situation from my friend Trevor. He loves playing basketball so much, and I know he was interested in trying out for the team. If you're still recruiting a player, he's most definitely available! I'll pass on the word to him. Just let* me *know.*

Hope I wasn't too bold about that.

I just really want things to work out for everyone. I guess there isn't a better time for me to give him this note than right now.

I poke him in the back. "Brett," I begin to whisper.

He reaches back and retrieves the note silently. He's reading it, obviously. I don't need to be psychic (or in my case, psychotic) to know that. I just hope that he's not going to react badly or anything. He's writing back now.

"Brooke? What's the answer?" Ms. Sanders asks, tapping on the chalkboard.

Oh, my God.

She totally caught me there. I *knew* I should have been doing the classwork. I guess all of this athletic drama is getting to me.

Well, there's no way to back out now.

Let's see what the problem is.

Thankfully it's just a simple quadratic equation. Given $3x^2 + 15y + 30 = 0$, I have to plug all of the values into the quadratic formula…

Oh, wait, there's the catch!

If I just divide the equation by 3, then…$x^2 + 5y + 10 = 0$

I think I've got it…

"Brooke?" Ms. Sanders prompts again.

Way to interrupt my train of thought.

"Negative five plus or minus the square root of negative fifteen all over two," I answer quickly.

"Good girl." Ms. Sanders smiles approvingly at me.

I can't help beaming back at her.

How absolutely perfect.

I could never mind having the coach of the cheerleading squad favor me. It's always fine that I'm kind of good at math.

But I did notice that Brett froze somewhat guiltily just as soon as Ms. Sanders called on me.

Even though he did whisper, "Nice one," back to me.

And I just beamed my thanks like an idiot.

How interesting.

Finally. He just passed back yet another note.

That's perfect! Sophia's going to be so happy! I don't

know when the tryouts are going to be, but I can get you in touch with Sophia. I'll tell her to call you. Write down your number and anything else she might need to know and I'll give it to her. Sophia also told me that she'd seen you with Trevor playing basketball. She told me he's really good, so we're probably going to let him try out just as a formality and let him on the team. She told me that he's better than most of the guys on the team, but I guess we'll just have to see how everything works out.

Yes! This is going to be so perfect, just like Brett said! But I do find it extremely interesting that he indirectly asked for my number. Maybe I'm reading into it too much, though. I usually tend to do that a lot, in addition to being paranoid. Replying to this is going to be so much fun. Well, here we go.

You can give my other note to Sophia. It has my cell phone number on it, plus a little idea of my experience.

Trevor really is a great basketball player. If you have any info that I should give to him, don't hesitate to pass it back.

I am so proud of myself sometimes. And yes, of course I did slip in my number. Hopefully he'll get my drift and slip in his. That would be great. Then I could have his number, too, since now I am so sure that he does have mine.

I just hope I won't kill his social status by becoming such good friends with him. Then again, I probably don't have the power to. It also helps that barely anyone knows who I am, of course.

Whew.

Brett's quick.

He's already hunched over on his desk, writing another note.

Anyway…next equation. I have to concentrate at least a little. In no way am I going to let Brett's distractions make me fail math. I still have to get on Ms. Sanders' good side – not only Sophia and Brett's.

Oops, never mind that.

I just got another note.

Give this to Trevor. If you have any questions, don't hesitate to call.

Okay, thanks!

No problem.

Well, that's the end of that exchange. I don't have to respond to that one at all, which is actually pretty good. Now I can direct my full attention to the board. Well, almost. I can't help being distracted by him even when he isn't even in any type of contact with me.

Maybe I had better take a look at what he wrote in that other note for me to give to Trevor…

Whoa. Not only is his cell phone number in it, but he also wrote this:

Hey Trevor –

I heard from trustworthy sources about your great

athletic abilities and that you want to try out for the basketball team. We've got one opening, as you know, and I'll definitely let you know when tryouts are going to be. If you have any questions, give me a call.

- Brett Evans

Ha!

Trustworthy sources!

That just cracks me up.

Apparently I'm one of those sources, along with Sophia. I never thought anyone would put me up to the rank of Sophia Garrison. It seems practically impossible, but I guess even the wildest things can come true.

So. Given that the above statement is true, x = the cheerleading tryouts, y = me, and therefore $x + y$ = *success.*

Another factor – only about ten minutes left to the period, which is equivalent to the ten minutes that are left till I can give this note to Trevor, plus give him the awesomely great news of all this.

I *so* like that.

Sophia

I'm so good sometimes. I can just tell.

Now that we're finally sitting quietly (well, almost) in English class with a few worksheets to do, I can relate a tale of genius. Okay, I'm exaggerating it. I always do, though. That's how you know you can't trust me with any story. Or even gossip. Oh, yes, especially gossip. I'll stretch it out a little (okay, a lot) just before

I pass it on to others. So I guess that makes me a gossip queen – kind of. After a few other cheerleaders, of course. But anyway.

The classroom was already so loud and so obnoxious that even I couldn't take it anymore. A quick glance at Trevor made me realize that he was feeling exactly the same way. Naturally, there was only one thing for me to do: make them shut up before Trevor and I went insane. Well, even if we did go insane, it would be together, so I doubt that it would be altogether *too* unpleasant. Yeah, yeah, I know how crazy you think I am. But you might think the same way, and I'd be kind enough to agree and allow you to go on thinking in your own ways of craziness. So none of us would need to go insane…we already would be insane.

Don't mind me.

But really, backtrack a bit and you'll understand. The din was enough to drive any girl (or guy, for that matter) insane. That's why I took charge by running to the front of the room before it got worse. I told everyone to sit down and shut up.

I mean, we all knew that their was nothing that Jackson's sub (as we have secretly dubbed her due to an incident involving Jackson tripping her in the hallway and consequently getting two and half weeks' worth of detention) was never going to do anything about the noise, let alone be able to. That's why the rest of those guys were all talking and yelling and acting like we were at a post-game party. There wasn't any music, yet the classroom felt like it was bursting at the seams.

So now everything's peaceful and quiet, and we're sitting in our regular seats since Jackson's sub insisted on checking the seating chart to make sure everything was in order. Personally, I have to admit that I'm actually honestly and truly happy about the seating chart.

This is one of my deepest, darkest secrets. I love sitting next to Trevor. He always makes me laugh, and he's really nice. Plus, I can totally surprise him today with some special information. That's part of the reason why I was so excited about coming to English today. Of course, another part of the reason is that I love seeing Trevor so much. He's really one of my greatest friends.

My plan is to be like, "So, Trevor, do you by any chance like to play basketball as much as it seems that you do?" and see what his response is. Somehow I know the conversation will just flow from there. I mean, it always does whenever we talk.

"So, Trevor, do you like to play basketball as much as it seems?"

Oh, my God.

Those words just flew out of my mouth completely on their own. I swear I didn't mean to say that yet.

He looks amazed. I honestly don't blame him. That must have seemed so *random*. I am so embarrassed right now…I can barely speak.

"Uh, yeah. It just so happens that I love playing basketball so much that I was considering trying out for the team." He looks really dazed.

What? Did I, like, read his mind or something?

Oh, my God.

That's so perfect! Brett will be so happy to hear about this. I can't wait to tell him. But, of course, I have to make sure that he doesn't figure out the other stuff about Trevor. You know what the other stuff is. But that doesn't mean I like him or anything… Ahem. You know what I mean.

"Really, Trevor?" I whisper. "That's so perfect!"

"Why?"

"Well, it just so happens that I was talking to Brett Evans last night, and he was saying..." I trail off for a second. Trevor has noticeably tensed up at the sound of Brett's name. Hmm, I wonder why...so I pause. "Trevor?"

"Yeah?" He doesn't look up.

"Is everything okay?"

"Oh, yeah, sure. Go on. What did Brett say?" He doesn't look extremely contented after hearing Brett's name, nor does he look me in the eye when he tells me that he's fine.

I can tell he's lying, even though I really don't know why. But that's not going to last once he hears why I'm talking to him about Brett Evans. "Brett was asking me if I knew anyone who played basketball really well," I say in a low tone.

He raises an eyebrow at me.

"So I told him that I knew how good you were at basketball," I barrel on, trying to ignore the bewildered look that has crossed his face. "He said that he would love to have you try out. I'm sure the tryouts will only be a formality, though, because as far as I'm concerned, you're going to be the varsity basketball team's latest addition!" I beam at him nervously.

Trevor's mouth falls open. I guess he just can't seem to believe the greatness of this all.

But then I realize that he might not be too happy about my big mouth spouting all of this to the star of the basketball team.

"I hope that's okay with you..." I venture.

"Okay?" He finds his voice. "It's more than okay. It's great. I'm just... surprised."

I laugh. "I can see that."

He manages to smile. "One question."

"Shoot."

"How did you find out that I even play basketball?"

I'm beginning to feel embarrassed again…

What do I say? That I was walking down his street just to see if I could catch a glimpse of his house, or even better, him?

That would be the truth, of course, but how awkward!

I settle for saying, "Oh, I was strolling around the area and I happened to see you playing basketball with your friend…Brooke, isn't it?"

He clearly brightens.

Maybe I was wrong about the whole 'Trevor not being interested in Brooke' thing.

Poor Brett. He definitely wouldn't be too happy about that. Neither would I, of course.

But maybe it's all for the best.

"Yeah, there was something I wanted to tell you too," Trevor suddenly says.

I look up quickly. So not going to miss a bit of this. "Oh, really?" This could be interesting. But I hope it's in a good way. I can't be disappointed here.

"Yeah. You're looking for an extra member on your cheerleading squad, aren't you?"

Ah. Just what I wanted to hear.

"Yeah, in fact, I was thinking of taking in Brooke."

"Really? That would be awesome!"

"I happened to see her doing some flips, too," I admit.

"Oh…" Trevor said knowingly.

Jackson's sub comes down the aisle. We both lean quickly over our papers in an attempt to make it look like we were working the whole time.

Too late.

She stops next to us. "I think we will have to collect these papers at the end of the period," she says, with an evil glare at us through narrowed eyes. "We will see whether you have been working or not."

As soon as she walks away, Trevor and I melt down into silent laughter. I can't help but think to myself how weird this woman is.

"She's so weird," Trevor whispers to me.

Oh, my God. He totally read my mind. But knowing me, I'm probably reading into it way too much. I think I was always kind of paranoid…or at least, my parents used to say that when I spazzed out a lot…but I don't know. Hmm.

We both start writing answers on our papers so when we do hand it in, we don't fail. But all the while, we're exchanging answers.

I can't wait to tell Brett that Trevor accepts *and* talk to Brooke! Even though I barely know her right now, I think we really might be the best of friends!

This is totally one of those rare times that I just love having Jackson's sub.

Brett

Well, I guess you could say that that was just…surreal.

Not only do I now have Brooke's number and she should have mine by now, but I also have proof for Sophia and myself, plus practically the rest of the members of the team and squad.

Perfect proof: Brooke wrote down in her own words that she wants to try out for the squad! This might be a connection for the two of us!

But now I can tell Sophia that she will definitely have a new member of the squad within the next few days! How perfect is that?

Oh, and that isn't all. I even managed to get it out of Brooke that Trevor Stevenson does want to try out for the basketball team!

It looks like things are going to be all set. All we've got to do is find a date to have the tryouts, run it all past Coach Davidson and Ms. Sanders (I refuse to call her Coach – she doesn't seem anything like a coach, and besides, I'm not one of her pom-pom waving cheerleaders…but maybe one of these days I'll just change my philosophy with no mention of it, so don't be surprised if I do), and recruit a few more people as a formality.

Then we can just take in Brooke and Trevor!

Yes!

Five minutes left of the period means that I can go meet Sophia outside in the hall after class, since she has English now… with Trevor. I'm guessing that Brooke's going to go meet Trevor, too. Maybe we can walk together.

Oh, I've got the smoothest idea.

Brooke usually takes a little while when she puts her notebooks and textbook in her bag. I'll just wait for her before I leave. Then somehow I can start up a good conversation and voila! she'll be walking with me.

There's the bell! A little early, but that works just fine.

Oh, no…scratch that plan, I guess. She just flew out of here, clutching my note to Trevor.

All I can do is catch up to her.

"Brooke!" I call, hurrying after her.

She pauses, glancing around.

"Brooke, wait up."

She turns. "Oh, hey, Brett."

"Hey," I greet her, but only for a display of politeness. Honestly, I didn't just approach her to say hello and walk away. That would be too lame for the popular basketball captain. I'm really not conceited, though. You've got to know that.

"What's up?"

"Nothing really after our barrage of notes."

She giggles, looking both surprised and impressed.

I guess she never thought I had a brain inside my head. I can only hope that she wasn't thinking that it was all air and fluff in here, though, because it isn't. At least, I don't think so.

We slip out of the classroom.

She finally starts talking in longer sentences. "Are you going to find Sophia?" she asks me.

How does she read my mind like that?

"Yeah! How did you know?"

"Oh, well, I think she was just in English next door, and that's where Trevor is, and I was going to meet him there." She looks really nervous.

I'm not that scary, am I? "Yeah. Is that how she knows Trevor?" I ask her casually.

"Yeah, I think so."

"Oh. That's cool. Nice way for them to meet, huh?"

She giggles again. And a surge of pride rushes through me. "Yeah. Nicer than Sanders."

I grin.

By now we're just outside Halitelli's English room. It's unusually quiet in there, but I can see everyone walking around the room.

Oh. That's why.

Jackson's sub, as we so affectionately call her, is in charge of Halitelli's classes today. She's handing out homework sheets. What a strange lady.

Finally, I see Sophia heading for the door. I also see Trevor copying me (not on purpose, though) by going after her and walking just on her heels.

The door swings open.

"Brett!" Sophia calls out, beaming.

Trevor slips out of the room. "Hey, Brooke," he says, and then, seeming kind of shy, he turns to me. "Hey. I'm Trevor."

"Yeah, I know. You probably know I'm Brett."

He grins. "How could I not? You're only the ever-famous and popular basketball captain."

Just my thoughts. Maybe I *am* right sometimes. But I've got to be modest.

"Come on, man, I'm not that important. But hey, I hear that you've got some athletic stuff going for you."

Trevor's ears turn red and he kicks at the ground, seeming embarrassed yet pleased at this compliment. But really, who wouldn't? He just got complimented by the star of the varsity basketball team. That's so cool for someone in our school who happens to be sitting on the middle branches of the social group tree, considering the fact that I'm practically at the top of it.

Brooke rolls her eyes.

Apparently Trevor's ears' turning red is something that happens quite often. Weirdly loser-like. I bet *my* ears don't turn red *that* much. But then again, I can't see them when I'm embarrassed, since I usually don't spend my most humiliating moments in front of a mirror. So I wouldn't know much about that. Usually my face gets red, but that's totally normal.

But I'm a cool guy. I won't judge this Trevor just yet. He

seems nice.

"Kind of," he finally says.

Sophia glances at him and smiles.

After being friends with her for so long, I can tell she might be dead gone on him. There's no reason why not, either. He could definitely pass as one of the cool guys on the basketball team, with his dark hair and green eyes. He's tall and well-built, too, I guess. In fact, he might be almost as good as me.

"Actually," Sophia says, "Trevor's going to be trying out for the basketball team, Brett."

"I heard," I reply.

"Oh, really?" She's definitely doubtful. But of me? Terrible of her. "From who?"

I gesture towards Brooke, who is still standing next to me.

"Oh. You must be Brooke." Sophia smiles in a friendly way. "You probably know that I'm Sophia."

"Yeah," Brooke says shyly.

"So," Sophia continues matter-of-factly, "you're going to be trying out for the cheerleading squad, aren't you?"

Brooke looks surprised. "Yeah, um, who told *you*?" She glances up at me almost accusingly. (Yes, I am about at least a half a foot taller than her, which makes our height difference almost perfect.)

I raise both hands in the air. "Don't look at me. I haven't had the chance to tell her anything yet."

Trevor admits, "It was me."

Brooke hurls him a look. "Thanks, Trevor."

"Hey, I did you a favor."

Brooke rolls her eyes again.

Sophia smiles. "Yeah, Brooke, it's actually a good thing. I'm probably just going to get you on the squad, just like Brett's going to make Trevor the newest addition to the team. Isn't that right, Brett?"

I admit it, I am listening, but at the same time I'm not paying enough attention to understand. That's really the only reason I'm forced to go, "Huh?"

The smile on Sophia's face is starting to look plastered on. "Trevor's going to be the new team member, right?"

"Oh, yeah, sure, I guess. As long as I get Coach Davidson's approval, and if no one better comes along, which I doubt will ever happen, you're officially on the team, Trevor."

Brooke beams. At least I pleased her and Sophia at the same time.

Even though I've never seen Trevor play, Sophia doesn't say many of the guys are good except me and Jackson. But Jackson got kicked off the team, so I guess that's where Trevor comes in.

Brooke glances at her watch. "The bell's going to ring soon. I've still got to go to my locker. Trevor, you want to go?"

Trevor nods rather reluctantly. He doesn't seem to want to leave.

Sophia doesn't seem to want them to go, either. "Wait!"

Trevor and Brooke turn back. They had only been a few steps away from Sophia and me in the first place.

"Where are you guys going now?"

Oh, please. It's not like Sophia and I didn't know that the two of them were in the same period as us for–

"Lunch," Trevor responds.

Well, yeah. That.

I want to tell them that it just so happens that Sophia and I are going to lunch as well. But somehow, I don't want to say that.

Sophia shoots me a warning glance as if to say, "Do something!"

Oh, believe me. I know that look very well, if not almost too well. It means if I don't salvage the situation, then I'm definitely going to regret it later in the form of Sophia punishing me somehow. Not fun.

"We're going there, too," I say.

"Really?" Brooke asks, stopping short. Yet somehow I know she's not really surprised.

Something tells me that she knew we were in her lunch period all along, just like we did. But I'm not going to say anything, of course.

"Yeah."

"That's cool." Trevor looks noticeably interested.

Sophia hasn't stopped firing those looks at me. I almost don't know what to do right now. But I guess there really is only one thing that I can say that would please Sophia and possibly the other two as well.

I take a deep breath. This question could change a lot of stuff. But hey, it might be worth it.

"So, would you guys care to join us at lunch today?"

Trevor

Well, here we are, just entering the cafeteria.

This time, it's not only just Brooke and me.

No, we've got two new friends to accompany us to lunch. They just happen to be the two most popular people in our entire grade, if not the whole school – Brett Evans and…the one and only Sophia Garrison.

How charming.

The four of us made it without incident to the concession line to buy our food. Sophia and Brooke both buy salads and bottles of iced tea. It turns out that Sophia is a vegetarian, just like Brooke, who just happens to be a health food freak. Sophia also doesn't believe in drinking sodas, which is just like Brooke once again. They both begin discussing the dangers of soft drinks.

Brett and I glance at each other and grin sheepishly, putting back the sodas we were about to buy with a trace of guilt. I sense that Brett had never listened to Sophia until Brooke came along, just like I hadn't ever paid much attention to Brooke until Sophia.

"It's also so wrong of you to eat meat!" Sophia emphasizes.

Brett simply raises an eyebrow skeptically.

I guess this is a speech that Sophia goes through a lot. I have to admit that I would gladly listen to it, in spite of the fact that it makes me look really, well, sycophantic – if that's a word. I guess I do listen to Miss Halitelli once in a while.

"Exactly!" Brooke cries out. She looks so happy to have someone who stands firm with her beliefs on her side. "No one has ever agreed with me on the whole vegetarian idea," she explains.

"Really?" Sophia tilts her head. "Same with me. But I honestly don't see why not. I mean, even as we speak, thousands of animals are being slaughtered all over the world. By eating the meat, you're encouraging the ending of so many lives. It's just wrong." She looks up at me. "Don't you understand? I know Brett won't listen to me much, but come on. At least maybe you, Trevor?"

I'm torn between the tacos on my plate and listening to my new friend. I know she's right, but I could never give up meat. It's really bad of me, but I just can't seem to go through with it.

Brooke rolls her eyes yet again. "Don't bother, Sophia. He never listens to me about the soda, the vegetarianism…basically anything."

Sophia laughs – music to my ears. "Hey, I wouldn't say that. He just put back that can of soda."

I can sense that my ears are turning red again. My hair isn't long enough to cover that up, but whatever. At least my whole head doesn't turn red. That would be too weird…even for me. But at least my ears had a right to turn red this time.

"Besides," Sophia continues, "I've tried so many times to convince Brett about the soda idea. I guess the two of us can be very convincing once we're put together." She winked.

Brett and I exchanged glances. I guess we both wanted to cover up the fact that it was Brooke who convinced him and Sophia who convinced me, so we both nodded really quickly in a successful attempt of shutting the two of them up. Well, at the very least, they changed the subject, since by then we were about to pay at the register.

Then the topic of where we were going to sit came up. This was a conversation that Brett began to take part in.

"I don't really want to sit at the table we usually sit at," Sophia proclaimed. "They're all going to be gossiping about what happened last night."

Brooke and I exchanged somewhat uneasy glances.

"That's so true," Brett says. "Hey, look." He begins to crane his neck. "I see Jackson. Whoa."

"What?" Sophia stands on tiptoe. She can't really see too well over all of these heads. It's not that she's short, though. Brett's just…tall. Like me, now that I come to think of it. How coincidental is that?

"Jackson's sitting practically all alone. The only person over there is kind of pale, has got straight black hair, she's shooting the nastiest looks at our normal table…" he trails off.

Now I see them. I know Jackson only too well from distance. But this girl? She looks like she flew straight out of a Clairol commercial, except she's got the meanest expression, which isn't attractive to anyone. Except maybe Jackson, judging by how interested he seems to be in her. But whatever.

"Oh, God," Sophia groans.

"What?" I ask. I can't help being concerned. Besides, Sophia rarely acts like this. So when she does, it means something is most definitely up.

"That's Daphne Carlisle. She is *such* a cruel person."

I'm more than appalled at this sudden display of hatred by such a sweet (seeming? I hope not) girl.

She sees the look on my face and quickly continues, "But you know I usually don't say those things about people. Daphne's just terrible."

"What did she do?" Brooke looks quite interested. She's getting too into this gossip business. I can't say I like it.

"She's tried out for cheerleading every single year since the seventh grade and she hasn't gotten in. Last night she started messaging me about the tryouts. She was practically threatening me, saying, 'If you don't accept me as being so much better at gymnastics than you are, you're going to regret it,' and stuff like that."

Brooke gasps and says, "Doesn't that freak you out?"

Sophia shrugs. "Oh, she's been stalking me down about getting on the squad for years. It's been ages since she started it, and even though it did bother me a little bit – all right, a lot – at first, I don't really care anymore. I doubt she'd do anything drastic that would really hurt me."

Brooke's eyes widen dramatically.

Sophia grins and teases, "If I were you, I'd watch out. Once you get taken onto the squad, she just might come after you. That would be one less thing for me to worry about."

Now Brooke's mouth falls open.

Sophia waits just the right amount of time before reassuring her. "Hey, chill. I was just kidding."

"Don't *do* that!"

I can already tell that these two are going to be best friends. I'm glad that Brooke approves of Sophia.

I guess Brett's cool. He might be a tad egotistic, but we can work around that, of course. I can definitely use a few extra friends.

"So, where are we going to sit?"

I glance around, glad for a chance to talk at last. "How about over there?" I point towards an empty table not too far away from Daphne and Jackson's.

"Sure."

The four of us walk across the cafeteria, aware of the buzz that is gradually being created. Everyone is staring at the two most popular people in the class walking with two formerly unknown social peasants.

The other cheerleaders and players on the basketball team are clearly considering waving us over to their table, but they also obviously don't want Brooke and me, who are just outsiders. Eventually they just decide on letting us walk by to the deserted little table, where we sit down and begin eating and chatting, ready to enjoy a great lunch period together.

The one thing that I can't help but notice is the pair of strange looks we receive from Jackson and Daphne. They glare at us, and I catch their stares, which send chills down my spine.

They look ready to kill.

Brooke

Today went *so* well. I'm officially best friends with Sophia Garrison, and I ate lunch with her, Trevor, and Brett Evans. We discussed the date of the tryouts, which will be next week, but for the rest of the day, I wasn't thinking about the tryouts, which is what I really *should* have been thinking about. I was too busy worrying about how I have two people to fear. Their names just happen to be Daphne Carlisle and Jackson Everett.

When we sat down at our table, I couldn't help seeing the death stares we got from those two. I'm guessing they figured Trevor and I were going to be the new additions to the team and squad, because they looked like they were going to do something drastic to hurt us, like Sophia said just before we went to sit down in the cafeteria.

But anyway, I'm actually interested in doing the math homework (I hope I wrote it down somewhere) since what we learned reminds me of the math class that I spent passing notes with Brett. But I assure you that I still learned a lot.

Can't you just tell how much I'm trying to distract myself from the thoughts of Jackson and Daphne?

"Brooke! Dinner!"

Looks like I'm going to be distracted for a little while at least. I didn't even realize that it was almost seven. I might as well tell my parents and thirteen-year-old sister Ashlynn about the latest news in school while we're eating together. Of course, I'll have to wait until Ashlynn finishes talking about her excitement. Usually it's a lot. You know how middle school drama goes.

"Coming!" I push my textbook away and flip off the light switch. I decide to leave my computer on, with my messenger minimized. If someone wants to instant message me, then they can. I'll just have to respond to them later.

I leave my room and meet Ashlynn coming out of her own bedroom, which is adjacent to mine.

"How was school?" I ask her, since I didn't get a chance to talk to her since this morning.

She sighs. "All right, I guess. I hate how the gossip and the drama keeps going around."

I pat her on the shoulder and try to sound wise. "Middle school drama," I tease. "You'll get out of it. Then comes high school."

She makes a face at me. "Ha, ha."

"But anyway, what's the gossip there?"

"Someone spread rumors about me liking Scott and Gwen liking Brad."

"Well, isn't all of that true?" I can't help thinking about the similarities between the names Brett and Brad.

"No! Gwen likes Scott and *I* like Brad!" my sister exclaims indignantly.

"Sorry. I don't keep up with these things."

To tell the truth, I vaguely remember hearing about Ashlynn's best friend Gwen a lot and how Ashlynn loves Brad.

Brad just happens to be Sophia's brother.

"Well, you should. I know everything about you."

Right. Because there is *so* much for her to know about me.

"My bad." I raise my hands defensively just like Brett did this morning outside Miss Halitelli's English classroom.

Copying the movements of the person you like supposedly means that you're 'in sync' with them. And yes, it is true. I didn't make it up, either. In fact, I actually read it online somewhere. If only I could remember where. Then I could translate everything Brett does.

Ashlynn rolls her eyes at me.

But before I can say anything back to her, I'm interrupted.

"Brooke! Ashlynn!" my mom calls from the foot of the stairs. "Hurry up! Dinner's getting cold!"

"We're coming!" I yell.

I guess our sister-to-sister tête-à-tête ends here.

The two of us hurry down the stairs and into the kitchen.

Our house is really rustic, with mostly wooden-paneled walls and floors with throw rugs here and there.

"Need any help setting the table?" I ask.

"No, silly, I set the table over twenty minutes ago. You two are just late," my mom scolds us. "But don't bother yourselves by worrying about it," she continues before we're even given a chance to apologize. "I'll only decrease your allowance if this keeps happening over and over."

We gasp.

"I'm only joking, sweeties. Just go sit down in the dining room. I'm going to call your father back in here. He went back to the den after you didn't come down right away."

Ashlynn and I sit down to dinner at the table and wait for our parents to enter the dining room.

Finally, at a quarter past seven, we all begin eating.

~ Chapter Two ~

"Wait," Ashlynn says all of a sudden. I put down my fork, and so does our mom. "Why are we here? It's Thursday!"

Mom smacks one hand to her forehead. "I knew I forgot something. I keep thinking that today's Wednesday. We'll go out to dinner next week, girls. I'm sorry. But we're all here. It's still a family dinner."

Ashlynn nods. "Yeah, I guess. Whatever."

Mom gives her a look. "Would you please quit it with the 'whatever' and the 'yeah'?"

"Sorry."

Silence for a few minutes.

"So, girls, how was school?"

Ashlynn glances at me with a significant look.

"Um, Ash, you first?" I say uncertainly.

She glares at me.

Come on. How on earth was I supposed to interpret *that*?

"Well? Ashlynn?" my mom prompts.

"It was fine."

"Nothing interesting happened?"

"No…just more rumors."

Oh, my God. She totally should *not* have said that. She could have just answered with a simple 'no.' But no…she doesn't have any common sense.

"Rumors? About who?"

"Oh, people."

I can tell that she doesn't want to tell Mom and Dad about the "who likes who" situations. I honestly don't blame her. They might blow it all out of proportion. So as a favor to her, I change the subject.

"Anyone want to know how my terrific day went?" I ask

cheerily. Corny, I know. But give me a break. I'm trying to save Ash.

"Oh, Brooke, please let Ashlynn finish," Dad says.

"But she was done," I protest.

"Brooke," Mom begins in a warning tone.

"All right, all right." I shrug at Ashlynn as if to say, 'I tried.'

She nods. But only slightly.

"Well, Ash, honey? What did you learn today?"

I roll my eyes at this standard show of parental concern. I tend to do that a lot. Roll my eyes, I mean.

"Nothing superbly motivating," my sister answers. "I'm sure what happened to Brooke today is so much more interesting," she hints.

Mom finally catches on to the fact that my sister doesn't really want to discuss her day as much as I do. It took her long enough. "Oh, all right, I give up. How was school, Brooke, dear?" she asks.

"Amazing!" I respond, beginning to highlight my day. Of course I leave out any information hinting about Brett. I don't want anything regarding me blown out of proportion, either. As I relate all of the greatest events, I watch with glee as my family's eyes all widen. After I finish, I pause for a dramatic effect.

Ashlynn's mouth is wide open. Luckily she had already finished chewing, so the rest of us aren't subject to the sight of food.

My parents look amazed yet proud.

My heart swells with pride.

Mom tries to summarize all of the stuff that happened. "So, honey," she begins slowly, "you're going to finally be trying out for this cheerleading squad?"

"Yes, and even better…it includes gymnastics!"

"That's wonderful!"

Suddenly the phone rings.

"Brooke, answer that. Ashlynn, help me clear the table so I can get dessert," Mom directs.

"Okay."

I leave the dining room and head into the den to pick up the phone. "Hello?"

"Hi, Brooke?"

I think it's– "Sophia?"

"Yeah, it's me. Am I calling at a bad time?"

Wow. "No, not at all. I've got about five minutes, though."

"That's fine. I got your number from the school directory."

"Oh. I gave Brett my cell phone number in a note that he was supposed to give to you," I explain.

"Oh. Well, he never gave it to me. You can't count on him much with stuff like that." She laughs. "Um, you know what? I'll call you later on your cell so we can discuss some tryout-related stuff, okay?"

"Sure. Here's my number…"

"Hang on a second. I need a pen and paper…"

I can hear her rummaging around somewhere on the other end of the line.

I'm so happy to finally have a best friend.

Within a couple minutes, we're off the phone and I return to the dinner table for a piece of chocolate cake.

"Who was that?" Dad asks.

"My new friend Sophia Garrison."

"*The* Sophia Garrison? Brad's sister?" Ashlynn echoes incredulously. Did she absolutely *need* to mention him? Now I have to clean up after her. Annoying child.

"Yeah," I say proudly.

"Brooke, is this Sophia girl replacing Trevor as your closest friend?" Mom says.

I can practically sense and hear a scolding coming along.

"No, Mom, Trevor's still my best guy friend."

But thankfully she caught onto the whole Sophia thing before she heard the mention of Brad. Time elapses long enough for her and Dad to forget things a little while after they've heard it, but the new subject of Brad Garrison wouldn't make the conversation go as I had planned.

"That's better." She sits back in her chair.

She really thinks Trevor's a good kid after he helped so much and he actually isn't 'chasing after' me, as she is so convinced a lot of guys will. But so far I've got no one. What a big surprise.

"How do you know her all of a sudden?" Ashlynn asks, sounding wary.

What? Does she suspect that I blackmailed Sophia into being my new best friend or something?

Oh, please.

"She's the captain of the cheerleading squad, and Trevor's friends with her."

"Ooh, has Trevor found a *friend*?" Ashlynn teases.

"I think so," I admit.

"Oh, honey, what about you?"

Ooh.

Trust Mom to bring up one of the most awkward subjects at the dinner table.

But I guess I might as well tell them the truth. What's the worst that could happen? It's not like I'm secretly dating him or anything. And besides, then I can actually talk to my family about the gossip.

If they care enough to listen, that is.

"Um, I don't know. Possibly Brett?"

My dad, needless to say, does not look too thrilled about my mention of a certain mystery guy.

I mean, come on, seriously.

He's my *dad.*

"Brooke, Trevor's a very good guy, you know," he begins.

Um, excuse me.

I know that's true, but…ew, that is so gross. I would never, *ever*, under *any* circumstances like Trevor *that way*.

"Yeah, Dad, I know that, but he just happens to be one of my very best friends. I would never like him like that."

"Oh. Well, I might as well ask before the situation keeps growing. Who exactly is this so-called 'Brett'?"

Ashlynn attempts to explain. "I only know of a certain Brett Evans, captain of the basketball team."

"And he's not with Sophia?" Mom questions.

"No. They're good friends, though. Kind of like Trevor and me."

"Wait a second…*that* Brett?" Ashlynn sounds even more skeptical than ever before as she asks me this.

How insulting. Does she honestly think I'm not good enough for someone of such a high social class as him?

"Yes…"

"Oh, I see," Mom says knowingly.

Ashlynn kicks me under the table with a mocking glance.

I can just feel my face getting hot.

There is definitely no way that I'm *not* blushing right now, thanks to them. This is so embarrassing.

"Is everyone done eating?" I ask, trying to change the subject.

"Yeah," Ashlynn grumbles, not too happy all of a sudden. She drops her fork on her plate with a clatter.

She couldn't be jealous of me and Brett when her situation with Brad isn't doing too well. It isn't *my* fault. Besides, I'm not even with Brett.

"Brooke? Brooke?"

Oops.

That would be my bad for zoning out.

"Yeah?"

"It's 'Yes,' not 'yeah.'"

"My apologies. Yes?"

"Help me clear the table."

"Oh, yeah, sure."

"Brooke…" Mom starts in a warning tone.

Oops.

That really was a total accident.

"Sorry." I reach for the platter with the remnants of cake on it and take it back into the kitchen.

I have to admit that I can't wait till Sophia calls back.

It's so good to finally have a best friend who's actually a girl.

Sophia

Brooke is so much nicer than the rest of those shallow girls on the squad. I'm so glad we started talking to each other. I'm going to call her back as soon as I can get back up to my bedroom. But I've got to finish washing the dinner dishes before I'm allowed to go.

So what do I do to get out of it?

Ooh! I know!

I'll just pay Brad to dry them up for me.

"Brad?"

He's halfway out of the kitchen. "What do you want now?" he mutters almost under his breath.

"I heard that."

"Okay, so?"

He is being such a spoiled pill of a thirteen-year-old.

"Can you do me a favor?"

"What? My day's been bad enough."

Ooh. That's not good. I need a happy kid drying the dishes for me. Otherwise he'll go rat me out. And I really don't need to be grounded.

"Oh…" I say sympathetically. I grab a towel and dry my hands. "Come sit down here and tell me about everything that happened today that's making you so upset."

I drag out a couple of stools at the island and make him sit down next to me.

Brad shuffles his feet over, but he does sit down.

"Well?"

"I hate hearing stuff about people through other people. It's so annoying."

Well, I can't say that I do, since thanks to that kind of stuff, I heard about Brooke, and Brett heard about Trevor. But I might as well take pity on the kid.

"Doesn't it stink?"

"Yeah."

"What did you hear that you aren't sure that you can believe?" Good thing I can somewhat relate to this stuff from my middle school days.

He looks up with renewed interest showing in his eyes. "How did you know?"

"Your big sister isn't all that stupid, you know."

"I wasn't too sure."

I know normally I would take offense at a comment like this, but it's a good sign that his 'great' sense of humor is coming back.

"Well?" How many times am I going to have to ask this?

"Okay, okay. My friend Eric told me that this girl Gwen liked me, and as far as I knew she didn't. I thought Ashlynn Dawson liked me, and I was really happy about that, and then I found out that–"

Whoa.

Wait a second.

Dawson?

"Dawson?"

"Yeah. Ashlynn Dawson." He's giving me a weird look, but I barely notice it.

"Is she the younger sister of my best friend Brooke Dawson?"

"I don't know."

"Well, what does she look like?"

"She has reddish-brown hair and it's kind of curly, and her eyes are really deep bluish-green. She's really pretty."

Oh, God. Here we go again.

Little Brad totally has a crush on this Ashlynn Dawson…Ooh la la.

But I've got to cover up my excitement.

"Okay, anyway…How do you know it really is Gwen who likes you and not this Ashlynn Dawson?"

Perfect masking, Sophia.

You're so good.

"I don't."

Wait. What? How is that supposed to make any sense? I'm already confused enough. He's making it worse.

"Wait a second, Brad. That doesn't make sense. I thought someone told you that Gwen liked you."

"Yeah, Eric did but I don't think it's true."

"So Ashlynn might like you instead."

"How would you know?"

"I'm not too sure. Describe how she acts when she's around you." After all, I've got to get all of this straight.

"She's always really nice to me, and when I asked her if it was true about Gwen liking me, she said that it wasn't."

"Okay…" That's not much info there. "Anything else?"

"She told me not to believe Eric, because he also spread the false rumor that she liked Scott."

"Does she give any other signs of liking you?"

"How am I supposed to know?"

"Well, I don't know," I defend myself.

This conversation isn't going very far.

I sit back (well, as far back as I can on a kitchen island stool, but you get the picture) to study my little brother.

He got the same genes and traits that I did. And they're not half bad, if I do say so myself.

He's got the tall (for his age), well built form. It's a nice advantage for him, but he's not too tough. A little sensitive, but in a good way.

Like me, he has blond hair, but his has streaks of very light brown here and there. And his isn't naturally super-straight like mine. Instead, it's kind of wavy. Not curly, but wavy. And it's not totally short, either. He's been begging Mom to let him grow it out a little, since I guess that whole side-swept thing is in for guys now, or whatever it was that all of the teen magazines have been claiming so strongly. But whatever the reason, Brad's clearly sick of the buzz cut he's had for all these years.

I've been trying to convince him that if he just grows it out a little and not *that* much, then he would totally be able to flip up the front – such a classic hot hairdo. But I'm sure that he'll look fine if he grows it out a bit. He's my brother, after all. He's got to look good. I'll take care of that.

We both have similar eyes in shape and color. Beautiful blue, of course. We both did get the long and curly eyelashes – not that *he* needs them. And it doesn't help me that much – they're still super light. So mascara is necessary, but Brad has no need to worry about that, luckily for him. And luckily for me, makeup is *so* advanced now. Waterproof, smudge-proof, et cetera, et cetera, et cetera. They might as well make a permanent kind. I mean, seriously. That's all they're missing right now.

But I definitely need to bring this conversation to an end.

Like, now.

"So…" I rap my manicured nails on the marble countertop. "Are there any other exciting details that I should know about?"

"Not really. But I know you."

"Um, okay, what?"

There is no way that he can be catching onto me already. He's not *supposed* to be that smart!

"You definitely didn't call me back in here just because you wanted to listen to stuff about my day."

Uh-oh.

"Brad! How could you say that?"

"Um, because it's true?"

Double uh-oh. I am so dead. What do I say to that?

"Uh…"

Intelligent, Sophia. *So* intelligent.

"See? I got you. Well, what do you want?"

Darn. I guess I might as well tell the truth.

"Well, I was kind of going to go call Brooke back, plus my hands were already tired from washing the dishes, so…"

"You want me to dry them because you're going to need your precious hands for talking to people online."

Oh…

Roar.

He does have me figured out.

But then again, I'm not that hard to figure out.

"Uh, yeah, well, something like that," I say in a small voice.

"Okay, then," he says slowly. "But wait, who are you calling?"

"Brooke Dawson…"

It clicks in my brain about Brooke and Ashlynn being sisters.

"Oh." He's silent for a second, thinking. "Well, if I do dry the dishes for you, what's in it for me, huh?"

Didn't I know this was coming?

"Um…"

"Whatever…" He gets up and walks across the kitchen to the sink, grabbing a dishcloth on his way.

Hmm, that's a good deal.

He's going to dry them anyway, whether or not I give him something in return for the job.

I drum my nails on the counter as I attempt to think this whole thing over once again.

Coming to a decision here…

No, I can't be that mean.

He's my little brother and I'm supposed to be there for him when he needs me.

And that's now, I guess.

But what can I do for him?

Oh, my God, I have the greatest idea.

I can find out for him whether or not Ashlynn likes him back. I already have proof that he likes her…so why not?

"How about I help you out a little?"

"Please. What could *you* do?"

That was harsh.

But I'll take it, since what I'm going to say is something he probably is going to like quite a lot.

"I can find out for you if Ashlynn likes you."

His eyes just totally lit up. "Okay!" But then his face falls. "Don't."

Now what?

"Why not?"

"I don't want her to think…well, whatever."

"If you don't want me to, I don't have to…"

"All right, all right, just do it. I'll be here drying the dishes," he mutters under his breath.

Oh, well, at least I got him to do what I wanted.

"Okay, that's cool. Thanks for drying them. I'll come back down here after I get off the phone," I promise.

"Yeah, right. I'll be done by then."

"Brad…"

"Okay, okay, I'll cool it."

"That's better."

I mean, honestly, I don't need my little brother being all high and mighty on me or whatever. He's *younger*. He's not allowed to talk back.

Okay, okay. I'm in the 21st century, I know.

I leave the kitchen and wander through the halls to the staircase. Finally, I'm in my room. I close the door behind me for some peace and quiet, since I can hear one of the TVs blaring from a nearby room.

After getting a hold of my phone, I dial Brooke's cell phone number.

"Hello?"

"Hey, Brooke."

"Oh, hey, Sophia."

"How was your dinner?"

Lame, I know, but I couldn't think of anything else casual enough to say. Besides, it just might be a good link for a conversation starter…well, for a conversation about this impending situation regarding Brad and Ashlynn, that is.

"Okay, I guess. I just finished the dishes."

"Oh…" I say knowingly. I totally understand. Too well, in fact. "That sucks," I continue on sympathetically – and cleverly. "I was actually supposed to wash and dry all of the dinner dishes, but I oh-so-cleverly bribed my little brother into drying them for me."

Brooke giggles. "Oh, yeah? How?"

Oh, yes.

How utterly perfect.

"He wants some information about a certain person…"

"Oh, really? Like who?"

"Your younger sister Ashlynn?"

"Oh…" She pauses and then lowers her voice to a whisper. "Well, it just so happens that Ashlynn clearly wants to know some stuff about Brad."

Oh, my God, really?

I don't know if I'm going to be able to answer her questions.

"Like…?"

"You first."

Darn.

Of course, that *was* pretty dumb of me to put myself in this position.

But then again, how else would anyone have brought up the topic?

I'm good, I'm good…

I guess.

"Um…Brad heard from his best friend Eric that a certain Gwen liked him."

Before I can go on, Brooke has to get the story straight, I guess.

It's actually a good thing she's interrupting me. It gives me a chance to get my own details right.

"Wait a second. That's the first part that's wrong."

"Okay. Is that a good thing, or what?"

"Um, I don't know. It depends on how your brother's looking at it. But Gwen does *not* like Brad. She likes Scott, but you *so* didn't hear that from me."

I chuckle.

At least she's good at keeping stories and pieces of gossip in order. That's so unlike me. Maybe that's why I'm always confused when fellow cheerleaders like, for example, Corinne Carlton, are talking to me.

"Brad probably heard a rumor that Ashlynn likes Scott, and that obviously is *not* true. Eric has been spreading all of these stories that aren't true."

"Okay…" I say slowly, still trying to get all of these so-called 'facts' straight. "So now you know that Brad wanted Ashlynn to like him, and Gwen likes Scott, which is who Ashlynn doesn't like, and Eric is this annoying little guy who's spreading the rumors."

"Right." She doesn't sound completely sure.

"Something like that, anyway." I can't have been totally right, after all. But I so totally just spilled the beans about Brad, just like Brooke told me her sister's secret.

She voices some of the thoughts going through my head. "Well, now we know that Brett – I mean, Brad, and Ashlynn like each other, but we shouldn't …" Suddenly she stops short and whispers, "Hang on just one second."

"Is everything okay?"

"Yeah, it's just that my *sister's* outside my *door*." She puts her phone down somewhere with a tiny clatter.

I hear a scuffling noise on the other end of the line as Brooke opens a door.

"Ash! What are you doing?"

"Nothing. I need the atlas."

"Nice excuse."

I hit the mute button and laugh to myself.

What I wouldn't give for a little sister in exchange for my brother.

Not.

"No, seriously. You took the atlas last night."

"Only for my World Geo homework – oh, yeah, right. It's on my desk. I'll go get it. No, you stay out of my room."

"All right. But who were you talking to?"

Uh-oh.

Someone's going to be in trouble.

"Ash, just mind your own business." She gets back on the phone. "Hey, Sophia?" she says.

I un-mute my phone. "Yeah, I'm here. Was she listening the whole time?"

"I don't know. You know what? We can let them worry about their problems, since we know everything and they can stumble around in the dark for a little while. After all, it gives everyone a sense of involvement.

"Besides, we do have our own problems to deal with, anyway. Like Miss Carlisle and Mr. Everett."

I smile at that one. Too bad it's so true.

"So how about we discuss the tryouts and stuff tomorrow at lunch when no one's listening to us, okay?"

I smile, happy that she still wants to sit together at lunch. "Okay, that's fine. See you tomorrow!"

I snap my phone shut.

Just in time, too, since there's a knock on my door.

I jump off the bed and walk over to the double doors.

"Sophia?"

It's Brad.

"Yeah?"

I open one of my bedroom doors, a little cautious after what happened with Brooke and Ashlynn.

"Are you done talking to Brooke yet?"

"Yes..."

Great.

Now I'm going to be in hot water.

"Well? What did she say?"

"Um...stuff about the cheerleading tryouts."

That really isn't a lie, you know.

"Yeah, uh-huh. Sure."

"Come on. What makes you say that? You're so clearly implying that you don't believe me."

I mean, seriously, come on.

It *is* kind of obvious, after all.

"Well, why should I believe you? You already had cheerleading tryouts at the beginning of the year, smart one."

Whoa.

He certainly thinks he's very smart.

But oh, please.

Ha, ha.

I've got a good comeback for that one.

"Hey, Brad, remember how Isabelle moved to New Jersey?"

"What–"

"That's why I'm holding tryouts for a replacement. Have a nice evening." I quickly close the door, leaving him standing out in the hall, mulling this new thought over in his amateur mind.

No offense meant, of course.

"Hey, wait!" He finally realizes that he's locked out of my room. "You have to tell me what she said!" He starts pounding on the door.

"Brad, she didn't say anything! I'll find out later, okay?"

"No! Tell me now!"

Oh, my God. What an immature little child.

"Brad, get away from my door!"

"No! I'll break it down if I have to! You are going to tell me!"

The beating doesn't stop.

I can almost see his fists gradually peeling away that once-perfect coat of smooth white paint.

Yes, I'm a little over-possessive about my doors. And anything that's part of my dear bedroom.

But I've got to stop him.

"Brad, I'm warning you. I'm going to tell Mom and Dad if you don't stop damaging my doors!"

I didn't mean to have to resort to that, but honestly, it's not my fault. He leaves me with no choice.

"You wouldn't dare. You know that I could totally tell on you for making me dry the dishes!"

My totally adorable West Highland white terrier, Sierra, starts barking, even though she's got to know it's Brad out there.

Barking, beating on the door, and voices clash together.

What an annoying mix.

Don't get me wrong; the barking is so cute, since I love Sierra so much, but the other stuff is driving me out of my mind.

Oh, my God, this is going to be such a long night.

Chapter 3:

Tryout Time

Brett

Well, here it is.

Today's the big day.

It was all decided last week, when on Friday, Sophia came stumbling into school and asked Ms. Sanders if she could hold tryouts for cheerleading after school on Monday instead of having practice, as long as she advertised it well. Ms. Sanders agreed, and Coach Davidson did, too, after I asked him.

So the four of us spent the weekend together, practicing for the tryouts. Well, Sophia and I were coaching Brooke and Trevor, but you get the picture.

I showed Trevor some of the coolest moves that would get the attention of Coach Davidson, and Sophia taught Brooke all of the stunts necessary for cheering. It doesn't take much to impress Ms. Sanders, I'm guessing, but Coach Davidson's a tough guy.

Sophia and I hung up signup sheets for the team and the squad on the main bulletin board just outside the cafeteria on Friday, and we had already gotten about twenty people signed up on each list by the end of the school day.

As Sophia had expected, Brooke's name was at the top of the cheerleading signup sheet, and Daphne Carlisle's was scrawled in obnoxious handwriting just below.

After school, the four of us headed to the main office to use the intercom system, which is where we are now.

"Ladies first." I hand the receiver to Sophia.

"Thanks." She unfolds a scrap of paper. "All students who are trying out for cheerleading, please report to the gymnasium at 2:45." She returns the receiver to me and whispers, "Your turn."

"All students who are trying out for boys' basketball, please head to the gym at 3:15. Thank you." Look who's more polite than Sophia.

Sophia and Brooke go off to the girls' locker room, and Trevor and I head for the boys' locker room.

It's 2:37. I can't wait.

Brooke

Breathe in, breathe out. Oh, my God. That's basically all I can think right now.

It's been five years since I first wanted to be a cheerleader or gymnast. That's five years that I've chickened out of trying out for the squad. It's so sad. I mean, it's cheerleading, for goodness' sake, not the Olympics. But I guess that the reason I want this so badly is because it's the only school sport that relates to gymnastics. I need it.

Oh, my God. It's 2:40. Five minutes left!

"Brooke? Are you ready?" Sophia comes around the corner.

I'm sitting on one of the benches, tying my shoe. I've just finished changing into my gym clothes. My regular clothes are in a pile next to me.

"There you are. It's time to go down now."

I don't budge.

"Brooke? You still in there?"

I manage to get out two words. "I'm nervous."

She laughs. Can you believe that? She *laughed.*

"Oh, come on, Brooke. You learned the moves, you're already a good gymnast, and you're going to make the most perfect cheerleader. Let's go."

I shove my clothes into my locker and snap the lock. "Okay."

We're almost at the door when all of a sudden it swings open and Daphne Carlisle comes bursting in.

Sophia glances at the clock. 2:42. She says smoothly, "You're going to be late, Daphne. All of the other girls are already down there."

Daphne hurls Sophia a nasty look. "I talked to Sanders. She said you can wait a minute or two. Get over it."

Sophia raises an eyebrow. I can't believe how coolly she handles the situation. "There's only one opening on the squad, Daphne. Lateness isn't going to get you anywhere. Besides, I'm doing the judging."

Daphne glares at her. "We'll see what Sanders says."

"*Coach. Coach* Sanders. Oh, wait, it would be *Ms.* Sanders to you, Daphne. You aren't on the squad."

"Yet." Daphne turns on her heel and stalks away.

The clock reads 2:44.

"She's *so* never going to get on the squad. She's always been jealous of me, as much as I hate to say it. I really don't see why. She would be pretty if she didn't always have that cruel look on her face." Sophia looks back at the clock. "It never hurts to be punctual, Brooke. Come on. Let's go."

We head down the stairs and into the gym.

Ms. Sanders is waiting in the center with more than fifteen other girls who are all stretching and acting like they are *so* going to be making it onto the squad.

"Just in time, Sophia, Brooke," Ms. Sanders says with a smile. "We're just going to be waiting on Daphne here. I'm sure most of you know the procedure for the tryouts by now, and I will be answering your questions after I refresh your memory."

She goes on to explain that we are going to need to exhibit our strengths and skills and tell why we think we uniquely qualify for the squad.

In the meantime, Sophia and I sit down and I start stretching.

Sophia keeps whispering notes to me. "Don't forget about how you have to tell everyone why you're a unique aspiring cheerleader," she reminds me.

"And what would that be again?" I can't help it – I'm blanking out.

Besides, Daphne just slipped into the gym. That's honestly not going to help me very much.

"You're a really good gymnast and you've been practicing for years," Sophia hisses in exasperation.

"Oh, right."

Ms. Sanders turns to us. "Sophia? Brooke?"

"Yes?"

"Is there something that you'd like to share with the rest of us?"

"No, Coach," Sophia answers without a flinch.

I can feel my face turning red as I hear Daphne snickering rudely.

"Daphne, that was uncalled for."

Score! But I definitely can't be wasting my time on thinking about warfare against Daphne Carlisle at a time like this.

"Besides," Ms. Sanders continues, "what I wanted to do was call up the captain of our cheerleading squad, Sophia Garrison."

Sophia smiles modestly as the rest of us clap and cheer for her. Daphne, of course, is an exception, given her never-ending deep resentment towards Sophia.

"Hey, girls," Sophia begins. "You all know why you're gathered here today. You all want that position on the squad. Needless to say, there is only one opening, so you can't all make it."

Daphne snorts and rolls her eyes. Honestly, there really are no words that are close to wholesome enough to describe that girl.

Sophia ignores her and keeps on talking. "Besides, in the end you all will know that you made a gallant effort and did a great job, but please don't come begging for another chance. Decisions will be made at the end of this session. Thank you all for showing up today. I'll turn this back over to Coach Sanders so we can begin the tryouts."

Oh, yeah! Righteous! But how many times could she possibly have said 'you all'?

"Thank you, Sophia. And now we'll begin." Ms. Sanders scans the tryout signup sheet carefully. "Well, I guess we can just take it from the top."

Oh, my God. My name is at the top of that list.

Please, Ms. Sanders, change your mind. Please, oh please, don't make me go first. Ms. Sanders, please understand–

"Brooke Dawson? Oh, there you are, Brooke. Well, you know the drill. Let's go, dear."

Darn. Did I ever know the drill. All those times I'd chickened out had led me to memorizing the procedures for the tryouts.

As I get up, I see Brett and Trevor peeking in through the windows at the main entrances to the gym, creaking the doors open bit by bit. Great. So now I know that they're going to be watching me as well as Sophia, Ms. Sanders, and the evil Daphne Carlisle, plus the rest of the girls who are trying out.

How consoling.

"Brooke? Come on. We haven't got all day, hon."

I hurry up to where she's standing.

"So tell us why you think you're uniquely qualified for the squad."

I wish I could just tell them my story and get it all over with.

"Well, for my whole life I've loved doing gymnastics. I wanted to try out for cheerleading since the seventh grade, but I always lacked self confidence. Finally, I realized that this was the only sport in school that I actually wanted to do. Plus, it was the closest thing to gymnastics that I could get, so my friends encouraged me to try out for this opening on the squad."

Oh, my God. What were all of those words that just randomly decided to spew out of my mouth?

Sophia smiles proudly. That seems to be an okay sign.

I glance over at the doors. Brett and Trevor are pretending to silently applaud me. How cute is that?

Ms. Sanders looks…impressed. I can't imagine why. "Well, Brooke, that sounded convincing."

Despite her praise, I can't help but feel embarrassed. My face feels hot, and I can just tell that I'm definitely blushing.

"So." Ms. Sanders claps her hands. "The stage is all yours, Brooke. Figuratively speaking, of course."

I half expect Daphne to exhibit some sort of snobby reaction, but she doesn't. It's probably only because Ms. Sanders is the coach of the squad, though. Daphne just doesn't know how to be nice.

"Thanks."

Okay. Going into routine.

Back handspring. Simple aerial cartwheel. Front split – easy enough. Now onto the more impressive stuff. Back flip. Aerial salto. Going on and on and on.

Time to take a quick glance at my friends and Ms. Sanders. If Sophia's gaping mouth is any hint, I'm doing well.

Maybe I'll throw in a stretch where I can arch all the way back and walk, then flip over into a standing position. Perfect! Brett and Trevor just started clapping for me!

Oh, no. Maybe that isn't such a good thing…

"Trevor, Brett…" Ms. Sanders begins in a warning voice. "You guys are going to have to find your coach or you won't be allowed here. We're holding tryouts here and we would appreciate if we could actually complete them without any interference."

Oops.

And Daphne just *has* to snicker again.

Um, hello.

We all know only too well that she totally used to be *obsessed* with all of those popular guys. But then again, I did happen to be one of the many people who knew that she was mainly in love with Jackson. Now he's on her side, so who knows what kind of dangerously evil couple they're going to end up being? Given the fact that they will get together, of course. But isn't that obvious?

But anyway, Brett handles the situation with Ms. Sanders suavely, which really doesn't surprise me. He holds up his hands defensively (like always – the whole 'my bad' event tells all) and replies so his voice carries all the way into the gym, "No problem, Ms. Sanders. We understand. We just wanted to see Brooke show off her absolutely amazing skills, but since that isn't allowed, I guess we can leave until Coach Davidson shows up. That is, if it really bothers you."

Ms. Sanders looks somewhat…guilty?

I guess she just can't turn down that face of Brett's.

And that voice.

But then again, who could?

That would definitely *not* be me. Oh, my God, he *always* manages to distract me. But not on purpose. If that makes any sense whatsoever.

God, I keep digressing.

"All right, all right, you can stay," she finally gives in. "Just don't make any more noise, okay?"

Trevor salutes her. Since when has he been daring enough to go through with something like that? Whatever.

"Yes, ma'am. Oh, look, there's Coach Davidson. Guess he's going to be a little late for *our* tryouts, so we might as well just hang here for a little while."

That kind of thing I would totally expect from Brett, but *Trevor* just said that.

Whoa.

At least he's coming out of his shell. I *guess* that's a good thing.

"Okay, that's fine, I don't care," Ms. Sanders says. She's starting to look just a little exasperated. "But if you *are* going to stay, just be quiet and let us go on with our tryouts! Otherwise we're going to have to share the gymnasium soon, and that won't be the easiest thing to do, gentlemen."

Trevor nods, looking a little like the phrase 'uh-oh' is playing through his head. Believe me, I can tell from his expression.

"Thank you. Go on, Brooke, dear."

Oh, God.

Here I go.

Sophia

Wow, Brooke is totally on a roll!

She's definitely going to make it on the squad, even if I don't have anything to do with the choosing.

Ms. Sanders clearly loves her.

Despite the fact that Brooke's using a lot of gymnastic moves.

Oh, good, she's continuing with her stunts.

No…

Why is she backing up?

She's going so far down the mat…there's a nice running start…but what is she going to do?

"Go, Brooke!" I can't help but cheer as she does a series of cartwheels and a flip, landing solidly and safely on both feet.

Ooh.

Daphne just gave me a death stare.

I'm so scared…not.

Honestly, what do you think she could do to hurt me? I've got my protective posse, right?

Ms. Sanders just glanced at me.

Brett and Trevor are silently clapping. That's so cute and sweet of them.

Ms. Sanders is writing on her clipboard now. She clears her throat.

Brooke is just going into a series of flips.

Wow. She is so good.

Looks like I've got some competition!

But that's all good since she's my best friend. I *love* being able to say that I actually have a best friend.

"Brooke?"

Brooke lands on the mat. "Yes?"

"That will be enough now, dear. Spectacular job, though." She smiles encouragingly. "Can we try some cheering, though?"

Brooke nods, breathing kind of heavily. But after doing such strenuous stunts, who wouldn't be?

Coach ruffles through some papers, and hands Brooke a scrap to read. "Think you've got it?"

Brooke nods.

Coach takes the paper back.

Brooke clears her throat and hurls a look at Daphne before smiling.

"Yell for the Scouts, because we can't be beat, so watch out Lions, we'll knock you off your feet!"

Her voice is surprisingly loud and clear. For Brooke, anyway.

But she was so perfect.

Take that.

"Thank you, Brooke. Next up – Daphne Carlisle."

Daphne smiles smugly and steps up to the front.

Brooke hurries back and sits down next to me. She's still practically gasping for air, despite her cheering.

"Good job!" I whisper to her. "That was totally amazing. You definitely made it onto the squad."

She takes a minute to respond, trying to catch her breath. "Thanks. I kind of messed up, though. I mean, if she didn't decide to interrupt that last one, I was totally going to toss in an aerial salto."

She really shouldn't look discouraged.

"Oh, come on, Brooke, you did really, really well. Daphne's going to be absolutely nothing compared to you."

"You think?" Her face brightens and she looks somewhat happier.

"Oh, please. I *know*. Whoa." I didn't see or hear Brett and Trevor slip into the gym and sneak up beside us.

"Hey," Brett whispers in Brooke's ear as he gives her a half hug, "you were amazing. You're on the squad."

Ha.

Someone was too nervous to give her a real hug. Scared it was going to be too awkward, little Brett? It might not have been if you actually did it…

Brooke smiles. "Thanks."

Ooh, she *so* likes him.

But I doubt he'll ever figure it out on his own.

I'm not going to interfere by butting in and telling him, though. Those two will work it out on their own.

After all, I've got Trevor to deal with.

Speaking of Trevor, he just leaned over to give Brooke a congratulatory hug. "You were awesome, Brooke," he says.

No competition there for me? At least, I really hope not. The last thing I need is to compete with my best friend for cheerleading *and* the guy we like.

But no. She likes Brett. I think. At least, I've definitely got to convince myself of that. Not that I have any proof of it, or anything. But believe me, I plan to find out the truth.

"Thank you!" Her smile widens.

"Tell me how glad you are that I convinced you to try out," he prompts her in a coaxing voice.

I guess I missed this part somehow.

"Very," Brooke responds, rolling her eyes jokingly.

Brett smiles and gazes at her. If I didn't have some idea that he was 'interested' in her, I probably wouldn't have seen the adoration glittering in his eyes.

I'm not too skilled with figuring out who likes who, but I'm working on brushing up on that stuff.

Hey, after all, I've got to be ready.

Trevor

Oh, yes!

I definitely knew Brooke was going to shine.

And guess what?

I was right, because she did!

Well, would you look at that. Daphne Carlisle is trying out for the squad now. At least I can sit back and know that Brooke basically just trounced all of those poor girls who barely have any idea of what hit them.

Whoa.

Not a bad speech, as much as I hate to admit it.

Really.

Here, plug this in along with a super snotty voice.

"I'm the best choice for an addition to the cheerleading squad for many reasons. Here are just a few."

Okay, first of all, that was way overly confident, plus way too conceited. She's also got that monotone but whiny "I've said this so many times that even *I* get sick of hearing myself say it" kind of voice that just irritates me beyond words.

Continuing on.

"I've tried out for the squad every year since seventh grade–"

And, if I might add, she never once made it, while Brooke is so going to make it on her first try.

"–and I feel that it's wrong for me not to have ever made it onto the squad."

Ha!

No matter how true that may be, you don't *advertise* it. I mean, duh. Even *I* knew that, and I'm supposedly unskilled with this stuff.

Want to know Ms. Sanders' reaction to that?

I can only too clearly describe it with relish.

She hears that part, raises both eyebrows till they're practically as high up as they could ever be on her forehead, and then begins to scribble something down on her clipboard frantically.

Wonder what that might be. I can just see it.

"Note to self: Never, ever, ever admit Daphne Carlisle onto the squad…even if it is to fetch pompoms from the supply closet."

Need I mention a reason?

She's so self-centered that she'd take all of the pompoms for herself and be like, "Oh, they're too good for *these* people. I think I should take them away." Really. I wouldn't put it past her.

"So I'll demonstrate a few of the supporting reasons of why I should have made the squad. Every single time I tried out."

That just cracks me up.

I'm sorry if I sound too sarcastic or anything, but that girl is by far the cattiest I have ever met. Not that I've ever spoken to her in person, or anything. But I also don't hope to in the near future.

I'm also sorry to say that I really did start snickering under my breath. It's too bad a lot of the girls (and Brett) around me heard me, right?

But it's even worse that Daphne heard me and gave me her only too well-known death stare.

Don't I just have this wonderfully pleasant feeling that I'm going to be one of the top people on her list to kill now?

Brett

I'm so proud of Brooke! She did so well! So did Trevor at our tryouts! They both definitely made it. I can't wait to see the list. Of course, I already know what the results are. Ha, ha.

Trevor showed off the really cool skills I showed him this weekend, and Brooke did more than Sophia had even taught her.

Sophia and I were so happy with the results of the tryouts that we decided to take Trevor and Brooke out to Giordano's for a celebratory pizza. The four of us make an awesome bunch. I wonder when we'll ever get the guts to admit the, um, *other* stuff to each other. That could definitely be awkward.

But right now, I can just sit back at my desk and relax, gloating over our success. I can't help but feel so triumphant.

Daphne was…okay, she was pretty good, but she's just so… malicious and spiteful, so I've just got to hate her. Besides, not only is she Sophia and Brooke's competition, but she's all close with Jackson, who I can't stand anymore because of what he did (not that anyone knows what he did to get kicked off the team, but he let down the rest of us), and she's so snotty about it! Seriously. What a cat.

Hang on…someone's messaging me.

Cool. Invite to a chat-room.

It's Sophia.

$0phi@ch33r: `hey brett want 2 join?`
brett_sp0rt_king: `duh`
$0phi@ch33r: `k, awesome`

Joining the chat-room…Can't wait to find out who's in this.

brett_sp0rt_king: `hey every1`
$0phi@ch33r: `brett's here. brooke?`
x0_br00ke_x0: `im here. hey brett`
brett_sp0rt_king: `hi`

Whoa.

Brooke's in this? Cool.

Wonder where Trevor is.

tr3v0r_tr0v3: `wait im here 2`
$0phi@ch33r: `great. so we're all here.`

Ah.

There he is.

And way to voice (well, write – type – type. At least, that's what I think) my thoughts, Sophia.

brett_sp0rt_king: yeah. any specific point 2 this or are we just here 2 chat?
$0phi@ch33r: um, chat, duh, but brett if u want 2 leave, u can.

Ooh.
Harsh.
Not taking that, though.

brett_sp0rt_king: hey. nothing personal im sure.
$0phi@ch33r: not at all. btw trevor cute s/n
tr3v0r_tr0v3: thanks. u get it?
$0phi@ch33r: yeah… trevor trove, treasure trove, right?
tr3v0r_tr0v3: yeah. i feel understood.
$0phi@ch33r: lol ☺
brett_sp0rt_king: brooke, getting bored?
x0_br00ke_x0: not 2 much or anything.
brett_sp0rt_king: yeah, right?
$0phi@ch33r: my apologies.
x0_br00ke_x0: no problem. so. how much hw do u guys have left?
$0phi@ch33r: nothing at all.
tr3v0r_tr0v3: yeah same
brett_sp0rt_king: well i still have the math hw… brooke did u finish it yet?
x0_br00ke_x0: no…didn't start yet.

actually i didn't write it down either.
brett_sp0rt_king: oh well that isn't a problem. pg.389 #1-50 p.401 #1-25
x0_br00ke_x0: what!?!?! that's sooooo much!!!
$0phi@ch33r: ha. now u bored, trevor?
tr3v0r_tr0v3: yeah…big surprise, huh?
brett_sp0rt_king: well, the 2nd part's only every other odd. So it's not bad.
$0phi@ch33r: totally
x0_br00ke_x0: oh yeah, that's sooo much better.
brett_sp0rt_king: well, yeah, i guess it is a lot. but I didn't hear u react earlier. weren't u paying attention when she wrote it on the board?
x0_br00ke_x0: no…on the contrary, i was 2 busy responding 2 all of ur notes…

Uh-oh. Busted.

Sophia's going to be so annoying tomorrow at school if and when Brooke and Trevor aren't around. I can just see her going, "You two were passing notes? Ooh!" and cooing and grilling me about it. I can't wait.

But I might as well take advantage of the moment's perfection.

brett_sp0rt_king: my bad
x0_br00ke_x0: yeah...but don't worry, ur totally forgiven. so want 2 do the hw together?

brett_sp0rt_king: sure.
$0phi@ch33r: ok guys im getting out of this. not rly in the mood 4 a study hall here
brett_sp0rt_king: sorry if we're about 2 ruin your chat room.
$0phi@ch33r: yeah w/e don't worry about it. i'll be online if any1 wants 2 talk.
tr3v0r_tr0v3: yeah well that's probably going 2 be me. im not rly in math mode at the moment.
$0phi@ch33r: cool.
$0phi@ch33r: *terminated.*
tr3v0r_tr0v3: bye guys have fun w/ the hw
brett_sp0rt_king: definitely thx see u 2mrw
x0_br00ke_x0: thx trev byeee
tr3v0r_tr0v3: yeah bye
tr3v0r_tr0v3: *terminated.*

Wow. That was the perfect setup.
So now it's just Brooke and me. How perfect.

brett_sp0rt_king: so brooke want 2 start #1?

Sophia

Well, so last night was pretty cool, and not just the tryouts. I actually liked the time I spent online a lot more than I usually do. And that really is saying a lot, considering the last conversation I had online other than last night wasn't really a conversation, since it was really just Daphne Carlisle's complete monologue of shooting all these insults at me in an attempt to have a place guaranteed for her on the squad.

Please.

Like I'm really going to get her a position on *the* cheerleading squad when Brooke is better *and* nicer than she is?

Not on my watch.

Besides, it isn't as if she really deserves it.

But anyway, onto more important stuff.

Trevor, Brooke, Brett, and I had a really long conversation last night online. Well, I spent more time talking to Trevor, since those other two were so set on doing their math homework together (of course, it totally helps that Trevor and I have Sanders *and* had already done the work, but whatever), but that's totally beside the point.

Anyway.

I can't wait to get to school and talk to my friends, plus see the list! It's probably posted up already.

Whoa.

Jackson does *not* live that near me. I never see him walking this way. So why on earth is he walking a constant thirty to forty feet behind me?

Wait…I'm not going to turn around, but still.

He's not following me, is he?

Why would he be following me?

Unless it's because he's all buddy-buddy with Daphne now, and since she hates me so much…

But seriously.

Does he think that's going to intimidate me?

Ugh, it's working.

I'm totally freaking out.

But who wouldn't?

He's big, muscular, he could crush me beneath his heel in a millisecond…but yeah, you get the picture.

Why on earth do I walk to school alone?

Okay, I just took a quick peek over my shoulder. He is still behind me. Obviously he's going to school, too, and he just happened to pick the same route as I did. It really isn't a big deal.

Then why does it seem so weird?

That's it.

I'm calling Brooke.

"Hello?"

"Hi, Brooke."

"Oh, hi, Sophia. What's the matter? You sound kind of… worried? Tense? What happened?"

Doesn't she just read my mind?

Okay. Now I have to test something. I make a quick turn at the nearest street.

I take another quick glance behind me.

Yeah.

Jackson's still there.

He's definitely following me.

I lower my voice. "You know Jackson?"

"Yeah, of course. Did something happen?"

"I know this might sound really paranoid of me, but he's never taken this route before, and he's been behind me for a while now. Maybe I'm overreacting, but I really do think he's following me."

"Oh, my God, really?"

Good old Brooke.

"Well, that's what I think, but I tend to overreact a lot…"

"Me, too. But be careful and check behind you every so often. I'll stay on the phone with you if you want."

"Thanks."

She is so sweet.

"Wait a second…" she says.

"Yeah?"

Anything to keep talking.

I've got to ward that freak off.

"Where are you?"

"I'm almost nearing the corner of Alpine and Valarian," I answer. "Why? Where are you?"

"Oh, hey, cool!"

"What?"

"I'm almost at Peregrine and Wilshire, and that's a block away from Rovenna, which is also a block away from Valarian and Alpine. I'll meet you somewhere on Rovenna. Look for me there."

I feel a surge of gratitude to such a great friend.

"Thank you so much. You have no idea how much I appreciate–"

Oh, my God.

Brooke

"Sophia? Sophia?"

I definitely couldn't have lost service. I'm in the open air, for God's sake. Plus I can see the sky. Let me try again.

"Sophia? Are you still there?"

I take a glance at my phone.

Weird.

It's saying the call has been disconnected from the other end. Even if she did disconnect it, what was the point of that?

Oh, my God.

I hope nothing happened.

What if Jackson snuck up on her from behind while I was talking to her and she couldn't hear him coming just because of my voice?

If something happened to her, I'll never forgive myself. It would totally be at least partly my fault, even if she is the one who called me in the first place.

I have to try calling her back.

No answer.

I'll try again in a minute.

No.

I can't wait any longer.

I'm dialing again.

This whole time I've been worrying that Jackson attacked her or something. And with good reason, too. Jackson is really strong. And scary. Besides, he would have been the best player on the basketball team…if it weren't for Brett. Of course I can't forget Brett! He's so…

Oh, my God, I'm such a terrible friend.

My only best friend (not counting Brett and Trevor) could be in serious danger, and all I can do is think about the guy I like and worry.

Plus listen to Sophia's phone ringing – and continuously getting her voicemail, which only makes me feel worse.

I've got to calm down. Got to stop freaking out and being so paranoid.

But what can I do?

I give up.

I'm calling Brett.

And no, this isn't just an opportunity for me to talk to him. Actually, we talked a lot online last night over the math homework.

Brett

So I'm walking to school, and my phone starts ringing.

The last person I expect to be calling me is Brooke.

So naturally you can imagine how incredulous and, well, ecstatic I am when I see her name on my caller ID. I just stop short and stare at my phone, letting it keep ringing.

Finally I decide that oh, hey, maybe it just might be a good idea for me to answer it. "Hello?"

"Brett, something happened to Sophia."

What?

No 'hello'?

But what she says doesn't click in my mind.

Wait…

"What?"

"I'm afraid that she's gotten into some type of danger." She sounds beyond freaked out.

Her voice makes me freeze. And it feels like my heart does, too.

She lowers her voice. "Jackson has been following her, and I was talking to her on the phone…" She pauses to shudder.

"And…?" I prompt.

It seems like she'll never continue.

"She just disconnected the call – or something else did."

Her words fall heavily – like hail.

I suddenly take note of the snow on the ground, seeing everything clearer. You would think I'd see red or something, or even a different color. But no. I see everything super clear. Weird, as you'd expect. It is me, after all.

But now…there is only cold silence.

"Well, that's it," I say, trying not to sound as nervous as I'm feeling. "I'm calling her."

"No, I tried that already. Three times." She brings silence onto me again. "She doesn't pick up."

Like I really needed confirmation of that.

"Well, if you're okay, just hurry up and get to school and I hope I'll see you there."

'I hope'? My own words are starting to scare me.

"Look, I'm going to call Trevor."

"Okay," she manages to say. "Hope to see you at school?"

"Yeah, hopefully," I mutter, trying not to sound as tense as I really feel.

Hopefully.

I can only hope Sophia's okay.

Trevor

Why would Brett be calling me before we even get to school?

Oh, well.

"Hey, Brett."

"Sophia's in trouble."

"What? She got grounded?"

"No. Jackson supposedly attacked her."

Oh, my God.

No.

She – I – but we were just talking at eleven last night.

She can't have been hurt.

"Brooke was talking to her on the phone because Sophia saw Jackson following her and flipped. Then the call just disconnected. Sophia cut it off. We can't reach her, and it seems like Jackson did attack her."

But Sophia's – I can't believe this.

I hope you haven't experienced talking to someone you know and making plans for the next time you're going to see them and then finding out the next day that something terrible happened to them.

I never felt anything as bad as that, so I wasn't prepared for hearing such terrible words as those.

They made me realize more than ever how much I really do love Sophia.

Sophia

You can't even imagine how freaked out I was once I figured out that Jackson was following me. I mean, I really would never have seen it coming.

But then everything got even worse.

I thought I was going to collapse with a heart attack or something. How often would you expect some guy to follow you along the way to school?

You'd almost definitely be thinking something along the lines of "Here? In Saffrondale? No way. There's no way anyone would bother following *me anywhere.*"

On top of that, all these other equally scary thoughts were hurtling around through the deepest, darkest corners of my mind. Questions, questions, questions. And they definitely were not comforting.

'Is he going to stay behind me in an attempt to scare me out of my wits? If so, it's definitely working well. Why would he be wasting his time on somebody like me? Is he going to try and hurt me?'

That last one had flown into one of the farthest corners of my mind once I realized Jackson was almost on my heels.

My mind was cleared of almost all of those totally creepy thoughts. And I really don't know how...but somehow I panicked anyway.

Brooke

I spent the rest of the walk to school completely freaking out.

What had Jackson done?

I kept worrying for Sophia's safety. After all, she *is* my best friend, even if we only started talking to each other last week.

I feel so bad for Trevor, though. I wonder how he's taking it. I wish I'd been the one to break the bad news to him. I've known him so much longer than Brett. Years and years longer, in fact. I know how to pass bad news on to him.

But I hate to say that no matter what Brett and Trevor do, they're not going to be able to amount to what friendship I shared with Sophia.

She was…different.

Brett

Oh, my God.

She called.

She's alive.

Better than that.

She's practically totally…

All right.

A little scratched up, and yes, her once-perfect outfit is covered in grass and mud stains. But who cares? She can change into something else if it matters that much to her. I'm sure Brooke or someone would be willing to help her out with her appearance.

But oh, if I ever get my hands on that Jackson…he's going down. Oh, wait, I forgot. I'm not allowed to hurt him. Darn. Sophia says to wait – we'll get back at Jackson and Daphne soon enough. I personally think that it's not a good idea – they might get to another one of us again before we can get revenge on them.

But hey, I guess it should be Sophia's call anyhow.

Ha, ha.

'Call.'

As in Sophia *called* me…?

It's funny how that's all she said to me about Jackson and Daphne, though. But she did remind me that she's going to be seeing me in school soon if nothing else happens.

Please. I *wanted* the details, but no. I'm not as special as *Trevor.* Watch – Sophia's going to go tell *him* everything.

No, I'm not jealous.

The truth is that I'd only be jealous if the situation involved Brooke.

Trevor

So I was so worried until I caught up with Sophia as I saw her staggering into one of the hidden side doors of the school. She seemed okay, I guess, but she looked totally terrible, and that isn't exactly normal for her.

I was waiting as far away as I could from where the two names were going to be posted – I didn't want to be alone when I celebrated after seeing my name up.

Not to sound stuck-up. But I already know I'm on the team.

Luckily, I caught sight of Sophia trying to sneak in.

Now all I've got to do is actually catch her.

"Sophia!"

She whirls around after hearing me call her name.

"Shh!"

I hold my hands up in the air defensively just like Brett would have done. I have to start being cool soon, anyhow. Now would be the perfect time to start.

"What?" I launch into a gentle scolding. "Do you have any idea how worried all three of us were about you?"

Obviously not.

She smacks her forehead in an exasperated way. "What?"

"We were worried…?" I notice her hand is covered in grass stains and…mud?

Whoa there.

The perfect Sophia Garrison should never be seen in public looking like such a…well, looking so bad. It just isn't her.

She stops short and leans against the wall tiredly, gradually sliding to the floor.

She is so lucky that no one's in this hall right now.

I walk over to her and sit down on the floor, too. "So. Want to tell me what happened to you on the way to school today? It seems to have been…unusually interesting."

She laughs.

Good sign, I guess.

"What did Brett or Brooke or whoever tell you? I'm way too tired to repeat all of this again."

"Um, Brett told me over the phone that Jackson might have hurt you, but that's pretty much it."

It's the truth, isn't it?

She begins laughing hysterically. Okay. That's not a good sign.

"Sophia…?" I really don't need an insane teenager having a spaz attack here. "Are you okay?"

"Ha! Of course he 'might have hurt' me. Of course."

I don't know what to say to that, so I stay silent.

"I'm going to tell you exactly what happened, but you're going to tell the others for me, okay?"

Duh. But I've got to be nice. "Sure."

"Good." She sighs. "Okay. So I was walking to school like I usually do, and then I noticed that Jackson, of all people, was following me. He never goes the same way I do to school. Actually, I always thought he took one of the buses, but whatever. Anyway. So I figured that maybe he was following me." She pauses.

I give her a second to breathe before reminding her, "You want to get to the part where you tell me how this happened to you?" waving my hand vaguely at her appearance. She *does* look weird.

"Sure, sure." She looks down regretfully at her outfit.

I roll my eyes. "Oh, my God, Sophia, I'm sure Brooke or

someone will help you fix up your outfit and accessories or whatever you call it. Clothes."

"Yeah, I know, I just – ugh."

Oh, my God! I didn't mean to let that out of my mouth! I would never choose to say something so mean to someone as important to me as Sophia! That's totally something I'd say to Brooke…not Sophia. I don't know how good or bad that is, though. Hmm.

"But that doesn't matter. You still look fine."

She snorts. "You think?"

Okay, maybe not.

"Well, all right, no, but we can fix that. Just tell me what happened so that I know who it is that I'm supposed to be watching out for."

Weirdly enough, I now have…competition? Ha! And now on top of all that, it's the strangest people, too.

I have the most random luck. I guess life can be randomly beautiful. But I guess staring at Sophia right now…isn't beautiful. How tragic.

"Fine, fine." She pauses again to think.

I know she's been through 'a lot,' but how much does it take to tell a story, for God's sake? "Sophia!"

She completely ignores and talks over me. "How about I tell all of you guys at lunch? Right now what is super important to me is fixing my personal appearance up." She lays a hand on my shoulder. "Popularity calls."

I roll my eyes like Brooke would have done. "All right. I understand that you've got to be perfect as always."

She beams, and despite how bedraggled she looks, she's glowing. And her hand hasn't left my shoulder. "Thanks, Trevor.

You're the best."

She's getting up to leave.

"No problem," I manage to say.

"So, have you seen Brooke?"

"No, she's probably still freaking out because she doesn't know what happened to you," I remind her.

A look of worry washes over Sophia's face. "Oh. That's not good. I have to find her now."

"Yeah, that might be a good idea."

"Want to come?"

I don't think I'm going to be able to stand up. In fact, I think that she's actually shocked me into staying put.

"No, that's okay. I'm not really in the mood for watching emergency makeup applications. Besides, I highly doubt that you'll be anywhere but the girls' room, and I can't exactly join you there."

She laughs, practically making me freeze. I made her laugh. And not for the first time, either.

"Okay, then, see you in English." Sophia slips off down the hall, clearly trying to hide from the others.

What a sweet girl.

Brooke

"Brooke! Brooke!"

Oh, my God. That can't be…"*Sophia!*" Oh, my God! She's back!

"You're okay! What happened to you? What did he do? You have to get help with that outfit now." I can't stop talking because I can barely believe she's actually standing right in front of me!

She looks happy to see me, too. "Yeah, actually, I was trying to find you. I really need to fix this, don't I?"

"Yeah, you don't want – um, ahem, *someone special* – to see you like this."

I almost said Trevor's name! Oops!

"Do you know something that I don't think you're supposed to know?"

And of course, she caught me.

Time to cover up my faux pas. "Um, well, you aren't too hard to figure out, Sophia. Actually, you're kind of transparent."

She stops and throws her hands up in despair. "Am I really? So, since you're so smart, Brooke, tell me who I like."

Okay, it was a command. And a compliment.

I open my mouth.

But before I can say his name, she interrupts me.

"No! Not here! We've got a lot of time before the bell." She grabs me by the arm and drags me through the hallways into a faraway bathroom that no one uses anymore just because it's, well, isolated from the other places.

So that's where we're headed now.

It's weird that no one is noticing us running. Or maybe everyone's trying to ignore us. I don't know and I guess I don't really care.

Funny that last week I would have cared so much what everyone else thought. But now it doesn't matter much. I guess that's okay.

We have about fifteen more minutes before the list is posted and then another ten before the first bell. That gives us time to fix Sophia's outfit and then head out to see my name on the list.

Not that we need to bother with the basketball list either. We all know it's Trevor and me!

So now we're safely in the bathroom.

As we presumed before heading here, no one is wasting their time by being in here, which gives us plenty of space and time.

"Oh, my God, Sophia, what did you do? Fight in the snow?"

Her outfit was cute once, but now kind of wet from the waist down and has a few dead blades of grass hanging around. There's a little mud here and there, and her hands haven't quite been cleaned of the earthly things it was smothered in.

Who knows what happened to her jacket during the scuffle that I know nothing about? She has it draped over one arm, and it looks a little worse for the wear.

"Kind of."

"Well, do you want to tell me what happened?" I pause. "Or not?"

"Yeah. Well, I was fighting Jackson off, and we landed in the snow. Like you said, I guess I did fight in the snow. That's what ruined this." She looks down at herself sadly. "I was trying to make it perfect. I guess it didn't last. Thanks to Jackson." She sighs, sounding so miserable that I can't help feeling sorry for her.

"That sucks."

"I know, doesn't it? He's such a retard. So is Daphne, now that I come to think of it," she added after some thought.

"Yeah, I guess. A smart retard, though, as much as I hate to admit it. But give me the details."

"I can't."

What?

"Why not? I'm your best friend!"

She chuckles, and so do I.

"Yeah, I know, but I promised Trevor that I would tell all of you guys at lunch. I was too tired to deal with everything three times or more."

Ooh.

The subject of Trevor and Sophia's varying relationship with Trevor awaits at my further discretion.

Ha, ha.

"Ooh, Sophia, so I was going to say Trevor's name as the guy you like."

Sophia opens her mouth.

"Oh, and don't you dare say anything to that. I know that I'm right. You so definitely like him."

She bites her lip and then gives up. "Okay, so maybe I do like him, but does he know about it? That's what I'm worrying about."

"Oh, don't worry, he'll never figure it out. Trevor's kind of a stupid guy sometimes when it comes to these things."

"Really?"

"Yeah, kind of." Not so true? Kind of. "If you want him to notice, it's going to take a lot of work. Just warning you, of course."

She groans. "That's good *and* bad."

"Yeah."

"So. What do I do to fix this?"

Oh. She's pointing back at her outfit.

How good of her to change the subject.

I'm definitely not going to tell Trevor that she likes him and I'm not telling her he likes her. It's too fun watching this as a kind of social experiment. Besides, it's better if they work it out on their own. Then it means more to them.

Besides, I have to figure out Brett.

And that's a tougher task than figuring out Trevor. At least, it is to me. Trevor's so random sometimes that I don't bother wasting my time.

"Um, I don't know."

She's wearing a cute white crop cardigan with a black tank underneath. I love the white twill pants that she's wearing. The embroidered black sash is cute, but it's got a little mud on it, which is going to have to go.

The jewelry is outrageous but matching. She's got black and white graduated necklace with unusually huge beads. Her earrings are white and black marbleized, and she's got this huge headband in her hair that's white with huge black polka dots.

Her purse is black and white. The shoes are black, shiny ballet flats. Very cute. Her standard huge Burberry tote bag is in surprisingly good condition, even though I have no idea how that managed to stay clean. There are really only a few problems altogether, but we can totally fix all of it.

"Okay," I say, "Let's get to work."

She points to the air-dryer hanging off the wall. "That's perfect for blow-drying clothes, you know."

I laugh. "Yeah. I know."

Sophia walks over and begins drying her pants. They've been patched with snow, which melted through into water spots.

"Wait!" I rush over to her with a wet paper towel and begin dabbing at one of the few muddy marks on her pants.

Brown, white. Not a good clash.

She's going to look like she's been fighting, and Sophia Garrison would never, ever do a thing like that.

Well, she did, but we don't want everyone else to know that.

She giggles. "This isn't going to look good after we're through with it."

I shake my head. "Of course not. It's going to look brilliant.

Brooke Dawson, at your service." I salute, and she smiles.

"Thanks, Brooke, I owe you one. What would I do without you…? Especially now?"

"I don't know, but duh, you owe me."

She nods.

Wow.

She's taking it seriously.

"God, Sophia, I'm kidding."

She laughs again. "Yeah, I know, but I really do owe you. But I could help you out by helping you get Brett."

I almost choke. "What?"

How did she figure *me* out?

She smirks knowingly. "I know you, Brooke Dawson. You like Brett. I *know* you do. Don't deny it."

"I won't. Instead, I'll ask you to prove it."

"Oh, please. I don't even need to."

"True." My face is red enough already. I don't think it will dare to get worse.

"Ha! I'm right!"

"Okay, okay, don't bother rubbing it in. Your outfitter might just walk out on you, you know."

"Oops, sorry, my bad."

"You sound like Brett."

"Ooh, you *so* love him."

"Shut up, Sophia Stevenson."

"Hey, don't bother even trying go there, missy. That's not even happening, so you can't say that."

"Only to shut you up. Besides, Brett and I aren't an item, either."

"Okay, you win."

"Oh, I always do, Sophia."

Sophia takes a glance at me and starts laughing.

"What are you doing?"

She is acting psychotic, after all.

"Brett's as stupid as Trevor. If he does figure out the girl, he finds it funny if she acts strange around him. It's so messed up, but it makes it so Brett. At least, that's what I think."

Helpful.

"Okay…you do that."

We're finally finished with her outfit, and I dab out the spots on her purse.

At last, we're ready to leave.

Now we can meet up with our dear Trevor and Brett (yes, I put Trevor's name first out of respect for my old friend).

And the four of us can go see the lists.

Sophia

Ooh, I'm so excited!

I feel so much better now that my outfit's perfect again and my hair is neat. Plus Brooke knows that I like Trevor and I officially have proof that she likes Brett. All in all, everything's pretty much good.

"Sophia! Brooke!"

"Brett! Trevor!"

It's the guys.

"How's everything going?"

All eyes in this hallway are on us.

The people here have got their ears open, too.

Given the conditions of our surroundings, I think it's best if I don't mention the incident that took place on my way to school.

"Don't mention the walk to school," I hiss at my friends.

Brett looks confused for a second, and then he nods. Maybe he really forgot about what happened, but I don't see how that could even be possible.

Trevor and Brooke quickly nod. *They're* smart enough to decode what I said – unlike Brett here.

Poor Brooke. I'm not too sure that she knows what she's getting into by liking Brett. He can be such a ditz sometimes.

Anyway, that's her problem. Her choice.

The four of us are on our way to see the postings, and we're almost there.

Suddenly Brooke pushes past the rest of us. "Hurry up."

Brett quickly follows on her heels.

Now I notice how cute Brooke's outfit is. She's finally beginning to wear more expressive clothing to school.

Today she's wearing a white tunic and dark jeans. She put her hair up so her bangs are down but everything else has been swept up by a black claw clip. Her earrings are black and white striped flat ovals with an oval-shaped hole cut out of each one, and her necklace is a thin black satin choker with a pendant matching her earrings dangling from it. The shoes…black stiletto boots.

Love it!

I mean, I'm wearing black and white, too, so we totally match, and that's perfectly fine. I would so rather accidentally dress like my best friend since we think so much alike than dress like my mortal enemy because *we* think alike. That would be freaky beyond words. Plus it would totally suck. Especially for my social life.

Finally…the postings.

Okay, so Trevor's on the basketball team. Celebrate! But that's old news…we all knew that was going to happen. There really was no competition.

But wait a second…

Oh, my God.

No way.

How could this happen?

Trevor

Yes!

I'm on the basketball team! It's officially posted on the wall, so it's got to be true! Finally. My time has come.

Hang on one second…

Sophia and Brooke are flipping out.

"Oh, my God, Brooke, I honestly don't know how that happened." Sophia jabs a finger at the cheerleading page.

My eyes scan the short printout.

What?

Daphne Carlisle?

That's definitely not Brooke Dawson's name there.

Brooke hasn't said anything. She's just staring at Daphne's name.

Oh, God.

We have company.

And this is so not a good time.

"Oh, hello, Garrison."

Sophia turns around to glare at Daphne as she pushes her way to see the so-called list. "Look who it is."

"Yeah, it's me. Face it, Garrison. I'm the best you've got. See you at practice today." She turns on her heel to walk away.

"Hold it, Carlisle. What do you have to say about this?"

Huh?

What is Sophia trying to get at?

"I'm so proud of myself. I've finally been shown justice. The best ones always win out in the end, Garrison."

Brooke's looking madder every second. Knowing her, she'll keep her cool and she won't explode at this girl.

Hmm…I don't know if I can say the same for Sophia here. She looks like she wants to strangle Daphne.

But then again, if she did, I wouldn't blame her.

"Yeah, Carlisle? Then you haven't seen the end of this cheerleading business. I'm sure we'll all be shown real justice when we're through with this."

Whoa.

Was that…Brooke?

"Yeah!" Brett lets out a word of encouragement.

Daphne just sneers and says, "Good luck with that, whoever you are. You're going to have a pretty tough time trying to change *Coach* Sanders' mind. Well, see you at practice, Garrison." She flips her hair over her shoulder, but I can see the tinge of fear in her eyes.

"Not if we have anything to do with it. Don't call her 'Coach' too soon, Carlisle. Nice outfit, by the way," Sophia calls as Daphne walks away.

"Thank you," Daphne replies, smiling down at her, um, apparel.

I'm guessing that blue and white thing's supposed to be called a tunic (gasp, it's similar to Brooke's, although Brooke makes it look good and Daphne does not), and she's got this weird belt thing around her waist. Her blue jeans are practically skin-tight, in an attempt to be cool, I guess, but they're destructed beyond coolness. Who knows what she was thinking when she bought those (or, knowing her, I wouldn't put it past her to *not* have paid for them)? I can't even describe those weird chains of blue and white plastic marbles around her neck, wrist, and dangling from her ears.

But no. She's not done trying to badmouth Sophia. "Nice mud on your face."

Brett tilts his head in a confused way. "What?"

Sophia groans and walks off down the corridor after snatching the short piece of paper off the wall.

Brooke follows her. "Sophia, wait."

"I'm going to talk to Coach Sanders. This is impossible."

"Sophia, it doesn't matter."

Sophia stops and whirls around, blue eyes blazing. "Oh, yes, it does. I have this feeling that this paper has been messed with. Coach Sanders would never have put Daphne on the squad instead of you. I'm going to settle a score with Carlisle. Besides, I detected at least a faint trace of guilt in her eyes. And what's with that mud thing? I do not have any dirt on my face. She planned that whole thing with Jackson, and that was her way of trying to show off her stupid scheme."

Brooke totally doesn't want to argue.

Brett looks at me and shrugs as if to say, "Let's go."

Sophia turns to us. "You guys can head to class. I don't think Coach Sanders would be too happy to have a whole bunch of us bothering her at once."

"All right." Brett clearly doesn't want to get involved.

I don't blame him, so I trail behind, and we head in our

separate ways to be early to homeroom while Sophia and Brooke stalk off to find Ms. Sanders.

I know this may be cruel of me, but I really do hope Jackson and Daphne get what they deserve.

It is only fair, after all.

Brooke

Daphne can*not* be a cheerleader. She was definitely not as good as I was. It's not fair! I should totally be the new cheerleader. And especially after all of my hard work!

That's why Sophia and I are on a quest to find Ms. Sanders and demand an explanation for the decision.

We're on our way to her classroom. Sophia's leading the way.

"Wait!" Sophia throws out an arm and blocks me from walking on any farther. She's peeking into the teachers' lounge.

"What?" I whisper.

"Coach is in there."

"But we can't go in, can we?"

"No." She appears to be mulling this over. "But we can – oh, no, wait, she's coming. Step back a little."

We pretend to have been walking innocently down the hallway.

Ms. Sanders emerges from the teachers' lounge, clutching a steaming stainless steel mug of coffee. Her coat is draped over one arm, and a tote bag is on her shoulder.

It appears that she just got here, but how would that make sense? She had to have been here to have posted that paper…

I'm slowly beginning to put things together.

"Sophia, I have proof–"

"Shh, Brooke, let me handle the first part."

I close my mouth. Guess I'm going to have to keep that little bit of information to myself for now.

"Coach Sanders, Coach Sanders!" Sophia runs to 'catch up' to Ms. Sanders.

The math teacher turns around. "Oh, hello, Sophia, Brooke. As you can see, I'm running a little later than usual this morning." She gives us a guilty smile. "I was up a little late grading papers, and I overslept."

Sophia stops short. I guess she's starting to piece everything together. "Wait a second…" she mumbles under her breath.

Ms. Sanders clearly doesn't hear her. But she does decide to say a few words that totally take me by surprise. "Oh, yes, congratulations on becoming the squad's newest cheerleader, Brooke. Practice will be today after school, but I'm sure Sophia can fill you in on all the details. Plus we have a game coming up tomorrow night. See you in class!" And with this, she hurries off so as not to be late to class.

Sophia's jaw about drops to her knees.

I'm confused. "What?"

"Wait, Coach." Sophia chases after her again.

"Yes?"

"What is this, then?" Sophia brandishes the 'list' in Ms. Sanders' face.

A bewildered look crosses my teacher's face as she reads the name on it. "Where did you get that?"

"It was hanging on the wall beside the basketball team's results," Sophia replies matter-of-factly. "Didn't you post it up?"

"Sophia, how could I have? I wasn't even here. But yesterday Daphne Carlisle followed me around after the tryouts, so I made up and gave her the printout to be hung up this morning just before homeroom. What is this?"

"This is what was posted," Sophia repeats.

"Daphne must have been behind this." Ms. Sanders shakes her head. "I'm going to have to have a word with that girl. She's taking this much too far. It's only high school cheerleading. She'll have other chances in life. Miss Carlisle is going to have to learn to be able to accept that. I understand that she was very upset about not making the squad for four years, and the fact that this is the fifth time she's tried out, but I can't do anything about it. She needs to learn to take rejection. What will she do come college application time?" Ms. Sanders throws her one free hand up in the air in desperation.

"I think you should talk to her," I suddenly hear myself saying. "She could probably use some help."

"Yes, well, I'm going to," Ms. Sanders responds. "I'm worried about her future, given that this continues. Well, girls, see you later." She finally manages to get away from us.

Sophia folds her arms across her chest smugly and looks at me slyly. "Well, we did it!" she says triumphantly.

I nod. "I know. Daphne is so, so busted."

"But I have a feeling that we're going to be seeing a lot more drama involving her and Jackson," Sophia declares.

I hang my head sorrowfully in recollection of what happened this morning. "Yeah. And that can't be good."

"No," Sophia agrees. "I also think Daphne will avoid Coach until practice, which she will show up at."

I glance up as we walk down the hall. "Really?"

"Trust me, Brooke, I know that girl. She will be at practice. But I don't know what scheme she's going to use." Sophia sighs deeply. "Anyway. Coming to French with me?"

"Yeah."

We're allowed to choose seats every day in Mademoiselle Sommers' class. Sophia and I have been sitting together for a few days now, and a bunch of the cheerleaders are there, but now I sit with all of them. This, of course, is somewhat interesting, since they spend a lot of time talking about their tans, their French manicures, and trivial things like that. So you can imagine exactly how much I fit in.

But anyway.

We walk together to French class. Once we get there, we realize that Mlle. Sommers isn't even there yet.

The first bell rings.

We find a row of seats and sit down where there will be enough room for the mob of Sophia's 'friends' – also known as the cheerleaders.

They come piling into the classroom.

"Brace yourself," Sophia hisses at me.

I'm confused. "What?"

She whispers, "They definitely got the word already. Just keep your cool when they attack you. Act like me."

See, if anyone else said that last bit, you and I would be thinking, 'What a stuck-up snob,' or something like that.

But the way Sophia said it was modest and not snobby at all. She was, after all, the most popular girl in our school, plus the best cheerleader and gymnast and everything, so naturally the rest of her clique looked up to her.

So obviously if I wanted to seem cool and relaxed to them, I had to act like Sophia.

Simple as that.

Brett

So I head to class. Trevor goes off to science class.

I'm on my way to history. Oh, joy.

But that's not what's on my mind right now. I mean, I actually finished the homework and some of it was kind of interesting. Weird.

I'm wondering if Sophia and Brooke ever did find Ms. Sanders, and if they did, I wonder if they managed to convince her about this whole 'truth' thing.

I really don't get what's going on.

I did figure out that Daphne did something to change who really is the cheerleader and that means Brooke isn't the–

Oh! I get it!

Daphne is such a…hmm. I can't even think of a word that would describe her exactly. At least, not a good one, anyway. Maybe I'll make up one. I'm sure the perfect word will just come to me one day.

Here comes Mr. Oakley. It sure took him long enough. I actually beat him to class for once. Wow.

Anyway, there's the second bell, and here come the pledge and the announcements over the loudspeaker.

If Sophia and Brooke were in the middle of their problem solving, then I hope they're going to finish up. They're late to French. Well, at the very least, Sanders *could* write them a late pass.

"I pledge allegiance to the flag of the United States of America, and to the republic for which it stands, one nation under God, indivisible, with liberty and justice for all."

Such loyal repetition.

I can't help tuning out these announcements.

But wait a second there…Listen up.

"Congratulations to Trevor Stevenson and Daph – oh, no, I mean, Brooke Dawson, new basketball player and new cheerleader respectively!"

Sophia

Well, as soon as Corinne and Kellie and the rest of the girls came bursting into the room, I knew they would all pounce upon Brooke.

I mean, they had to have heard the news.

They're all so into gossip and everything. And besides, news like that would be bound to spread faster than poison ivy.

So I decided that it would be oh-so-kind if I whispered a little warning to Brooke, and when I did? Boy, did she look scared and confused.

But *I* wasn't surprised when they all attacked. *I'm* the one who totally felt like saying "I told you so." But, just kidding, I didn't.

"Oh, my God, Brooke, congrats!"

"Good job, Brooke!"

"You're finally on the squad!"

"You're totally one of us at heart!"

I just watch her eyes get wider and wider.

It is quite entertaining that she didn't get it at first.

Finally she decides that it just might be a good idea if she responded to the barrage of comments.

"Um, thanks?"

Oh, *so* intelligent.

Ha, ha.

Of course, typical girls, they all keep talking over her.

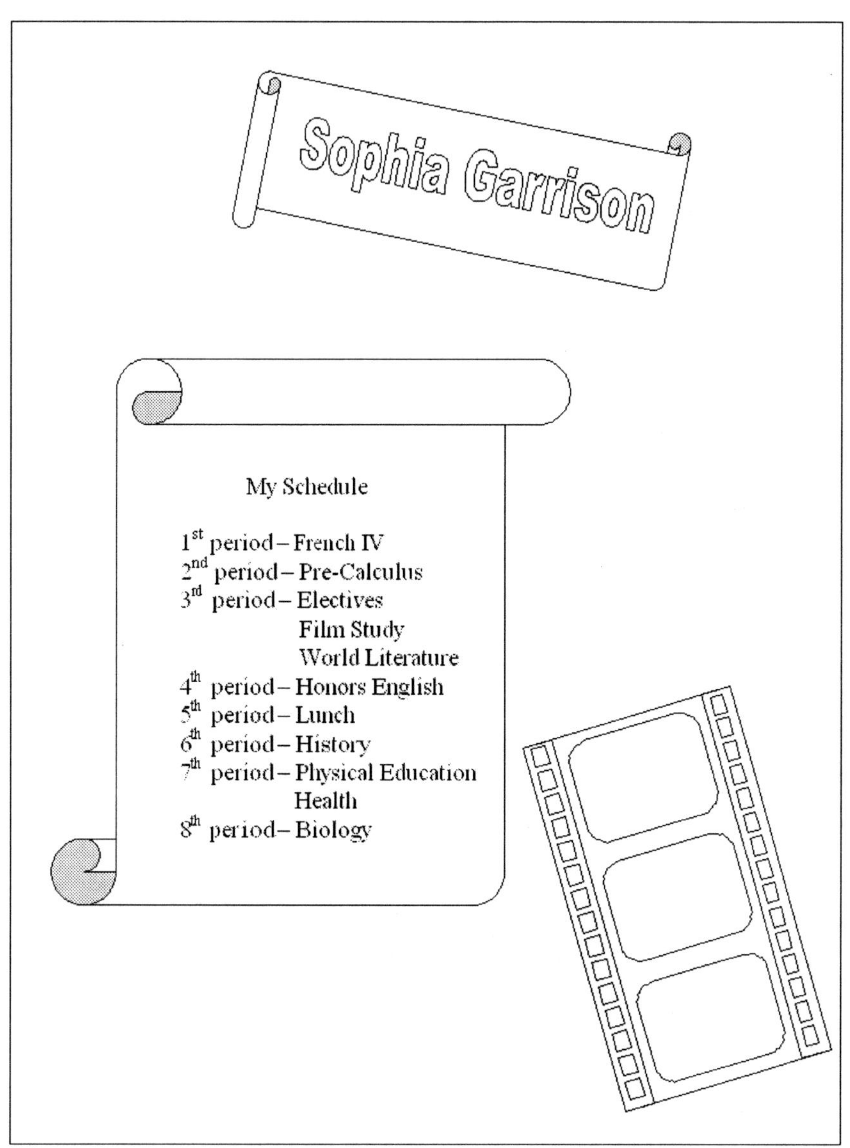
Sophia Garrison
My Schedule
1st period – French IV
2nd period – Pre-Calculus
3rd period – Electives
Film Study
World Literature
4th period – Honors English
5th period – Lunch
6th period – History
7th period – Physical Education
Health
8th period – Biology

Suddenly…Corinne comes to her senses. Or, at least, she *thinks* she does.

Please excuse my cynical ways.

I really don't have too many hard feelings towards them. They're just so preppy only to the extent of wanting to be…*me.*

Not to be conceited or anything. I'm just feeling so smug about our victory over that Daphne Carlisle.

Anyway.

Corinne manages to shut them all up. "Hey!" she calls so expressively.

Everyone glances up.

"What?" Kellie asks, looking around worriedly.

"Um, hello? Announcements…" Corinne hints, getting back up out of her seat to pledge allegiance to the flag.

They all follow suit.

Brooke is finally able to stand up after the other girls back a little bit away from her and give her some breathing room.

I, of course, have been pledging while keeping a hawk's eye on all of those other girls attacking Brooke.

That poor girl.

She's a celebrity just like me now.

Just kidding, just kidding.

Mlle. Sommers slips into the room and up front to her desk.

How sneaky. We all know she's late, anyway.

Funny that she was late *and* so was Coach Sanders, *and* I was plagued by that terrible incident on my way to school, and *then* there was that whole thing about the cheerleading earlier…

Is everyone around here having an awkward morning?

Brooke

Wow.

I totally did *not* expect to be mobbed by all of those popular preppy girls. It was actually really scary.

At least now I know that I don't want to be one of them. I'm perfectly happy in my own skin.

So now we're done with the pledge.

But no one can figure out why Corinne Carlton tried to hush us all up.

Was it because Mlle. Sommers was right about to come in?

Or…

"Congratulations to Trevor Stevenson and Daph – oh, no, I mean, Brooke Dawson, new basketball player on the team and new cheerleader respectively!"

Oh. That's why.

All of the girls start clapping and cheering.

"Go, Brooke!"

Applause, applause.

And it's all for me.

Yippee!

Mme. Sommers looks up, confused. "Ah, oui, félicitations, Mlle. Dawson."

Okay, then.

"Merci beaucoup, Mlle. Sommers."

"Oui, oui, oui, devoir."

Um, all right.

Someone's a little out of it today. I think she still has to have her coffee pick-me-up from the teachers' lounge.

Everyone stares at her.

"Devoir?" she repeats her voice rising higher and higher as the announcements fade away. "Homework? Take it out!"

Everyone starts scuffling around, trying to find the translations we were supposed to have for today.

"I'll be around to check it in a few minutes. Brooke, take charge of the class until I get back from the teachers' lounge. I need a cup of coffee…" She practically races out of the room.

As soon as the door to the classroom swings shut, everyone starts talking really, really loudly. God forbid another teacher hears us being so loud and unsupervised.

I look over at Sophia helplessly. "What am I supposed to do?"

She smiles at me and shrugs kind of vaguely. "Go up to the board and try to get their attention. You're going to have to work on your voice projection one of these days, anyway," she points out.

Great help.

Of course, Sophia jumps up to give some assistance just as I start making my way to the front. Apparently she got one of her superbly fantastic ideas after she gave me that useless advice.

"I'll keep a lookout," she calls.

Suddenly everyone shuts up.

"What?"

"Huh?"

They're all totally confused. But at least they're quiet.

Sophia comes to sit down in a hurry. "Go to the front," she hisses at me.

I obey, and within good time, since Mlle. Sommers is walking through the door, sipping a cup of coffee.

"Bien!" She smiles at me. "You may sit down, Brooke. Merci

beaucoup."

Amazing what coffee can do to transform a person in the morning.

"De rien, Mlle. Sommers," I respond dutifully. After all, I need to keep my grades in this class up in the atmosphere, if not in space. Just kidding. I'm not *that* concerned about my grades, except in the super-important classes.

Anyway…

"I'm coming around to check your homework."

Another great day has begun.

Soon enough we're going to be heading off to cheerleading practice, and Daphne Carlisle will definitely make a scene.

And I can't wait.

Chapter 4:

Practice Makes Perfect

Trevor

So I can proudly and safely declare that the four of us all survived the school day without any negative events, since we're in eighth period now, and nothing bad can *really* happen to us in here.

Translation: Brett and I are in Spanish class, Brooke's in whatever elective she's taking now (I think that's either web design or photography – I can't remember), and Sophia is in biology.

Señora Lopez is up at the front of the room jabbering in Spanish to one of the girls whose parents are from Mexico. That makes her bilingual in Spanish and English and whatever else.

Lucky girl. She aces everything so easily en esta clase.

Anyway.

I'm going to be a superbly good kid and take out my homework and wait for class to start.

Brett, on the other hand, is practically half-asleep next to me. He must have been up so late talking to Brooke online.

Ooh.

"Buenas tardes, clase."

"Hola, Señora Lopez."

"Ahora…Yo voy a chequear su tarea."

Everyone but Brett and me hurries to take out their homework.

Of course, I'm already prepared.

But Brett? He's still taking a nap on top of his stack of books.

"Brett?" I whisper.

No response.

"Hey, Brett."

How sleepy was he?

I poke him. "Brett. Wake up."

"Huh?"

Finally. A response.

"Okay, let's take it slow. Take. Out. Your. Homework."

"What homework?"

"Oh, my God. Spanish? Textbook pages? Does any of it ring a bell?"

"Kind of."

"So, Brett, did you actually do the homework, or since you were up so late instant messaging Brooke about your math homework and all that other stuff, did you not do it? I mean, I'm sure *you* would know only way too well that Brooke has always been taking French, *and* she's not *that* multilingual, *and* therefore would *not* be able to help you much with Spanish."

Boy, does that wake him up.

"Hey. Hey."

Well, all right, then. Way too expressive. I just can't handle it. "You okay?"

"No, no, no, you listen."

Huh?

"Brooke and I weren't up *that* late and–" He stops, staring at me confusedly.

I honestly don't know what's wrong with him, so I just raise one eyebrow and stare right back.

"Whatever, man. But I did do the homework. See here?"

"See what?"

He yanks out a wrinkled piece of paper from one of his many folders.

What a messy kid.

Wait a second…

"What's that?" I grab the paper from him.

Oh, my God.

Brooke:

Letter to Brooke?

Whoa there.

Before I can read any more, Brett snatches the note back.

"Hey! That's not it!" he hisses indignantly.

"I know *that.* But what *is* it?"

Oh, boy, I can't help but tease him.

"Nothing." He gets pinkish in the face.

Caught!

But I'll let him off easy this time…only this time.

"So?" I prompt. "Where is it?"

"Oh, right, the homework." He rummages around and I catch another glimpse of the note.

Congratulations on the cheerleading squad position! I knew you'd make it, just like I told you last night.

Ha! He doesn't even notice me reading!

Amazing that we got all of the answers right on the math homework. Well, then again, smarts go far with great minds. ☺

I'm really trying not to laugh.

I hope he won't give this to her, because if he does, I will die of laughter. I would so honestly crack up right then and there.

It's just so *stupid.* I'm biting my lip.

"Got it!"

I'm distracted by another piece of paper with all of the answers to his homework written down on it.

Suddenly he realizes what I've been doing. "No! I told you not to!"

Señora Lopez glances over at us, looking just a little concerned, and with good reason. "Chicos? Is everything okay?"

"Yeah, Señora, don't worry."

Brett, though, looks like he's going to attack me.

"Brett! Chill!"

"You can*not* tell *anyone*."

"Okay, okay, I wasn't going to, anyway."

He doesn't look too convinced.

"Chill!" I repeat, desperate to calm him down.

"Okay." He sits back and doesn't say anything else.

"You mad?"

"No…I'm actually excited about practice."

Hmm. Strange. It seems like he completely forgot about this entire note thing.

Señora Lopez comes by. "Chicos? Tarea?"

"Sí, Señora." I hold up my homework.

Brett shows her what's left of his.

"Muy bien." She moves on after raising an eyebrow at the state of Brett's somewhat tattered tarea.

"I can't wait for practice, either," I admit.

And it's true.

It's my first practice for the team!

I can't wait.

Brooke

Oh, my God!

First practice!

We're all in the locker room, getting changed for the first cheerleading practice with *me* on the squad.

Sophia just swung the door to her locker open to take out her sneakers.

No one bothers locking these lockers because we all have the same cheering uniforms and no one comes in here while we're practicing to steal our regular clothes – especially since we're after school.

Besides, who does that? I mean, seriously. Who is stupid enough and has so small of a life to vandalize or steal other people's gym clothes?

Exactly. Not really anyone.

"Oh, my God!" she squeals.

"What?" I ask.

"Someone..." She holds out her sneaker to me.

The inside sole has been torn out of the shoe.

Whoa...

"Who has no life to do that?" she asks me rhetorically.

My thoughts exactly.

But boy, oh, boy, do I have a fantastic idea of what the answer to that question just might be...

Even though it's totally unnecessary, I answer anyway in a low, dramatic voice. "Someone like Daphne."

Her eyes widen. "No way. You think?"

"Totally."

Daphne comes strolling by. "Loser," she mutters at Sophia.

Suddenly I hear myself retorting, "Go look in the mirror, Carlisle." I stare her down with my most evil glare.

She finally sees me. "Oh, look who it is...the wannabe."

Ha!

I'm not the wannabe...*She* is!

"Yeah, well, I wouldn't talk if I were you," I say nonchalantly.

"Oh, really?" She stops and folds her arms across her chest. "And do I *want* to know why *that* would be?"

Um, I don't know.

"Who cares?"

Sophia shoots a look at me.

Daphne flips her hair around and looks at herself in the

mirror. "Well, since no one cares, I don't have time to talk to you people."

Sophia can't help getting ticked off at that one. "Yeah? Then get out of here and never darken this place again."

Not such a good move.

Daphne sneers. "It's not like I'd want to stay here anyway." She goes off to a different corner of the locker room.

Sophia and I couldn't care less.

Sophia whispers, "Close one. I'm glad you didn't let her onto the fact that *she isn't a cheerleader*!"

We share a quick laugh.

"But I think it's really just way too tough to figure out who might have done this…" I say sarcastically, indicating the shoe.

She sobers up. "Yeah. She really needs to get a life."

"Totally. But for now…what do we do?"

She pauses. "I don't know. Is there any way to put these back together?" she wonders aloud, picking up her sneakers.

"I think so." I manage to slip one of the soles back into a shoe. "Here. Try it on and see if it will stay in place."

She puts on the sneaker and walks around a little. "Yeah, it's okay, I guess. Here, let me fix the other one. You get ready. Here's your uniform." She hands it to me.

"Thanks. Wow." I stare at the package.

It's wrapped in cellophane so I can see its perfection clearly. The top is a nearly full length tank in yellow, gold, and white for the Saffrondale Scouts. The skirt, I can see as I flip the package over, matches perfectly.

"We're going to be practicing in our uniforms today and tomorrow because of the game. That's usually the drill. On all the other days except the day of and the day before each game, we just wear gym shorts and a shirt. It's really simple stuff. Got it?"

I nod.

"Oh, yeah, here, take these, too." Sophia hands me a pair of pompoms that are encased in more cellophane.

They're brand new. Gold, yellow, and white to match the outfit, too. The gold shimmers and rustles as I take the pompoms out.

"Wow," I repeat.

"Oh, come on, Brooke," Sophia teases. "Don't tell me you've never seen pompoms and uniforms exactly like these before."

I shake my head vigorously.

"That's what I thought. I mean, I know you've been to *some* games before," she says with a smile.

"Yeah."

"Well, hurry up. I'm going to go talk to Coach Sanders. I doubt she noticed that we've got an extra unwanted 'wannabe' here."

I crack a smile.

Unlike the last time I was up here after school, I'm totally not nervous. Instead, I'm actually excited!

Brett

First practice with our newest team member!

Coach seems really happy, too.

"Okay, team, we've got our newest team member, Trevor Stevenson, to welcome. He's a great basketball player and our team's only going to do better with him. Now. Every one of you guys should be done with your stretching, so let's move it and hit some lay-ups!"

Yeah.

Coach loves lay-ups.

"We're supposed to be done stretching?" Trevor whispers to me.

"Um, yeah. Beginning before the drills."

"Huh?"

"We get here before practice to stretch. If you're exactly on time, you miss the stretching. We start with the drills."

"Oh. Okay."

Hmm. This guy really must be an amateur.

"Have you *ever* played?"

"Well, yeah, but not on any real teams," he admits.

"Oh," I say knowingly. "Well, don't be nervous. It's just practice. You can get nervous before a game."

"Who said I was nervous?" he asks.

Nice play. I'm not *that* stupid.

"No one. But I can tell you are."

"Snap."

I grin.

We get in line for lay-ups.

"Go! Go!" Coach is yelling from the opposite basket. "Come on, guys! Pick up the pace here!"

Everyone makes an effort to hurry up and the line starts moving a tad faster, but not fast enough.

Coach keeps on yelling 'encouragements.'

Trevor's in line right behind me, and he doesn't seem to want to stop talking to me during the warm-ups. But that's just fine.

He pokes me in the shoulder.

"What?" I turn around.

"If we're in here, where are the cheerleaders?" he asks.

That's actually a pretty good question. And I hate to admit it, but I'm not too sure where they are, either.

God. I really have to start keeping better track of my friends.

"Hmm," I say intelligently. "I don't know."

"Well, any guesses?"

"I have no clue. Maybe the cafeteria? Or the halls? Or the auditorium? I don't know. You guess."

"Just wondering. You took all my guesses."

I smile.

It's almost my turn.

"You remember how to do this, right?" I ask Trevor.

"Yeah. I'm not that stupid."

"Just checking." I grin.

"Go!"

Oops, my bad.

I run up to the basket while dribbling and take a shot.

Score!

Trevor does the same and makes it in.

Pretty good for an amateur.

Cough.

"Nice one," I say to him.

"Thanks, man, you too."

Trevor's a good guy. I've decided.

Sophia

This is totally going to be interesting.

I'm waiting for Coach Sanders downstairs outside the locker room.

The guys on the basketball team are in the gym stretching. I don't see Trevor or Brett, but then again, I don't see much of anything.

Oh, and here she is!

"Hi, Coach!" I bounce up to her, pompoms behind my back.

"Oh, hello there, Sophia."

"How is everything?"

"Fine, actually. The day's been better than the morning, thankfully. No more rushing and hectic craziness."

"That's good. But I think some of the girls are running late."

"Oh, well, what can I do about that? The question is, do we have any extra cheerleaders hanging around?"

She reads my mind sometimes, I swear! But then again, a lot of people tend to do that. Am I really as transparent as Brooke says I am?

"Why, yes, we do."

"Well, I guess I'll handle that somehow."

The basis of another conflict begins to rise up inside my mind.

"Uh, Coach?"

"Yes…?"

"Where are we going to practice?"

She begins to point towards the gym.

"Um, I don't think so."

"Since when have we had any conflict with practicing in the gym, Sophia?" She hasn't noticed anything yet.

"Well, never, but what about the basketball team?"

"Oh, that's right. I completely forgot about that. Hmm." She pauses and leans against the wall to think it over.

I peek into the gym. "There's no space for us to practice. We can't spread out now. They've just started doing lay-ups or whatever those things are called." I stab a finger at the court.

"Yes, that would be a problem. Well, I'll go talk to Coach Davidson." She slings her tote bag over one shoulder and heads for the gym.

"Need any company?" I ask helpfully.

"That would be just fine," she answers absent-mindedly.

That works for me.

I can check to see where Trevor and Brett are.

Slick. Oh, yes. How very slick.

We step into the gym.

Coach Davidson looks up from where he's been yelling stuff to the guys.

"Hello there, Sanders," he greets Coach Sanders cordially. And why shouldn't he? I mean, it's not like they're rivals. They work together.

Coach Sanders, of course, has to cut right to the chase. "Davidson, where will the squad practice?"

Apparently it's become their custom to call each other by their last names. I guess it's a Coach thing?

"I don't know, but definitely not in here."

"I figured that out, but where do we go? The team usually doesn't practice at the exact same time as the squad, you know."

"Yes, I know that. But with both the squad and the team making additions, and that big game coming up tomorrow, we don't have much choice. We have to practice today and tomorrow, plus run overtime for practice."

I'm trying to keep up with the conversation, plus understand everything that's going on, when I hear a voice interfering.

"Sophia!"

I whirl around.

It's Brett and Trevor.

"Hey!"

I glance at the two coaches to make sure they're still totally occupied with all their talking, and then I hurry over to where the guys are jogging in place extremely slowly and dribbling their basketballs in complete synchronization.

"Why aren't you with the squad?" Brett asks.

"Yeah, and where's Brooke?" Trevor says.

"We didn't start practice yet, since we now have nowhere to go," I say pointedly, with a disapproving glance towards the two.

"Hey!"

"Brooke's upstairs," I continue. "No one's ready except for me, anyway."

I involuntarily shake my foot, since the sneakers are kind of bothering me. I can't help thinking about how stupid Daphne ruins everything.

"Uh, Sophia, what're you doing?" Brett asks, looking down.

"Oh, sorry. It's just my sneaker."

"Your sneaker?" Trevor echoes, looking at me like I've lost a few marbles.

It finally dawns on me that they have no idea what Daphne seems to have done to my sneaker.

I relate the story to them dramatically.

Trevor's eyes widen as he shoots another lay-up.

"I just *know* it was her," I say.

Brett starts laughing.

"What's your problem?" I ask indignantly. "Those were new sneakers!"

"I'm sure they were," Brett says solemnly. "But who *does* that?"

Now I'm just confused.

"What?" Trevor obviously feels the same way.

"Okay, think about it."

The three of us slow down as we realize that the other guys have given up with the tiring lay-ups.

The coaches are still talking.

Brett barrels on. "So you open your locker and you find that the interior soles of your sneakers have been taken out. Someone has been desperate enough to try and 'bring you down' and they apparently thought that there was no other way except to break into your *gym* locker and take time to rip the soles out of your *sneakers*. Not that I'm implying anything mean about your sneakers or anything. But still. Who even bothers to *do* that?"

Trevor and I finally see the funny side of it all.

"Yeah, I guess it *is* really stupid," I agree.

"It really is," Brett says.

Trevor adds, "Of all the things she could have possibly done to actually hurt you, she picks ruining your sneakers."

"And they aren't even ruined!" I pipe up.

We come to a stop by the entrance to the gym.

Coach Sanders suddenly turns around.

Brooke storms into the gym, looking livid.

"Uh-oh," Trevor mutters under his breath.

I jump up and hurry over to Coach Sanders, grabbing Brooke and dragging her along with me.

"Come along, girls," Coach says in exasperation. "We're going to find a place to practice. Get the squad. Tell them we're going to be running late. Listen for an announcement telling the cheerleaders where to go."

"Yes, ma'am."

Coach shifts her bag from one shoulder to the other and hurries off down the hall, ponytail swinging back and forth.

We watch her dash into the distance of the corridor. She turns the corner and we run up the stairs to the locker room.

Of course, knowing our luck, we've got to run right into our nemesis.

"Look who it is. Don't run, you might trip and hurt yourselves. But it's not like anyone would care."

Brooke waits till Daphne passes to make faces at her retreating back.

I giggle. I can't help it.

But Daphne hears me.

Brooke starts laughing along with me for solidarity, even though it does sound somewhat shaky.

How nice of her, but I doubt she's ever held any type of insulting competition, let alone anything like this.

Not to exaggerate or anything, but life with Daphne being part of it? It's like a never-ending dis-off.

"What is your *problem*?" Daphne hisses.

"I could ask you the very same question," Brooke says with a stare equivalent to that of Daphne's evil.

"Oh, shut up," Daphne shoots back.

I hold up my hands defensively. "Ooh, I'm so scared, Carlisle."

Daphne mutters something under her breath and Brooke and I decide not to respond to it, not knowing exactly what she said.

Suddenly, I pause at the landing. "Oh, hey, Carlisle!" I call, remembering what I'm supposed to tell all the cheerleaders.

She's clearly debating whether or not she should stop. "What?" she answers back. "I don't have time for this."

"Yeah, well, practice won't start until there's an announcement over the loudspeaker," I tell her.

"I'm not stupid, okay? Stop trying to get me off the squad.

It's her who shouldn't be here." She takes a jab at Brooke.

"You're welcome. Just thought you might want to know that we don't have a place to practice yet."

She sniffs and stomps off, no doubt heading for the gym.

What can I say?

Oh, right.

That stupid girl.

As soon as she's gone, Brooke lays in on me.

"What did you do that for? She's going to think that she's actually on the cheerleading squad!" she says.

I smile slyly. "That's the point."

She stares at me in total astonishment, and then cracks up. "You're so mean."

"Hey, hey, hey," I begin, feeling the need to defend myself. "Don't go around getting the wrong impression there. I'm not mean. Remember the golden rule? Treat others the way you want to be treated?"

"Yeah, well, do you want to be treated badly?"

"Well, no, but still. She's being mean, so that's got to mean that she wants mean treatment back, so I might as well be kind and generous and give her exactly what she wants, right?"

Brooke starts laughing again. "Oh, my God, Sophia…"

"Oh, well, let's just forget it and forge ahead."

"Uh, yeah, sure."

We hurry up the rest of the stairs, and just before we step into the locker room, a bunch of the other cheerleaders come pouring out.

"Sophia! Brooke!"

"Hey!"

"How are you guys?"

"What's up?"

"What are you doing?"

"Why are you going back up?"

Flood of greetings. Plus some of the girls were quiet and just waved. Basically? We got a flurry of joy.

You just gotta love high school.

Brooke seems too stunned to respond. She totally needs to get used to her newfound popularity.

So naturally, I've got to talk for her.

"Oh, hey!" I greet them all back.

And since they all love me I get their full attention.

"We were just heading back up to let you all know that practice is delayed until further notice," I say.

Their eyes widen.

"What?"

"Why?"

"What happened?"

"How long is it going to be *now*?"

I hold up one hand in an attempt to stop the flow of questions. And miraculously, it does a pretty good job of working.

Brooke finally digs her voice up from the bottom of her vocal cords. "Wait," she calls out. "Sophia knows. Let her talk."

They all shut up instantly and gaze upon her in awe.

I almost start laughing.

Brooke shoots me a look. "Go on, Sophia," she says authoritatively.

"Right. Well, the basketball team's in the gym practicing right now, and that means that we don't have anywhere to go at the moment. Plus, both of our practices are going to be running way overtime, so we can't just wait till they're done. Coach Sanders went off to find somewhere for us to go. In the meantime, we're supposed to wait until she announces our new location over the intercom."

This information is received quietly. But the tranquility doesn't last long. The girls start chattering again as we move back down the stairs to wait in the hall outside the gym.

Just before we get there, we hear a door slam loudly.

Everyone hushes up for a second, and then they all break out in a flurry of careful whispering.

"Who *was* that?"

"Wasn't me."

"Um, duh, it wasn't any of us…we're all here!"

"Oh, yeah…"

"That would make sense."

"Then what was it?"

"*Who* was that?"

"*Now* what?"

"Okay, people, I'll go find out. Stay here," I command.

Brooke starts to follow. "Want me to stay with them? I don't feel like dealing with whoever it was," she mutters.

"Sure, that's fine." I flounce off.

But once I see who just stormed her way out of the gym, I stop and turn back into a little alcove lined by a wall, vending machine, and water fountain.

Who wants to be seen by none other than Miss Daphne Carlisle?

"Look, Mr. Davidson, I figured out that Coach Sanders isn't in there," she's saying angrily.

Coach?

How insulting!

"But practice is in the gym!" She stomps past the place where the hulking vending machine is sheltering me.

Her eyes are flashing fury.

"Listen, Miss Carlisle, I just sent Coach Sanders out. She went to find a place for you girls to practice! Now, please don't interfere with my basketball practice again! We have work to do!" He stalks away and into the gym.

Daphne whirls around without giving me any warning, perhaps feeling someone's stare upon her back.

And then?

She catches sight of me.

I quickly pretend to be straightening up just after 'getting a drink of water' from the fountain.

"What are you staring at?" She sneers.

"You don't want to be drawing attention to yourself," I say quietly, and keep on looking intently at her.

She seems to freak out a little.

I don't soften my gaze.

"What's your problem?" she says, and not for the first time.

I just raise an eyebrow at her and leave my safe house to circle around her with a final, strong stare.

"Get away." She pulls out of reach.

Seriously.

Like I would bother wasting my time on hurting her.

"Daphne!" a deep voice calls down the hall.

Daphne and I both freeze and whirl around.

Guess who? Oh, no one but Jackson Everett.

"Oh, God," I moan under my breath in exasperation.

Thankfully, Daphne doesn't hear me. No, she's too busy fawning over the fact that Jackson *Everett* came to see her after school *and in* school.

How very, very sweet.

Not.

"Jackson!" she cries.

I can practically hear the girls at the stairwell sighing in irritation. And, of course, I can't help it. I've got to join them.

But just my luck.

With my noise and the rest of the girls, Daphne hears one whole collective sigh of, uh, jealousy.

Like that seriously happened, but anyway.

"Shut up," she says to me.

At first I almost don't react, but Jackson hears and starts laughing. And boy, hearing that formerly-popular-only-thanks-to-Brett-and-me-and-I-don't-even-have-a-clue-why guy making fun of me totally ticked me off.

"Who was talking to you, wannabe?" I retort.

"Hey, Jackson, I wonder who that could be directed at..."

Lame...

Jackson finally catches up with her and swings a well-defined and well-toned (as much as I hate to admit it) arm around her shoulder. "I don't know, Daph. Can't have been you. You're definitely not a wannabe."

Ugh.

Since when were they officially a couple? With the two of them together, you'd practically expect them to throw a super-splashy engagement party for themselves just so the whole world would be able to know about their getting together.

She smiles up at him.

It's so disgusting.

"I know, right?" she says. She's practically melting in

mushiness.

"You know what?" I hear myself saying.

"What?" Daphne spits out.

"You two make such a lovely – sick, *nasty* – couple."

Jackson starts to say, "Why, thank you," when Daphne stops him by laying a finger across his lips.

Oh, how romantic.

Ew, no!

"Yeah? Well, just because you don't have a boyfriend, I'm sure you can't help being jealous."

I laugh bitterly. "Oh, sure, Carlisle, I mean, *Mrs. Everett.* Well, I really hope you have fun with your new boyfriend. That is, if he really does like you. Oh, and don't talk trash about me when you don't even know the partial truth. The lies will come hurtling back at you. In fact, it's called bad karma, I believe."

Daphne's eyes narrow in rage.

As for me? I couldn't care less.

I turn on my heel to stalk away to the stairwell and have a great grand exit, but before I can take a single step, so many things start happening at once.

One of the doors to the gym swings open, and Trevor slips out, only looking a little bit exhausted.

Poor thing.

"Sophia?"

"Trevor!"

I was honestly never so glad to see him.

Daphne interrupts in rage. "Better to have a boyfriend than to be single. You would know how important it is in the social life of popularity.

"Oh, yeah, and be careful. I'm going to rise higher than you."

"Yeah, well, you won't ever get invited to the best parties," I warn her. "My friends stay loyal, and besides, the official bouncers will keep you out."

Trevor chuckles. "Ooh, ouch."

Jackson has to speak up, of course, and interfere. "Look, *dude*. I belong on that team." He steps dangerously close.

I can only remember too clearly what happened this morning.

I tried so hard to get away from him, but I'm not used to doing that kind of stuff. He stepped behind a fence after he overtook me, and next thing I knew, he had overpowered me and I was on the snowy grass.

Surrounded by mud.

Yuck.

"Yeah?" Trevor says bravely, stepping right up so he and Jackson are face to face and pretty close.

Daphne doesn't do anything to stop either one of them.

She just smirks.

You'd think she'd want to try and protect her precious boyfriend, but no, she just stands back.

Is she scared of Trevor?

Ooh!

Or maybe she just is totally positive that Jackson could take on a million Trevors. But then again, maybe he could. And doesn't that sting me to know?

"Well, look, you obviously weren't good enough for the team," Trevor goes on. He's getting a little too toughened up.

I don't know how good this is.

"Oh, yeah? And you think you are?"

"Yeah, actually, I do." Trevor's starting to sound ticked off.

I don't really think a fistfight breaking out would be the best idea.

Daphne's looking a little worse for the wear.

We're both standing on opposite sides of the two guys. And she's starting to look a little worried.

Maybe she knows as well as I do that Jackson blows his top pretty easily.

But what she doesn't know is that Trevor's always going to stay cool.

One of the things about him to be admired.

And believe me, there's so many that they're practically countless.

Brooke

Oh, my God.

Trevor, why do you do this to us?

I can just feel the tension outside the locker room stairwell.

Trevor and Jackson just started arguing.

We all know how Jackson gets fired up. It wouldn't be pretty if they started fighting. But Trevor doesn't fight. He never has. And therefore? He has absolutely zero experience, which totally isn't good if he's going to have to fight a guy like Jackson.

Oh, my God, I'm so scared.

"Girls," I whisper.

Everyone looks at me nervously.

"This is the plan."

They crane their necks and ears to hear our only hope of saving Trevor from this terrible danger.

How sweet.

"Tiptoe upstairs."

They start to move.

"No, no, no, not yet. First listen."

They're listening intently.

I love this feeling of superiority that I get.

And it's sad that I've been popular for less than a week, while they've been up here forever and haven't gotten this much attention.

Ah, well, life isn't fair, as we all know.

It works in my favor?

I like it.

Who wouldn't?

"Okay. When you go up, open and slam the main door to the locker room. Make a lot of noise and start talking and laughing and whatever it is that you do so well to be loud. Come down the stairs and out into the hall and start staring and everything. I'll stay down here to execute the plan."

Kellie Hamilton whispers back, "But are you sure this will work? We have to stop them from arguing."

I shrug. "There's only one way to find out."

They all bob their heads.

Case dismissed.

"Then we'll hope for the best."

Trevor

"Look, man, you only got picked for the team because there was no one else left. All the good guys except me were always on the team. You're not good."

"How would you know? You've never even seen me play." I can't help sounding stone cold. My voice is iced…frosty.

You can't play nice with Jackson Everett.

He's just too bad.

"Dude, I *know*. You're only on the team because of Brett Evans, that loser of a captain." His face moves in on me, eyes flashing…riveting…dark evil.

Okay, okay, I'm exaggerating a tad.

But he does look really scary.

The first time I actually noticed him in the cafeteria, I noticed something else. I've said it once, I'll say it again – a dozen times or more – that guy looks ready to kill.

I admit it. I'm a little scared.

But does that stop me? Heck, no.

"Okay, say whatever you want about me, because I know it's not true and I don't care, because there's nothing that I need to prove to you."

Daphne snickers. "Yeah, you've got nothing to prove."

"But when you start talking trash about my friends, that's when there's going to be trouble," I continue angrily.

"Oh, so you think he's your friend, huh?"

Sophia steps in. "Yeah, he does, because Brett is his friend. Just like Brooke and I and the rest of the team and squad are."

Daphne butts in. "Oh, please. There has got to be at least one person on the squad who would never be his friend."

"Oh, really?"

"Yeah. Me."

"Sure, Carlisle. Keep thinking that. Keep dreaming."

"Shut up, Garrison."

"Yeah? Make me."

Not such a smart one.

Daphne steps forward as if she's going to try and hurt Sophia. She wouldn't. She couldn't. She'd never dare.

I want to raise a hand to block or somehow stop her, but I couldn't ever hit a girl. I'd break the codes of social life. Well, life in general, actually.

Sophia moves in, too. Jackson starts backing a little away. I do, too.

Sophia's blue eyes are blazing. But I see a faint sparkle in them. She'd never hurt anyone except when self-defense is necessary.

Daphne doesn't know that. She's definitely not sure whether or not she should attack, but she's also prepared to defend herself as well.

Suddenly a door slams upstairs. I can hear a mob of the cheerleaders coming down the stairs.

All at once, I wonder where Brooke is.

Then I hear her voice.

The crew comes out from the area where the stairwell is.

"*What* is going *on*?" Brooke asks, and the familiar look in her eyes tells me that she's known what's been going on all along.

What a good friend.

But what was her plan?

"No one asked you," Daphne snapped.

Brooke looks around, mocking confusion. "Since when could such an unimportant thing as the wind talk? Especially since no one wants to hear it!? It's most important on the sea…as far away from here as possible."

"What the–" Jackson starts to say, totally confused.

I have to admit, we're all confused. So he's excused – sadly.

I back away.

Suddenly Coach Davidson comes out of the gym.

Jackson's eyes widen and then narrow again. He's definitely

not going to let this go without putting up a fight. That's your typical loser.

"Trevor!" Coach calls. "What is going on?"

I hold my hands up defensively, just like Brett would have done in such a situation, and step aside, revealing Jackson.

Coach catches sight of Jackson. "Jackson Everett! You were kicked off the team, and my intention is to keep you away from it."

Coach has no idea what has been going on in the past few minutes. So he really has an excuse for making Jackson madder.

Jackson looks like steam is about to start billowing out of his ears. He clenches his fists and steps forward – up to Coach Davidson.

"Mr. Everett, I've warned you before. Leave."

Jackson narrows his eyes. "You know that when you kicked me off your team, you lost one of the best players."

"Oh, really?" Coach folds his arms across his chest and says sardonically, "Well, I guess that's the consequence that I was willing to face. Besides, I have replaced you. And I've replaced you well." He throws an arm around my shoulder.

Sophia and Brooke beam.

The rest of the girls on the squad (and I don't count Daphne, because she's not on the squad) grin too.

"Trevor, back inside. I want to see this guy leave." Coach gives me a friendly thump on the shoulder and sends me back into the gym.

I start to wave to the girls.

Surprisingly, every single one beams brightly and waves back.

Wow.

Now that is something that totally would not have happened

before I became the popular second star of the basketball team.

I head into the gym.

Brett greets me with a whack on the back

"Hey," I say, disguising my almost-choke.

"Where were you?" he asks. "I thought you were going to get a bottle of water or something."

"Yeah, I was, but we had an incident with a few people," I say subtly.

The rest of the team is listening in, after all. I don't think I should have to worry them about Jackson and Daphne.

Nothing they can't handle, anyway.

Maybe we should tell them…

Oh, well, all in good time.

All in good time.

Sophia

Well, that girl could just drive me straight out of my mind without even using much effort!

And even the thought of that ticks me off.

But anyway.

I'm going to try not to blow my own top.

Trevor's back in the gym. Safe?

Oh, God, I hope so.

But Coach Davidson is hanging around here just to watch Jackson retreat down the corridor and leave us alone.

Daphne looks so sad to see him go.

Ha, ha, ha, ha.

I'm so mean.

But she totally deserves it.

Corinne raises a hand and waves. "'Bye, Jackson!" she giggles goodbye behind her other hand.

I can't help it. I smile, too.

Soon Kellie is beaming along with Brooke.

Daphne has gone from looking sad to furious in a heartbeat. "Mr. Davidson!" she whines, stamping her foot.

He holds up his hands in the air. "Hey, I really am super-sorry, kid, but it's officially part of my job!" He grins and winks at the rest of us.

I laugh aloud, totally relieved.

"Now. Where are you all headed?"

"We actually don't know yet."

Just as soon as those words finish flying out of my mouth, the intercom finally crackles back to life once again.

"All cheerleaders, please report to the auditorium with your gear. Bring along a supply of gymnastic mats."

There's a beeping noise as the loudspeaker gets turned off.

Everyone looks around, totally mystified.

Well, everyone except for Daphne. She's just way too busy acting all irritated at Coach Davidson and everyone else for so clearly 'ruining her life.'

Doesn't that just make the rest of us want to laugh? Oh, yes, oh, yes.

Coach Davidson swings open the door to the gym.

I glance over at him.

"So, girls, it looks like you're going to be headed to the auditorium," he proclaims so intelligently.

"Yeah," I say.

Corinne is as confused as everyone else. "But how are we going to practice in the auditorium?" she asks Coach Davidson.

He shrugs. "Well, I wouldn't know. But I'm assuming you're going to spread out mats on the stage."

"Oh."

"Okay."

"Sure."

"Whatever."

"By the way, speaking of the gymnastic mats, you're going to need quite a few of them. I'll get you a cart to put them on. But you're going to have to pitch in." He holds the door to the gym open for us.

"Of course!" Duh. That was Corinne.

"Okay."

"Sure."

"Whatever."

We all file into the gym, leaving Daphne behind.

But, of course, she finally changes her mind and hurries to follow the squad inside the gym, but it sure doesn't take a genius to figure out that she isn't going to be helping us out very much.

Coach helps us load a bunch of the mats onto one of those big slabs of steel on wheels (just kidding, it's probably just tin or something), so we can cart it to the auditorium.

The guys are on a seven-minute break. You'd think Brett or Trevor would pitch in to help a little, but no, I guess their break is much too precious.

As soon as we manage to push the cart out into the hallway, the guys are forced to get back to their drills. The poor players.

Wink, wink. Yeah, I'm totally kidding on that one.

But before the door swings shut, Corinne, Kellie, and a few other cheerleaders manage to blow kisses to their boyfriends.

Brooke catches my eye and nods slightly.

So we both do the same for Trevor and Brett.

Brooke

Okay, so pushing a cart of gymnastic mats on your own isn't really quite a small feat to accomplish.

Especially alone.

Well, okay, we are taking turns, since the auditorium is all the way on the other side of the building. It's literally the opposite annex from the gym.

Plus, since our school isn't normally shaped, we can't go straight there. Instead, we have to go all the way around.

Yeah.

Just a little tiring.

Sophia catches up to me.

Corinne, Kellie, and the others are in a deep, quiet discussion about the most recent events involving Jackson and Daphne Everett (ha, ha).

In other words, they're occupied enough for Sophia and me to talk… without any unwanted ears listening.

Plus, Daphne decided to take the other hallway. And there's no need to worry…I made sure of it.

"Oh, my God, Brooke!" Sophia whispers excitedly.

"What's that about? The fight? The kisses blown by half of the squad? What, Sophia, *what?*" I tease.

"Everything!" she cries out quietly.

"Yeah, I know. It was so…"

"…Weird," she finishes.

"Yeah. Couldn't have thought of a more expressive word myself," I joke.

"Thank you." She sweeps into a dramatic bow.

I drop my pompoms on top of the cart.

"So, you like your uniform?"

"Totally! But you know what 'happened' to your sneakers?" I ask, pausing to let the cart move along on its own.

"Yeah…we discussed this already, remember?"

"Yeah. But it happened to mine, too."

"No!" Sophia takes over pushing the cart, much to my gratitude, and she does so with ease. She must be stronger than I am, or something.

"Yeah, actually, it did."

A look of realization passes over Sophia's face.

I stare at her.

"Oh," she says knowingly. "That's why you stormed into the gym looking so livid and furious."

"Yeah…"

Did I really look that mad?

Uh-oh!

An image of Brett's smiling face flashes through my mind.

God.

He's going to think I'm a spastic freak now.

And I am so not.

"Well, it's okay. It was righteous anger."

Relief washes over me. At least she agrees.

Corinne bounces up to us.

I shut my mouth.

"Hey, you two!"

"Hi," I manage to say.

Sophia greets her.

"So, did you guys get a load of that whole Daphne-Jackson

thing?" she asks in a low voice.

This girl is clearly like the rest. They all have a taste for gossip.

"How could we not, Corinne?" Sophia asks.

"True, true."

The three of us walk together in silence for a moment.

"So," Corinne goes on, "do you know what happened to her, anyway? Because she's not here."

"Oh, she went the other way," I say.

"Oh."

By now we're just a little ways from the auditorium. Sophia's been pushing the cart.

I pick up my pompoms and tighten my ponytail a bit.

Suddenly, Coach Sanders comes hurtling around the corner, with Daphne just on her heels.

"There you are!" she cries. "Let's get in quickly. It's already almost half past three. We only have till five thirty."

Everyone's eyes widen.

Five thirty?

Coach Sanders seems to notice.

After all, I'm sure we all looked incredulous.

"I tried to go till six, but you all have to be out of here by five thirty. We do have a lot to practice. The game's tomorrow and we have a new cheerleader to work with!" she reminds all of us.

Everyone looks from me to Daphne.

Sophia says to Coach Sanders, "We can stop before five, Coach. I'll teach Brooke everything for tomorrow."

Coach gives in reluctantly. "Well, all right, then."

The rest of the girls sigh their relief.

"Coach?"

Oh, joy. Carlisle has something to say.

"Yes?" Coach turns around. "Daphne? What are you doing here?" she asks, feigning confusion.

Daphne opens and closes her mouth in her own (fake) confusion. "Coach Sanders, I'm the new cheerleader."

"No, you're not. Brooke Dawson is the newest cheerleader, as if you didn't hear that already."

Daphne's mouth drops open.

What. A. Loser.

"What? Coach!"

"Daphne, I am not your coach. What you did with the lists was wrong. Completely wrong. And you have to learn to take rejection." Coach points in the opposite direction. "Now go!"

Daphne's eyes narrow into tiny slits.

First instinct? Run! At least, that's totally what I would be thinking. But does she? No.

"Coach!"

"Stop. Go."

Daphne hurls a look at Sophia and me. She mouths, "I'll get you for this," and whirls away.

"Daphne…"

"I'm going!"

"Now!"

So then the next thing we know, the wicked witch is gone. But she'll be back. We all know it.

Brett

Well, practice was extra tiring today.

We finished at five. Usually we're done by four or half past at the latest.

But since we have a new team member, namely, Trevor, we had to spend more time on the court before the big game tomorrow than ever before.

Now the team and the squad are at Giordano's Pizza Ristorante for a quick early dinner with one another. But for the first time, we split into more than one long table. The main table that we usually sit at was taken by some group from out of town, and so we had to break into groups and sit at booths. But we're still all together, so it's okay.

Sophia, Brooke, Trevor, and I are sitting in a booth together, waiting for our pizza.

Sophia says, "Look, guys, I don't think Daphne and Jackson were just fooling around when they made their last threats."

I have to agree with that, and it seems as if Brooke and Trevor do, too.

Trevor says, "Yeah, but what do we do?"

"I guess we should stay on guard?" Brooke asks tentatively.

"Yeah," Sophia says. "But we've also got to be extremely careful."

I nod.

Trevor adds, "I have a feeling that they aren't going to be too nice tomorrow, especially since the game's tomorrow."

I finally have something to say. "Yeah, because thanks to Trevor and Brooke, they can't be in a game together."

Brooke looks alarmed.

"I'm not saying I think that," I quickly reassure her. "But in those two's eyes? It's the truth."

Brooke nods. "I guess."

The waiter comes by with a steaming pizza pie. "Half vegetarian, half supreme," he says, "just as you ordered."

"Thank you," Trevor says.

The waiter smiles. "Enjoy!"

We wait till he hurries off before we continue our conversation, for some odd reason.

"So tomorrow's the game," Sophia counters. "Brooke, I promised I'd teach you everything you're supposed to know."

Brooke nods.

"You want to come over to my place after dinner?" Sophia says.

Brooke exchanges a glance with Trevor and smiles. "Actually," she says, "I think my house would work fine."

Trevor laughs aloud. "The shed!"

Sophia looks confused. I probably do, too. "What shed?" she asks for me.

Brooke proceeds to explain. "Well, there's this shed in my backyard, and Trevor and I fixed it up so it's like a place for me to practice gymnastics and stuff like that. It'd be the perfect place for us to practice."

I take a slice of steaming pizza and fold it in half, taking a bite.

"Okay, that works!" Sophia says with a grin. "I doubt you'd want to run into Brad. We won't have problems with Ashlynn, I'm sure."

Brooke beams back at her. "Well, not many, anyway. We'd be avoiding her pretty well, I think."

"Perfect."

Trevor clears his throat. "Brett, you too tired to practice at my place later?" he asks, looking nervous.

Sometimes I could really swear that I'm a scary guy. But I'm not. Brooke and Trevor just act a little nervous around me sometimes. What did I do!?

I swallow a bite and shake my head. "Not at all."

Sophia and Brooke smile.

"Trevor's got an awesome basketball court," Sophia says.

Trevor's ears turn a little pink. "Thanks."

Sophia doesn't seem to notice.

What a blind blonde. Not dumb at all, but totally blind. I can't believe her sometimes.

Just kidding. I'd never say anything cruel about any of my friends and actually mean it. It would just be a joke.

Brooke breaks the awkward silence. "Well, Trevor, I'm glad you survived that face-off with Jackson. You did well." She nods her approval.

He grins. "Thanks. Nothing I couldn't handle." He pretends to brush imaginary dust off his shoulder.

Sophia shakes her head critically. "You stepped into danger there, Trevor. I'm only glad you got out safely."

Brooke nods emphatically.

Trevor looks down at his plate solemnly. "Yeah, I know."

It all looks so stupid. I crack up.

Sophia leans over and punches me playfully on the shoulder. "Brett!" she scolds me.

I try to muffle my laughter. "Sorry. But you all looked like part of some reality show or soap or something."

Brooke smiles along. "I guess."

I'm suddenly distracted. We've got company here. Thankfully it's a good person.

Brandon Sullivan, an okay buddy of mine, strolls over to our booth. "Hey," he says, glancing at Brooke and Sophia and flashing a perfect smile that would disarm girls as great as them.

"Hey, Brandon," I return, trying to keep my cool.

He wouldn't try to steal either one of them, I'm sure.

Besides, he's dating Corinne Carlton.

Isn't he?

Oh, yes.

There's Corinne watching closely from their table…and taking such good care of her boyfriend by letting him stray so far away.

Brooke smiles back at him, though to me it seems a little forced, and not as open as it could have been.

But maybe that's because whenever she smiles at or for me, it's totally genuine, and I can tell when it is or when it isn't.

Ha, ha.

But anyway.

She distracts me way too much. I wonder if I'm as good at distracting her. I highly doubt it.

"So, you guys ready for that big game tomorrow?"

Hmm…that was too random.

"Yeah," Sophia says. "We just have some work to do to touch everything up, but we're good to go."

"That's cool." He leans in and lowers his voice, clearly for an attempted dramatic effect. "I hear that Everett and his new girlfriend might be there tomorrow night to do some damage to the rest of us."

So that's what he wanted to talk about.

What a big deal.

Not.

But I have absolutely got to brush off that nonsensical, newfangled notion (don't ask where that one came from: I really don't have a clue) in less than an instant.

"Nah," I say, "I don't think so."

"Why not?" he demands. "You've got to admit, it is a pretty

reasonable thing for anyone to assume."

"Well, okay, then, I'll credit you for that, but what would they do? We're all going to be on our guards."

"True."

Brooke edges a little into the seat surreptitiously enough so that only I actually notice her doing so.

I move in a bit so she can get farther away from Brandon, since that's totally fine with me. Closer to me, farther away from him. Perfect arrangement – at least, as far as I'm concerned.

Trevor says confidently, "But whatever happens, we'll definitely be ready."

And all I can do is nod my agreement to how right he is about that.

Chapter 5:

Scouting a Game of Disaster

Trevor

Okay, so last night Brett and I practiced our basketball plays and moves, just so everything would be perfect for today's game. Brooke and Sophia worked on their cheers, or whatever it is they were supposed to be practicing in Brooke's shed.

Everyone's super keyed up for the game. And in addition to being a little nervous about everything, I'm really excited, too!

We all hung around in the halls before homeroom, which is when we were so thrilled to hear that Sophia made it to school this morning safely and without any incidents involving Jackson and/or Daphne. That's definitely good news.

She and Brooke are wearing their cheerleading uniforms, just like the rest of the squad members. The whole basketball team is dressed up: pants, shoes, button down collared shirt, and a tie. It's a custom on game day, as we all know.

Now the morning announcements are over, along with the pledge of allegiance. Ms. Sanders is saying, "Extra credit to anyone who comes to the game tonight and gets an orange ticket from me!"

Ha!

I'll get more than what everyone else does, and so will Brett, Brooke, and Sophia! We're *in* the game.

I'm so hyped up.

This time?

I swear…

I really can*not* wait.

Sophia

Wow, so it's really going to be spreading fast that Coach (well, 'Ms.' to most people) Sanders is giving all her students orange tickets that are worth extra credit points if they show up at the game. That's interesting, since she's never done anything like it before.

All the more reason for this game to have a super-huge turnout.

I hear that some of the other teachers may be benefiting from this wonderful new idea that Coach has thought of. Maybe they'll copy it and have more people turn up at this 'totally huge' game.

Again, all the more reason. All the more reason.

But I hear that the Lodi Valley Lions are really good. They

haven't had a single loss the whole season – players or games. Then again, neither have we – about the games, anyway. And our team is even better than before. But their record is also pretty good from the past several years. They apparently have some kind of trophy that claims that they're the best, since the cheerleading squad there won the upstate New York cheering competition every single year. The funny thing is that I don't remember playing them out of all my years of high school and the two in middle school. But I don't remember that many. There aren't too many memorable ones that actually do stick out in my mind. Even then I can barely remember who's who. I get them all mixed up.

"Sophia!"

"Oh, hey, Kellie, what's up?"

"Nothing, just going to math next period. Is it really true about that whole extra credit thing with Madame Coach?"

Yes. But I'll let her flip about the worksheets once she comes to it. And I'm not going to say anything about them.

"Yeah. I already had math. I'm going to English now."

"Oh, that's cool. You have…?"

"Halitelli."

"Oh…" Kellie says knowingly.

Apparently she's one of many who thoroughly understands how, um, interesting Miss Halitelli can get, what with her strangely 'great' ideas and everything that she stirs up into one big mess we're forced to call English class. But she's still fabulous – don't get me wrong.

We near Coach Sanders' room.

"Well, I'm going to go in now," Kellie tells me. "I'll see you later? At lunch, maybe? You need to come back."

I nod. "I will. But Brett, Trevor, and Brooke are going to have to come along with me," I say, keeping my loyalty to them in mind.

"Sure, of course! If anyone at the table has a problem with that, which I'm sure they won't, I promise that I'll do my best to sort them out." She smiles and bounces into the classroom.

Kellie's a good person, I tell you. She's one of those shy girls who is really nice and turns out to be a popular cheerleader anyway, despite what it may seem. Plus she can be really outgoing if she puts her mind to it.

On the other hand, Kellie's best friend, Corinne, is bubbly all the time. She's a little too lively sometimes – for my taste, at least. But her boyfriend Brandon definitely likes that about her, so that's nice for the both of them. And it's also good that she's one of our cheerleaders – that means she gets a free way to let out a lot of her pent-up energy, all while we succeed with flying colors in getting the crowds super excited. But Corinne's still nice, so I guess that's fine, too.

"Sophia!"

I turn around and beam. "Hey, Trevor!"

"Ready for Halitelli?"

"Sure."

We slip into Miss Halitelli's classroom, only to be stunned by the brightness of her fashion choices for the day.

She's wearing only our school colors.

The outfit itself?

Oh, she's donning a yellow blazer, her usual I'm-in-law-school skirt, but in yellow, mind you, creamy yellow pumps, a pale, pale silk shirt, and her straight dirty blonde hair is swept up into a French twist, with a sparkling ornament of yellow and white stones.

You'd expect someone in that kind of outfit to look something along the lines of utterly repulsive, but somehow it just wasn't true.

See, Miss Halitelli is really kind of pretty, as strange as that may sound to your average outsider. She's young and a little sophisticated, being from Manhattan or SoHo or Brooklyn, or wherever it is in those parts of New York that she came from. Normally, she manages to look a little dull, but she pulls off something similar to the latest trends for her age, whatever that is.

But today?

Her blue eyes seem to be sparkling more than usual, and she's definitely wearing a little extra makeup. "Good morning, class!" she says cheerily as the bell rings. "Today I'm sure many of you are feeling peppy!" She winks at Trevor and me. "After all, this evening is *the* basketball game against Lodi Valley High! Oh, I can't *wait* to beat that school!"

Well, okay, then.

I think it should be quite safe to assume that someone's extremely excited about the game.

And I think there's an extra reason behind it.

Brooke

"Many of you have probably already heard that each of my students who I see at the game will receive an orange ticket," Coach – well, for now, it's Ms. – Sanders, says and holds up a roll of what suspiciously looks like the type of average raffle tickets that you can buy in just about any party store. "Each orange ticket is going to be worth a certain amount of extra credit points."

"How much?" someone calls out.

She holds up a hand to stop them. As if that's going to work a single little bit. But I can totally tell she's having fun with this.

"I haven't decided yet," she admits, but not without great self confidence. "It all depends on how many people show up, and how impressed I am in general."

Everyone immediately starts whispering.

"Are you going?"

"We should totally wear something *extra* school spirited for more extra credit," someone says with a giggle.

Mocking?

Not necessarily.

Brett turns around. "So I'm guessing we're going to get extra tickets," he says with a smile.

That smile. So cute.

"Extra tickets?" I repeat, faking confusion. "*What* are you *talk*ing about, Brett?"

He gives me a weird look for a second until he finally realizes that I'm just playing around.

And then the moment passes.

A bit of a delayed reaction, but we can work around that.

Besides, there are other things I'm worried about.

Ms. Sanders comes around, passing out worksheets.

Worksheets? Well, this is new.

Brett stifles a chuckle and passes me back a pair of worksheets.

"What are you laughing about?"

He doesn't say anything, just turns around and smiles again.

I look at the worksheets to see what's so funny.

They're those types of busy-work handouts that substitutes are supposed to give out to math classes, but they've got those riddles that you fill in as you do the work.

Suddenly, I see it.

On one of the worksheets is a basketball player with a Saffrondale Scouts uniform on. He looks something like…Brett? And there's another guy who looks like Trevor! Plus, there's the rest of the team…it's a caricature!

"Funny?" Brett asks. He's not super pleased.

I nod, trying to conceal my laughter.

"Okay."

Wait. He's definitely not done. What else is there to make fun of?

"What?"

"Look at the other one."

I turn to the next worksheet.

Oh, my God.

One cheerleader…Sophia.

The other? Me.

Oh, my God.

The rest of the squad is pictured below it.

Brett starts laughing. "Surprised?"

What?

"Don't tell me you knew about this."

"No, I swear I didn't," he responds with his classic defensive 'hands in the air.'

"Okay, okay."

"You may work with a partner," Ms. Sanders suddenly announces.

Brett turns around completely. "So, partner, let's start working."

"We're definitely going to get everything right," I hear myself saying, "since our faces are on the pages."

~ Chapter Five ~

Trevor

Well.

Something is most definitely up with Miss Halitelli.

She's super excited about the game, plus she is extremely hyped about beating the Lodi Valley High Lions.

Sophia just leaned over to whisper to me, "There's got to be something behind this whole thing."

I nod. "It's weird."

"I want to go find out."

"Sophia, wait!"

Too late.

She's already out of her seat and walking up to Miss Halitelli's desk.

No one else notices her going up to the front of the room. They're all too busy working on the grammar worksheets (easy stuff!) that Miss Halitelli handed out.

Speaking of worksheets, math class was too weird.

A drawing of *my face* was on one of them.

Brett was on the same page, along with a miniature picture of the rest of the team, and Sophia and Brooke were on the other worksheet, near another smaller caricature of the cheering squad.

Imagine that. Finding your own face on your math class work. So scary!

But anyway.

Now I'm trying to forget the creepiness of first finding my face there, and then the untold embarrassment of everyone watching me afterwards. I am a shy kind of guy, after all. I don't like that much attention for stupid reasons.

I'm waiting for Sophia to finish talking to Miss Halitelli.

Hmm. That actually doesn't look like it's going to be happening anytime soon.

Sophia's yanking over a chair and sitting down beside Miss Halitelli's desk to have a chat with her. Teacher's pet? I don't want to say that just yet. But we'll find out soon. We'll see how true it is.

Sophia

Well, Miss Halitelli certainly has an…interesting story to tell.

It turns out that when she went to college, she was taking all that stuff and getting the requirements and stuff she needed to become a teacher.

She always loved to write. In fact, some of her work got published here and there and she was pretty well known in college.

One of the guys that she went to school with just happened to go to college with her, plus live in her dorm wing.

He was a cool one in high school, she wasn't as much. Then, behind his friends' back, he started trying to 'connect' with her, since they'd both be going to the same college and all. They'd exchange writing, talk a lot, and they became really close, spending time together when he wasn't so busy being popular.

His friends found out, though, and started encouraging him to associate with girls who were of as high social status as he was, and so their high school friendship pretty much dwindled to an end.

But then, come 'the commencement of college,' when she actually thought he might like her for her and as more than a friend, he dropped her almost instantly and fell hard for her drop-dead gorgeous roommate.

Miss Halitelli's friendship with him fell apart, and he became the principal of Lodi Valley High, while she's an English teacher here.

I think that's just a horrible way to end an unofficial relationship – or, as it seems to have been, a 'fantastically irreplaceable friendship,' but she seems like she wants to kill him right now.

That's the interesting part.

I mean, you'd never expect your English teacher to have such a twisted personal past in college and high school.

Who ever knew?

But the thing is, Miss Halitelli is super excited not only about the game, but about us beating her now archenemy.

She let me in on a little secret.

He's supposedly been trying to find a way to contact her, but she refuses to ever speak to him until *after* we crush his school.

Ha!

I would probably do something similar, but I'd let him fawn a little over me before I decided whether or not I was going to forgive him. Plus, maybe I'd give him some time to let him feel so bad about himself for betraying me the way he did. Let him wallow in guilt a bit, too.

I know, I know, now *you* know that I can be so totally bad, but hey, he would totally deserve it.

Trevor isn't anything like that, though, so I wouldn't have to worry about that kind of thing.

Besides, I'm never going to be in that kind of situation (I hope), since I'm already the social queen.

"Well, Sophia," Miss Halitelli says, "I guess you and I can just watch, wait, and see our victory tonight. Make me proud so I can snub him to his face."

I can barely stifle a laugh at that. "Of course, Miss Halitelli, of course." I glance at the clock, and then at Trevor.

Miss Halitelli doesn't say anything else.

Maybe I should go do that class work.

"Well, I'm going to get to those grammar worksheets," I say, edging away to put the chair back.

"Sure, dear." She glances up. "Go Scouts!"

"Yeah," I say, sort of half-heartedly. "Go Scouts."

She turns back to her work, and I make my way down the aisles back to where Trevor's waiting.

"Well?" he asks, unable to contain his curiosity.

"Well, what?" I say innocently.

He rolls his eyes.

Apparently the innocence is an old joke to him.

"Come on, Sophia."

I stare back at him unblinkingly.

"Fine. Don't tell me."

Aw, he knows I'm going to tell him now.

"Okay, you win."

He grins like a little kid.

I add, "Just like you *knew* you would."

He nods proudly.

I sigh.

"Continue?"

"Right. Sure." I relate the entire story of what I found out to him, and what do I get as a response?

A plain, boring sigh, and he turns right back to his worksheets.

Are guys as perfect as Trevor *this* uninterested in a story so heatedly romantic and dramatic?

Sigh.

That strikes a blow on my love life.

"Oh, so that's it?"

"Hey, it's just not something that's superbly interesting and gripping, you know?" he defends.

"No!"

"Well, fine," he admits. "Of course you're against the *guy* in all of this…" He clicks his tongue reprovingly.

"Oh, please! You *know* he did the wrong thing, Trevor."

I look him in the eye, and by the way his eyes are sparkling, I can finally figure out that he's teasing me.

"Trevor!"

He laughs and hands me one of his finished worksheets. "Here. Hurry up and copy it so we can work on the others."

I stare at him. "What?"

"Copy it?"

"Trevor, that's your work. I can do it myself."

"Sophia…"

"Okay, okay." I finally take his work from him and start jotting down the answers quickly.

Suddenly a shadow looms over me.

I quickly shove his paper over.

False alarm.

Miss Halitelli is just walking – well, skipping, weirdly enough – down one of the aisles.

Weirdly enough, she doesn't even take so much as a glance at me.

Usually, she's got her eye on everyone and she combs the class for copying and cheating with the eye of a hawk.

She's way too excited about seeing this so-called totally nameless Mr. Lodi Valley Principal.

I would promise that I'll prove it, but guess what?

I don't need to.

Brett

So math was pretty fun, what with the strangely interesting worksheets that I finished with Brooke.

Well, okay, I admit it.

Hanging with Brooke was the best part of all the fun.

We're out in the hallway now, waiting for Trevor and Sophia to come out of English. Our waiting for them has become a customary day-to-day thing now, since we're all the best of friends.

"There you are!" Brooke says with a smile as Sophia and Trevor pile out with the rest of their class after the bell.

Sophia grins. "Yeah. And I have an exciting story for you, Brooke. I doubt Brett would be interested."

Trevor says disapprovingly, "Sophia, it's not nice to gossip about other people's personal lives."

"Sure, Trevor, sure. After all, you are the one who was begging me to tell you the story after I chatted with Miss Halitelli."

I give her a weird look, only on account of who she claims to have chatted with. "Uh, Sophia, are you sure you're feeling okay? Because I would understand if you're extremely worked up about the game…"

She scowls. "Of course I'm okay. There was just an interesting tale behind Miss Halitelli's extraordinary attitude, you know."

"Um, okay, then."

I was kidding.

Brooke says in hopes of defending Sophia and in hopes of

salvaging the moment, "I'd love to hear it at lunch, Sophia," with a sweet smile.

Sophia beams. "Thank you, *Brooke*."

Trevor chuckles. "Sophia, Sophia, what are we going to do with you?" He lays a hand on her shoulder.

The smile remains on her face. "Love me for me!" She skips away with Brooke right behind her.

Trevor glances at me.

I shrug.

"Let's go."

Brooke

Well, Sophia told me about the whole thing with Miss Halitelli during lunch, and I thought it was…interesting.

In other words, I can't wait to find out what happens at the game!

Thankfully, I won't have to wait too long. Right now, we're pretty much through with practice, and the game is scheduled to begin very soon.

The guys are sitting off to the side, doing some last minute stretches and stuff like that to prepare. The girls are all stretching, too.

Sophia returns from the bathroom. "Hey," she says, looking around. "Where'd my pompoms go?"

The basketball team leaves.

The gym starts filling up with eager fans.

"I don't know," I respond. "Didn't you leave them right here?" I turn to the bench only to see that they clearly aren't where she put them.

"Yeah, but I can't find them."

Coach Sanders hurries up to the squad. "Girls, get ready. The game's going to start soon. Start some of the pre-game chants."

Corinne and Kellie glance at each other nervously.

"Which ones?"

Coach bites her lip. "I don't know, but come up with something good. I'll be right back in a second to give you an outline." She rushes off.

I glance at Corinne.

She shrugs.

"Kellie?"

"I don't know. What are they doing?"

Sophia says, "I'm going to go find new pompoms. Someone obviously took mine. I'll be back." She leaves.

I'm thinking this might be the work of Daphne Carlisle, but I don't see her anywhere nearby.

Still, I won't rule out that suspect.

Suddenly, the Lodi Valley High cheerleaders start their chants.

"The power, the might, can you believe the hype? Let's go Lions, let us fight. The Lions will rock you tonight!"

Corinne's eyebrows shoot up.

Kellie narrows her eyes determinedly. She gathers everyone together. "Scouts fans, let's hear it."

Everyone nods.

I remember this one.

We burst out with, "Scouts fans, let's hear it. Yell with great spirit. Yell 'Go!'"

A bunch of people respond.

"Yell 'Fight!'"

"Fight!"

"Yell 'Win!'"

"Win!"

"All right!"

I glance around in search of Sophia.

She's not back yet.

Corinne leans in. "Fans, get ready!"

Nod, nod.

"Scouts fans, get ready! Let us hear you cheer! Stand up, show your spirit, and yell real loud and clear! Yell Scouts, Scouts, #1! Yell Scouts, Scouts, #1!"

"Scouts, Scouts, #1! Scouts, Scouts, #1!" a lot of people yell, drowning out the somewhat sparsely scattered Lodi Valley fans.

Oh, yeah!

We are so good!

I soon get caught up in the excitement of the cheers that I almost forget why I kept glancing at the doors.

Coach returns. "Girls! Head count!"

She counts the heads, and we're all accounted for.

I guess Sophia showed up after all.

Coach directs us with what cheers and chants to use, and we all go through an entire routine.

Suddenly, we've got a surprise.

Apparently the musicians who live in the band room (not trying to bring on any stereotypical offense, but in our school, they are pretty much the only ones around, and they totally do spend way too much time there) have been practicing more than just simple sheet music.

No, they've actually been putting together a mini marching band!

Seriously. No kidding.

They come in through the gym doors wearing yellow, um, 'uniforms.' I guess that's what those are.

Well, the girls are wearing short yellow skirts and tanks – wait a second! Those are…some of our cheerleading uniforms!

Aw, Coach Sanders must have made a deal with them. They get to be cheerleaders for a day, plus do what they do best!

How cute!

The guys are wearing the extra basketball uniforms, since there's only about five of them and five of the girls.

Their names aren't on the backs, are they?

Wait, yes, they are!

That's adorable! They taped them on!

Ha!

The girl at the front, whose name, I think, is Michele Clarke, is directing them. She's really pretty, plus I think she's a senior. She took over leading the band, I guess since she's so musically talented, plus a great singer and composer.

She turns, nods, and the group bursts into song.

The crowd is clearly as impressed as the rest of us who play spectators to this intriguing event.

And weirdly enough, the game hasn't even started yet.

But we're still awing the Lodi Valley High visitors and fans. The cheerleaders have stopped short and are staring. Gaping.

Lodi Valley High…

Suddenly, I remember the story of Miss Halitelli.

I glance around for her and don't see her anywhere.

Strange.

You would expect her to be here, considering her great enthusiasm about the big game tonight.

I scan the area for the principal, but I can't identify him, since first of all, I've never seen him before, and second of all, I have no idea what he looks like, even though I got the story out of Miss Halitelli during my sixth period English class.

Wait a second…

Who is that woman?

She's standing a little ways off to the side of the squad, watching the band go by with great interest.

She's got beautifully straight, shining blonde hair, and blue eyes (from what I can see, anyway). She's wearing a really nice pale yellow silk shirt that I wouldn't be able to find anywhere, and low rise cream-colored pants. Her designer handbag is draped casually over one arm.

Oh, my God.

That's Miss *Halitelli*!

Whoever would have guessed?

No offense, or anything.

Coach Sanders hushes us all up. "Time to let the band play and, well, sing. Please remain in motion, though!"

A couple of the girls giggle, but I'm too busy gawking at Miss Halitelli to see the humor of it all.

Miss Halitelli must be feeling my stare on her, because she turns to the side, and once she catches sight of me, she smiles.

She wasn't wearing that in school! And she wasn't wearing so little but such complimentary makeup, either.

"Hear the drums," Michele suddenly sings, "the Scouts will come!"

Wow.

Suddenly my mind plays a snippet of music. *'Hear the drums, Hannibal comes!'*

Hey.

Wait a second.

She's singing a spoof of…the Phantom of the Opera music?

Interesting.

Of course, it's still amazingly good.

Better than the nothingness of the Lodi Valley Losers.

Well, I can't say that just yet since we haven't exactly played the game yet.

Plus, it won't be nice.

But don't you worry. I'll be thinking it in my head as soon as we win!

Go Scouts!

Sophia

I'm trying to open the door to the supply closet.

Somebody picked up my pompoms, or worse, stole them. It doesn't matter to me that much, except for the fact that I'm totally missing the pre-game glory. It's not like the pompoms were extremely special to me, either.

I just have a terrible feeling Daphne's behind this. But how? I haven't seen her since during school, so I don't think she's actually anywhere near here.

Finally, the door's actually opening.

I slip inside.

Of course, it would help a lot if I actually knew where the storage of extra pompoms were going to be.

A rustle from a near corner startles me.

I'm not alone here.

This thought totally freaks me out.

Suddenly I let out a small scream.

~ Chapter Five ~

Someone covers my mouth with their hand.

I struggle to get away.

The vise-like grip on my arms is too strong…but in a way, too familiar.

Too…"Jackson!" I mumble faintly. That's not the first time this creep has snuck up on me…

I pause for a few seconds to distract him. Maybe he'll think I fainted.

Sure enough, his grasp loosens a tiny bit, which equals my chance to break free from his clutches.

Thankfully, I took a little karate when I was eight.

Can I try something a little smarter…?

I shoot away from him…

And straight into a metal shelf.

Ouch.

Despite the sting of pain on the back of my head, I hurry and charge back to attack him the best I can.

He's standing there, with a black baseball cap pulled down low over his eyes, in an attempt to disguise himself, I guess. Lame how he's wearing black jeans, black sneakers, and a black sweatshirt.

Danger in black.

I stifle a laugh at this totally random thought.

He tilts his head, clearly confused. And then he pauses to look down at himself, wondering what's funny. Is it his appearance?

Clearly.

I take advantage of the moment, trying my very best to ignore the back of my throbbing skull. I hurl myself at him, kicking my leg up for no absolute reason.

Of course, he's too smart for me.

He merely steps aside…

And I'll be quite honest and straightforward and admit that I totally didn't think of him doing that.

I go hurtling at the door, which is also made of metal and wood. My foot slams straight into it, and I go down.

I'm sitting on the floor. "Ow," I say inadvertently.

Jackson waits for me to stop moving.

I start scuttling away.

"Oh, no, you don't," he mutters.

First time he's spoken during this whole little scuffle.

Anyway.

Maybe I can get away.

He isn't too near me…

I reach for the doorknob as surreptitiously as possible.

Not hidden enough for him not to see.

"I don't think so." He steps forward with one big stride and yanks me away, tossing me with incredible strength into a corner.

Thud.

I'm actually getting used to the pain, most of which was self-inflicted, as sad as it is for me to admit it.

He reaches over to the top of a shelf and says, "Here's what you've been looking for." And then he knocks a stack of boxes down.

Pompoms come fluttering down (gee, I wonder how *he* knew that's what I was looking for – cough, Daphne), and the next thing I know? I'm buried under a whole lot of cartons and pompoms and dusty clouds.

I hear Jackson slip out and the lock clicks in place.

It hits me hard that I'm going to be stuck in here until someone opens the door, digs through the stuff, and finds me. And that could take a while.

What about the game?

What about my cheerleading?

What about the rest of the squad surviving without me?

What about the special cheers that we so carefully put together?

What about Brooke and Trevor's first game?

What about…

Suddenly I figure out that I really can't breathe well, being totally overwhelmed by the strong fake smell of whatever they made all of those pompoms that smell so weirdly disgusting out of, and then…

The world…goes…

Black.

Trevor

"Time to fly," Coach Davidson says and claps his hands once.

"Let's go!" Brett yells.

Coach smiles. "Go, Scouts!"

We hurtle out of the locker room and into the hall.

I hear a crash of – it sounds like cartons – somewhere nearby, but apparently no one else does. I guess it's probably just a strange case of pre-game nerves.

Brett leans over. "You okay?"

"Sure. Why not?"

"Well, I don't know. First game…Aren't you a little nervous?" he asks curiously.

I guess when it was his first game (must have been so long ago…) he was 'a little nervous, too.' He probably remembers.

"Not really," I lie.

He grins, but I think he knows that I'm lying. He should know. "That's cool."

"Go!"

We run into the gym.

The cheerleaders and the fans start cheering.

The Lodi Valley Lions enter…

To less cheering.

Ha!

In their faces!

We're going to start the game now.

I catch a quick glimpse Brooke cheering for me…well, really for Brett, but me, too.

Wow!

Since when do we have a mini marching band?

Oh, well, I'll definitely take that. What a cool surprise!

Who the heck is…whoa. Miss *Halitelli*?

Wow. I wonder how Sophia must be taking that drastic change. Wherever she is. I mean, I don't exactly see her. Whatever. She's probably mixed in somewhere with the rest of the girls.

But Brooke, too, actually. She's doing very well with this cheering thing. I'm so proud of her.

Almost as proud as I am of myself.

Ha, ha.

And the game begins.

Brooke

Here's my big performance!

I'm so nervous that I can't even get up on top of the girls

without completely ignoring them.

I memorized my chant word for word. But then again, the rest of the girls did, too.

Here we go!

I'm up top.

Too scared to look down for fear I'll fall.

Well, let's go.

"Brett Evans makes every play, and he can confuse you all the way! Trevor and Brandon, they're super quick, and to make the baskets, they're our pick! The rest of our team can totally attack, and tonight they're gonna take your trophy back!"

I breathe a sigh of relief.

It's done. The hardest part.

Now all I have to do is stand up here and get the crowd cheering.

"Go Scouts! Go Scouts! Go, go, go, Sc–"

Whoa.

That was definitely a shift that I felt.

Sophia?

Oh, my God.

No!

That's not Sophia.

Daphne?!

Shift again.

Slipping…

Falling…

Wait.

Falling?

I let out a scream. "No, Daphne, *no*!"

Chapter 6:

Salvaging the Ruins

Brett

I can't believe the four of us are at the hospital.

And there I was, talking about how all of us would be on our guards tonight, looking out for danger. And then even I get all caught up in the excitement of the game and I regret admitting that even *I* forgot.

I shudder.

It's so scary how everything happens in seconds. A split second, and the pain of danger strikes.

~ Chapter Six ~

You can imagine that it all happened so quickly.

It all started when I had turned to glance over at the cheerleaders to watch as they chanted out a really cute cheer.

"Brett Evans will call each play, and he can beat you all the way! Trevor and Brandon are so quick, and to make the baskets, they're our pick! The rest of our team can really attack, and tonight they will grab your trophy back!"

Or something like that.

It had been really cute, plus they mentioned a few of our names. The important ones, anyway.

So I was shooting glances back and forth from the game to Brooke, who was at the very top of the pyramid, and I was also kind of wondering where Sophia was.

In other words, I was multi-tasking.

Since I was pretty far away, I assumed that Sophia was the one right below Brooke, supporting her.

Then, just as I got a closer look at the girl's heavily made-up face, I realized that it wasn't Sophia.

It was none other than the source of evil…Daphne Carlisle.

And no, I am not exaggerating even the tiniest bit. She really is the Wicked Witch of the West – only we were the ones who had to be burdened the great misfortune of having her move all the way to the East.

If that makes any sense.

But anyway.

Just as it clicked in my mind that Daphne was right below Brooke – which was where Sophia was supposed to be – I saw Daphne shift a little in her place, and before I could move a single muscle, Brooke let out a scream and was suddenly seen crumpled in a heap on the gym floor.

Chaos broke out just as Trevor passed the ball to me, unaware of what was going on since he was clearly concentrating too hard on the game.

I was barely paying any attention, but I hurled the basketball at the backboard in hopes of letting out my suddenly accumulated emotions, and I almost didn't hear the buzzer sound as it went through the hoop.

I started to run off the court, with Trevor hot on my heels. Neither of us got very far, though. Within seconds, there was a blockade formed by the administrators. Trevor and I were held back by a few pairs of arms. Luckily for us, we had a good view of the scene.

Brooke was staggering to her feet, gingerly moving each limb. Her face suddenly was contorted in pain when she attempted to move her left arm.

Ms. Sanders pushed her way back to Brooke. "Can you move the arm at all, honey?" she asked.

Brooke shrugged and winced again as she rolled her shoulder back. "I don't know," she said shakily. "It hurts."

Ms. Sanders put a comforting arm around Brooke's right shoulder. "I'm sure it does, honey," she said. "Do you think a trip to the hospital would be in order?"

Trevor and I exchanged a glance.

The hospital?

If only it wasn't that bad.

Brooke's eyes widened almost fearfully. "No, no, no," she answered quickly, "that's okay. It isn't *that* bad. Maybe after the game?"

Ms. Sanders looked like she was going to argue, but Brooke stared back pleadingly, almost insisting that she would be allowed to remain at the game.

"I'll stay on the bench," Brooke begged.

"Hon, you really shouldn't stay."

"I want to," Brooke answered. She opened her mouth to say more, but she was interrupted by a figure of authority.

Coach Davidson pushed in. "I understand that there's an injury, but we have to continue the game or forfeit, pushing us out."

Ms. Sanders nodded. "I understand, too. Brooke, are you sure?"

Brooke nodded. "Definitely." She cradled her arm carefully. "But I'd like some kind of sling or something, if possible."

"Of course."

"And," Brooke continued, "I'd like to see that this, uh, 'cheerleader' gets unmasked." She led Ms. Sanders over to where the disguised Daphne was trying to hide inside the bunch of other cheerleaders.

Ms. Sanders looked confused. "Who?"

"This wannabe Sophia." Brooke reached out with her good arm and dragged Daphne out into the open.

A bunch of people gasped dramatically.

Trevor was one of them, since he apparently didn't notice much of this. What a committed basketball player.

Brooke maintained a firm grip on Daphne's arm, yanked off the blonde wig, and wiped off some of the makeup.

Ms. Sanders' face grew stern. "Daphne Carlisle. What is the meaning of this?" she demanded.

Daphne stayed sour and silent.

The crowd suddenly grew quieter.

I heard the gym doors creak open.

Trevor and I automatically tilted our heads to see who was entering, as was our automatic custom at all times.

There we were surprised to see a sneaky Jackson trying to fit in with the remainder of the crowd.

"Jackson Everett!" Trevor called out.

Everyone's heads turned to stare him down.

"Sorry," he said, shrinking back behind me.

"No," I said suddenly, "he's right. Look over there." As I pointed, a whole bunch of people turned to follow my gaze.

Coach Davidson happened to be one of them.

Sucks for Everett.

"Jackson!" he boomed. "Are you involved in this?"

Jackson had been trying to slip past, but saw that he was cornered. "What?" he said innocently.

I broke away from the rest of the people to confront the idiot. "What have you done with Sophia?" I demanded.

"What have I–?" It suddenly dawned on him that he was in serious trouble. "I haven't done anything!"

Everyone turned back from me to Daphne.

She narrowed her eyes and didn't speak.

Ms. Sanders tried again for the last time. "Daphne, I'm warning you, it's either now or never."

Brooke decided to speak up. "Daphne, let's just put it this way. You just ruined your only chances of ever getting anywhere athletically. You only have one way of attempting to get out of this mess. So perhaps you'd like to share a small piece of information with the rest of us. Where is Sophia?"

Daphne turned to Jackson, her resentment clearly directed at anyone but him, despite the amount of hot water she was in.

He wearily gave up. "Supply closet." He sank against the wall.

~ Chapter Six ~

I about shot out of the room. I was seeing red.

"Brett!"

I saw Coach Davidson come chasing after me.

But I barely looked back.

Trevor had gotten Brooke out of the barricaded area and was bringing her along on the rescue chase.

Coach Davidson remained right behind me as I made my way through the empty, dimly lit halls.

It's funny how I was rushing to find Sophia while it really is true that I like Brooke and I didn't bother to stop and check on her. But the thing is, I knew Brooke was alive and well (almost, anyway).

But Sophia?

She could be terribly injured for all I knew. It was totally possible – probable, sadly enough to admit, now that I knew for certain who had been involved.

I finally reached the only door Sophia could have been stowed behind, skidding to a stop just in front of it.

I tried the doorknob with the sinking feeling that it would be locked.

It didn't budge.

My stomach gave a sudden lurch of fear.

A strong arm pushed me away – I guess it was Coach Davidson – and I caught a glimpse of Trevor opening the door with surprisingly great ease.

Amazing how sweaty palms can deprive you of what you need most: a hand that can actually twist a doorknob right.

I pushed my way inside before anyone else could even blink an eye. "Sophia? Sophia?"

Trevor joined in with my calls.

I seriously felt like I was calling some kind of pet – cat, dog, whatever. It felt so weird to be calling for her like in hide-and-seek or something random like that. For our age and maturity, anyway.

Ahem.

Finally I just shoved him aside when I detected a faint hint of movement beneath a bunch of boxes.

"Sophia!"

Trevor gave me a weird look.

So maybe I should have been exhibiting more concern towards Brooke, since I like her, but Sophia was missing in action.

Well, she *was* definitely somewhere – buried or hidden – inside the supply closet, but still… You know what I mean.

"Brooke, you okay?" Trevor asked kindly.

Yawn.

I saw Brooke nod and motion with her good hand for us to keep looking for Sophia under the junk.

Trevor gave me this infuriating stare and as soon as Brooke looked away, he jerked his head at her.

I finally figured out that I was supposed to go to her.

I really did want to look for Sophia, but I decided to give the poor guy a chance and go to Brooke, even though my conscience told me that it was a bad thing to do. But I really didn't have much of a choice.

Brooke stepped in before I could get out. "I'm coming in to find her," she insisted defiantly, staring into the darkened corners of the tiny room with a determined look on her face.

I shrugged and stepped back with a sweeping bow to let her in. "Yes, ma'am. Are you sure you okay, though?"

"Of course. It's just a sprain, I guess." She moved her arm and winced. "It doesn't hurt too much. It could have been worse."

Her arm didn't look too good, but she didn't seem to care much.

Coach Davidson cleared his throat a tad impatiently. "Hurry it up, guys. We're going to have to go on with the game."

Trevor said, "Yes, Coach, we're trying to hurry," sounding a little rude, but definitely trying to use tact.

I was impressed.

The three of us dug away the cardboard boxes and pairs of pompoms that had been scattered on the once-neat floor.

Beneath the mess lay a crumpled up figure.

It could only be one person.

Sophia.

Brooke let out a little cry of excitement.

Trevor dove down on the floor with a rushed sigh of relief.

I joined him, but not without some sophistication.

In other words, I didn't just fly down there. Impressive of Trevor, but also a little too eager.

We knelt down around Sophia, waiting for any sign of movement from her – a sign of hope.

Finally she moved a little, but didn't wake up.

I sighed, relieved.

"She's going to be fine," I said.

It was more of a self-reassuring statement than fact, as much as I hated to admit it to myself. But I didn't dare to admit it to anyone else for fear of worrying them even more, and possible beyond the limit.

In the end, we did manage to revive her with water and stuff or whatever it was that Miss Halitelli (who totally didn't look anything like she usually does) gladly provided and administered.

Sophia and Brooke sat out for the rest of the game.

Well, Brooke sat out, and Sophia kind of lounged out, since she was a little out of it after inhaling all those weird cleaners and then the mustiness and all that stuff. But she was pretty okay after the whole ordeal.

And it turns out that Daphne didn't really mean to hurt Brooke that badly – she just couldn't bear the weight.

Another sign that she could never be a cheerleader.

Ha, ha.

Oh yeah, and she and Jackson are scheduled for some kind of hearing thing sometime soon.

Oh, the sweetness of vindication.

Not revenge, mind you, but pure vindication.

Anyway, we had won the game (which was cut in half due to what had happened) in the end of it all, but that's pretty unimportant compared to the rest of the events.

Sophia's doing fine now, but she's just a little out if it.

The three of us are sitting in the hospital waiting room, waiting for Brooke's medical verdict.

Sophia's family and Brooke's family are on their way here to meet us, having just recently found out about what happened.

That's going to be…interesting.

We're completely silent.

There really isn't much for any of us to say, after all. We were all at the game and we all know what happened.

Suddenly, we hear a nurse's voice.

Of course, the three of us all have to lean forward in our chairs in eager anticipation of the results.

"Honey, are you sure your parents are coming?" she asks as she steps out of one of the doorways.

"Of course. They're on their way – in fact, they should be here any minute now," another voice says.

Wait a second…

That's Brooke's voice!

She steps out, wearing a simple bandage (one of those Ace things) around her hand and wrist.

"Brooke!"

Well.

That wasn't just us.

Whoa.

Las familias están aquí.

Sophia

"Sophia! Are you all right?" My mother hurls herself at me, having clearly been worrying herself to death.

"Yes, Mom, I'm okay," I answer, since I really am.

I'm just a little zoned out, and my head hurts, along with my foot.

Brad gives me a little punch on the arm as a greeting.

"Brad!" Mom scolds. "She's been through enough already!"

I stifle a smile as Brad rolls his eyes and gives me an awkward fake hug. "My bad," he says. He straightens up and suddenly his eyes widen. He practically collapses down on the chair next to me, quickly shooting looks at a something that must be somewhere over my shoulder.

I narrow my eyes and my forehead creases up. "Hey," I say to him, "are you feeling okay?"

He shakes his head furtively and hisses, "Help me. Get me out of here," in this weird voice.

Trevor and Brett have gone over to Brooke, who just was freed from the doctor and nurses. She's got some type of brace wrapped around her wrist, hand and forearm or whatever now. I wanted to go over there, but Brett and Trevor insisted that Brooke would understand if I stayed put. After all, they said, she wants you to feel better more than anything else.

Our parents have gone over to the reception desk to sign in and identify themselves as my parents or whatever it is you're supposed to do when you arrive at a hospital. I wouldn't know, since nothing like this has ever happened in all of my years of being the captain of the cheerleading squad.

Oh, well. Times have changed. It's modern now.

But Brad is acting so weird now, though.

"Brad?" I shake him gently by the shoulder. "What is wrong with you?" I turn around to see what he's staring at.

Oh.

That must be Brooke's family.

The girl standing a little ways away looks like a miniature clone of Brooke, and she and Brooke are spitting images of the almost middle-aged woman standing there. So those are Mr. and Mrs. Dawson, and the famous Ashlynn.

Ashlynn finally gets over to Brooke, and the family starts chattering away rather excitedly.

Mrs. Dawson gives Trevor a hug.

Apparently Brooke and Trevor are closer than I thought.

Brett slips away. Funny thing if he wants to get out of having to meet the Dawsons.

Hmm. I doubt that Ashlynn has even noticed Brad sitting next to me. She's too busy greeting her sister and all that.

I mention this to Brad, but he doesn't believe me, I guess.

"Sophia! That doesn't matter! She's gonna see me eventually!"

Okay, he believes me, but even though I think I made a pretty good point, it means absolutely nothing to him.

But seriously?

He's spazzing out way too much.

"Okay, then what does?" I ask reasonably.

"I don't *want* her to see me!"

"Why not?"

He could actually talk to her, after all, plus tell her the truth if he wanted to. It could all work for the better, in fact.

"Oh, *my* God." He turns his head to the side and pulls down on the bill of his baseball cap.

As if *that* will suffice to conceal him.

Dream on, little boy.

"Tell me?"

"It's going to be so awkward!"

Great explanation.

And excuse.

"Oh, please, Brad," I begin, only to be interrupted.

"Shut up!"

"What a nice way to treat me after all that I've been through," I say, making a sad puppy dog face.

I catch him rolling his eyes.

"Please. You can't guilt me into talking to her. In fact, I'm not planning on staying here."

"Fine. That wasn't my plan, but go right ahead."

Not to worry.

He'd never leave.

Or would he?

"Sophia!"

Great. It's Mom.

"Yeah?"

She gives me a look. "Come over here."

I realize that she's standing with Mrs. Dawson, Brooke, and Ashlynn.

Trevor and Brett are close by, and Mr. Dawson and my dad are off in another corner, talking.

Ashlynn looks up.

And catches sight of Brad.

Brad gets up and walks away.

What an idiot.

He's a Garrison.

He's a *guy*.

He's *supposed* to be *tough*.

Come on, Brad.

I grab him surreptitiously by the sleeve of his coat. "Come on," I hiss. "You're going to have to deal with this sooner or later. There couldn't be a more perfect time than *right now*. Now move!"

He glares at me formidably, but like I even care.

"I'm going to kill you."

"You'll thank me later."

"Yeah, right."

I do not appreciate all this sarcasm.

Apparently he doesn't appreciate the fact that I'm trying to help him here.

Not for long.

Brooke

Well, my left wrist is mildly sprained or strained or something.

I have no idea exactly what happened, though.

In fact, I actually tuned out of what the nurse and the doctor were telling me until I heard the part about the bandage thing.

Yeah, that's all. I have an Ace bandage wrapped around my forearm and hand. No big deal. I guess.

I mean, I can still do gym. I just can't take part in any activity that might injure me even more.

My family's here now, and we're talking to Sophia's family.

I already introduced Brett and the Garrisons to my family.

Dad actually liked Brett.

Score!

But the awkward part?

Ashlynn.

Not her alone.

Add in Brad Garrison.

How totally uncomfortable.

They've been shooting looks at each other and then looking away every time one caught the other. You know. What happens with your crush in class. Embarrassing at points, but also never-ending. So they kept on glancing at each other for about a full ten minutes of awkwardness before Mom and Mrs. Garrison realized that they haven't introduced their younger kids to each other yet. And now they decide to do so.

"Oh, by the way, this is my youngest, Brad," Mrs. Garrison says. "He's almost fourteen."

"Why, what a coincidence!" Mom exclaims. She's calmed down quite a lot after seeing that the only result of the great disaster is a bandage on my arm. "Ashlynn here is thirteen, too."

Ashlynn switches a phony smile on and off within seconds.

I could slap her for that. I really could. I mean, seriously.

She's making it all worse than it already is.

Instead of coming close to committing what could generate into a huge social gaffe, I gently nudged her with my foot (the one that wasn't feeling so sore). Nothing too conspicuous or anything.

Brad gives her a quick jerk of the head in return – a nod of curt greeting. He doesn't even make much eye contact.

I really like this kid. He must know Ashlynn truly well or that was a lucky shot. She hates it when guys act all gruff.

Then again, she wasn't being too friendly herself, so she's pretty much driving a nail into her own coffin.

Well, sort of.

Anyway.

"You're in the same grade, right?" Sophia asks.

Smart.

Brad clearly doesn't appreciate his sister's attempt to salvage the situation. He tries to mask the scowl that's trying to take control of his face.

"Yes, Sophia," Ashlynn answers sweetly. What a suck up.

Either my stepping on the toe of her shoe worked, or she's trying to endear herself to her crush's older sister and mother. I doubt her sudden change in behavior is to make me look good in front of Sophia and the Garrisons.

I mean, if she did, it would have been way too considerate of her to be anywhere near true.

Besides, I don't see her being nearly as nice to Brad.

The poor guy. I mean, he likes her.

And since she likes him, you'd think she could be nice.

This whole thing is so entertaining. I can't wait to find out what happens in the end. It's like a real live good book. You don't come across that too often. And now that I have, I'm determined to enjoy it.

While helping out a little so the plot goes as planned, of course. You can't expect me to just sit back and watch a movie while I could actually do what I want and make a great story go my way.

Um, hello.

Not going to happen.

Trevor

Well, I've got to admit that everything happening within the past few hours was really scary, and I'm still a little shaken up.

Everything has been way too crazy to outline, so I'll just start with what's actually happening.

First the basics – I'm almost too tired and worn out to think. I actually can't wait to go home for once.

Sad.

Who: Sophia and the Garrisons (!), Brooke and the Dawsons (no big deal – I spend enough time with them already, and they love me), Brett (which is totally awkward for him, since he's got to meet the Dawsons. Not that I'm not having trouble with this whole Garrison thing, but still…you know what I mean), and me (duh). Plus the nurses and doctors that are walking around, but they don't count because none of the rest of us are personally acquainted with them or anything.

What: well, we're all bunched together here in little groups, talking and waiting for whatever extra stuff Brooke and Sophia are going to need, and what they're going to have to get checked up.

Where: the hospital.

When: now (duh again).

Why: because Sophia and Brooke were both hurt in the first game they had with Brett and me.

Okay.

So now we're all still hanging around here, talking awkwardly.

Well, Brett and me are pretending to be talking, while Brooke and Sophia are with their moms and siblings.

Mr. Garrison (help!) is talking to Mr. Dawson…and the plus is that while they haven't even met before, they seem to be getting along pretty well.

Too much to think about right now.

This is really getting boring.

"Sophia Garrison?"

Finally.

It's only about time.

Sophia ambles over to the reception desk pretty casually for someone who's been injured. "Yes?"

"A nurse is waiting for you just inside that room." The lady sitting behind the desk points at an open door, and sure enough, a nurse steps out.

"Thank you." Sophia strolls into the room.

The nurse smiles reassuringly at Mrs. Garrison and then follows Sophia into the small office.

The second the door swings shut, Mrs. Garrison and Mrs. Dawson immediately launch into a discussion about how worried they were about the outcome of the whole ordeal and how cheerleading never used to be this dangerous all because of events like this and jealousy and stuff like that.

They're going to be the best of friends – well, despite the fact that they are parents, anyway, and that they both have sixteen-year-old daughters who happen to be the best of pals as well.

Plus, I have this feeling that something odd is going on between Ashlynn, Brooke's little sister, and Brad, Sophia's little brother. They're in the same grade, and apparently they do know each other.

But that, of course, is beside the point.

I'm guessing Sophia is going to be okay, but she may have hurt her foot a little, if the way she was wincing as she stumbled around everywhere is any indication. I have no idea how that happened, but with Jackson around, a lot is possible.

Brooke slips away from the adults and younger ones and joins Brett and me with a soft smile.

"You feeling okay?" Brett finally says.

Brooke nods. "It hurts a little, but the doctor said it should be better pretty soon."

"That's good."

"Yeah."

Well, there isn't really much to say anyway.

"You think Sophia's going to be all right?" I say in an attempt to break the ice and make conversation.

Surprisingly Brett and Brooke exchange glances, and each tries not to smile. Their eyes sparkle.

"What?"

"Nothing," Brooke says teasingly.

"*What?*"

Brett says after a moment's worth of an awkward silence, "Come on, man. If you're not going to make a move, then cover it all up."

"Huh?"

Brooke giggles and punches me lightly on the shoulder with her right fist – the one that isn't injured.

It's nice to hear her laughing like everything's going just fine, but what are they talking about? I'm going to *pretend* that I don't know.

"Come on, Trevor, it isn't that tough to figure out."

I shoot her a look. She better not have told him… "Brooke!"

"What?" she goes all innocently.

"Did you…?"

She shakes her head. "Never!"

Brett catches on. "Dude, I figured it out."

I blush. "Am I that obvious?"

"No," Brooke says. "I almost wouldn't have figured it out before."

I'm filled with hope for a second. And then I see the twinkle in Brooke's eyes. And only now do I realize that she's kidding.

Darn.

I turn to Brett and ask in a tone that I hope sounds casual, "How did *you* figure it out, huh?"

Okay. Not too casual.

I guess I just can't seem to pull off a Brett Evans type of persona. Apparently it's not…'me' enough.

He shrugs.

"Is there some kind of guy to guy understanding going on here between the two of you?" Brooke suggests only half-jokingly. "Because I have no idea what's going on, just so you know."

"Good," I say, oddly relieved.

Brett chuckles. "Sure."

Like *he* doesn't like Brooke, and *she* doesn't like him back. Of course, I'm the one that gets dumped on.

They shouldn't be using my personal life to get closer to each other. It just isn't fair to me. Oh, well. There are bigger fish to fry, I guess.

Suddenly Sophia returns, accompanied by the same nurse. Here we go. Time to hear the verdict.

I hope I'm not red still…

Sophia

So all I have is a bit of a twisted ankle. All I have to do is not put too much pressure on it for a while. But I'm going to be fine.

I really want to know why Trevor was blushing so much when I got back into the waiting room.

Okay, I know I'm probably being paranoid, but tell me why he wouldn't meet my gaze afterwards.

Yeah. Exactly.

Now Brad isn't too happy with me, and we're all in the car going home. My parents offered to give Trevor and Brett a lift home, since we live somewhat nearby, so it's all of us except the Dawsons.

Awkward?

I think not.

Of course, this can only be thanks to Trevor and Brett, who decided that they'd get in back with me.

Thankfully, that means that I don't have to sit with Brad…and I can ignore him completely.

Life is so good.

Brett

Well, today was crazy.

But I'm finally at home.

Normally after any big game – especially a win over Lodi Valley – we would throw a huge celebration by going to Giordano's and really have a great pizza party or something fun like that.

But after what happened today? No one was so hyped up that they still wanted to go out for dinner.

Daphne and Jackson killed the excitement.

But anyway.

Moving onto a neutral topic.

I just had a quick dinner.

By the time I actually got back from the hospital (Sophia's family dropped me off), it was a little past nine. That meant my parents had already eaten dinner – but my dog hadn't, since I'm the one who feeds him.

So I went downstairs after putting all my stuff away and found my parents watching some random show on TV. They've given up on coming to every game, since my dad gets home pretty late most days.

I didn't bother filling them in on everything that happened. They were too immersed in whatever was on, and I was hungry. All that worrying can make a person practically starve to death.

I wandered off into the kitchen.

Our place is so high-tech. My dad insisted on a state-of-the-art home theater and totally modernized kitchen and all that stuff.

Great, I know.

But I can barely find anything in the refrigerator, let alone cook by myself. I'll basically be able to make some simple stuff – you know, heating up casseroles or previously prepared things.

And that's just what I did for my dinner.

I found one of those frozen prepared meals in the freezer after digging through a bunch of plastic drawers.

Duffy, the lovable wire fox terrier that I've had for years, came padding into the kitchen, slipping and sliding and wobbling on the smooth tiled floor. He had been waiting to have his dinner.

The poor old thing.

So I had to explain to him why he hadn't gotten his dinner earlier, and he listened very faithfully and then sat at my feet while I put my Salisbury steak and mashed potatoes meal in the oven to be heated up.

Yes, I'm guilty. Even though Brooke and Sophia won't stop pestering me (and Trevor, for that matter), I still eat meat. I can't help it. I need that extra strength.

But Duffy's needs called.

"Oh, all right, boy," I finally said, and went over to the pantry to get out his bag of dog food.

Duffy followed me around until his dish was filled to the brim. Only then did he actually sit down and pay attention to something other than begging me for his dinner. He dug right into that pile of dry food, and I refilled his water dish as he munched. Soon Duffy was lapping up the water, too.

I sat down at the island with my own dinner a few minutes later, and ate my meal, also munching over thoughts in my mind.

Then Duffy started scratching at my stool.

I looked down at his furry face.

He wanted a treat.

Lucky dog.

He gets me giving him food, playing with him, and he gets to be lazy all day, with no worries about evil cheerleader wannabes and former basketball players plotting against him and trying to do bodily harm to him.

Nope, I'm the one who has to deal with that stuff.

Sorry, Duffy, but you're going to have to stay here. Be happy with your little rawhide toys and whatever it is that you love to play with so much.

Anyway.

So I did play with him for a little bit in the kitchen, and I threw around one of those treats of Pup-eroni or whatever it's called that he loves so much until he finally got it.

Duffy's a good dog.

He's always awesome to hang around with.

He also did a pretty good job of distracting me from the subject of Daphne and Jackson and that whole…thing.

Oh, my God, I have nothing more to say about this that wouldn't be too…um, well, negative.

Now it's way past ten.

I've spent plenty of time surfing the channels up in my room, and I've sent one email each to Brooke and Sophia just to check up on them and see how everything was going (by the way, I hope I wasn't too bold with what I said in my email to Brooke. I don't want to seem too obvious, but I'm not going to hang around doing absolutely nothing forever. I'm going to make a move sometime or the other).

Oh, yeah, and I figured I might as well forget homework, too.

So why not get some sleep?

Brooke

I'll admit I was a little worried about going back to school this morning, what with all the danger of last night.

Plus I've got to have this brace on.

But I don't know how long it's going to last. I mean, I don't have a note or anything (I conveniently forgot it at home) so I can take part in some of practice. I just can't put too much weight on my wrist.

But Coach Sanders will definitely understand about that.

"Brooke!"

"There you are!"

"Oh, my God, are you okay?"

Yeah, guess who?

The squad… every single one of the *real* Saffrondale High cheerleaders. Except for Sophia, that is.

Hmm. Wonder where she is.

Oh, well. I have no time to worry about her whereabouts at the current moment. Right now, duty calls.

"Hi, you guys," I say, turning to face them.

Kellie hurries over to me, smiling.

Last night, I signed on to check my messages, and surprisingly, there was a ton of them waiting for me.

Sophia, I guess, must have been too tired to even type a message out. Besides, she could have called me, but maybe she was too worn out for that, too. Poor girl.

A lot of the girls had sent me messages, and a few of the guys, too.

It was actually pretty weird.

I mean, I guess it's possible that they could have bummed my screen name off of each other, but even the thought of that is strange.

But anyway.

Back to what they wrote.

It's so sweet.

Kellie had written a whole long note.

smile4kellie: hi brooke, it's kellie hamilton. just wanted 2 check up on you since what happened at tonight's game was sooooo incredibly scary... um, i guess you went 2 the hospital afterwards, so i won't really worry if you don't reply to this but i hope you're okay and i guess i'll just see you in school 2mrw. hope you're feeling better and that your arm doesn't hurt 2 much. it would really stink if you couldn't cheer anymore, since this was only your 1st game and that totally isn't fair. you must have such a bad impression on cheerleading now. but we're not all mean like daphne, so don't worry. ☺ your place on the squad will always be there. we def would nvr replace you w/ anybody like daphne. that would like ttly kill the squad. well, i guess that's about it, so i'll talk 2 u 2mrw! bye!
<3 kellie

Kellie is so sweet. She's probably the nicest, most innocent girl on the squad – with the possible exception of Sophia, of course.

Corinne sent me a really quick note.

~ Chapter Six ~

cee2cee: heyy brooke!! hope ur feelin better & that ur doin well & i'll cya tmrw!
<3 cor

At first I was wondering who on earth 'cee2cee' was, but then I remembered that Corinne's first and last name both begin with 'C,' so she sometimes goes by any variant of 'Cee Cee.' It is a little scary, but it's rare that she calls herself that. Usually it's simply 'Corinne' or 'Cor.'

But anyway.

It was really nice of Corinne to send me a message, considering I barely even talk to her in the first place.

And Michele Clarke?

I have never said a single word to that girl, let alone talked to her online.

I mean, first of all, she's a senior.

Second, she's way too smart for me.

Third? She isn't even the type of person I'd hang out with.

I'm not saying that she isn't a totally terrific and sweet person. We're just so different from each other.

I'm a cheerleader (online speak: OMG can u believe it!?!) and she's a singer and band conductor.

She's so much smarter than I am and belongs in her sophomore or junior year of college, not her senior year of high school.

She's an upper, *upper*classman, and I'm just an upperclassman, if you get what I'm trying to say here.

And there's so much more.

Yeah.
Major differences there.
But here you go anyway.

sing2be_michele: Hi, Brooke, it's Michele Clarke. Maybe you saw me at the great basketball game against Lodi Valley High School this evening. I just wanted to check up on you and find out how you were feeling, since the last I saw of you was an injured cheerleader hobbling her way out of the gym right in the middle of the game, and then later on sitting out to the side with Sophia Garrison. I extend only my very best wishes to her as well. Anyway, feel better, Brooke, and I hope to see you back in school by tomorrow morning! Hope to see you bright and early!
All of my very best wishes,
Michele

Wow.

She sounds so smart. I mean, only someone as perfect and proper and *smart* as Michele would capitalize and punctuate everything correctly online. Everyone else is just, like, so informal because it's online. But not Michele.

Trevor sent me something, too, but I expected that. I mean, he *had* to. It's part of his duty to me as my childhood best friend. Duh.

tr3v0r_tr0v3: brooke! ok, so i know i just saw u a little while ago back up in the hospital, but i just wanted 2 check in on u again & find out how u were doing since i know u were traumatized by tonight's events. oh yeah, & i hope ash isn't driving u 2 crazy! well, i gtg now, so i'll def c u tmrw!
-trevor

Good kid, good kid. He'll always be my favorite childhood friend (and that's not only because he's the only one – I promise).

But anyway.

Last but not least.

My favorite…

Brett was the best of all.

I mean, I hate to admit it and everything, but his really was.

Here you go.

Cherish it the way I did – and I still am loving it, believe me.

br3tt_sp0rt_king: hey brooke, it's brett...as if u didn't know that. anyway...um, i just wanted 2 find out how u were doing. i got home about 1½ hrs ago - sophia's rents dropped me off... but that's pretty much it about me. can't wait till tmrw, even though i will admit i don't plan on doing any of my hw even if i didn't get much. guilty as

charged, but i think i'll manage 2 get away w/ it. you prlly will 2 although since you're such a good girl i guess you're gonna do all your hw anyway. well, you don't have 2 reply 2 this...i understand that you're probably really tired, so i guess i'll just be seeing u tmrw morning in school...i especially can't wait 2 c mr and mrs everett get knocked out cold when they see you and sophia alive and well and in school, walking around...lol. plus i can't wait 2 see them when they find out what's gonna happen 2 them...not that i know either lol well anyway, since that's really about it, i guess i'll just see u tmrw...oh, yeah, & good night.
love ya, brett

Oh, my God!

Every single time I even think about what he wrote, I feel so… incredibly good about myself to know that I'm that loved and I'm just so *happy* about it!

Especially that last part…

…"oh, yeah, & good night. love ya, brett"…

Oh, my God!

How amazing!!

Could there be anything sweeter for a guy who I'm not even dating…yet?

Trevor

Well, today's been pretty uneventful so far. I mean, sure, I've got a bunch of people coming up to me and congratulating me on a job well done with last night's game against Lodi Valley, but that's it.

Brooke and Sophia have crowds buzzing around them, all because of that cheerleading drama.

Sophia's used to all the rush, but Brooke? She's all excited because so many more people are paying attention to her.

Brett's bored, too, and a little cranky since he still has to make up all the homework that he didn't do last night.

But that's just karma.

I think.

Ms. Sanders seems a little drained after all that excitement last night, but she's still her happy self, I guess.

I heard from Sophia on the way back home that Miss Halitelli had an interesting reaction after the game.

Actually, Sophia did, too.

But then we took her to the hospital.

Ha, ha.

So slick.

I guess soon I'll be getting used to this newfound 'fame' that isn't *really* fame, but whatever.

It isn't as if it even matters much.

Life goes on.

Sophia

Well, in addition to the bunch of messages in my email

inbox, I also found a ton of them when I signed onto my instant messenger for a few minutes.

I understand how loved I am. Really, I do.

But to tell the truth? It's just stupid.

I mean, seriously.

I didn't even do anything – good *or* bad – to deserve so much attention. All I did was get attacked and faint in a supply closet.

Fantastic feat.

Here I was thinking that it was so amazing how many people actually cared enough about me to want to check on my mental health. It was actually pretty weird, in fact.

I really have to admit that I do feel kind of bad for Trevor and Brett – especially Trevor, since it was a strange first game for him – since they're the ones who actually helped us win the game, in addition the rest of the team – but not the squad.

I mean, sure, we did cheer those guys on, but to the extent of just that.

Cheering.

Yippee.

And I spent the game in *the* most *un*traditional way – on the sidelines and in the depths of the junk (not that I don't appreciate pompoms, or anything, but you'd understand if you were in the same quagmire) Jackson had thrown on top of me under his dearly beloved Daphne's command.

So you can pretty much imagine how much of a help to everyone else *I* was. I mean, seriously. Since I was the stupid damsel in distress, they had to send out a rescue search party for me. Well, practically.

Wow. That's really sad. Which totally makes me a helpful angel sent all the way down from heaven above. Unless you count extra time to make up some more of those defensive and/or offensive plays, or whatever I'm supposed to call those things. But I totally don't.

Anyway. Enough wallowing in guilt.

What was really interesting was that since I was forced to hang around on that stupid bench all night through the game yesterday, I caught all the drama without having to bounce around with pompoms at the same time.

At the end of the game, I looked on with interest as Miss Halitelli (who looked totally incredible and unbelievably not like herself) sat way up front and close to all the action.

Finally, she bounced up.

I looked around, confused at first, but then the whole thing with Mr. Lodi Valley came flooding back. And then my interest was regained.

I immediately recognized the guy who had to be the principal. He was wearing a suit and had that professional look to him.

Miss Halitelli flipped her hair over her shoulder in one motion and practically stepped right up to him in smiling silence.

Yeah, well, don't ask me what that was supposed to do. I really don't understand her either.

But I think her plan was to let him notice her on his own.

And of course, it kind of worked as most of her, um, 'plans' do.

Kind of.

Brett

Well, unlike Trevor, I'm totally not concerned about how much attention I'm getting because I, as captain of the basketball team, led our school to a wondrous victory over Lodi Valley High.

No. I'm totally used to that.

I'm just a little ticked off about the fact that despite how wonderfully I played last night, I am *still* being forced to make up all of the homework that I skipped out on that had been assigned yesterday.

It sucks.

I mean, come on.

You would think that by now they would have agreed to cutting some slack for captains and star players of the basketball team and other important sports stars that happen to be leading the school to so many triumphs.

Oh, yeah, and that definitely should include any specific cheerleaders who were so dreadfully traumatized by last night's horrendous (oh, yes, you've got to love the fantastic vocabulary; it's a result of actually listening to someone smart like Brooke, and not just because I like her) events.

But that's not intended for implying that two girls as angelic as they didn't do their homework.

I think.

Brooke

Like everyone else in school, my teachers totally see fit to treat me so well. It's weird – not being that practically invisible girl-next-door anymore. I could definitely get used to all of this, though.

But hey, at least there's some interesting gossip going on with our beloved staff members. Well, that's what Sophia tells me anyway, and I guess it really isn't like I didn't see it myself, but still.

~ Chapter Six ~

I caught all this excitement from the bench last night. I just completely forgot about it after the hospital stuff and the messages and all that.

Mr. Winston Romero, or so it just happens to turn out, is the current principal of Lodi Valley High.

He's also the same guy Miss Halitelli has been spazzing out over for the past couple of days.

Sophia had nudged me weakly and whispered in a faint voice, "Brooke, that's him…I think."

I looked back at the tall guy in the suit with renewed interest.

So *this* was the guy who had flipped Miss Halitelli's life around from simple, only-okay shambles to fabulous and back to shambles.

And then to sheer anger.

He seemed almost like your average, tough-guy principal. You know the drill. Brown hair, green eyes, tall and athletically built just in case the occasion arises during which he's forced to ward off an insane student or faculty member...yeah, the usual.

But now that I knew everything about what he'd done in his past, I was much, much more intrigued.

It was pretty funny how Miss Halitelli jumped right up off her little designated bench as he strode by.

He seemed a little dazed. I don't know if that was because his team had lost a game to us, or because he seemed to be searching for someone.

Gee, yeah, I really wondered who.

So Miss Halitelli was totally being all coquettish, but he didn't even notice. You'd think that since she was so eager to beat his school down and everything, she wouldn't treat him so well and be so…flirty.

But no.

I guess he really didn't notice her standing right at his shoulder at first. He was clearly way too busy combing the crowds for her.

Strange, that Romero guy. He barely even noticed Miss Halitelli call out his name…faintly.

I mean, sure, he turned around a little bit, but he couldn't seem to figure out who was speaking.

All I could think about was how they must have not seen each other for so long for him to not even recognize or notice her. And of course, my mind lingered on how much that would suck if something similar happened between me and Brett.

Hey.

It could happen…

…As much as I hate imagining it.

But I don't think it would happen. Brett's way too nice of a guy to do something like that to me. He's already sky-high popular. Besides, he and I are such good friends with Sophia and Trevor, plus everyone knows we're friends. So I think everything should last nicely for quite some time.

I hope.

Anyway.

Miss Halitelli finally decided that it just might be a good idea to call out, "Winston!" a little louder.

Yes, apparently she calls him Winston, that being his first name, obviously.

Too bad he doesn't even look like a Winston. But then again, maybe even less of a Mr. Romero.

Or more.

I can't decide.

Hmm.

~ Chapter Six ~

Just her luck that he turned around and stared at her, but didn't recognize her *and* didn't figure out that she had said his name.

I swear…the guy's got to be at least a little insane. That's the only explanation for his odd lack of common sense as a certified principal.

God.

Some things in life are just *so* weird.

So he randomly asks her, "Excuse me, but do you happen to know an English teacher here by the name of Miss Halitelli?"

She opens her mouth, totally stunned.

He pauses. "She may have gotten married."

A dismayed look slowly spreads across his face at this terrifying thought.

Ha, ha.

She finally regains her powers of speech. "Um, Winston…?"

His eyes widen drastically. "*Heather*?"

Yeah, that's right.

Heather.

Heather Halitelli.

Funny if her middle name was Rachael or Roxanne or something else starting with an 'R.' Then she'd be H.R.H.

Her Royal Highness, my English teacher, Miss Halitelli.

Anyway…

"Heather Halitelli. Really?" He sounds skeptical.

As if Miss Halitelli couldn't be that pretty or something.

Or maybe she was less than he expected.

Hmm.

Either way, it does come out as an insult.

Best not to mention it to Miss Halitelli.

Clearly she didn't notice yet, anyway.

"Yes…" Miss Halitelli says slowly, as if she's talking to a young child.

Perfect fit. He *is* acting like one.

He's speechless.

Practically.

"Oh, my God," he gushes in a weird voice. "I really cannot believe it."

A smile slowly beams its way across Miss Halitelli's face. "It's been too long," she says softly.

Eww…

Way too mushy gushy for my taste.

But not enough for little old Winston Romero.

"Much too long," he whispers back, gazing into her eyes.

She breaks the eye contact.

No more connection.

She whips her head away. "I can't, Winston," she whispers faintly.

"What?" he asks, concerned.

She looks back up at him – yes, into his eyes, folks – seeming a little defiant.

"Heather, *what?*" he repeats. "I don't get it."

"*You* wouldn't understand," she says irritably.

He's getting a little ticked off now. "Understand *what*, Heather? Tell me what's going on."

"Miss Halitelli, Miss Halitelli!" A yearbook representative rushes up, camera in hand. "Would you please pose for a photo with the mascot? We're getting all the pictures of one of the many easy victories in Saffrondale High history."

Winston looks downcast, even though it's a little unclear whether his expression is caused by the pomposity of the

Saffrondale student or by the totally strange way his ex is treating him.

Miss Halitelli looks somewhat dazed.

The eager little cameraman finally notices the principal of the defeated team's school. "Oh, I'm sorry, but we can never help but celebrate, you know."

Principal Romero nods slowly. "Heather, could you at least tell me why you're acting like–"

"If you'd just give me a moment, I'd be happy to explain, but right now I have to oblige to this young man's request." She smiles graciously at the yearbook geek. And then she turns back to her old buddy with seemingly cold eyes. "Wait here." She clicks off in her shiny designer stilettos to take a picture with the furry bear in the Scouts uniform.

Designer? Miss *Halitelli*? Yeah, that's what I thought, too. But even more interesting…

Wait. Winston looks impressed? Okay. This guy has got to be a freak. No offense meant, but is it any wonder why he hung out with Miss Halitelli in high school sometimes?

But if you think about it in our terms, it's kind of more like… Why do Brett, Sophia, and even Trevor hang out with me? Ew, I don't even want to think about that.

Back to the tales of romance.

So anyway, Mr. Romero's just waiting there for her, and, um, watching Miss Halitelli a little closely as she poses for the photo and smiles brightly.

I'll admit it. She does look really pretty. If you flashed back to her high school days and got rid of whatever, uh, 'funky' trends they were going through, she'd probably have been drop-dead gorgeous to the people of her time…and maybe to a few of us, too.

But this guy? I'm sorry, but I just don't see it. Maybe he was a total knock-out way back in whatever day it was then, but right now, he isn't much of a hottie. I apologize, but if you had seen him, you'd know it's true. Anyway, I guess that doesn't matter. Miss Halitelli clearly has cared somewhat for him, and does care for him at least a little bit right now, so that's all that does matter.

Coach Sanders suddenly flits by, and shoves four extra credit tickets in my hand and four in Sophia's.

We glance at each other, confused, dazed, and stunned.

Four?!

Miss Halitelli returns to Mr. Romero.

He gathers himself together and becomes much more poised. "What were you saying, Heather?" he asks politely.

Miss Halitelli retorts coolly, "Winston, do you even remember how we ended our connection?"

Mr. Romero sighs. "Heather…listen."

Miss Halitelli narrows her eyes. "No, Winston, *you* listen."

He's beginning to look the slightest bit uncomfortable. And believe me, he should.

That little rat.

Miss Halitelli continues. "*You* were the one who was so *fake* and *pretended* to like me for some odd and unclear reason and–"

Mr. Romero has to interrupt.

Sophia glances at me and nods significantly.

We both know now that this is going to get pretty interesting.

"Heather!"

Miss Halitelli pauses to glare formidably at him. "*What*?!"

Mr. Romero seems a little scared. "I never *pretended.* I really did like you. I swear."

Her eyes narrow to tiny slits.

Now Sophia and I can make a mental note not to ever mess with this woman's personal life…although I doubt we'll bother remembering it.

"Oh, really?" she challenges him. "Then why, may I ask, did you be so cold and shallow ever since the beginning (when we met), and date every single one of my pretty friends and *never me*!?!"

He pauses. "Well. I, uh…"

Ha! Busted!!

Miss Halitelli seems to think so, too. She folds her arms triumphantly across her chest and stands back to survey her opponent.

"Heather…" he starts up again, "I don't know…I guess I just was blind to the treasure I had right in front of me."

"Exactly. You were always so…" she pauses to think. "Stupid."

He raises one eyebrow, seeming almost amused that he basically just told her '*how he truly feels about her*' and she barely even reacted.

Sophia and I glance at each other, both equally surprised.

Miss Halitelli?

Not notice a detail as important as that?

Wow…

She really did get into that tirade of hers…

Continuing on.

Mr. Romero smiles faintly.

So maybe he might have been at least a little cute.

Miss Halitelli stops short right in the middle of her ranting. "What are you smiling at?" she demands, more than just a little irritated.

He doesn't stop with the smile. In fact, he's practically beaming now. "Nothing," he answers quickly.

"Oh?" You can tell she totally doesn't believe him.

But then again…who would?

"Well. Fine. You."

"What?"

"You. I'm smiling at you."

"Oh, please, Winston." She turns on her stiletto heel to stalk away from the heated discussion.

Maybe I wouldn't do *that.*

The smile fades.

"Heather. Heather! Heather, *wait!*" He follows her in total desperation.

Aww…

How cute.

Sophia and I glance at each other yet again.

If they leave the gym, how are we supposed to keep an eye – okay, eavesdrop – on the conversation?

He stops her before she gets too far away.

Still in earshot.

Score!

"Heather." He grabs her arm.

She tries to shake away. "Let *go*, Winston. I told you so many times. I'm *through* wasting my time on you. You never cared like I did."

He looks as if he's been stabbed through the heart. The poor guy's been dreadfully wounded, and his voice tells of all his pain as he says, "Heather! How could you even think that?"

She tries to look cool and nonchalant, as if she really does staunchly believe in what she's saying. "It's true."

"No, it isn't. And you know it."

She jerks away. "Oh, I knew it all this time, did I? Then what happened to Ali Avery? Hmm?"

He uncertainly opens his mouth and then closes it again, realizing that it's better for him to stay silent and let her cry out at him.

"If I knew it so well, then why did you have to go around with all of the girls I was friends with and drop me as a *friend*?" Her eyes are practically blazing. "Tell me that. Tell me *why*."

Now he's getting a little irritated. And I probably would be feeling the same way, too.

"Heather!" he says, almost scolding her. "How was I supposed to know that you liked me?"

Miss Halitelli's totally ticked off now. And it shows. "Well, I don't know!" she retorts. "But how stupid could you really have been, Winston?" She whirls away.

Anger, anger, anger.

A certain couple doesn't need to communicate more.

No, they need counseling. Not that they're a couple, or anything. At least, not just yet.

"Heather. Heather, please."

"What?" she whips around.

"I'm sorry. For everything."

"It's about what you do, not what you say."

"Fine. Here." He hands her a folded piece of paper.

Don't ask me where that came from. I'm just about as clueless as you are in this whole situation.

She takes the paper gingerly, as if it might suddenly explode in her hand and turn to ashes, just like her anger.

"Look, Heather. I've made my apology. You don't seem to want to accept it. And now I'm just tired of being sorry. Sorry that I lost one of my most valuable, treasured friends. Sorry I lost someone I loved."

And with that concise speech of total righteousness, he turns on his heel and walks away, blending into the crowd.

Oh! Ouch, Miss Halitelli!

She's totally stunned.

Sophia and I exchange glances.

And you can tell we're both thinking the same thing: this is going to get even more interesting… if that's even possible.

Anyway…

Miss Halitelli unfolds the paper carefully and gives it the once-over. Her eyes get this confused look, and then she actually reads it instead of skimming it. Her expression softens, and she looks sad. Then a faint smile creeps over her face.

You and I can only imagine what it said on that little piece of paper. But one thing I do know very well? It had to have been incredible. And romantic.

At least, romantic and incredible enough for her to go chasing after him, stumbling in her stilettos all of a sudden, going "Winston! Winston! Wait for me!"

Yeah.

Goodness knows what happened next.

Sophia

Hmm…

Miss Halitelli is in a fantastic mood today.

And gee, I wonder why.

~ Chapter Six ~

Cough, cough, Winston Romero, cough, cough.

But, of course, nobody knows what really went on after Miss Halitelli chased Mr. Romero out of the gym and off to who-knows-where. I mean, Brooke and I were the only ones who were actually watching the little exchange. And if we don't know what happened in the end, then who does?

However, we think it's safe to assume that something incredibly good must have happened. And I really want to find out what it was.

So now I'm waiting in the English classroom. The first bell has already rung (I mean, duh, why else would I be waiting here?) but the second bell hasn't, and I just happened to get here a little earlier than usual…rather than hang around in the hallways like I usually do and risk a chance of getting hurt.

Trevor isn't here yet.

Miss Halitelli is hopping around the classroom like a little psychopathic maniac. She is way too happy.

I really want to find out why…

"Hey, Sophia."

Oh my God, it's Trevor!

"Trevor! Hey!"

He sits down next to me. "So. Anything interesting happen recently?"

I open and close my mouth quickly upon noticing the faint traces of a smile crossing his lips.

He's so teasing me about what happened last night. And that totally isn't fair to me! I mean, I've been through a lot. Being attacked by Jackson Everett totally isn't fun. And I'd think Trevor would know that after arguing with him a few days ago.

So I think of a snappy response. "Yeah, well, exactly a week ago, I became best friends with these two totally awesome people and someone else I was already friends with, and now my life is so totally perfect and complete!"

He stares at me really strangely. Too strangely. That's really weird. This is getting to be way too awkward of a moment here. Why?

"What?" I ask.

"Nothing. I, uh, just can't believe it's been a whole week," he covers up really quickly and carefully.

Yeah. Sure. That's so definitely not it.

But I really want to find out what it actually was, in addition to wanting to find out what happened with Miss Halitelli and Mr. Romero.

First things first.

I've got to deal with Trevor.

"Okay, sure, Trevor. But anyway…" I trail off, trying to search for the exact right words to say.

He's making me so confused!

"Oh, did you see Miss H. with that Lodi Valley guy last night?" I lower my voice to a mere whisper for fear that Miss Halitelli might hear us talking about her. "It was right after the game."

He rolls his eyes. "Sophia…" he says, almost chiding. "You know I didn't. But since you seem so interested in the subject, tell me what happened. Just don't let the lady know that we're talking about her."

Way to steal my exact thoughts!

I mean, I totally knew how he would react to that. I just *understand* him like that. Seriously.

When is he going to *realize* that we are totally meant to be?

I just hope he has realized it already and just doesn't want to say anything just yet…just like Winston Romero!

Except I don't want it to take seven years or whatever.

That would totally break my heart…or anything even nearly equivalent to it would, at least.

So I hope he'll say something someday soon.

"Sure."

And so I relate the entire story to him.

Well, what I can, anyway.

After all, the second bell rings, and we've got to get in our seats…and off the tops of the desks.

Miss Halitelli skips up to the front of the room.

Trevor and I stare at her sudden morphing of personality.

Even though I know something incredibly good must have happened to her yesterday…she's still changed a lot.

Way too much.

Although it is very nice, I'm not going to lie.

I need a cheerful English teacher…

It boosts all of our moods.

But that new persona…

The rest of the class does not seem to notice it, however. Then again, what *do* they ever notice?

"Good morning, class!"

Okay.

That's normal enough, I guess.

"Well, first of all, congratulations to our basketball team and cheerleading squad on a fabulous game last night!"

I can't help but raise my hand.

Daring, yes, I know.

"Sophia! Yes, to anyone who was at the game last night, you know what Sophia went through! Congratulations to a fantastically brave young lady! And to Trevor! Our newest basketball player and just as good as our star, Brett! Congratulations, congratulations! I'm *so* proud!"

Oh.

My.

God.

Not this again…

Didn't I just recently mention that I didn't want to be the center of attention for being the damsel in distress?

I mean, seriously.

What about the people who actually were useful?

It's like Paris Hilton once said…She was like, "I hope going forward that the public and the media will focus on more important things, like the men and women serving our country in Iraq, Afghanistan and other places around the world." Or it was something like that. But anyway, whatever it was that she said, she was totally right about it.

And here I am, getting all the attention for being attacked by Jackson, when here we have Trevor and Brett going off and winning a tough basketball game against one of the best high schools in the area…plus it just happened to be the very first time Trevor played for our school's team.

You tell me which one should (by the judgment of any smart person's common sense) be branded as the more important issue.

Okay, I guess people tend to like the gossip more, but still. It's who's going around in the world doing great things that should have all the attention, not the ones who didn't do anything except get assaulted.

I mean, it's not like I wasn't already embarrassed enough.

I actually got attacked by Jackson. Jackson Everett, my former 'friend.' And a snotty girl was in charge of the whole plot.

Against me.

Me.

Who really didn't do anything wrong except not let her onto the squad because she wasn't as good as Brooke.

Oh, and against Brooke.

Who didn't do anything except rightfully make her way onto Saffrondale High's varsity cheerleading squad and be totally innocent and sweet.

So you can tell I'm ranting inside my mind.

But I get completely distracted by Trevor elbowing me.

I turn my head slightly.

I'm definitely blushing with embarrassment since the whole class is staring at me for a reason I don't exactly like.

But then I see that Trevor's grinning.

Yeah, that's right.

He's pleased.

Happy.

Whatever.

But I really don't see why.

And now I suddenly remember. How he got all the attention for being the newest second star on the basketball team. How he had helped the captain lead the team to a victory over Lodi Valley. How he had gotten so much glory that he had never ever felt before. How he deserved it.

And now I see why he's happy. And you know what? He definitely should be. Because that's exactly how I would feel.

Of course, I was completely useless last night. As if that really matters anymore. Because apparently, to everyone else, I'm something of a heroine, too, in addition to Brooke, since we were both brave in situations of peril and danger or whatever they're all saying about us.

And then there's Trevor and Brett, who were such amazing players, and the rest of the team and the squad.

But Miss Halitelli finally remembers why she first noticed me after temporarily leaving her dream land for the real world.

"Oh, Sophia, you had a question?"

I can no longer remember what witty comment I was going to question her with. So I quickly answer, "Oh, no, never mind."

She shrugs. "Okay. Anyway, class, I have no idea what we should do today, so I guess we can have some more busy work. How's that?"

A murmur of agreement flutters through the class.

Busy work, as we all know only much too well, couldn't be any better. After all, it gives us all a chance to talk amongst ourselves while getting an easy 'A+' on a simple class work assignment.

"Well, then, that is absolutely perfect. But I must admit that I don't have any copies made already, so I can either put up the transparencies of the worksheets on the overhead projector, or I can go make the copies." She brushes back a strand of hair.

I have to admit, she looks as perfect as she did last night at the great game she had waited so long for.

"Take your pick," she says.

Everyone says collectively, "Copies."

"Well, then, in that case, I'll be back in less than five minutes." She hurries to her desk and picks up a thin manila folder and rushes out of the room, only stopping to give us a final command: "Be good."

As if we'd be anything but that.

Trevor immediately starts talking to me as soon as the door

swings closed, just like the rest of the class.

Except they're all talking amongst themselves, and not to me or Trevor. No, they're all talking about me and Trevor. And Brooke, and Brett, and about what happened at last night's game.

"So, did you hear what happened with Daphne and Jackson?" Trevor asks me, seeming as if he's got a pretty good bit of gossip to hand over to me.

He sounds way too proud about it, considering neither of us are supposed to be interested in listening to gossip.

"Uh, no," I answer truthfully.

The plain thoughts of Daphne or Jackson's verdicts haven't even dared to cross my mind.

I seriously wonder why.

"Well, rumor has it that they're supposed to have some sort of hearing or trial or something to decide what is supposed to be done with them. In the meantime, they're being kept away from people like us," Trevor explains.

This is good news, I guess.

Although it is sad to hear about what has happened to our classmates, but what can you do? Life is…life. It's unfair, as much as I hate to admit it. Why else would we have so much insanity in the world?

"Oh, wow," I say, being somewhat speechless. "That's really sad."

"Yeah," he agrees. "Over cheerleading and basketball? In high school? It's not *that* important. But after what they did, I guess that it is."

I nod.

And then I think over the meaning of his words.

"Well, maybe to them it is. And maybe to a lot of other

people, too. I mean, to us it's just, like, whatever. But I guess that's just because we take our positions on the team or squad for granted. To others, it must mean a lot. I guess a lot of people get really mad that we get all the credit."

Trevor nods. "I guess so. I remember what it was like to not be on the team but to be in the crowd – only too clearly. But I was never that jealous. In fact, I don't think I was jealous at all. I was just mad at myself because it wasn't that I couldn't do what you all were doing. It was that I hadn't been able to gather up the self confidence that I needed to even try to aim for my goals. That was sad to me. And yet, even now, I know that those guys and girls never felt superior to everyone else. They were just a little proud of themselves. And that's fine. It's not that they ever wanted to make anyone else feel bad. Those others just seemed to do that to themselves…and it wasn't even on purpose."

I nod again, this time more understandingly.

God, do I feel for the kid. Even though I've never exactly known a situation like that, having been in the land of almost-perfection for some time now.

But about that jealousy thing…

It's starting to make more sense to me now, but I can't believe anyone would waste their time and risk a scarring impact upon their life and their future just to do something as cruel as that.

But then again, I suppose anything's possible, when you look back on all the crazy things that have happened in the world.

We've got the evil wars going on all over the place, acts of terrorism, cruelty to animals, abuse to almost every species of life, genocides of entire races, racism, murder and robbery, news coverage on personal lives of celebrities instead of the really important things going on, and all of that.

Question: what is wrong with the world we live in?

Answer: almost everything.

I mean, sure, we're making such great advances in technology and all that, plus we can leave our planet, but still. If we're making plans to figure out how we can get off the planet and onto others and create biospheres on different planets, then shouldn't we be able to have world peace and learn how to live with one another first?

Life *so* doesn't make sense.

"I just don't understand," I say aloud suddenly.

God. Trevor must totally think I'm insane now.

I glance up at him. "Sorry," I say quickly. "I was just thinking to myself about how crazy the entire world is."

He smiles and shakes his head. "No, it's okay. I understand. You know," he says quietly and kind of…uncertainly, "you can always think aloud if I'm around to listen to you."

Lame as that may sound, I can't help smiling. "Thanks, Trevor."

"Class! I'm so glad you listened to me and you were so good while I was gone!" A whirl of blonde hair swoops into the classroom.

Time to find out what happened last night.

Miss Halitelli has returned.

Trevor

Sophia took that well.

She and I were just having a conversation before little Miss Halitelli returned from the copy room, which, by the way, was moved to a mysterious location after a graduating class photocopied some stupid montage of class pictures and plastered the school as their senior prank – how retarded.

But Sophia and I were talking about what happened with Jackson and Daphne and all that stuff, and how the world is crazy.

Then she was silent for a few minutes, clearly thinking to herself.

And then, all of a sudden and out of the blue, she goes, "I just don't understand," with this distressed look on her face.

And at that exact moment, I wanted to make her feel better. Like I wanted to get rid of whatever was making her so sad.

So I told her.

No, I didn't tell her that I like her as more than a friend.

But when she apologized for thinking aloud, I told her that it was okay, that I understood how she was feeling completely, and that she could always think aloud if I was around to listen to all of her thoughts.

And I know that sounds really lame, and as soon as it came out of my mouth, that's exactly what I thought, too, but I guess to her it really meant something.

I don't know how. And I don't know why.

But she looked happy and she smiled and thanked me.

And maybe I'm reading into this (well, scratch that, I probably am, but still) but something about that last bit of our conversation was…

Different.

Special.

And I still can't figure out why.

But now Sophia is on her way to talk to Miss Halitelli about what happened last night with Mr. Winslow Romeo or whoever that Loser Valley High principal (I'm sorry, but they lost and we won – I'm not trying to be conceited, but they hated us so I don't like them very much) was.

I'll be totally honest with you and admit that I really don't care much about this whole romance story or whatever it is. I'd be interested if it involved someone other than my English teacher.

In fact, the only reason I *am* interested in this is because Sophia's telling me all about it and she's very interested.

That's why, and that's it.

Otherwise?

I wouldn't care at all.

Well, fine, if something actually came out of it, I'd be thinking, 'All right, this is cool, and I hope Miss Halitelli will be so superbly happy that she'll ditch that homework idea for a little while.'

And I'd definitely be happy for her.

But right now?

Yippee.

No big deal.

It wouldn't be as important to me as Sophia telling me she liked me as more than a friend, too.

But then again, I'd definitely get completely blown away into a different world if she ever did that.

And I wouldn't mind if it happened, because I could always come back to her…how perfect.

But now.

Now I must get to this stack of worksheets so I can guarantee a happier Sophia when she returns.

Not that she would ever, *ever* use me like that.

I just love doing all that I can to impress her and get on her very best side, if you know what I mean.

I mean, really.

Isn't that what a guy is supposed to do for the girl he really, truly loves?

Brett

Okay, so I'll admit that things are going pretty well, despite that homework business in my classes. That wasn't so fun. And then I was kind of worried about Brooke and Sophia's safety, in addition to Trevor's and my own.

But it apparently turns out that Daphne and Jackson are being kept away from the four of us.

Then again, it's not as if I've had any classes with them yet today, so I wouldn't know if they're currently present in the building or not. And I haven't checked up on the others by consulting with them, since I haven't seen them since before homeroom.

Not true, actually.

Brooke's here, of course.

We're in math with Sanders.

She was extremely happy when we walked into the room, and I guess that's because everything worked out with the athletic drama. Even though I really don't know what happened in the end with the couple of cruelty.

Guess I'll find out after the bell rings.

We're actually learning in class right now, and I'm supposed to be taking notes on the rest of this quadratic equation stuff, but I'm way too lazy. Plus I'm so very exhausted after last night's events.

Thank God Ms. Sanders didn't decide to give us homework last night. But then again, she shouldn't have. It *was* our game, after all. And she was the one with all of those extra credit tickets.

Which, by the way, she did hand out after the game. It was kind of interesting, since she was keeping one eye on the tickets and line and stuff and the other eye on Brooke and Sophia and the rest of the cheerleaders.

Oh, my God.

It's not that I don't like math. It's just that I'm getting really bored with this formula thing. I mean, how many of these equations do you want us to solve, Ms. Sanders? If we don't get it now, I doubt we'll ever get it.

"Brett?"

Oh, whoop-de-do.

"Yeah?" I answer. Daring and witty.

Brooke had better be impressed.

She lets out a tiny giggle as do a few other people who are scattered around the classroom.

I glance back at her out of the corner of my eye.

Yeah, one hand is covering her mouth, but the way the corners of her gorgeous eyes are tilted, I can tell that she definitely is smiling.

Score!

Ms. Sanders rolls her eyes at me and smiles, too. "Brett," she chides, sounding way too forgiving. "Now I'm going to have to make you come up to the board and solve the problem yourself."

"All right, all right." I take my time getting out of my chair and dragging my feet up the aisle to the board.

She offers me a piece of chalk. "Get started."

"Ms. Sanders," I begin pleadingly, "you have no idea how tired I am after that entire ordeal last night."

She rolls her eyes again. "Oh, please, Brett, put a sock in it and just solve the problem before I bestow an even worse fate upon you."

I yawn and take the piece of chalk from her. "Fine." And I solve the problem correctly with great ease. So simple.

"Fine job," Ms. Sanders says to me somewhat reluctantly.

Isn't it her job to make sure I get my questions right? She didn't sound super happy. But then again, I guess I can drive her crazy.

But since I'm Brett Evans, I guess I can also get away with it pretty easily. Not to be conceited or anything.

But it is true.

"Thank you, Ms. Sanders," I reply to her in an attempt to be courteous.

I really do try sometimes.

Ms. Sanders eyes me warily in return. "Hmm…Well, you may go sit down now, Mr. Evans."

I hold up my hands in the air defensively and stroll casually back to my seat, getting a laugh out of the class, even though it is somewhat weak.

I have to admit, that felt really good. I haven't dared to do anything like that since Brooke first caught my eye.

And believe me, now that was quite some time ago.

I sit down in my seat and lean back comfortably.

Well, as comfortable as it is possible to get in a chair like the ones we have in our classrooms.

I can tell that Brooke is faintly smiling. "What brought you to do that?" she whispers in my ear.

"I don't know, I guess I just felt like it," I respond.

She beams and sits back.

Well, I did manage to entertain the lady.

Oh, and I did a pretty fabulous job of it.

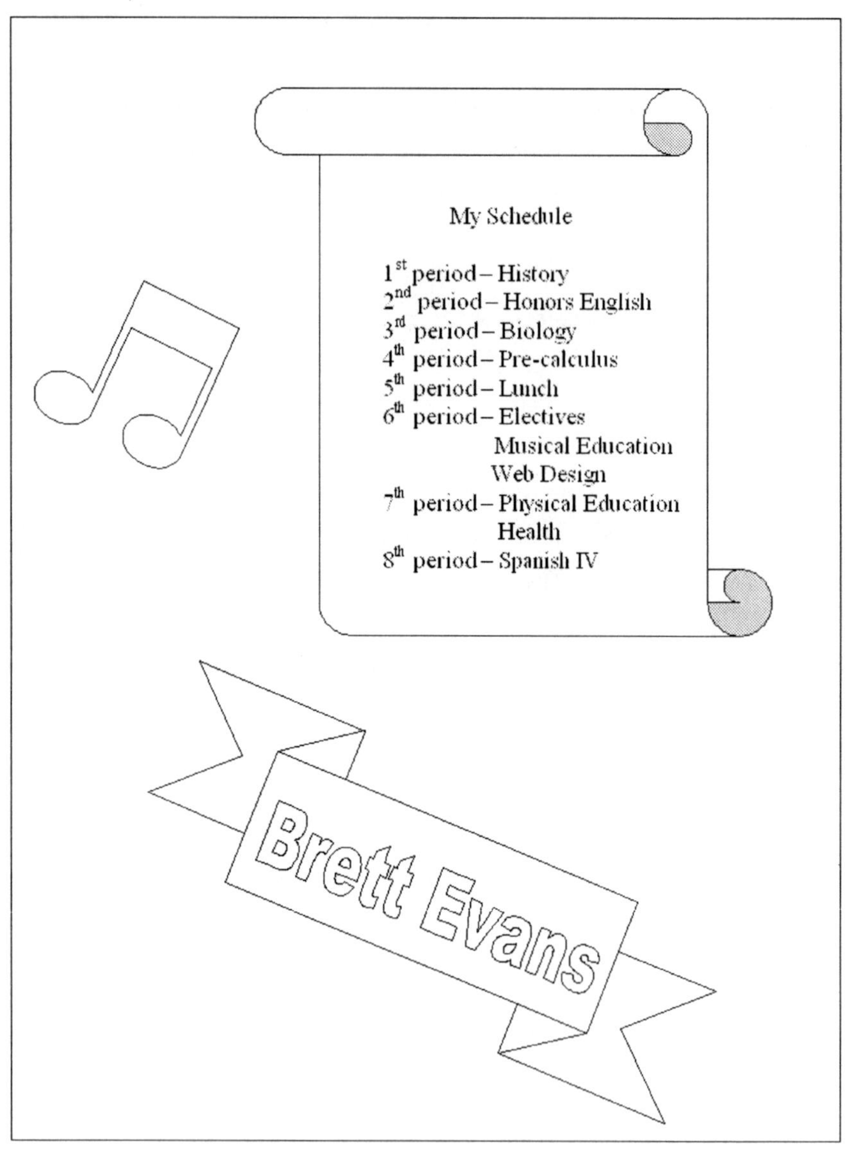
My Schedule
1st period – History
2nd period – Honors English
3rd period – Biology
4th period – Pre-calculus
5th period – Lunch
6th period – Electives
Musical Education
Web Design
7th period – Physical Education
Health
8th period – Spanish IV
Brett Evans

I think it just might be safe to say it now…

Mission accomplished.

Brooke

Wow, math is so much fun today!

Brett was totally way too smart for Ms. (Coach?) Sanders. Except not intelligence smart. Attitude smart.

He's lucky she wasn't too tough on him. He totally could have gotten in trouble for being so sassy.

But since he's Brett…

She tolerated him.

And he didn't get in trouble.

How adorable.

"Homework for tonight…" Ms. Sanders begins to announce.

Ugh, how boring is that?

But on the bright side, Brett will probably want to do the homework together tonight online…

"Brooke."

And what do you know?

"Yeah?" I whisper.

"Homework together?"

I told you so.

"Definitely."

The bell rings before I can say anything else.

The whole class shoots out of their seats and straight out the door.

Guess not that many people favor math with Ms. Sanders over some of their other classes.

Cough, cough, lunch.

~ Chapter Six ~

Brett and I walk out of the room together, as has become our daily custom over the past week.

And I've got to admit it…

I really do treasure it.

We walk next door, almost completely silent.

Trevor and Sophia exit Miss Halitelli's room momentarily, walking side by side, and smiling.

Sophia's bubbling over with enthusiasm.

And then I remember that we never found out what happened after the game with Miss Halitelli and her Romeo – Mr. Romero.

"Oh, my God, Sophia! What happened? Did she tell you?" I gush, hurrying over to Sophia.

Sophia nods, looking totally triumphant.

"Well?" I prompt, "What did she say?"

Sophia's taking her sweet old time.

I glance at Trevor questioningly.

He shrugs and rolls his eyes at me in response. "If you ask me, I think you two are making way too huge of a deal out of all of this stuff."

And now it's my turn to roll my eyes at *him* and say scornfully, "Oh, please, Trevor. No one asked you."

He says defensively, "Okay, okay. Go right ahead, Sophia."

Sophia smiles at him.

Yawn.

"So according to Miss Halitelli, the two of them left the premises for dinner somewhere – I think at Giordano's, which is so totally *un*romantic, but whatever. They've already made plans for their next, uh, '*date*,' which is going to be tomorrow night."

Hmm…

Impressive?

Sure, I guess.

"Oh," I say carefully. "Is that it?"

Sophia nods. "Well, yeah, pretty much. There wasn't really anything super interesting...she was just really happy and excited."

I nod.

Because really...

What else is there for me to say or do?

"But," Sophia continues, "I have a feeling that something incredibly good is going to happen on their date tomorrow night."

"Oh, really? Why's that?"

"They just happen to be going to a romantic restaurant by the lake and to spend some time walking around the Village," Sophia announces proudly.

Wait a second...

Romantic restaurant?

By the lake?

The Village?!

Oh, my goodness gracious...

Wow.

I should probably explain a few details about the lake.

Here in Saffrondale, we're totally landlocked, as you would imagine, being in northwestern upstate New York.

But a little farther away from Saffrondale, we've got this gorgeous lake in the middle of nowhere.

Kentvale is kind of between Saffrondale and Lodi Valley. And Kentvale just happens to be the home of the gorgeous lake. And perched right by the edge of the lake is a small 'classic' village (called the Kentvale Village, no surprise, but nicknamed by the rest of us normal people 'The Village') that's totally trying to be colonial or at the very least, artsy or super-elegant. It's up to you to pick what it really seems to be.

Personally, I think there is absolutely no point in going to the Village unless you've got a significant other to go to the Village with. It isn't even fun to go there with a bunch of your closest friends…unless you're, like, double dating or triple or quadruple dating, or something. And then you've got to be somewhat into each other as a couple…not just as friends. Believe me, I went there with Trevor once, and it was like we had to be dating or something…it was way freaky the way everyone was acting around us.

But I definitely wouldn't mind going there to visit with Brett…and maybe taking Sophia and Trevor along together as well.

Here.

You've got to get an idea of what's in the village before you start making any decisions or opinions about it.

We've got a romantic restaurant where you can usually eat by candlelight or by the fireside, and that's called – gee, we'd never have guessed – The Candlelight Inn, one of many in the country, even though none of them are affiliated with this one. I mean, this one isn't even an inn. It's really just a restaurant with a few rooms on the third floor for the owners and family to live in.

Then there's a jewelry place called Symington Jewelers. It's so old-fashioned. You walk in, go down a few steps, and it's all wood and silver and gold. Seriously. It's really gorgeous, but it's so…"What would you like to get for the lady, sir? We've got a great selection of absolutely divine engagement rings over here, and each one comes with a bouquet of the most lush and sweet-smelling red roses for an additional charge of a mere $9.99…"

Yeah.

Way too romantic for most teens' taste.

But I can almost guarantee that if Jackson and Daphne get suspended, that's where you're going to find them spending the day.

Ha, ha.

And then you've got the flower shop. Chandler's Florist. Quaint-looking little blue and white house with a pretty little garden of flowers around it. The radius around the place smells so sweet, if at all a little too sweet. And once you go inside, they're all for buying a bouquet of mixed flowers or roses for your loved one. Plus they're tied with a printed ribbon with romantic messages.

Hmm…

What else?

Oh, my God, the gazebo! How could I forget?! Okay, so the gazebo's basically this wooden…gazebo on a small hilltop for people to look out over the lake and take in the beauty. That's pretty much it, but it means a lot to Kentvale Village, being a nice attraction and all.

But whatever.

Oh, yeah, and then you have the souvenir shop. Also known to the public as Eli's Souvenirs. Who runs the place? You guessed it right: Eli. Eli Whitman. He's an old guy who tries to sell you everything in the entire place – stuff that has 'Kentvale Village' emblazoned on it, and all that insanity.

Just kidding. I mean, who am I to talk about what I think of Kentvale Village? I've only been there once, and that was without anyone 'significant' except Trevor. Maybe if I went there with someone special, like…Brett, for example, I'd have a whole new perspective on the place…

Not that it's wishful thinking or anything.

"Wow," I suddenly say aloud, realizing that a lot could come out of this prospective date of theirs tomorrow night.

"Yeah," Brett agrees, speaking totally out of the blue. I would have expected him to be silent during this whole conversation, but apparently that isn't going to be so. "Well, the four of us should go there one day. Maybe even with Brandon and Corinne. Or maybe even just us. You know?" He turns to the rest of us only to find us staring at him as if he's just lost his last marble.

Which, you know, as much as I hate to admit it, he just might have.

Sophia snickers in a way that almost doesn't sound like her, even though she does speak the truth. "Oh, come on, Brett. You *know* that only super-romantic *couples* go there. Why would *we* bother wasting our time by doing *that*?"

Ooh…Shut down! Or maybe not…

"I don't know…It might be fun just to go there to make fun of. You know?" He looks at me hopefully.

Wait…me? Why *me*?!

I look away quickly, pretending to be distracted by someone else walking down the hallway.

Despite the fact that we all know (most of us, anyway) that no one else could distract me from him. A small detail, but a solid fact. If that makes any sense.

"Sure, Brett, sure." Sophia turns her head away and we all continue walking off to the cafeteria.

Dismissive.

But what brought Brett to say that?

He *knows* about that whole "couples only in Kentvale Village" thing.

And I *know* he does.
So why?
I know what I want to be the reason.
But could it be true?

Chapter 7:

Battling the Enemies

Brett

Okay, so after Trevor and I had to listen to that whole story about Miss Halitelli and her new boyfriend (ew), and after I was stupid and blabbed out what I was thinking – which just happened to be something about going to the Kentvale Village with Brooke and with Trevor and Sophia coming along (yeah, how could I even dare to think that *aloud*?) – we actually made it to the cafeteria without further incident.

Or so we hoped…

I mean, we still didn't know if Daphne and Jackson were in

school or not. We definitely hadn't seen them at all yet.

So since we usually see them in the halls giving us nasty looks, or at least before homeroom, we assumed that neither of them was here.

Boy, were we wrong.

We walked into the cafeteria, scanning the crowd.

But then we saw a bunch of people.

People older than us.

Adults.

They were, or so it just happened to turn out, monitoring the cafeteria for any signs of arguments or brawling due to last night's events.

Daphne and Jackson were sitting by themselves at a small table in the very center of the cafeteria with totally evil looks etched upon their faces. The teenage delinquents sitting at the delinquent table.

That was almost a really good laugh.

But then we also saw that there were a good amount of monitor people standing around their table.

And I guess that was really when the danger of the whole entire situation started to make sense.

Sophia

Oh, my God.

Saffrondale High has never had such an incident.

I mean, even though I was one of the central victims of last night's catastrophic event, I didn't think it would be *that* important.

But apparently to the administration, it was important.

So important that they now have tons of people – adults –

monitoring everywhere Jackson and Daphne go.

That's so scary.

I mean, really.

It's almost as if they're terrorists, or something.

Except instead of giving everyone else in school bodyguards, I guess since they have pretty easily identified who the main suspects – okay, culprits – are (and they know who the evil pair is without a doubt) they're having the couple watched, so they can't cause any more damage to the school or its occupants.

Of course, the administrators could have just suspended or even expelled Jackson and Daphne, but it's true enough that anyone could just sneak back into the school. Disguised by a bit of makeup, any former student can make it past the security.

And even *that* is scary.

But anyway…

Off with the worrying thoughts.

Now the four of us (yeah, that's Trevor, Brett, Brooke, and I) are sitting here at our regular table. The cheerleading and basketball table.

Also known as the popular table.

Ah, yes, that's us.

But it's not like anyone really hates us, or anything. No, they're just…I don't know. But they definitely don't hate us.

Besides, it's not like we hate any of them, either.

The only ones that really hate us are Jackson and Daphne. And I doubt they're even human, so they don't count.

Just kidding.

They're more real than I'd like to imagine…and admit.

I mean, seriously.

If things are like this in high school, then what the heck is the real world going to be like?

That's so scary.

On to normal stuff?

Corinne and Kellie and the rest of the girls from the squad that are sitting with us are being totally sweet, trying to help us ignore the new changes that have been made to our everyday surroundings.

And the guys – like Brandon and them – are being just as nice. Well, they really are trying, and I can tell.

And now we've also got this new thing where they're only letting a certain amount of people go up to get their lunches at a time.

They're calling us up by table.

Guess who's last?

No, not our table.

Jackson and Daphne.

Delinquents come last.

And that's the only consoling part.

Yeah.

That they get denied of their lunch until the rest of us start eating.

But weirdly enough, other than this whole thing inside school, everything else is being hushed up from the general public. I don't know how the school plans to do that, but I guess they're just going to be, like, "Oh, yeah, we've got it all under control. There's no situation going on here."

I just wonder if anyone's really going to buy all that.

I mean, there was an incident at the game last night. No one can really hide or deny that. It's totally impossible. But I guess they can cover it up somehow. They do have the authority.

But it's not up to me to worry about that.

All I have to think about is my safety, Brett's, Trevor's, and Brooke's safety. And the rest of my family and friends.

Anyway.

Distraction.

Must distract myself.

A monitor walks over to our table.

We all look up at her.

"You may go buy your lunches now," she tells us. She's right about to walk away, when she turns back and adds, "Thank you for cooperating."

Now we're all staring since nothing like this ever happens or has happened in the history of Saffrondale High.

At least, that's what I think.

Finally I stand up.

Everyone follows, one by one.

We walk over to the kitchen area in almost complete silence, just like the rest of the cafeteria's occupants.

Finally Corinne speaks up.

Figures it would be *her* to talk first.

Not to be mean.

But even she can only say one short thing, even if it is what we're all thinking inside our minds.

"This is so weird, you guys."

But the thing is…it's so totally true.

Trevor

I can't stand this.

The cafeteria has never been this quiet.

And one of the worst things about it is everyone's either staring at Jackson and Daphne (which is totally fine with us, since they definitely deserve the humiliation) or they've got their eyes glued to our table.

And let me tell you, that isn't fun.

Is it our fault Jackson and Daphne have such serious issues? Is it our fault they want something that they just can't have and they keep becoming more and more desperate to get it? Is anything about them our fault?

We're all sitting here, trying to eat.

Corinne suddenly whispers, "Oh, my God, I can't take this."

Everyone at our table bobs their head in agreement.

Brooke, of all people, decides to speak out. "You think we can get out of here and head somewhere else?"

We all glance at one another, thinking this over.

But I doubt it would ever work.

"Brooke," I begin.

"Yeah, I know," she cuts me off. "They probably wouldn't let us out of here." She pauses.

Sophia exchanges a look with Brooke. "We could try," she says.

I glance at Brett, who's sitting next to me. "I don't think so," I whisper to him under my breath.

He nods. "I know," he whispers back to me. "But let them try."

"Sure." I turn back to my Boca cheeseburger with pickles, lettuce, and tomatoes and corn and baked beans on the side (new cafeteria specialty!) and give it a look of pure disgust.

Sophia, of course, catches me.

I quickly pick up my fork and try to eat some of the side

veggies.

She laughs. "Keep trying, Trevor. I'm proud of you."

More will power!

Brooke turns her head and giggles, too. "Nice, Trevor. Keep up the good work. You're making progress."

Brett gives me a dirty look.

I stare at him right back.

He groans and turns to his burger (yeah, he's the one eating meat).

I pick up my Boca burger and finally try it.

Hmm…

Not bad.

I tell Sophia and Brooke, "This is pretty good," and continue eating.

They exchange glances and smile. "Told ya."

I smile back and soon the burger's gone.

Brooke waves at one of the monitors (one who looks extra-nice and lenient, I can't help but noticing) and beckons her over to our table.

"Yes?" the aide asks.

Brooke lowers her voice and puts on a pleading façade.

I have to admit it…

She *is* a good actress.

"Um, we were involved in the incident last night," Brooke begins in a sad, 'oh, poor me,' little voice.

The lady raises her eyebrows. Way up.

It's not that stunning.

Is it?

She lifts up her hand and points at the table of two delinquents. "Go!" she commands authoritatively.

It suddenly dawns on us that she thinks we were in on the whole evil plan with Jackson and Daphne. As if.

I'd sooner have stuck pins in my eyes. And I'm sure that's how the rest of the team and squad would have felt about such a thing.

"Oh!" Brooke's eyes widen drastically. "Oh! No! That's not what I meant!"

The monitor places a hand on one hip. "Oh, really? Then what did you mean?" she asks skeptically.

"We were involved as victims," Brooke attempts carefully, and then pauses for a few seconds just to allow that information to sink in.

The lady's eyes widen all of a sudden. "Oh, my! Oh, my goodness!"

This is interesting.

I put down my fork for a moment.

She lays a hand on Brooke's shoulder. "Honey–"

'*Honey*'!?!

Oh, well.

Guess I'll have to take it silently.

"–I am so sorry…You must be Brooke, right?"

Brooke looks surprised.

And why in heaven's name shouldn't she?

Just kidding.

"Yeah, I am," Brooke answers. Slowly.

"And you're Sophie?" The lady turns to Sophia.

"Sophia," she corrects. "Well, yeah, I am."

"That's just terrible," the monitor says.

Um, okay.

We all glance at one another uncertainly.

"Uh, yeah," Brooke tries. "And since it's kind of hard on us to stay in here, we were wondering if we could–"

"Leave?" the woman interrupts her.

"Yeah," Brett suddenly answers.

The aide shakes her head, looking apologetic and almost regretful. "No, kids, I'm sorry, but you can't."

We all sigh our disappointment instantly.

Corinne pouts and looks at Brandon significantly.

God.

All this to get out of lunch?

Normally we'd do this to get *to* lunch.

How strange. Anyway.

Brandon finally talks for Corinne. "Aw, come on," he says. Totally convincing. In fact, the monitor just gives him a look. And he's almost silenced. "Don't you think we've been through enough?" he pleads. "It's so tough on us having them all staring."

She pauses. "Well, look. They're also staring at those two kids." She points at Daphne and Jackson – not surreptitiously at all, if I might add.

All the people who have been watching (and trying to eavesdrop on) our conversation look over at the delinquents quickly, and then back at us.

"Well, wouldn't you rather have them staring at those two as punishment for their behavior?" Kellie, of all people, suddenly points out.

The woman nods. "Well, yes…that would be nice. Guilt them into begging forgiveness, maybe…"

"So…?" Corinne asks somewhat rudely.

"So what?"

"So if we're gone, then what is there to stare at other than those two?" Corinne says, all matter-of-factly.

True, true.

Corinne Carlton finally made her point.

Whoopee.

Too bad it just won't work.

"I know, sweetheart, but orders are orders, and rules are rules. You've got to stay here. I'm sorry, but that's all I can do for you."

We stare at her, open-mouthed.

I told them so.

But I won't say it out loud.

Brett elbows me.

"We were right."

"I know," I hiss back, taking a sip of water and grimacing a little.

I love water (you have to if you're an athletic type of person), but once you get used to having a soda, or a fruit punch drink, or something with more flavor than *water* ever day at lunch, it's a big letdown.

Sophia elbows me.

How many people are going to elbow me in one day!?

"Here," she whispers.

"What?"

She tries to slip me a tiny packet, holding it out in her outstretched hand.

Doesn't she *know* sugar is disgusting when mixed with water?

Oh.

Wait.

That's not sugar.

What is it??

Oh…

Crystal Light.

Sweetness.

"Thanks," I whisper.

She beams that perfect smile at me. "You've made a lot of changes for one day," she says quietly.

Yet I can tell she's pleased with my progress.

I have to admit, I am, too.

She glances at Corinne, who has started an animated conversation with Brooke and Kellie and the rest of the girls at our table.

Brett starts talking to Brandon and the rest of the guys.

Sophia starts talking in a normal voice again. "I know it's been tough to switch from all this stuff you loved to eat," she says.

I nod.

It's so true.

"But you'll get used to it eventually. And if you can't stick it out for that long, that's okay. I understand. At least you'll have tried." She smiles yet again.

But wait.

If she thinks that I'm even close to giving up this 'no soda, no junk, no meat' diet, then she's definitely got another think coming.

Or whatever it is that they say.

I guess it's just that whenever Brooke tried to tell me all about her latest vegetarian diet or sugarless techniques, I never really wanted to listen. I had my own principles, and it seemed like Brooke was the only one who wanted to get away from those foods.

But then when I met Sophia and really got to know her as a best friend, I realized that more people I knew were on this idea, and it wasn't just another one of Brooke's insane new-fangled notions - thank you, Miss Halitelli.

I mean, I knew it was a good idea, but I didn't want to consider it because it seemed so tough to do. Yet I never admired Brooke for sticking with her principles, although I really should have. But I have to admit…it just never crossed my mind.

But don't think that I just decided to try it for Sophia because I like her and everything. When she and Brooke ganged up on me, I gave in quickly, although it is taking me some time to adjust to these new ways.

But I guess in a way, that's just how I am.

Always.

Hmm…

Wait a second.

I realize now that something's different around here.

Chatter has broken out at our entire table…

…Finally.

And soon enough, everyone in the rest of the cafeteria's talking like everything is back to normal. Oh, and they're done staring.

But I guess none of us realized that lunch can really always end quickly. Time really flew by…

Because now it's time to leave for our next class.

Oh, my God.

This is so stupid.

We're getting dismissed by table.

One of the monitors waves us out of the cafeteria.

We (the, uh, 'P0Pu1@R$', or so the online reference to us is at times – @ +!m3$, actually) walk out together and go our separate ways.

"Oh, my God," Corinne says. "This is so stupid."

Way to steal my thoughts and say them out loud. But I guess

everyone's pretty much thinking the same thing at a time like this.

"I feel like we're in kindergarten again," I say.

She smiles. "Totally."

Wow.

I had even the simplest conversation with Corinne Carlton in which we actually *agreed* on something.

I'm impressed beyond words.

I never thought I'd see eye-to-eye on *anything* with a girl like her.

Not that I actually like her.

God.

Life can be so strange yet beautiful sometimes.

It's so weird…

Brooke

Hmm…

Lunch was really weird…but interesting.

I mean, it was silent in the entire cafeteria for so long. It was so…uncomfortable for everyone.

But a little later into the lunch period everything went back to normal, and sixth period was okay, too, I guess.

So now I'm right about to meet up with Sophia, Trevor, and Brett (oh, my God once again) and we're going to head off to gym.

That should be even more interesting than lunch, since the teenage delinquents, namely, Jackson and Daphne, are in our gym class.

I think we're going to have a lot in store.

"Brooke? Brooke! Brooke Dawson! Over here!"

I turn around to see who's calling my name and I find Sophia waving at me crazily.

I hurry over to where she's standing by the gym. "Hey, Sophia. What's the matter with you? You're, like, spazzing out all of a sudden."

Her blue eyes are wide, and the sparkle is gone.

Something strange has got to be going on here.

"Sophia? Sophia! What's the matter?" I repeat, anxious.

"Rumor has it in the halls and in class that Jackson and Daphne – well, mainly Daphne, I think – are planning to start something huge during gym class," she reports worriedly, chewing on one of her expensive-looking acrylic French tips.

I grab her hand and take it away from her mouth. "Stop it."

Then it registers in my mind what she just said. "Wait. What?!?"

She stamps her foot. "They're going to 'start something,'" she repeats, making quotation marks out of her fingers as she says 'start something.'

"Meaning…?" I ask, still totally confused.

"They're going to try to start a fight or something."

Oh, please.

And that's it?

"A fight," I repeat skeptically. "Yeah, right."

I look her in the eye and realize that she's serious.

"Sophia," I begin again, this time feeling just the slightest bit nervous about this whole thing.

"Seriously," she says. "I'm not kidding. That's what everyone has been saying. During sixth period, too. And they've all been looking at me nervously in the hallways. It's freaking me out."

Whoa…

That's her proof?

"Please, Sophia. Think about it. Who do you really think started this rumor?"

She shrugs. "How am *I* supposed to know? I take in what I hear and judge it logically. And this makes sense!"

I grab her by the shoulders gently, still looking her square in the eye.

Many people pass, and she's not lying about the staring part. They're all giving us scared looks.

But what should they be scared for?

"Sophia."

"What? I'm not lying."

"I know you aren't lying, but how would any of those people know what Jackson and Daphne have planned for the rest of us? They don't talk to them!"

I know I have a point.

Totally.

She pauses, thinking this new bit of information over.

"I'm right," I say. "And I know it."

"Okay," she says after a few seconds of mulling it over in her mind. "But still. I'm not totally convinced."

"Why not?" I guide her towards the girls' locker room.

Okay, come on.

Let's face it.

If we don't hurry, we're going to be late, and God knows what's going to happen after that.

"Brooke!" she exclaims. "They would know. After spending so much time staring at them, I would expect them to know. And you should, too. All I wanted was for us to be prepared for whatever they have in store."

"Okay," I say slowly. "I can understand that. But I'm just saying not to believe everything you hear. Gossip isn't the answer."

"Oh, please," she scoffs right back. "Gossip isn't the answer to what?"

I pause for a second.

She's right.

That made no sense whatsoever.

"Okay," I admit. "You're right. But I know for a fact that you have a little bit of Corinne Carlson in you. And that's the gossiping part. You don't spread the word around much, but you do take it in. And sometimes, you take it a little too seriously."

She gives me a look.

"Come on, Sophia. Own up to it."

"Okay, fine, maybe I do. But still. That has absolutely nothing to do with the current situation. I– "

Suddenly she shuts up automatically and starts staring at something – someone? – over my shoulder.

I whirl around, totally freaked out.

Daphne and Jackson are walking down the hallway, getting all the stares in the history of Saffrondale High. They both are wearing the most evil looks I have ever seen. Evil enough for even them.

Daphne struts down the hall with a weird air for someone who's a total delinquent and is in so much trouble.

She walks past us…

Almost.

First – before she walks into the locker room – she just has to jolt right into me and Sophia.

She gives us a look and *then* walks into the locker room.

Jackson goes into the guys' locker room without even so much as a glance at us – an act, I must say, that I personally don't mind at all.

The monitors that have been keeping watch in the hallways leave, no doubt to go on their lunch break, since Daphne and Jackson are safely in their gym class. At least that's what they think. But they think wrong.

As soon as they're gone, Sophia gives *me* a look.

It's almost as if she's dying to say, "I told you so."

No.

Instead, she says, "I warned you. We're both half right. Now come on. Let's go change for class."

She leads me up the stairs and into the locker room.

She *is* right.

Something strange is definitely in store for us.

Sophia

Oh, my God.

Don't I wish that Brooke had just believed me.

I told her that Daphne – the witch – had something terrible planned for us. I knew it. I knew it.

And maybe I was a little too overdramatic about it. But still.

I knew the truth.

And Brooke just couldn't believe me.

But since she's my best friend, I'm not going to hold it against her.

I guess I didn't sound too…believable?

Either way, when we entered the locker room, which was about a couple minutes ago, Daphne was just standing there.

She was leaning against the wall, one foot propped up against the whiteness, and a bottle of Mountain Dew in her hand, from which she was taking long drinks.

Brooke hissed under her breath, although not loud enough for Daphne to hear her, "Ugh. Company."

I sighed and stared Daphne down with a glare almost equally nasty as the one she was shooting at me.

And that's where we are now.

Yeah…

Giving each other the evil eye.

That's all.

My apologies if I got your hopes up.

Suddenly she kicks a foot off the wall, clearly seething.

Brooke and I hear a clicking sound as the heel of her neon orange (yeah, that's right – neon orange) knee-high boot kicks off the wall.

She takes yet another long sip of Mountain Dew (ew!) and sneers, the glare not softening at all.

Brooke jumps momentarily.

Daphne snickers.

But she doesn't say anything else at all.

We pass her without incident.

In my opinion?

Brush with danger…

Brush with luck.

As soon as we get to our designated area of the locker room, Brooke hisses at me, "I told you she wasn't going to do anything!"

I roll my eyes at her with a shrug.

Can she prove that?

I don't *think* so.

Suddenly an empty green bottle flies into our alcove, bouncing off a row of lockers and smacking off the bench in the middle.

Brooke gives off a sudden squeal.

Daphne clicks her way by, letting out a sinister laugh.

God.

She would play a perfect villain in any movie, despite the fact that's she's probably one of the world's worst actresses.

And by worst actress, I don't mean what the tabloids keep saying about Jessica Simpson, and celebrities like her, because that is totally not true. Jessica *is* a good actress. Those people are just way too jealous to admit it. And they just need something to write about, so they make it all up as they go along. There isn't always truth in the tabloids. I mean, duh.

But anyway.

Daphne wouldn't even have to do any acting. But then that would totally be typecasting, and I doubt many people would be happy about that.

I have a feeling that a lot of people in our area would, though. Myself and my friends included.

Brooke has a nasty look on her face now. And I honestly don't blame her.

She picks up the soda bottle gingerly, given how much she hates soda.

"Here, you can have that back!" she yells out, chucking the plastic bottle at Daphne's retreating back.

It hits the wicked witch's giant Prada bag (um, excuse me, but it's so totally *fake* since it belongs to *Daphne*, so let's call that Frada).

Daphne just turns around in a circle and smirks, and she keeps on walking away, leaving the bottle lying there on the clay tiles.

That has some effect on the rest of us.

Well, it has some effect on all the girls in the locker room who are watching, anyway. As expected.

But Daphne's reaction to Brooke throwing the bottle at her?

Now *that* was very…

Impressive.

I mean, her typical reaction would be something along the lines of her completely blowing up and shooting at Brooke (and me, just for the heck of it) like an uncontrollable fireball.

Well, at least that's what I'd expect her to do, anyway.

And I'm sure a lot of girls I know (and guys, too, for that matter) would totally agree with me.

It's so typical.

But something different is going on now.

And I'm almost scared – terrified, actually – to find out what this depraved girl is going to do next.

Brett

Well, let me just start off by saying that when Jackson came into the locker room quietly and coolly (not popularity-wise, let me assure you; he was still hated), both Trevor and I knew that something was different.

So when he took out a bottle of Mountain Dew and sat down on the bench between two of the rows of lockers to drink it, I was totally thinking, 'What is going *on*?!'

I glanced at Trevor quickly and he just gave me a quick nod in return.

I had no idea exactly what he was thinking at the moment, but we both changed extremely quickly and locked *all* of our stuff in our gym lockers.

~ Chapter Seven ~

Can't trust a delinquent (as the others call him and Daphne, and it does have a funnily great ring to it) alone with my prized possessions.

I mean, really.

Notes and letters that I've drafted to Brooke that contain very important and classified information about, well, how much I like her and stuff like that, but also about what we plan to do to protect ourselves, are scattered all over the place inside all my binders and notebooks and things.

I'm not so stupid that I'd leave Jackson, of all people, alone with my stuff. Definitely not.

Not that I have my books with me, but still.

So now I'm just waiting for Trevor to finish locking up all of his things, all the while keeping a wary eye on Jackson, who's still drinking all that Mountain Dew.

Sometimes I really wonder exactly how stupid he is.

You know?

I mean, not only is he – well, he *was* – an athlete, but he's clearly lacking a lot of necessary common sense that even *I* have.

Any idiot would know that Mountain Dew has even more caffeine than Coca Cola does. And let me tell you, that's a lot – not even to compare it to Coke.

Plus, you shouldn't drink soda directly before, during, or after taking part in athletic events.

Everyone knows that you should drink water and have an intake of salt, or just drink good old Gatorade or Powerade or whatever sports drink you prefer.

And I'd expect even Jackson to know that after so much time spent playing basketball with Coach Davidson and the rest of the team.

Wait.

He's got to know by now.

I know he isn't *that* stupid.

But why?

Why?

Maybe Brooke, Sophia, and Trevor will have a more reasonable explanation for this weirdness…

Of course, I'd ask Trevor now, but I can't.

And it's all because of one thing:

Stupid Jackson is sitting right in front of us…

…but he's not even trying to do anything to hurt us.

Isn't that so strangely incredible?

Trevor

That whole silence in the locker room just now was so weird. And so…abnormal. For our school, anyway.

But as soon as Brett and I finished changing into our gym clothes and locking our stuff away just for safety, we rushed out of the locker room and into the hall and met up with Brooke and Sophia, who come downstairs from the girls' locker room a few minutes after we stepped out, just as the second bell rings.

Who knows why we're so early?

None of us do, anyway.

"Oh, my God," Sophia gushes as soon as she and Brooke catch up with us. "Did he have a Mountain Dew?"

Brett and I exchange surprised and suspicious looks.

How did *they* know?

Brett still looks confused, so I take over, nodding slowly.

Brooke narrows her eyes. "What was *with* that?" she asks

furiously, her brown eyes blazing.

Brett does happen to notice that Brooke has practically got smoke pouring straight out of her ears.

"Hey," he says to her, laying one hand on her shoulder.

She looks up at him, still seeming a little ticked off.

Aw…

How cute.

"What's up with you?" he asks her.

Ouch.

Not so kind there.

In fact, a little harsh.

Brooke rolls her eyes. "Oh, *nothing*," she shoots back, a little too sarcastically for a girl like her.

I mean, I definitely would never treat Sophia like that.

But all Brett does in reaction is draw his hand away from her.

Smart move.

It's not a good idea to keep bothering Brooke when she's mad.

Not a good idea at all.

Sophia decides that she should answer for boiling Brooke. "Oh, she's just a little ticked off because the wicked witch just chucked her empty soda bottle at us and scared Brooke. And then when Brooke threw it back and yelled back, the wannabe only smirked and walked away after it hit her *Frada* bag."

Um, nice emphasis on Frada?

"Oh." Brett pauses. "Frada?" he repeats.

"Yeah!" Sophia insists. "Her bag. She's totally trying to pretend that it's Prada, but it's clearly a fake. Like Daphne Carlisle would ever carry a real Prada bag."

A brunette pushes her way past us. "Actually, it is authentic, Garrison. Only a poseur like *you* would ever carry a Frada bag."

Sophia gasps, most definitely beyond ticked off.

And then I realize who just said that.

Oh, none other than the rightfully so-called wicked witch herself.

Little Miss Daphne Carlisle.

Brooke

Applause, applause.

All hollow.

And all because that just might have been Daphne Carlisle's best comeback yet.

How sad.

Okay, okay, so it wasn't that bad.

It's just that it was so…

Witch-y.

Or worse, if you get what I mean.

But that's kind of beside the point now.

I mean, we're inside the gym.

Well, the four of us anyway – Sophia, Trevor, Brett, and me.

That's not to say that we're the only ones that are in here…oh, no. That's far from the truth, let me tell you.

Daphne's in a corner by herself, extremely busied by the burden of having to tie her hair up while waiting for her dear Jackson.

And there are a bunch of others here, scattered around, whispering in awe about all of the most recent events.

This whispering thing is just starting to get kind of annoying, though – and a little bit out of hand.

I mean, I feel all of them staring at me, and since I'm not used to being seen, let alone a gossip topic, it totally bothers me.

But to stop it from bothering me, I've got to forget about it.

Forget the staring.

Forget the whispering.

Hard as that may be.

Brett!

Brett, distract me.

"Hey. Brooke."

Oh, my God.

Talk about random wishes coming true.

"Yeah?" I say, trying to be all nonchalant or whatever it is I'm supposed to be around the one I like.

"Don't worry about it."

What?

"Don't worry about what?"

"Her," Brett says to me meaningfully, looking me right in the eye.

His eyes are so blue.

Dazzling.

"Oh," I say, stiffening up automatically at the mention of Daphne. "Don't worry about it. I'm fine. I don't care."

He smiles.

Equally daz– oh, forget it.

"I'm sure you don't, Brooke."

Oh, please.

Sassy much?

Then again, judging by his actions during math, that was expected.

"Yeah," I say, crossing my arms. "I don't."

He smiles again.

I don't even react.

Instead I keep a close and wary eye on Daphne.

Take the high road.

Be the bigger one.

Ignore her.

It's tough.

I just want to get up off this stupid stack of gymnastic mats (no offense or anything), walk over to her, and smack her stupid face.

But I'm not going to.

So you've got no need to worry.

Except about my mental health, of course.

"I think I might be going insane."

Suddenly there's a comforting hand laid on my shoulder.

"You're not going insane, Brooke," Brett assures me.

Oh, my God.

I *so* did not mean to say that out loud!

"Maybe not," I agree.

Oh, wow.

That was so witty.

"You aren't," he says. "But look."

I turn back to look at him.

I can't help it.

I'm still way ticked off at Daphne.

But then again, who wouldn't be?

"This is *so* not fair," I say all of a sudden.

He puts an arm around my shoulders.

Oh, my God!

Brett Evans' arm is around my shoulders?!?

Wow…

Maybe this isn't so unfair after all…

"I know," he says. "But you're doing the right thing. Staying out of everything the best you can, at least."

"Yeah, I guess," I reply, trying to enjoy the comforting ways of his voice and of him being nearby.

"You are," he reassures me. "Believe it."

I turn my head a little. "Okay." I see Trevor trying his best to soothe Sophia's nerves.

"So. Onto other, uh, more important topics?"

"Sure, why not?" I say, sounding a little dull.

I'm so sorry, but I can't help that, either.

"What are you doing tonight?"

What!?

Why does he want to know?

Unless…

He can't possibly want to go out with me tonight!

Or can he?

I have to play this cool.

I don't want to, anyway.

As weird as that must seem.

But now?

Tonight?

When things are so crazy and hectic what with all of the drama that I'm trying to swim out of?

What could he be *thinking*?!

"Oh, Brett, I don't know."

I pause.

All of a sudden, and in a matter of seconds, I remember something quite important in a situation such as this.

Every Thursday, my parents insist that our whole family has

dinner together – and we have to go out.

Perfect excuse.

Thank God he didn't ask if I wanted to go out with him sometime. But that would be fine since I could say, 'Absolutely, but not just yet.'

But then again, he didn't ask at all yet.

So I might be making a mountain out of no molehill.

"Every Thursday my parents insist on going out to dinner with my sister and me," I explain.

His face falls. "Oh."

"Why?" I ask.

Even though I guess I really probably shouldn't have.

Sudden hope washes over his face.

Hmm…

"You think you could get out of it? Maybe?" he asks.

I shake my head, feeling at least a little regretful. "Why?" I repeat.

"I was wondering if you wanted to, like, maybe go see a movie together or something. Dinner, too?"

Oh.

My.

God.

He's serious.

Brett Evans just asked me out.

But I can't.

I can't.

"Brett, I'm sorry. But I really can't."

He looks disappointed.

It's actually kind of amazing.

I mean, seriously.

This is *me* we're talking about.

"Tomorrow night, maybe?"

I really would love to.

But how can I?

I mean, there's all this drama going on now…

Daphne.

Jackson.

Fighting.

Everything.

It's just too much for me to handle.

Can I really turn him down?

Completely?

"Look, Brett," I begin. "There's so much going on. Too much. All of this drama. I can't really…"

He holds one hand up as if to stop my words. "No. It's okay. Don't worry about it. You're right. There *is* too much going on right now."

He turns his head a little bit.

Ugh.

Now I feel so bad.

And mad at myself.

I mean, seriously.

How long have I been dreaming of this? How much of a dream come true does this seem to be? How could I be so *stupid*?!

"Wait, Brett, I –"

Before I can finish what I'm about to say (whatever that would have been), Mr. Davidson comes into the gym and makes us all sit in our assigned spots.

Alphabetical, as usual.

And that's just my luck, as usual.

Which means…

Alphabetically, let's list some people who just happen to be extremely vital to the current situation at hand.

Carlisle, Daphne.

Definition: wicked, evil, vicious, witch. Current status: Oh, my God. No comment to make here.

Dawson, Brooke.

Definition: me! Current status: extremely aggravated at herself and Daphne for her blunder and for the insanity.

Evans, Brett.

Definition: such a sweetheart. Current status: must be the slightest bit irritated because Dawson, Brooke rejected him.

Um, hello.

Think about it.

Awkward much?

Brett

I don't think this has ever happened before.

I really don't.

Not that I've ever actually found anyone that I really liked – enough to want to ask them out, that is.

But when I make my first attempt, I get rejected. Flat-out.

I might as well admit it. That really stings. I'm hurt. But what can I do about it?

I guess that means Brooke doesn't like me. Ouch.

I mean, all those girls that claim to love me so much? Why can't Brooke be one of them?

But that's not right, I guess. I wouldn't want her to be like that

– grossly infatuated with someone she doesn't even know. And she would never be happy like that either.

And if it makes her happy (not liking me, I mean), then so be it.

If she's happy, then I guess I should be happy. And maybe if I'm lucky, she doesn't think I like her that way. Maybe she thinks I just wanted to spend time with her as friends. Maybe. Most likely not. But maybe. I've got to have hope.

This is how it's going to be. Guess sometimes everyone goes through stuff like this. I was just lucky until junior year.

Oh, well. I guess no matter what happens, you know it…

You just gotta love high school.

Sophia

Well…

Mr. Davidson is clearly feeling good about himself.

And yesterday's game must be having the perfect effect on him.

But he still decides that we can have a free period of gym… playing basketball.

Ha, ha.

Trevor and Brett are definitely going to be having fun with this.

But Mr. Davidson has some cleaning to do so he's leaving us alone here. But we're not really alone. He's cleaning out one of the adjoining supply closets.

Just not the one that Jackson and I, um, made a mess in when we were fighting each other off.

It hasn't been decided who's going to have to clean that up.

But I have a feeling Daphne and Jackson are.

In shifts, of course.

Not together.

That would be a gift to them – something they totally do not deserve.

Suddenly music is blaring (not loud enough to travel far away from the gym) from the overhead speakers.

Sweet!

But what is this?

"I'm goin' home…to the place where I belong…and where your love has always been enough for me…"

"Home"?

By Daughtry!?

Why does Mr. *Davidson* have this music?

Everyone's staring at each other, confused and surprised…but happy.

Brooke comes hopping over to me and Trevor.

Brett slowly lopes after her.

What's up with him?

He's acting so weird.

Actually, so is Brooke…

"Trevor, want to go get the basketball?" I hint with a smile.

He grins back at me. "Sure. Come on, Brett."

Brett nods, seeming more than a little out of it. "Okay." He follows, looking somewhat dazed.

Dazed?

Why?

Brooke steps over to me, with a weird look on her face.

What is going on?

Something strange definitely happened between her and Brett.

But what?

Brooke smiles.

Good sign.

"Send the guys to do the work," she says.

I nod and beam right back. "Yeah, of course. What else are they good for?"

God.

This feels like we just met and we're trying our best to make awkward bits of conversation come to life.

Is she still ticked about that whole thing with Daphne? That's totally history right now. I'm trying to forget about it. And I would think that she would be trying to do the same thing, too.

"Brooke."

She looks up. "What?"

"What's the matter with you?"

"Nothing," she says, looking all innocent. "Why?"

She's faking it.

I know my best friend.

So nice to actually be able to know that.

"Come on, Brooke. Tell me. What happened?"

"Nothing," she insists.

"Want me to ask Brett?"

Her indifferent pose cracks.

Score.

"How did you know it had anything to do with him?" she asks, looking way beyond surprised.

"Easy. You both are acting weird."

"Oh." She pauses for a second.

"Well…?" I prompt her.

"Right. Um…" she sighs. "He kind of, well, sort of, actually, not really, asked me out…"

I stare at her for a second.

Oh, my God!

That is so good!

How sweet!

That's just…perfect!!

"Wanting you to be wanting me, no that ain't no way to be, how I feel? Read my lips, because I'm so over…I'm so…movin' on, it's my time, you never were a friend of mine…hurt at first, a little bit, and now I'm so over… so over it."

My mind automatically registers what song this is. I almost wouldn't have realized the song had changed if I didn't love this song so much.

'Over it.'

Katharine McPhee.

Former *American Idol* contestants and their successes?

Nice…

But Brett asking Brooke out?

That's even better!

"Brooke!" I cry out. "That's fabulous!"

She nods slowly. "Yeah, I guess, but I couldn't go."

What!?!

"Why not?"

"There's so much going on right now, plus I've got so much that I've got to deal with these days…"

"Oh, Brooke!" I sigh.

"I know. I feel so bad now. But I don't think…I mean, I just don't think now is a good time for either one of us."

"Yeah," I agree slowly, "I guess. But when you said whatever you said to *reject* him, how did he react?"

She sighs.

Again.

"He was like, 'Yeah, okay, you're right.' And he brushed it off completely. And then we went and sat in our spots for attendance."

"Oh."

He's probably a little hurt about it.

Knowing Brett Evans, I can definitely attest to that.

But that totally sucks.

"Do you think he's–"

"So you think you can just get away with all this?"

Brooke and I whirl around, completely caught off guard.

"All what?" Brooke asks calmly.

Daphne's standing right behind us.

"Throwing the blame on Jackson and me."

I let out a laugh. "Throwing the blame on you? What blame was there to throw except what really belonged to you?"

I half-expect Daphne to blow her top, but she totally doesn't.

What a big surprise.

Instead, she steps closer to me, her eyes narrowed, but she's faintly…

Smiling!?

How does that make sense?

Oh, no.

But wait.

It's one of those totally evil, 'I'm gonna get you so you better watch out' smiles.

God.

I hate those.

Oh, here we go again.

Change of song!

It's Kelly Clarkson…

Hmm.

I vaguely remember this song.

I mean, I have Kelly's album 'My December' and everything… so I guess that's probably why…

"Don't waste your time trying to fix what I want to erase, what I need to forget. Don't waste your time on me, my friend. Friend, what does that even mean? I don't want your hand, you'll only pull me down. So save your breath, don't waste your song on me, on me…Don't waste your time."

Don't waste your time.

Duh.

'Don't waste your time.'

Hmm…

Isn't this the perfect song of the moment?

Daphne finally opens her mouth – no doubt to yell at me for what I just said to her because…oh, I don't know, it stung so badly.

"Listen." She looks me in the eye.

Ooh.

Searing pain.

Not.

"It so is not my fault that you were so selfish your entire life and that you grew up a spoiled brat who was only concerned about what was best for your stupid self and not for the welfare of others."

Um, excuse me.

But that is so not true.

She's worse than the tabloids. Well, maybe not. I mean, she says all of this where I can fix the damage she does. Unlike what the tabloids do to Britney. I mean, Britney's fabulous. She's just got a lot to deal with. Most of us are nothing compared to how famous she is. It's got to be tough living a life like that. We all wish for fame once in a while, but that's too much.

God.

Where are those monitors when you really need them?

"You're calling, you're talking, you're trying…trying to get in. But it's over, it's over, it's over, friend."

Believe me.

It is so over.

My tolerating of this stupid time of arguments and verbal fighting is over.

Not to say she ever was a friend of mine.

But come on.

Let's start with giving her a stare down.

She wants to pick a fight with me?

She better be ready.

Because she's so gonna get a show.

Trevor

You can only imagine how surprised I was when Brett and I stepped out of the supply closet with a decent basketball to the voice of Kelly Clarkson belting out a song that could only be called 'Don't Waste Your Time.'

But that's not the reason we were surprised.

No.

When we walked out, Kelly's anger and hurt and confusion in her voice was being depicted by Sophia and Brooke and…

Daphne.

Except the weird thing was that they weren't really yelling at each other. They were…talking?

And Brett and I are just staring, totally confused.

Why would they be talking and not fighting or arguing?

"Let's go," Brett says to me with a nod.

I follow.

"But it's over, it's over, it's over, my friend…Don't waste my time."

The song ends.

Finally.

But the seemingly serene discussion among the three girls doesn't end. In fact, it does nothing but continue.

We reach them.

A few – well, more like a lot – of our gym classmates have gathered around to watch the event.

"Distract them, Brett, distract them," I whisper, since most of them are girls who happen to love Brett the basketball star.

"With pleasure."

He shoots the basketball he's been holding and it slips through the net easily.

"Score!" he triumphs.

Almost all of the girls smile.

"Do me a huge favor and someone go get that," he says, flashing them one of his stunning smiles that always makes them all want to swoon.

A few of the girls leave the scene to try to retrieve the basketball first in order to endear themselves to Brett.

Yeah, right.

Like that's ever going to happen.

We all know he likes Brooke.

Well, at least, Sophia and I do.

But no one else does…

I turn to Brett.

He's tilted his head to one side and is now staring confusedly at Brooke, Sophia, and Daphne.

I quickly start listening in on the heated conversation that's going on just like everyone else is doing.

"Look," Sophia says suddenly, eyes flashing. "You. You are just a…stuck-up, self-centered wannabe who is never going to get what you want by using the ways you tend to use. You can't win with your methods, Carlisle."

A few of the people around gasp.

I guess that wasn't the type of thing that Sophia could say and improve her public image, but she doesn't seem to care.

Daphne, however, is clearly keeping her cool.

Brooke is definitely steaming fury.

"Oh, really, Sophia?" Daphne challenges.

Hmm…

Interesting.

Sophia's the one referring to Daphne by her last name and is totally being overwhelmed with anger while Daphne has the grace to talk to Sophia with ease and call her by her given first name.

That *is* very interesting.

I think of mentioning this to Brett.

But Daphne's got more to say.

And she won't be silenced.

"Sophia, you think that you can get around by acting like just because you're the cheerleading captain, and just because you might have gotten better genes than some of the rest of us, and just because you think you're all that, you can convince everyone that you're better than everyone else."

Sophia's eyes narrow even more and she opens her mouth to

respond.

But she can't say anything.

Daphne keeps barreling on.

"And maybe you've been able to pull all of this off for all these years, but it's got to stop. You've got to realize that there are other people in this world that you've got to think about. People other than yourself."

Sophia's fists are clenched.

Brooke looks as if she could smack Daphne.

But Daphne seems to have a point.

At least, the other girls are starting to look like they're believing her.

But how could they!?

Sophia isn't like that. Sophia is in no way related to the girl Daphne's talking about right now. Sophia does care about others.

"You can't go on like this forever. We all know the truth now. You're not someone to be admired and idolized."

"She never said she was to be idolized," someone suddenly calls out. "And she was only well-liked. Is that a crime?"

Heads turn. It's Brett speaking. Rightfully said. He would know the truth. Don't they see that?

Some of the onlookers are murmuring, and shaking their heads. Shaking their heads…?

Wait. What?!?

Daphne goes on. "You're just like her," she accuses smoothly. "And so are those two," she says, indicating Brooke and me. "You're fakes. Poseurs."

Oh, my God.

That little…

Wow.

It's just like Sophia's been saying.

That girl is such a wicked witch.

Not that I didn't know that already.

But anyway.

"It's true."

Another voice has joined the conversation.

Aha.

Brett

I was wondering where Jackson had gotten to.

And now he's here to back Daphne's points up.

"Yeah," Daphne says. "*Poseurs.*"

That little rat of a wannabe.

Suddenly all insanity breaks out.

Sophia launches herself at Daphne, fists first.

Daphne squeals and wheels back to hide behind Jackson.

What a baby.

Scaredy-cat.

But that definitely doesn't stop Sophia.

She pushes Jackson aside.

He falls to the floor with a little yelp.

Weak.

I glance at Brooke. She looks stunned and dazed. I'm almost scared she's going to join Sophia.

Sophia. Who, by the way, is now on the ground, wrestling with Daphne.

Daphne. Who happens to be doing quite a good job of defending herself and throwing in a few aimless punches at the same time.

I don't know what to do, I don't know what to do…What do I do!?

I don't want Sophia to get beaten up! Not that Daphne could do any damage, but still.

Ooh.

Jackson just kicked Sophia.

He's going down.

Trevor

Why are Brett and I standing by idly, you may ask?

You may well ask.

Brett seems to be lost completely.

His eyes are glazed over…

Wait.

No.

He has his eye on Jackson.

"Brett, don't," I whisper without moving my lips, for fear that anything the rest of them hears me say will be misinterpreted.

He doesn't seem to hear me.

"*You say I'm your best friend…you know that you can count on me. You say I'm nice, I'm funny…is that why I'm not the girl of your dreams? You say that I'm the only one who understands you. But I'm the one on Friday nights with nothing to do…I don't think so…*"

These songs are so random…

"Brett!" I whisper, a little more loudly this time over the voice of who I think is Diana DeGarmo. I tug on his sleeve.

"*We both know that you've been cheating off my paper since the seventh grade…you know you do it...*"

Oh, my God.

There is way too much going on here…

Can't concentrate…

He shrugs away from me, trying to break free.

But are you kidding?

The grip that I have on him is not going anywhere.

And neither is he.

Brooke

"*I'm just the fool that you can kick around. The loser who picks you up when you are down. The girl in glasses who sits next to you. Who always tells you that you're great and fixes all your big mistakes and when she goes and breaks your heart, I get the call… you fall apart…I don't think so.*"

I don't think so, either.

Why am I standing here?

Why can't I do anything for myself here?

Why can't I just help my friends?

Why am I so *stupid* and *spineless*?

Of course Daphne can kick me around. She just did.

That song…

Perfect.

Too bad I don't have glasses.

Too bad I could have had Brett.

Too bad it's not his fault that I don't.

Too bad there was no other girl to begin with.

Too bad…

Too bad.

"*This is for every girl alive who's heart's been broken by a boy like you…*"

He never broke my heart. I dented his. But a girl like me

shouldn't ever dent a heart like his.

Not even a dent.

"*Loser.*"

Ha.

I'm the loser.

But now I can't help tuning in to everything else that's going on in an attempt to stop thinking about my personal issues with my life's connection to this song (even if it does make absolutely no sense).

Trevor's trying his best to maintain a grip on Brett – if Brett can't maintain a grip on himself.

Brett is definitely aiming himself at Jackson.

And I guess I should go help Sophia.

Daphne pulls herself away from Sophia.

Maybe there's no need for me here.

Suddenly Brett breaks free.

Jackson's just getting up.

Dusting himself off after Sophia knocked him down.

And now he's down again.

Brett's on top of him.

"Brett!"

He turns his head slightly and catches sight of me.

And then he turns away. Sob.

Suddenly Jackson's on top of Brett.

His face is contorted with anger.

"You know what?" he hisses at Brett.

The two of them are only inches apart.

And Jackson's looking pretty murderous.

"What?" Brett heaves back.

"I knew that this whole–"

Jackson's on the floor.

Brett's dominating.

"–idea of staying calm was–"

Brett's down.

"–not going to work with you people–"

Brett's on top.

"Yeah?"

Brett pins him down on the gym floor.

I'm finally propelled towards them.

"Well, then maybe for once in your entire useless little life," Brett continues, "you were *right*!"

Ooh!

Shut down–

Suddenly a force knocks me over – and takes all the wind out of me.

I'm surrounded by a never-ending curtain of black hair.

Not too tough to identify…

Daphne.

Thanks a lot, Sophia.

I manage to throw her off of me for a second and I look around.

Brett and Jackson are still attempting to punch each other out.

Trevor is trying to help Sophia up.

Her eyes are blazing, but icy blue at the same time.

Daphne tries to take me down again, but I knock her off just like I did only a few seconds ago.

"You–"

She can't find a word to describe me. But then again, she doesn't even know me.

"Yeah?" I hurl back. "If you don't know what – or even who

– *I* am, then what do you think *you* are?"

"Better than you," she spits out, flying at me again.

Nice comeback?

I merely stagger aside, and she shoots right into Sophia.

Oops.

Sophia flies to the floor with a thud.

A few of the spectators gasp and step back.

Trevor groans and throws his hands up in the air desperately.

Apparently he isn't going to try and do anything about that. What a bad boy. Just kidding. He did his part. I guess. Although he didn't try to rescue me yet. And it's not like I didn't get hurt.

Trevor! Help!

I sink to the floor, trying to suppress a moan.

"Ow."

Trevor finally turns to me.

I mean, it's about time.

"You okay?"

"Do I *look* okay?" is all I can think of to say.

"Well, no," he answers uncomfortably. "Come on. Get up." He extends a hand to help me.

Maybe I mean as much to him as Sophia after all.

Boy, does that make me feel special.

Sophia

You'd think that the sounds of four – maybe even five – teenagers fighting in the middle of a high school gymnasium would be louder than the Kellie Pickler singing her heart out, but oh, no.

And you also may wonder how, in the midst of all this insanity,

I knew who was singing 'Red High Heels.'

But as a dedicated fan of *American Idol*, I believe it is my duty to know the contestants who have succeeded in getting their hands on a record deal.

And this particular song by Kellie Pickler may not be what I usually would listen to, but it still is a great song.

"*Baby, I got plans tonight you don't know nothin' about. And I've been sittin' 'round way too long tryin' to figure you out.*"

Where in the world is Mr. Davidson when you need him?!

"All right, break it up, break it up," someone says, sounding all authoritative.

"*Nobody holds a candle to me in my red high heels.*"

Ha!

Wish I was wearing red high heels now.

Then Daphne wouldn't be able to lay a single finger on me.

Or wouldn't she do that anyway?

Knowing her?

Of course.

"*And you can watch me walk if you want to, want to. I bet you want me back now, don't you, don't you?*"

Thank God.

It's Mr. Davidson.

"*I'm about to show you just how missin' me feels…*"

"Daphne!"

I try to shove her away from me, and she staggers away a bit, looking completely disoriented.

"All those games you tried to play, well, they ain't gonna work on me now. I put a barbed wire fence around my heart, baby, just to keep you out. Well, you thought I'd wait around forever, but baby, get real. I just kicked you to the curb...in my red high heels."

Don't need those red high heels to kick that witch away.

Daphne curses vehemently under her breath, but Mr. Davidson hears her and drags her away from me.

I examine the damage that she's done to me.

At least I was wearing my gym clothes and not what I wore to school today.

Although this is a Hollister shirt…but whatever. It's only a little wrinkled, so I'm sure it'll survive.

It's gonna have to.

And the Soffe shorts? They'll be fine. They were meant for activity, after all, so I guess that could've been like some random sport in gym class.

Not.

"Out. All of you."

Everyone stares at Mr. Davidson, confused.

"Not you," he says in exasperation, waving in the direction of the rest of the class.

"Then…?" a hidden member of the gathered onlookers calls out. "Who?"

Mr. Davidson turns.

And he points at the six of us:

Trevor. The almost innocent one who fought absolutely no one.

Daphne. The wicked witch who provoked all of us.

Brett. The one who attacked Jackson – rightfully, of course.

Brooke. The poor girl who got attacked by Daphne.

Jackson. The stupid – idiot who deserves anything terrible.

And…

Me.

Yes.

Me.

I'm the one who started the fighting, as anyone in the gym can so easily confirm – all because it's true.

"Us?" Daphne croaks out.

Hmm.

I have to agree with her.

All of us?

I was *provoked.*

God.

Does no one in this stupid place understand that?

"Coach," Brett begins. "It wasn't–"

"I can't handle this," Coach Davidson spits out, wiping his forehead. "Get out. Go to the office."

"Office?" Brooke squeaks.

"Yes," he repeats angrily. "The main office? Go!"

We pick ourselves up off the floor and meekly gather together.

Well, at least, the four of us do.

Jackson and Daphne step next to each other. Both of them are looking extremely livid about the whole thing.

And in a way I guess that they should be. I mean, I was the one who jumped her when she was trying her best to talk all reasonably, even if her plan didn't work.

Oh, well.

Sucks for them.

And for the rest of us.

"Go!" he repeats furiously.

"Do we at least change first?" I ask.

"I don't care! Just go to the office. I can only hope they will know what to do and how to deal with you people."

Daphne, Brooke and I walk off, eying each other.

Well, more like Brooke and I are giving Daphne wary looks and Daphne's looking right back at us.

Trevor has grabbed Brett by the arm and is now dragging him along a little farther behind.

And they've got Jackson just on their heels.

Oh, God.

Jackson's on their heels, looking totally menacing just like he did that morning when he was following me.

Good times, guys, good times.

Thanks *so* much for all of those totally sweet memories.

Not.

Brett

The thing that sucks about this the most is that I didn't even get in enough good punches to hit Jackson with. I know, I know. That's bad morals or whatever. But I can't help it. He's a jerk, and he deserves anything bad that comes his way, and even though I shouldn't be the reason anything bad is coming his way (and especially not the source of his problems), I can't help it!

So now we got sent out of gym and we have to change out of our gym clothes and into our regular clothes. And then? We get to take a trip down the hallways to the main office for proper punishment right after that.

Yippee.

Jackson looks like he's going to try and get in another shot at me. Not literally. But he definitely wants to really hurt me.

I hope they take him and his girlfriend off to a mental hospital or something. Or at least into counseling. They really need help.

And maybe Sophia was the one who started the whole physical

fighting part of the argument. But she had a right to do it. And she has an excuse. Daphne provoked her. That better be good enough for those air headed administrators of ours. And if it's not, I don't know what we'll do.

To really tell the truth?

Sometimes…I'd really rather have that Winston Romero guy as our principal. He actually listens (if the way he dealt with our dear English teacher Miss Heather Halitelli is any indication) and he'd actually try to deal with the situation. And it definitely wouldn't end with "Detention for a few weeks or so and we'll work from there" if we were working with old Winston. Then again, he's probably flying on the wings of love right now, so I doubt he'd be much help, either. And I haven't exactly talked to our Principal Walker that much. I can't make any judgments, I guess. We'll see how this goes.

God.

If we get in trouble with the law because of this, I'm gonna sue.

Trevor

Wow.

I cannot believe that we're in this much trouble right now.

I mean, now that we're in the locker room, changing in silence, and preparing to go up to the main office to be punished for our bad behavior (oh, please), I can actually reflect on this entire stupid situation.

I am beyond irritated. Beyond angry at this stupidity.

If someone – no, make that anyone – thinks that I am not fully innocent in this entire thing, then they are…

They are definitely going to have another think coming.

Brooke

Oh.

My.

God.

I have never been in any trouble before.

I have always been the innocent, adorable, lovable one.

Always the sweet girl next door.

Totally perfect.

With no reason for anyone not to like me.

I have never had any problems with needing to forge a path for all high school girls. Never, never.

And now? Oh, yeah, I'm just getting sent to the principal's office (totally no biggie) for behind knocked down by an angry wannabe cheerleader.

How does this happen to me?!?

The six of us were sent out of gym class to change back into our regular clothes.

And now Daphne (ew!), Sophia, and I are up in the girls' locker room, changing and giving one another significantly nasty looks.

Except it's Daphne versus me and Sophia, of course. That's a given.

But this is so not going to be good.

Sophia

So now here we are, on our way to the principal's office.

I had totally expected Daphne and Jackson to start something again while we were all alone in the hallways, but instead they conveniently decided to take a different route to the office.

That's when Brett started acting weird.

I could totally tell something weird was going on once his eyes started narrowing and he had that look on his face that I know only too well.

And now I've been spending the past few minutes watching his face get even more contorted.

Things are somewhat awkward between him and Brooke, or so I'm guessing. But then again, they haven't exactly gotten a chance to even talk yet ever since that whole asking out incident before gym.

Trevor and I are walking in between the two of them, so as to keep as much distance between them in case things aren't going so well.

Of course, Trevor knows nothing about the date situation.

Not that it's my fault.

He wasn't there when Brooke told me, and I never exactly got the chance to tell him myself.

But I'm sure that Brooke will tell him as soon as she can.

But I can no longer stand this.

Brett's face is looking really weird now.

"Okay, Brett," I say finally. "What's up?"

"Nothing," he says stiffly.

"Brett, none of us are mad at you, if that's what you're thinking," I try telling him to no avail.

"That's not what I'm thinking, but that's reassuring." He turns his head away from me to look the opposite way.

Oh, God.

Please don't let this be about Brooke…

I switch my place to be beside him, and beside him only.

He looks down at me. "What?"

"Tell me."

"Nothing. It's just that I wouldn't be surprised if that stupid couple doesn't even show up at the office." He clenches his fists. And his teeth. And boy, does he not look a single bit happy.

My eyes widen suddenly as I realize that those two could only so easily slip out of trouble this way. "No…"

He nods.

I turn to Trevor and Brooke, who are walking in silence, but listening to our conversation at the same time.

"You think?" I ask.

Trevor nods slowly. "Why not? It's possible."

Brooke sighs heavily. "And, of course, by letting them go around 'the other way,' we just let them slip away."

Brett winces. "Exactly."

"And that isn't good."

"So now what?" I ask.

Brett narrows his eyes once again.

Trevor and Brooke turn to look at him.

"We'll split up, I guess," Trevor says slowly.

"Two and two, since there are two of them to, uh, take on," Brooke adds in, speaking so softly.

"A girl for Daphne, a guy for Jackson," I chime in.

"Obviously," says Brett.

"Come on," I say to Trevor, grabbing him by the arm. "We'll go this way," I tell Brett and Brooke as I point down the hallway we just walked through.

Brett bites on his lip for a second. "Okay," he says.

"Yeah, that's fine," Brooke says with a smile.

Is she serious?

Brooke

I seriously thought that Brett wouldn't want to speak to me ever again after how mean I had been to him.

And believe me, I really felt terrible about how I had been like, "Oh, yeah, sorry, no can do. I've got to go out to dinner with my family tonight. It's gonna be the event of the century. Well, gotta go. See ya 'round."

I really was sorry. And I didn't mean to hurt his feelings but I guess that that's just how it had to go down.

It kills, it kills.

So now Sophia and Trevor have skipped off (yes, they practically did skip…I'm not kidding) in the direction from which we came in hopes of catching Daphne and Jackson by following them in their tracks.

Our plan is to try to catch them and then corner them so that they have to come with us to the office. I mean, if we're going to get in trouble, they might as well receive the same treatment. It's what they deserve.

If Sophia and Trevor catch sight of them, they're going to call either Brett or me by cell, and we're going to meet up.

But in the two minutes that have passed since the four of us split up, there's been absolutely no sign.

Oh, yeah, and there's just one more thing…now it's just Brett and me here.

"So," Brett says.

I turn to him quickly with a surprised glance, naturally stunned that he's even speaking to me.

He looks a little nervous.

Maybe even shy.

But that fleeting moment's expression quickly passes on his face.

Or did I imagine all of it?

"Putting aside all of the insane events from gym," he continues, "let's focus on the situation at hand, okay?"

Um, okay.

"Yeah." I nod. "Sure."

We walk on through the hallways in silence.

There's absolutely nothing to say.

"Look," he begins to say, looking as if he really doesn't know what to say.

Appropriate.

Suddenly Brett pulls his phone out of his pocket. I realize that it's been vibrating. He fumbles with it for a minute. And I have to admit it: he's acting unusually strange – especially for a perfect guy like him. Well, as perfect as you can be when a girl (even a loser like me) turns you down.

Oh, my God.

How could I have done that!?

Seriously, every single time I remember that, I feel like slapping myself, even though I'd never think of taking it back or trying to change what I said.

Not that I could do anything stupid in front of Brett. Then he would feel so bad about having asked out a lunatic.

And the awkwardness would increase – extremely.

"Hey," he says into his phone, clearly trying hard to sound calm.

Too bad it's barely working.

"Hey!" Sophia's bright and cheery voice sings out brightly. I can even hear it from the tiny speaker even though she's whispering.

"So," Brett says. "Did you find them yet?"

This time he sounds a little more like himself.

The way he should.

He hasn't really suffered much at all.

Rejection?

Get over it, boy.

I'll be back before you know it.

Sophia

Good news, good answer.

"Yeah, actually, we did find them," I whisper back in a low tone.

Extremely low.

There's a risk of Daphne and Jackson hearing us. They are only just around the corner, after all.

"Where are you?" Brett asks.

I can almost see him looking around as if he expects to practically appear out of nowhere.

"East side, second corner," I say, trying to sound like a professional spy or something.

He laughs. "Okay. Be there in a few," he returns.

Mission accomplished?

Maybe not.

Trevor's tugging on my sleeve urgently.

Brett hangs up.

I snap my phone shut and snap at Trevor. "What?"

"Listen," he commands, fear suddenly lighting up his (did I mention gorgeous?) eyes.

I pause, still staring into his eyes. "What?" I repeat. "I seriously do not hear anything."

He lays a finger across my lips for a fleeting moment of perfection.

Time to pass out.

Of incredulity.

And amazement.

And excitement.

And it's actually almost as if my senses have been sharpened by that one sudden movement of his.

Amazing.

The effect it has on me.

Sad, too.

And now I hear what Trevor's been hearing this whole time.

Heels.

Clicking.

As if someone – oh, a certain and *specific* someone – is tiptoeing over in our direction wearing heels that aren't supposed to be silent.

Gee. I wonder who that could be?

Brett

Text message!

Brooke lays a hand on my shoulder gently.

I almost freeze in my tracks.

She's acting…

Normal?

And that's how I should be acting.

"What's that?" she asks me. "Text?"

I nod. "Yeah," I manage to say.

I flip open my phone, tapping a few keys.

```
From: Sophia_G

cornr 2 ASAP. company.

<3 always, Sophia G
```

"Let's go," I say to Brooke, barely looking at her.

She gives me a weird look. "Where?" she asks. "I thought we would meet up with them."

"Yeah, we're supposed to. And they just happen to be needing our help at the moment."

Her eyes widen.

Finally: the desired reaction.

"Come on." She starts running the best she can.

"Between the second and third corner, I'm guessing," I tell her.

"Okay."

We pass by the office, completely heedless to the fact that we could get caught. Not to say we weren't thinking about it. At least I am.

"Brooke," I say.

She turns her head, not showing the slightest sign of wanting to stop. "We can talk when we get there," she responds.

I shrug and give up.

Her problem.

Her fault.

If we don't manage to slip by, that is.

Trevor

Where are those two when you need them most?

I mean, here we are, waiting for them, trying to squeeze into that little alcove where the old copper statue of some great administrator is poised on a pedestal, with our enemies, Daphne and Jackson, clearly getting closer to us.

And Brett and Brooke aren't even near us!

Wait.

There's different footsteps coming now.

Quicker ones.

Lighter ones.

As if someone's running.

But there's two someones.

Brett.

Brooke.

"Where are they?" I hear Brooke whisper, panting.

I'm completely comfortable where I am. I mean, I'm with Sophia, safe behind this statue.

Yet I have to get out of here.

"There they are," Sophia breathes into my ear, peering out through the space between this guy's ear and the chipping white paint coating the wall.

I nod.

This is really the closest we've ever been to each other. It's getting to be kind of awkward.

Brooke and Brett are facing the opposite direction.

As I step out from behind the statue and tap her on the shoulder.

She whirls around, hands covering her mouth, eyes wide, and lets out a tiny little squeak of shock.

And then she sees that it's only me.

She glares at me.

"Trevor! Don't you dare do that ever again!" She's breathing kind of heavily. And it's not just because she ran all the way over here. I *scared* her.

Ha, ha.

I crack a smile.

"Trevor!" she hisses, still looking mad. But her eyes are twinkling.

"Oops. Sorry," I say, half-heartedly. Like she even cares.

"So?" she asks. "What's the emergency?"

"Emergency? How did you know they were coming to get us?" I whisper back to her, surprised.

She gives me a weird look. "What do you mean?"

Brett steps forward and gives me a friendly slap of greeting on the back, as is his custom nowadays.

Sophia emerges from behind the statue.

Brooke's eyes widen once again. She starts shaking her head and smiling disbelievingly. "Only you two would have come up with that hiding place," she declares.

"Oh, really?" Sophia asks with a smile. "Then where would you have hidden?" she challenges.

Brooke raises one eyebrow. And then she stabs one finger in the direction of a somewhat decrepit door.

"The supply closet?" Sophia says skeptically.

Brooke beams. "One of many, yes."

Sophia rolls her eyes. "Yeah. Great choice. I just didn't feel like going back in one of those. After all, *he* knows how to take people down in a supply closet. I just know how to try and do a karate kick and end up crashing into the door."

I crack a smile.

Brett laughs.

"Oh, isn't that right, Sophia?"

So much for hiding.

Sophia

"What were you doing following us, huh?" Daphne circles around the four of us tauntingly, with a sneer on her face, while Jackson just stands there smirking like the giant idiot that he always has been.

"Following you?" Trevor repeats, trying to sound tougher than he actually is (oh, and believe me, I know it).

Daphne glares at him.

But why would he stop talking?

"Why would *we* waste our time following *you*?" he asks.

Seriously.

It's actually kind of true.

But we kind of did waste our time, I guess.

Smart of Trevor to flaunt it, of course. Good old guy.

"Oh, gee, I don't know," Daphne retorts. "It's not up to me to try and decode what's going through your little minds."

Brett snorts, seemingly involuntarily, if it's any indication by the way his eyes widen suddenly and he covers his mouth with his hands.

Jackson steps up to him.

Finally. I mean, it's about time.

"Look, *buddy*," he says menacingly, fists clenched. "I'm not even close to forgiving you for anything."

Brett stiffens up. "I never asked you to forgive me for anything. And I wasn't expecting it, either. And besides, I'm not going to forgive you for all that you've done, either."

Either, either, either.

How boring.

But Jackson certainly doesn't think so.

And neither does Daphne.

"How low," Daphne spits out.

What?

'How low'!?

"What…?" Trevor says.

Brett and Brooke exchange confused glances.

"Huh?" Jackson says, turning to look at Daphne. "What was that?"

She shrugs, pouting. "I don't know!"

What a stupid girl.

It's like she just says whatever pops into her mind as soon as she thinks it. Come to think of it, that sounds like a perfect description for what she does. Hmm.

He gives her a weird look. "Okay. Back to business, then." He turns back to face Brett, sneering.

Suddenly Brooke snaps into action.

I blink.

In the past split second, she's now restraining Brett with one hand, which is snapped onto his wrist.

Although, of course, Brett hasn't exactly shown a sign of wanting to hurt Jackson just yet. But I'm sure he really does want to not too deep down inside.

Then again, I'd love it if Jackson fell off the face of the earth, too. So who am I to say anything?

Brooke's got her other arm up for self defense.

And Trevor creeps behind her.

Little scaredy-cat.

It's so funny.

Not the "Mean Girls" look on Brooke's face.

And not Brett's squirming.

Well, okay, maybe that, too.

But Trevor's seriously trying to protect himself…

Using Brooke and Brett?!?!

Oh, *please.*

Wait, no, he isn't.

He's…

Coming over here?

Aww, that is just *so* sweet.

And it is kind of sad that while Brett and Brooke are struggling through their own difficult times, what with Brooke rejecting Brett and their not having any time to talk at all and all this awkwardness between them, Trevor and I are totally bonding and we're becoming even closer than ever before.

And I know that really sucks for them, but it's totally working out for me. So while I do feel really, really bad for them, I'm super happy at the same time.

God, I'm such a bad friend.

But only to make it up to them, I'm going to step up.

To their defense.

Oh, yes. I'm so going to risk my life for them.

As if it's going to make much of a difference, but can't I at least try? They'll at least appreciate it.

I hope.

"Back off," I say, sounding oh-so-lame.

Daphne snickers. "Wow, Sophia, that was, like, even stupider than what I just said," she says.

I give her a silencing look.

At least, that's what I wanted it to do.

And I also feel the urge to open her eyes to reality.

"Carlisle, nothing could be stupider than you, your boyfriend, and your pointless little comments."

She shoots a nasty look at me effortlessly.

What?

I mean, it isn't as if she has to make any effort whatsoever to be a witch. She's just so – like that.

"You have always gotten on my nerves, Garrison," she says, seething way beyond description.

She steps up to me. Her pointy nose is only inches away from mine.

I can see her face only too clearly.

It's too much of a close up view.

It's too much…

Oh, my God.

How much eye makeup does she wear?

I mean, seriously.

If you're going to wear makeup, okay. That's your choice, and if you wear it right, then it's fine. It'll look good on you, and therefore you will look good, and then there are absolutely no worries.

Right?

But making the cosmetic stuff look good on you? Wearing it

right? That's not too tough, but for Daphne Carlisle, it clearly is a difficult task.

The key to makeup is to not put on so much of it on that it's quite noticeable. You're supposed to put it on so that it enhances your features – not so that all a person sees when they look at your face is how much makeup you're wearing. It's supposed to be there but not be noticeable because it'll just make your beauty look natural.

At least, so I've heard.

I'd kind of expect Daphne to know that, but no.

She's got so much eyeliner on, some weird color of eyeshadow (which, by the way, has been applied so much that it looks terrible) that I can't even describe, let alone name, tons and tons of mascara (and it's gotten a little clumpy here and there, which is so unattractive) and her eyes look so big and scary now.

Then again, the scariness does suit her, I suppose. It's exactly like her personality, if you give it a little thought.

"Great," I say, trying to sound perky, when I'm really a tiny bit scared of what she might do.

I mean, I can't help remembering what happened about ten or fifteen minutes ago in the gym, even if I did start it.

That girl's such a beast. And I don't even mean it in a good way, as some guys like to say.

"At least I've accomplished something, then," I say. "And that's good to know." I beam at her, trying to have this whole sunshiny thing going for me.

And it only makes her madder.

"Now nothing can stop me," she says.

And I realize that she's got hurting me in mind.

No!

Wait!

What did I do?!

I'm just a cheerleader!

Brooke flips in front of me. "Don't you dare lay a finger on her," she hisses through clenched teeth.

Daphne folds her arms across her chest and gives Brooke one of those once-over looks, smirking at what she's wearing (a cute white halter top and black jeans with black heels, but she does still have that bandage on from last night's events…and maybe that's what Daphne's staring at, but I can't be sure). "Oh, yeah?"

Brooke's fingers slip away from Brett's wrist. "Yeah."

"And like you're going to stop me?"

"Isn't that a given?" Brooke retorts coolly.

How sweet of her.

And how true.

But maybe I can protect myself?

Or am I a damsel in distress and another possible damsel is coming to save me?

Wait. How does that make sense?!?

"Well, I don't know. Maybe it is. But I'll just go through you first. Like I'm not going to get revenge for all that this girl has done to me? Please. Think again, Lawson."

Brooke doesn't flinch. "It's Dawson."

"Whatever, freak."

Brooke's hand swings a little. And then the next thing we all know…Brett's hand is entwined in hers.

Brett

Okay, so I know I shouldn't have done that.

She already rejected me and yet I go right ahead and grab her hand when there's a possibility that she doesn't like me.

But she's the one who technically started it by trying to, uh, 'restrain' me by grabbing my wrist. So what's the diff?

I mean, all I did was take her hand.

My bad.

And now Daphne is totally stunned.

Come to think of it…

Everyone else is, too.

Well, except for that stupid Jackson.

Brooke hasn't made a single move.

No reaction.

But whatever.

At least she's not flipping out like anyone else would.

And?

She doesn't move to free her hand.

Ha!

Instead, she starts walking, leading me with her. "Meet you in the office, Carlisle," she calmly throws over her shoulder.

Daphne stares at her as if she's lost her mind.

And I'll admit that I'm a little bit stunned that Brooke just walked away from the perfect chance to silence that brat for good. But then again, it *is* in her blood to do something like that, so I'm not *super* surprised.

Trevor beckons to Sophia, who instantly goes to his side (how cute), and the two of them follow us.

Daphne finally finds her voice. "Like, you seriously think we're going to the office?" she scoffs.

Brooke pauses and turns around again, placing her free hand on her hip. "Oh, believe me, you will, or we'll have to tell Mr.

Davidson how much we missed you there."

Score!

Daphne's jaw drops, and she stares at Brooke, completely taken aback.

The seconds pass.

"Fine," she says through gritted teeth. "But you four are walking in front."

Oh, please.

That totally gives away all her plans, now, doesn't it?

"Oh, no," Brooke replies lightly, "you'll walk in front with your fiancée."

Daphne blushes.

Ha, ha.

Way to make her feel a little embarrassed?

At least, I hope that worked the way it should have.

"No threat there," Jackson mutters under his breath.

"What was that, Jackson?" Brooke's voice is super sweet.

Cough.

Super fake.

"You can't make us do that."

"Did I mention that we'll also be forced to tell Mr. Davidson *and* the office how you were threatening *us* only a few minutes ago?" Brooke adds in.

You've gotta love this girl.

Just maybe not the way I do.

A crease has formed on Daphne's forehead. "I – that is so not fair – you can't do that–"

"Oh, yeah?" Brooke walks up to Daphne and looks her straight in the eye. "Try me, Carlisle."

Daphne gasps – and it's a gasp of pure rage, let me tell you.

I half-expect her to explode or something, but no.

No such luck.

"I thought so." Brooke crosses her arms and smirks.

I have to admit…I never saw this side of her before.

"Now step right up, if you please." She tilts her head to one side and watches the cruel couple move up the hallway.

A slow, proud smile spreads across her face.

Sophia lifts her hands and pretends to be applauding Brooke's great job well done. "Nice one!" she whispers.

Brooke beams. "Thanks!"

And then, wonder of all wonders, she surprises us.

And slips her hand into mine and gives me a little smile right before she skips off down the hall, dragging me with her.

Trevor

Okay.

I clearly missed something very important.

I mean, really.

That whole thing with Brett plus Brooke equals heart? That was definitely not happening about an hour ago.

I really need to get caught up on this stuff.

And my best friend…she didn't even tell me anything! And on top of that? She's acting like Brett and her holding hands is absolutely nothing!

After how long she's been crushing on him?

Oh, God, it's definitely not nothing.

And now they're lagging behind a bit. Sophia and I have almost passed by the two of them.

I give Sophia a little nudge with my elbow.

She looks up at me. "Hmm?"

And she's clearly off in her own little world, if that little happy smile on her face explains anything.

Should I ask now?

"Uh…"

"What, Trevor?"

Okay, fine.

I lower my voice to a mere whisper. "Since when…?" I give a quick jerk of my head, indicating that I'm talking about Brett and Brooke.

"Oh!" She tosses her head in acknowledgment. "That's a long story."

We glance over our shoulders at them.

They seem to be just beginning to get deeply involved in a heated conversation of their own.

And then they feel us staring at them.

I think.

I mean, you know that kind of sixth sense you have where you can just feel someone staring at you? Well, yeah. That's what I mean.

So anyway, they look up at us.

And I realize that Brooke has let go of his hand. Apparently, she did so quite some time ago, and I just missed it.

Once again, last to know.

We casually turn our heads back to face front.

"What?" Brooke asks, sounding a little bit defensive.

"Nothing, nothing," I reassure her.

Brett tilts his head at me, seeming somewhat confused.

Brooke gives me a weird look that lasts less than a second – so short that I can't even be sure of its existence.

"So, Trevor," Sophia says, acting like she's about to start a conversation with me just to get rid of Brett and Brooke staring.

"So, Sophia," I imitate.

She punches me on the arm playfully, and we continue walking as if there was no break in our discourse.

Brett rolls his eyes and he and Brooke resume their conversation. Or so it seems…they begin it.

And now here we are.

Not too far from the office.

Not too far from our fates.

Brooke

Brett finally did it.

He brought it up.

"Brooke," he said, "what was that?"

And duh, I knew what he was talking about. Not too tough to figure out.

I shrug. "I don't know. What seemed right at the moment."

And because it seems right at this moment, I move my hands even farther away from him (yes, I let go a while ago) and sweep my hair up into a twist and hold it up with one hand.

Hair sticks, hair sticks, I need a pair of them. Otherwise this hairdo is so not going to stay up, and that's definitely not good…

I shift my shoulder until my purse slides down my shoulder.

He nods. So understanding. I'm starting to hate it. But that's only because of my stupidity, of course.

"Okay. I see."

I dig through my purse with one hand, the other holding up my hair.

"Yeah."

Stupid, is that all I can say?

Finally!

I jab a pair of brown hair sticks through my hair. Lucky my purse is always full of so much stuff…

Brett gives me the once-over.

Like I don't get that enough from Daphne.

But at least he does it with a better attitude than her.

"Nice," he says somewhat shyly.

"Thanks."

What else am I supposed to say to a comment like that?

"Look," I say suddenly. "I'm sorry about what happened right before gym, Brett. It's not that I don't like you. Really."

He brightens…somewhat.

Wow. He's actually happy to hear that.

Good sign, good sign!

"Good to know," he says, clearly trying to sound nonchalant.

"Yeah," I say, not looking at him. "Definitely."

He smiles to himself. It's one of those secret smiles that he thinks I don't see. As if. It's one that I rarely *get* to see, but whatever. More points for me!

Take that, Carlisle.

You just know I'm better than you.

Sophia

Trevor and I keep walking on in silence, just thinking to ourselves.

It's good company – having him around, I mean. Even if we don't talk much, it's still very nice to be hanging out with him.

Although we are walking to the principal's office to be properly punished for brawling in gym class.

How weird does that sound?

But weird or not, here we are.

And now it's time for me to take over with Brooke's style of friendliness that's dripping with sarcasm.

I leave Trevor's side and step up to the door to the main office. I swing it open and prop it there with my foot, pointing one hand into the waiting room in invitation. "After you, Mr. and Mrs. Everett. Welcome to the principal's office."

This makes Daphne blush (oh, yes!), and I feel a fleeting moment's worth of pure satisfaction.

And really, why shouldn't I?

Jackson just rolls his eyes at me, seeming bored, as I beam proudly over my win.

"Freak," Daphne mutters under her breath.

"Come again?" I cup one hand around my ear.

She rolls her eyes and sighs, sounding totally frustrated.

This couldn't get better.

Except for the fact that there's a high possibility that my three best friends and I may get into deep trouble for fighting.

But like I could care less…

Brett

Here we are.

Sitting in the waiting area of the main office.

How terribly gripping.

Miss Warner, who happens to be one of the secretaries, was mad shocked to see us when we all walked in.

I'm sure she knew about all the drama that had been going on. And maybe that's why she was stunned that we were all walking together – and not fighting. But little did she know that only about twenty minutes or so ago, we were in the middle of one of our worst battles ever.

Ha, ha, ha. That's not even funny.

Trevor

"What – I – this is – do you have an appointment?"

That's all Miss Warner could say when the six of us entered the main office. She was not expecting us.

Which meant that Coach Davidson hadn't called ahead…

And we could have easily gotten away with not going to the office.

No one would have known.

Daphne hurled yet another glare at Sophia and Brooke.

Brett merely cracked his knuckles at her. Lame, but it worked well enough.

Daphne whipped her head back around to face Miss Warner. "No, we don't. Jackson and I just stopped by to say 'hi.' We'll be going now." She grabbed Jackson's wrist and beat a path to the exit.

Miss Warner stood up with great agility for a woman who sits at a desk all the time. "I think not."

Daphne ignored her.

And Jackson apparently didn't even hear her.

Why anyone would want to date anyone like Jackson is beyond me.

But anyway.

Brett and I made for the door as well, beating them there. And all we had to do was bar across the double doors using the both of us.

Daphne stepped back into Jackson.

Miss Warner came out from behind her desk and walked out to the waiting area, leaving her safe haven behind the glass.

Daphne and Jackson slowly turned around to face her.

Miss Warner pointed at the seats lining the walls. "Sit."

They slink over to a pair of seats and burrow into them. Well, not literally, but practically.

"You have clearly got some explaining to do," Miss Warner deducted smoothly, "or you wouldn't be here."

And now we all have yet to discover what exactly our explaining is supposed to – or is going to – be.

Brooke smiles a little shakily.

"Now." Miss Warner purses her lips and narrows her eyes. "Who exactly was it that sent you here?"

"Mr. – oh, my apologies. *Coach*, to *some* people here," Sophia volunteers with a smirk, "Davidson."

Miss Warner nods. "I see. And he must have had a good reason to do so, I would imagine?"

"You imagine correctly," Brooke pipes up.

Brooke, Brooke, Brooke.

Your newfound attitude is surprising us all.

But I already knew it was there, of course. I just didn't expect her to start using it in public so soon.

But what must happen will happen, I guess.

"No," Daphne shoots back, "you imagine wrong."

"Way to break the streak," Brett mutters under his breath, but only I hear him.

"Oh, really, Miss Carlisle?" Miss Warner turns to Daphne with a kind of amused look on her face. "Pray tell why I'm incorrect."

"Jackson and I did not do anything wrong," Daphne insists.

"Who accused you of doing anything wrong?" Miss Warner asks icily.

Oh!

Shut *down*!

"I, uh, no one, but that's what these four are gonna do in about two seconds," Daphne stutters.

How accusing.

It's not like I was going to do anything, but…you know…I might as well. Just to tick the two of them off a little bit.

"One Mississippi…"

Brett joins me, a smile creeping onto his face to tilt up the corners of his mouth.

Brooke must be swooning.

"Two Mississippi…"

Daphne's eyes narrow more and more until they're the tiniest slits ever. I'm almost wondering how she can even see.

"Oh, shut up," she finally hisses.

As if I'm really going to listen to her.

Brooke and Sophia are smiling, too.

"We didn't do anything," Jackson defends. "Quit it."

Brett and I both hold our hands up in the air simultaneously (now a trademark of both of us!) and give an innocent shrug.

"Nothing doing."

Miss Warner sighs in exasperation and gives us a smile, rolling her eyes. It's a small one, but it's still a smile.

"What happened in gym class?" she asks.

Brooke and Sophia both stare at Miss Warner, very doe-eyed and completely clear of suspicious actions.

"I think *they* can explain," Daphne says, jabbing a finger at Brooke and Sophia. "They're the ones that started it, after all."

"Okay, cut the drama, please." Miss Warner steps into the dangerous zone between the enemy camps. "Sit," she tells the four of us.

So we do.

"Now, then, Brooke, dear," she smiles sweetly at her favorite out of all.

Brooke can be such a girl next door sometimes.

Brown hair, greenish eyes, loved by all of the parents, the teachers, but unknown by those her age…although that last part has changed.

But it's useful.

I think Miss Warner was especially stunned to see Brooke *Dawson* walking into the *principal's* office. I mean, how horrifying. What happened to the perfect girl who never got in trouble?

Who knows?

Brooke just looks at her.

"Explain to me exactly what happened, dear?" Miss Warner prompts, like this is a 'duh' suggestion.

"Oh."

Relive the moments.

And how I could have helped Brett with Jackson.

Brooke

Well, I just explained everything in as much detail possible to Miss Warner, who just happens to love me.

And she looked beyond astonished. But I guess that should have been expected, since our story was kind of…interesting.

Her reaction was just like, 'Um, okay.'

And then she decided that this situation was out of her hands (again, that should have been expected, since we came to see the principal, not her secretary) and told us to sit tight, since Principal Walker was in a meeting.

Now she's gone back through the glass door and is sitting at her desk again, typing away frantically.

Wouldn't you expect her to be sending out a mass email to the entire staff warning them about the six insane students who see fit to torment one another daily and make attempts on one another's lives?

I kind of would.

Sophia

Finally.

We're now sitting safely inside Principal Walker's office.

At least, Trevor, Brett, Brooke and I are. Daphne and Jackson are still in the waiting area. Who knows what will happen in there with the two of them on the loose?

I mean, I fully tried to slip Miss Warner a thought of warning (coincidental name) by mouthing, 'Be careful,' to her, but all she did in response was raise one eyebrow at me skeptically.

I tried.

I really did.

"So," Principal Walker is saying kindly. "One of you. Please enlighten me by telling me what exactly happened to make you all end up here."

Brooke sighs, sounding oh-so-pitiful. "Someone else can go this time. My mouth is too tired."

Principal Walker smiles, tucking one of her brown curls behind her left ear. "That's perfectly fine with me. I don't mind who tells the tale, as long as someone does."

Trevor clears his throat and starts to speak.

I'm not even listening to him.

Just watching him.

Moments before the story is finished (oh, God, finally!) we hear sudden commotion in the main area.

"No!" Miss Warner shrieks. Her voice sounds muffled, but I guess that must be because of the walls. "You two get back here this instant!"

Doors open and slam.

Didn't I tip her off?

Brett

We all stood up once we heard all that racket going on outside Principal Walker's personal office.

Silence reigned over the five of us.

There was only one thing that could have possibly been happening.

I mean, Vice Principal Mackenzie was out to lunch, since it was time for her break, and so was her secretary, for the same reason.

Think about it.

The person you play secretary to is out to lunch? Well, then, there's no reason why *you* shouldn't go out to lunch.

Or run off to Nordstrom or wherever you needed to go to exchange that black sweater you needed the smaller size of because you need to wear it to your husband's company dinner on Saturday night.

But anyway. Bottom line of that is…the secretary's gone, too. I think her name is Mrs. Carson.

And no other teacher had entered the office at all. If they had, we would have known, because they would have said 'hi' to Miss Warner, and then we would have overheard their conversation.

So it was just Daphne, Jackson, and Miss Warner out in the main waiting area. And that was for sure. Well, Miss Warner was in the secretaries' area behind the glass doors, and the other two were in the waiting area. Which was right nearby the main entrance to the entire office.

Perfect time for them to beat a quick retreat, don't you think?

Principal Walker shoots towards the door suddenly and flies out.

Sophia shakes her head disapprovingly.

I give her a look.

I mean, really.

What's her problem?

"She's going to do the right thing, you know," I tell her.

Sophia nods. "I know. But I told her so."

"Who?"

"Miss Warner."

"Huh?" Trevor asks, taking the word right out of my mouth.

"I told her to be careful. I mean, I knew just as well as anyone that those two would try to pull something once we were out of the room. It's just logical thinking. And I told her. 'Be careful.' Those were my exact two words."

I snicker. "Ooh, Sophia, two words."

She smiles, taking it good-naturedly, like I knew she would. As always. "Laugh all you want, but I did. And did she listen to me and keep a hawk's eye on them like I would have done? No. I don't think so. And where did it get her?"

She pokes her head out the door.

And her eyebrows shoot up on her forehead like mad.

"Where did it get her…?" Brooke prompts.

The first words she's spoken since she claimed that her mouth was 'tired.'

Too cute.

"Out the doors and into the halls, chasing after them in her heels?"

Trevor

Well, I guess Sophia was right in expecting that those two would attempt to escape from the clutches of Principal Walker, but wow.

They made it.

Well…almost.

It's been a few minutes or so since Principal Walker shot out of her private office. And now she's gone off to help Miss Warner. At least, she's definitely disappeared from sight.

So now we're alone in the main office.

Completely alone.

Brett starts sneaking around the room. "Maybe they have test answers and stuff like that stored in here," he hints.

Sophia reaches over and slaps him on the arm.

"Ow." He rubs his shoulder, pretending to be hurt. "No need for that, Garrison."

Sophia rolls her eyes. "First of all, that's so wrong of you, and you shouldn't even be thinking of trying to cheat on anything. Second of all, they don't keep test answers here, partly because that would be the stupidest thing that they could possibly do, and because teachers keep their own test answers and the standardized test answers are with the people who create the tests – and that's not anywhere in Saffrondale. And third of all, don't you dare call me Garrison, because you know who calls me that. And fourth, that definitely did not even hurt. So don't you dare try to fool around with me."

Brett's eyes are wide, but it's all fake. "Chill out, Soph," he says. "I'm only kidding, and you know it."

"Yeah, well, I can never be sure," she mutters.

"What's the matter with you?" Brooke asks. "Don't worry about anything. Principal Walker's so on our side. No matter what. I mean, like she would trust Daphne and Jackson. *So* not going to happen, especially after how they acted at the game last night. She was there, she saw it all, and she knows that we're the ones who are right, and they are so wrong. So don't worry."

"I'm not," Sophia says with a sigh. "But come on, let's go track them down." She heads for the back door to the office. The one that no students are allowed to go through. Tsk, tsk. Bad Sophia.

Brett follows her eagerly. "Yeah! I've always wanted to go through that door! But it's, like, off-limits to students or whatever." He makes a face – someone's acting a little immature…

Brooke starts to walk off in the same direction.

And then she notices that I'm not going anywhere.

"Hurry up, Trevor," she tells me. "We haven't got all day, you know. And I personally don't feel like chasing them around the entire building when we just had enough exercise in gym and I might have to do practice today."

I barely hear her.

I've been standing next to Mrs. Carson's desk (she's Vice Principal Mackenzie's secretary), and I can't help taking a glance at her computer. I notice that there's no screensaver playing, which means she can't have left the office too long ago, and therefore she won't be back too soon – a guarantee of at *least* an hour of her desk and her computer being all by its lonesome, and then we've got the principal and her secretary off on the chase while Vice Principal Mackenzie is out to lunch.

Decoding...

So we'll be alone in the office for quite some time, unless a teacher barges in here. And that's pretty unlikely, since at this hour teachers are usually doing their job and teaching or having their lunch break, since it's now the second lunch period out of three.

And then I take a closer look at the screen.

It's divided up into several small boxes, and the boxes all have a different scene being played in them.

They're all scenes of different parts of the school building, and the school grounds and surroundings.

Score. I know only too well what those are.

Cameras.

Security cameras.

Brooke

"Oh, my God, Trevor, you are such a genius!" I cry out in as low a whisper as I possibly can use.

He smiles, but doesn't look at me. His eyes are fixated at the computer screen. "Thank you very much, thank you, thank you."

Sophia comes over and leans over my shoulder, trying to get a view of what we're watching.

"What is that?" she asks. "We have to get out of here!"

"No," Trevor says.

"Come on," Brett complains in a kind of whiny tone. "I wanted to go through this!" he gestures toward the back door.

"Then go ahead," Sophia says to him. "Walk out and walk back in just for your own pleasure, but quit with the whining. We're busy."

He pauses, clearly thinking about it, but then he comes over to the desk.

Trevor lowers himself down into the chair behind the desk.

"Well?" he asks. "What you got there, Trevor?"

Trevor rolls his eyes and smiles. "Security cameras. Maybe this way we can find out where in the building Daphne, Jackson, Miss Warner, and Principal Walker are."

"Not only that," I add. "We can just watch what's going on without having to leave the room."

"True," Brett agrees, finally getting into the spirit of things and forgetting about his precious door. "But that's only if we're fortunate enough."

"What do you mean?"

"I mean, that's only going to happen if Daphne and Jackson get cornered right in front of one of the cameras."

"Oh."

Trevor's face falls.

"Not to crush anything here, buddy," Brett adds in quickly, obviously feeling guilty since that's exactly what he just did.

"No problem. I didn't think of that."

"Neither did I," Sophia admits.

"Ditto," I add in.

"Anyway, we'd better keep a lookout," Trevor says.

"A lookout," Sophia repeats slowly.

"Yeah, like in case they're coming back already and we don't know it because they haven't passed by the cameras we're watching at the moment? I mean, it is possible since I've been switching cameras."

Brett nods. "I'll go."

But before he can head out through the glass door to cross through the empty waiting area, Trevor stops him.

"Wait. Never mind that. There's another camera here that just happens to be positioned right outside the office. So I'll just keep an eye on that while I'm sifting through the rest of the camera's views."

Brett's still confused.

"Wait, what?"

"Don't worry about it," I translate to him.

What a cutie.

"So I can just sit here and relax?"

I nod. "Yeah, pretty much. Just chill."

He beams. "Okay. That works for me."

I smile back.

He's so sweet.

Sophia perches herself on the edge of Mrs. Carson's desk.

I gingerly sit down on one corner of Miss Warner's seat and glance at her computer screen. She's been typing some letter for Principal Walker. Boring.

"Here they are," Trevor triumphs all of a sudden.

Sophia turns to look back at the screen. "Where?"

He points at a small box. "Here."

I step over to the desk and look over Sophia's shoulder.

Brett joins me a few seconds later.

Glory, glory.

The two of them have been cornered by Miss Warner and Principal Walker, although I can't exactly tell where in the school building they are…

"Oh, my God, how ironic is that!?" Sophia exclaims, her hands flying to her mouth all of a sudden.

"What?"

"They're right where we had that conversation with them."

"Wow, you're right."

And it's so true.

How ironic.

Sophia

Principal Walker dresses kind of like you'd expect a lawyer to.

You know the drill. The knee-length skirt, heels, professional blouse, et cetera, et cetera, et cetera.

And she acts somewhat like a police officer. With all that 'Okay, this is what we're going to do with you. We're going to punish you like this. Now.' You know. She's just a very… executive kind of person.

Except she's really nice.

Well, nice until the point where you've done something wrong, of course. In that case, then you're never going to hear the end of it. But that's beside the point.

On the cameras, we can now see Jackson and Daphne against the wall, with Miss Warner standing nearby and Principal Walker talking to them sternly.

Too bad we can't hear anything they're saying, but still. Beggars can't be choosers, and this is more than good enough.

At least we didn't have to leave the office…and risk getting caught roaming the halls during class time and getting in more trouble for leaving the office when we're supposed to be getting punished for our wrong actions.

Plus we don't miss out on much.

Brooke and I are pretty good at lip-reading, after all.

Daphne looks like she wants to kill someone (probably one or all of us, and maybe Principal Walker, Mr. Davidson, Ms. Sanders, Miss Warner, and the rest of the squad and team as well) and Jackson's got a protective arm around her shoulder.

Tear, tear, little baby Daphne, why don't you go cry about it in your crib?

Brett

Too bad Principal Walker has her back to the camera. We're totally missing out on everything thanks to that.

But, of course, we do have the perfect view of Daphne and Jackson's faces – and their horrified expressions.

Boy, do I want to know what's going to happen to them.

Trevor

Wow.

Wow, wow, wow.

That's pretty much all I can think (and have been thinking for the past few minutes that have gone by since we found out about the news).

God.

Those two little *idiots*.

I wonder how happy their parents are going to be when they find out about their teenager's…

Suspension!?

Brooke

So we watched the screen for about five more minutes, although we had no idea what was going on.

But what we did know was that a few teachers had poked their heads out into the hallway just to see what was causing all the commotion. And they had smirked and returned to teaching their classes.

And something Principal Walker had said with such dramatic effects caused Daphne and Jackson's mouths to drop wide open.

They were speechless.

And then I was pretty much *dying* to find out what had just happened.

And it turned out that Sophia was, too.

Rightfully, of course.

"Trevor," she said, "are you sure there isn't some kind of option? Like, on that specific camera? Where you can turn the sound on?"

"I don't know," he admitted. "Let me check."

He started fiddling around with some of the options listed beside the box of the camera we were watching. And he clicked on one option with a small musical note symbol on it. And then there was sound.

Do I sound like Agatha Christie or what?!

Sophia

"There's no way you can do that!" Jackson was yelling. "You can't *suspend* us! That's not fair!"

Okay. Maybe not yelling, but he was close to it. Very close.

Daphne seemed totally incapable of speech. She was just standing there, opening and closing her mouth, staring at Principal Walker like she couldn't believe her ears.

Then again, if I was being suspended, I wouldn't believe it, either.

But that's a whole different story.

I mean, Daphne's the type of girl I can see getting suspended (or even expelled, but that just might be asking a little too much), now that I know her so well. Or rather, a little bit too well.

"Oh, yes," Brooke muttered under her breath. "That's what you get for trying to hurt my friends, Jackson."

I smiled at her, and she smiled back.

We watched for a few more minutes, and then the four of them disappeared from the camera's view.

"Trevor!" Brooke chided. "What did you do?"

"Nothing," he defended himself. "They walked away from the view of that camera, that's all."

"Well, then, come on. Let's follow them!" Brett commanded.

I smiled.

He does the most random things sometimes, but I guess that one flowed with the moment, in a way.

Trevor switched the cameras, and we caught a few cuts of them walking through the hallways.

"All sound on?" Brooke suggested.

Trevor fiddled around with the controls a bit, and then said, "Nope. That wouldn't work. Then we'd hear all the sound going on around the whole school. And that's not what we want, now is it?"

"No…"

"Let me try this…" he clicked on another button.

There was a camera fixated on the area where the four had stopped. It was a little off-centered on our subject, and it cut off Miss Warner, but like she seriously even mattered at the moment.

No offense, or anything, of course.

"Get your things, and then get out of the building. I'll have all your records filed again with this new occurrence, and there will be no need of you for the next few days," Principal Walker announced.

We were all completely silent.

Could it really be true?

Two full days (or maybe even more, if we were lucky) without Jackson and Daphne? Two full days of freedom!?!?

I swear, birds could have started singing at that moment, the sun could have come out, and all of that great stuff that's native to springtime could have happened, and it wouldn't have seemed more right.

Never more right.

Chapter 8:

Living the Life...

Brett

I was never so happy in the entirety of the past week as when I heard those four words.

"You can't *suspend* us!"

Oh, yeah?

Well, guess what, Jackson?

Yes, she can.

Trevor

I never really felt like such a genius.

And okay, so I wasn't really a genius.

It doesn't take a rocket scientist to figure out how to use a simple security camera system on a computer.

But it was still all me who so smoothly discovered the cameras opened up on the computer. All me, all me. And I'm still very proud of myself. And all my hard work (okay, maybe not, but still).

And then seeing Daphne lay one hand gently (gently!? My thoughts exactly…but then again, think of whose arm she's going to be laying her hand on) on Jackson's arm (ha) just as he was going to start yelling at Principal Walker some more.

"Whatever, Jackson. Think about it," she breathed in his ear. "No school. You'd like that, wouldn't you? We could hang out together for so long…I mean, how fun would that be?"

Yuck.

He managed a smile. "Yeah. I guess."

Okay.

Is that guy stupid, or what?

"I'll also be calling your parents to inform them about your new schedule. They are not to let you out of their sight."

"What!?" Daphne squealed, letting go of Jackson's arm.

It was at this point that Miss Halitelli stuck her head out of her English classroom, clearly about to ask whoever was cutting class to settle down. Her eyes widened and she slipped back into the room, suppressing a smile.

Principal Walker smiled. "That's right, Daphne. After all, such actions call for these measures."

Daphne gasped. "That's too much."

"Oh, really? I don't think so."

Miss Warner giggled a little.

And now the bell rings.

Students flood out into the hallways and are stunned to see the two biggest delinquents in our entire school standing in the middle of the corridor, accompanied by the principal and her secretary.

Oh, wow.

That's definitely a surprise.

"Miss Warner, if you'll be so kind as to escort these two students to their lockers so they may gather their belongings and then take them to the main entrance to the building so as to see them off?"

"With pleasure, Principal Walker."

I half expect Miss Warner to sweep into a bow or something, but she doesn't. Thankfully. That would have be kind of weird.

The three of them disappear out of sight and Principal Walker mutters, "After all, I've got some other students to talk to," and smiles, walking off in the opposite direction. There's no doubt that she's returning to the office.

Everyone's gaping.

At least we know now that Principal Walker is definitely on our side.

As if that one's a shocker.

Brooke

"Hurry up!" I hiss at Trevor. "Reset everything back to the way it was before Principal Walker gets back!"

I readjust Miss Warner's seat so she won't notice any difference when (and if…no, just kidding) she returns to her desk.

Trevor smiles. "That's not a problem. Mrs. Carson obviously never uses these cameras personally, yet she *is* always required to keep them open, so she hasn't fiddled around with them in a while."

Fiddled?

"Trevor…" I say in a warning tone, hurrying to the waiting area.

Brett and Sophia have already seated themselves there, seeing as Principal Walker would probably like it if we were there instead of nosing around in her personal office. I sit down beside them.

"I'm hurrying, I'm hurrying," he mutters.

"Are you using a tone with me?"

Sophia and Brett smile.

"No…" Trevor trails off. "Done!"

He restores everything back to its original condition and rushes over to where the rest of us are sitting.

Just in time.

Sophia

Oh, God.

I thought Trevor wouldn't get back here in time.

I mean, he sat down seconds ago, and now one of the two doorknobs to the main entrance is twisting.

Principal Walker enters the waiting area.

"Oh, hello," she greets us.

Didn't she expect us to be waiting here?

The second bell rings.

Brooke looks at her, confused. "Aren't we supposed to be here?"

"I would imagine so..." Principal Walker says. "Unless you would rather be in class?" Her mouth twitches: she's definitely smiling – teasing.

Brett shakes his head. "Oh, no," he answers with one of his dazzling smiles that all the teachers love him for.

Sickening.

"Now, then," she continues, "shall we meet in my office after you all pick up a refreshing drink in the staff room?"

I'm sure my mouth has dropped open.

"No need to look so incredulous, Sophia. The four of you have been through much excitement in the past twenty-four – make that forty-eight – hours, haven't you?"

We all bob our heads, still amazed.

At least, I know I am.

"Well, then, you deserve a little something. Help yourself to whatever's on the table or in the fridge or freezer. As long as it doesn't have a staff member's name marked on it, that is. We don't want any unhappy campers around here."

"Not at all," Trevor manages to say.

Has this ever happened before?

We've just had a fight with two of our classmates (allow me to enlighten you – a fight that *I*, one of the four against two, started) and the other two get suspended when we had the advantage in the fight, *and* we're getting rewarded (well, in a way)?

Um, hello?

No.

I think not.

Brett

Hmm.

Even though for the past two years, I've been the one to win all the basketball games for Saffrondale High School, I've never gotten this treatment before.

I mean, seriously.

We were all surprised.

"Here, kids, why don't you go into the teacher's lounge and help yourselves to whatever food is in there, hmm? And then we'll have our little meeting about who punched who in your fistfight. After all, I just suspended your opponents."

That?

Coming from the principal of your high school?

Also known as a very important person who rules over about one thousand two hundred students?

Wow…

I'd half-expect the food to be, like, fake, or poisoned, or something.

But no.

It just turns out that Principal Walker loves us because we're angels compared to Daphne Carlisle and Jackson Everett.

Oh, well.

Works for me.

Trevor

So we've had our little chat with Principal Walker…

And it lasted almost until the end of Spanish.

Yeah, I missed a pop quiz, too, apparently. So did Brett, of course, but that's beside the point.

And then when we finally walked into Spanish class, we found Señora Lopez sitting at her desk, working, and the whole rest of the class working diligently away on a pop quiz. Of course, once we entered, they all glanced up and stared in awe, since we were the two guys who had just caused the suspension of Daphne Carlisle and Jackson Everett. And then they all started whispering like crazy.

Once Señora Lopez finally got them all to settle down, she decided that we could make up the pop quiz some other time.

Skipping out on a pop quiz?

That has never – ever – happened to me. I mean, I was never a bad boy who tried to sneak out to the nurse's office or anything during a quiz or test time. And I never had an excuse – or made up one.

And now here I am, missing a pop quiz in Spanish. And thank God, since I didn't exactly review what we've learned.

But you know what I think about it?

Sweetness.

Oh, sweetness.

Brooke

Time for cheerleading practice.

It feels so much…I don't know. Different.

At least I know that this time, I'm safe.

Safe.

That word has so much meaning now. I just never thought I'd be unsafe with only one or two of my classmates around.

I never.

Brett

I had half a mind (not literally, of course, but I picked this one up from Principal Walker, since during our little meeting she was saying, "I had half a mind to suspend them for a week, but given the conditions, I don't think that will be allowed…") to skip basketball practice and drag Trevor with me, especially after what happened during gym class only about a couple of hours ago, but truth be told, I can't exactly do that.

So here we are, waiting in the gym for Coach Davidson, racking up the memories of our little fistfight.

In other words, we're getting a little too swamped by the recollection (source of new word: Brooke) of gym class.

Time couldn't tick any faster, now, could it?

Trevor

Well.

All the guys came up to Brett and me at practice and were all, "Way to go! You got Everett and his girl suspended!"

And I was never more surprised.

I mean, let's just say that I didn't exactly think of Jackson and Daphne's suspensions that way. Well, as thanks to Brett, Sophia, Brooke, and me, that is.

Brett seemed a little dazed, too. He just stared at Brandon Sullivan when Brandon thumped him on the back in celebration or whatever. He looked so confused.

And then, a few minutes later, he went, "Wait, you think that was all thanks to the four of *us*?"

The guys just stopped short and all said, "Well, yeah…"

"But it wasn't us," Brett quickly said. "That was Principal Walker who actually got them suspended – "

They all started laughing really loudly, and Brett's voice ended up getting completely drowned out.

"Yeah, right, it was all Principal Walker, Evans."

"You're hilarious."

"But either way, you're a hero."

"You too, Stevenson."

Me?

A hero?

Ha, now *that's* hilarious.

Brooke

Practice was the usual. I did take part in it, but only to some extent. Coach Sanders drew the limit in certain areas, so it all worked out fine.

And I'm happy to say that I felt completely comfortable at practice today. For once. The girls were super nice and didn't even mention anything about the suspension or the fight or anything. They were just the usual. Nice. Overly obsessed with Sophia. And now me, of course. But it was good to have all that without Daphne and Jackson to worry about. As long as I was in school, I was safe.

And home's good, too.

The four of us split up after practice and headed home, just as it should have happened.

I guess we had enough of one another's company for today.

But then again, maybe not.

Trevor's calling.

"Hello?"

"Brooke!? What's going on with you and Brett? You never mentioned any of this to me!"

"Sorry," I say sheepishly. "But I told Sophia everything when you and Brett went to get the basketball during gym."

"So that's when everything started?"

"Well, no," I admit. "It was before that. Like right before Mr. Davidson took attendance."

"So what happened? I don't get it."

"Well, Brett asked me out."

I can practically see him grinning.

"That's great, Brooke!"

Time to take the poor guy by surprise.

"Yeah, I guess it is, but it probably would have turned out better if I hadn't turned him down, right?"

Silence for a moment.

"What? You're joking, right, Brooke? Because this is one of your worst jokes, okay? It's not funny." No emotion in his voice. It's totally flat.

"No, seriously. I'm not kidding."

"Really? Why?" Now the emotion's mixed. Confusing.

"Well, I felt like it was – I don't know. Moving too fast?"

He sighs in exasperation. "Brooke…haven't you been, like, dreaming about this since forever?"

Hey! No! Well, all right. Maybe I have. But still. That's not fair.

"No!"

"Come on, Brooke. It's me. You don't need to lie. Especially when I know the real truth. But you really felt like that?"

"Yeah, that, and I just had too much to worry about. Too

much to deal with. Look, Trevor, either you get what I'm saying, or you don't."

"No, no, no, Brooke, I get it. It's just that…I don't know. Wow. You really make your choices…interestingly, don't you?"

"Yeah, Trevor, I guess I do."

I guess I do.

Sophia

I just barely settled into my bed with my iPod and my cell phone next to me. Plus, I had Shadowland, the first book of the *Mediator* series. I've had all six books for a while now, and I've been meaning to read them, but I never had the time to relax. I was always so busy with cheering or whatever that I never had any time to myself.

Oh, and I think I forgot to mention that when you're reading, and you're on page six, and you're really getting to like the main character a lot, and you want to find out about the hot ghost guy that's going to show up in her bedroom, and what else is going to happen, you really don't want to hear your little brother pounding on your bedroom doors, yelling at the top of his lungs.

Seriously.

I heard him *over* the voice of Alicia Keys belting out 'Diary.' Such a beautiful song. And such a beautiful voice.

But, of course, Brad has to ruin it.

"Open the door! Open the door! Sophia, Sophia, Sophia! Open the door! Open the door!"

Um, hello?

Can you say spaz?

He's worse than I thought *I* was. And that's sad.

"What do you want?" I yell, although I don't hear myself too clearly. I rip my ear-buds out of my ears.

No problem now.

All I can hear is pounding sounds on the door.

"Let me in! Let me in! Sophia! Open the door and let me in!" he keeps crying out. "Sophia!"

"Hey. Brad."

He stops for a second only to snarl, "WHAT?"

"It's unlocked."

Silence for a moment in the hall.

And then the door bursts open and a red-faced Brad is bouncing on my bed, hyper beyond description.

I take one look at him.

"Do I *want* to know?"

Brett

Sigh.

If only.

Brooke and I would probably be relaxing together and having so much fun at Giordano's right now.

Or actually, we might even be somewhere better, if I'd been able to come up with it in time for what could have been our first date.

Of course, we aren't going out tonight. We would have been, but Brooke crushed the idea.

But it's all good.

Only because I know something better is true.

And I can't help but smile because of it.

Trevor

So now that I know all of the details about Brett and Brooke and their status together, I'm content.

Of course, it did take a lot to get it all out of Brooke. I mean, I tell her that she makes interesting decisions, and she sighs so pitifully and goes, "Yeah, Trevor, I guess I do." Like she totally wanted to end the conversation there.

But I made sure she told me every single last detail.

And then she had to go out to dinner with her family.

Yet I knew that was going to happen already.

After all…

What are friends for?

Brooke

I cannot believe this.

We didn't go out to our stupid little Thursday dinner.

Seriously.

Mom was like, "Oh, I have a headache. I think we can afford to skip dinner for another week."

But what she meant was, "Let's not go out to dinner this week. I'm just feeling too lazy."

And then my dad was like, "Oh, that's fine. You go rest. I have some work to do. I'll just have something to eat later."

So I had to cook.

Seriously.

I made macaroni and cheese.

For myself and Ashlynn.

And okay, I know that doesn't really count as cooking dinner.

~ Chapter Eight ~

I mean, for one thing, it was disgusting. Not to mention it was total embarrassment to my healthy diet.

But the other thing is, Ashlynn was acting really weird during our sad excuse for a dinner…like she didn't want to talk about anything at all.

I didn't get why.

Although it was probably about Brad. Brad Garrison.

Aww.

Adorable.

There's a soft knock at my door.

I'm sitting at my computer. Staring at the screen. I have to message him. I have to. But now I can't. And it's all because of someone outside my door.

"What?"

"Can I come in?"

Gee, it's Ashlynn.

Wonder what she wants.

"Yeah, sure. It's not locked."

I minimize my messenger.

She clearly needs someone to talk to, so I don't need any distractions. God forbid Brett does send me a message after noticing that I'm online. I know he is.

She comes in and sits down on my bed.

Her face has the same strange expression from when we ate.

"Okay, what's up?"

She gives me a weird look. "What's up?" she repeats.

"Yeah…"

"You never really say that."

"Well, whatever. What's wrong?"

"I don't know what to do!" she wails.

Um, okay.

About…?

Well, duh. Brad, Brad, Brad.

"About Brad?" I guess so ingeniously.

She gives me a withering look. "No duh."

"Okay." I swing around on my desk chair. "Tell me everything. I'm all ears."

She rolls her eyes, but she's definitely ready to begin.

Brett

Okay.

If I were going out to dinner, I wouldn't bother signing on to my messenger. Right? Doesn't that make sense?

At the very least, I'd have put up some kind of away message.

So why is Brooke signed on?

And if she'd signed on a while ago and hadn't done anything, she'd be listed as idle or something.

So she's online.

Hmm…

Where is she?

Let's test if she was lying before.

Because I really don't like a girl that lies to me.

Sophia

"I haven't talked to her all day."

So?

It's not like you're going to die because of it, Brad.

But then again, I'm not going to dare say that to him. He'll have a spaz attack or whatever.

"And…?"

"I don't know what to do!"

I get up and go over to my computer and sit down there. What can I do? He's invaded the bed.

"Well, neither do I."

Hmm…

Brooke's online.

I wonder what happened to dinner.

I mean, she isn't idle.

I turn around.

He's not looking.

I carefully begin to type out a message.

$0phi@ch33r: brooke? u there? what happened 2 dinner?

And I receive a quick response.

x0_br00ke_x0: yeah, im here. dinner got canceled. what's up w/ u? im listening 2 ashlynn complain.
$0phi@ch33r: oh that sucks. listening 2 brad complain about ash. =P
x0_br00ke_x0: lol yeah. nothing new, huh?
$0phi@ch33r: yeah. pretty much.

"Sophia!"

I snap back to attention. "What?"

"You're not listening!"

He bounds off my bed (ugh, messing up all of my covers in the process) and hurries over to my computer. "What are you doing?"

I quickly minimize my messenger so that it goes straight back into its tray. "Nothing! Now go on, go on, I'm listening."

"Well, I'm staying right here."

"Fine. See if I care."

He starts talking again, but I tune out completely.

Suddenly another message pops up.

Darn.

x0_br00ke_x0:omg she's like, i didn't tlk 2 him all day...it was sooo awkward and i h8 it. blah blah blah.

Brad shoots up at the computer.

I exit out of the window, but not soon enough.

"Is that Brooke?"

"That is none of your business," I inform him authoritatively. "Now hurry up. You're wasting my time."

He glares at me in disgust. "Please. You were reading when I came in."

"Yeah! And in case you don't pay attention, that just happens to be something that *I* rarely get to do!"

He doesn't soften his glare. "Yeah. Uh huh. Right."

"Brad, I am this close to kicking you out of my room right now. Just warning you," I say.

My patience with this kid is seriously waning.

Fading.

Whatever.

God forbid Brooke sends me another message.

Maybe this mental telepathy thing might work…

Please, Brooke, understand this situation and don't send me a message until he leaves.

Please.

Don't.

My messenger beeps.

So much for that.

x0_br00ke_x0: OMG ashlynn SHUT UP!!!!! SOPHIA HELP!

I can't help smiling.

She is so stupid.

And so very, very dead.

Brooke

Okay.

So Sophia stopped sending me messages.

Whatever.

Maybe Brad caught her.

Oops.

Oh, well.

I guess I'll hear from her eventually.

I swing around in my desk chair a few times, bored out of my mind.

I've done all my homework, and in less time than usual, since I didn't waste time eating dinner and I didn't bother going out to the shed after school. There was no point in practicing, anyway. After all, my wrist still hurts a little bit, although I did remove the bandage on it.

Oh, great.

A message.

Maybe I won't be so bored anymore.

Wait.

It's definitely not from Sophia.

Oh, God.

It's Brett.

I'm in for it now.

Brett

It took me forever to think of what I could possibly say in a message to Brooke.

I mean, what could I say?

So then I finally gave up on thinking up things that I might be able to say to her and just sent her something.

br3tt_sp0rt_king: hey brooke, jw if u were home or something

But now it's been about a minute since I sent that. And I feel really bad that I ever doubted her. I mean, why would she have to lie to me about her plans for tonight? She's not that type of girl.

So I send her another message.

br3tt_sp0rt_king: but nvm i guess u arent

br3tt_sp0rt_king: so i guess i'll just ttyl

And now I guess I might as well sign off.

No point bothering Sophia.

I don't have anything that I absolutely need to say to her. And there's no small talk to make, either.

And Trevor isn't online.

No point in staying online.

x0_br00ke_x0: no, brett, wait. im here.

Oh.

Hmm.

br3tt_sp0rt_king: oh. what happened 2 dinner?
x0_br00ke_x0: already got back.

Oh, please, Brooke. Don't lie.

That's the first step to ruining a relationship. Unless, of course, that's what you want. It would kill me to understand that, but I can. I really can.

br3tt_sp0rt_king: oh really?

Brooke

He so does not believe me. But I don't blame him. And I really can't lie.

x0_br00ke_x0: no...jk.
br3tt_sp0rt_king: oh.

He's so confused.
I've got to explain.

x0_br00ke_x0: my mom has a headache...so we didn't go. =(
br3tt_sp0rt_king: oh. =(hope she feels better
x0_br00ke_x0: i think she's actually feeling fine right now. no one really wanted 2 go.
br3tt_sp0rt_king: oh...so what're u doing right now?

Oh. It's so intelligent, Brett.

"Who are you talking to?" Ashlynn asks, walking over to my desk.

I minimize my messenger. "No one."

"Yeah, right. Trevor?"

I shake my head.

"Sophia?"

I nod, and then shake my head. "I was, but she stopped talking. I think she's busy," I fib about that last part, since I know what she's doing (who she's dealing with) and I can't exactly mention his name to Ashlynn here.

"Okay..." She pauses. And then gets a sudden inspiration. "Brett Evans!?"

I nod kind of sheepishly. "Yeah."

She bites her lip, like she's trying not to laugh.

"What about?"

"What!?"

"What are you two talking about?"

Why not blow it all out of proportion and watch Ashlynn blow a few capillaries?

"Oh, just how our plans for tonight got screwed up and all. You know, for our first date."

Trevor

I'm beyond bored.

I would sign online, but I don't feel like it.

Maybe I'll just study…it can't hurt.

God, I'm such a freak.

Sophia

"I give up with you!" Brad stomps out of my room.

"Well, you said what you wanted to say!" I call back.

Oops. Not my bad. Brooke…

But it was me. Can't blame her.

Back to the tales of everyone's favorite mediator…

Finally!

Brett

Where is she?

Did I scare her away or something by asking her what she was doing? I mean, I wasn't going to ask if she wanted to hang out or anything. I got what she said. Even if it didn't make much sense. But I respect her thoughts. Maybe she was overwhelmed with everything that's going on now. I understand that.

Am I really a suck up???

Brooke

"What!? Your first *date*!?!?" Ashlynn practically screamed.

Oops. Don't want the rents hearing that…I think.

"Well, okay, not really," I admit.

"What happened?" she squeals, jumping back onto my bed and grabbing a pillow. "Tell me everything."

She's a good sister. Not like me.

So I start tell her most of it. Well, okay, everything. But right when I've gotten to the part where he asks me out, my messenger beeps at me.

Oh, God, it's Brett.

br3tt_sp0rt_king: brooke? u still there? im gonna sign off...

No! Don't! Well, okay, whatever. Maybe it *is* a good idea.

I start typing aloud.

x0_br00ke_x0: yeah, im here, but my sis wants 2 tlk 2 me...

"No!" Ashlynn cries out, but she doesn't move from her perch, so I know it's okay.

br3tt_sp0rt_king: oh got it. so i'll c u tmrw?

Short and sweet. Loving it.

x0_br00ke_x0: definitely. ttyl
br3tt_sp0rt_king: yeah
br3tt_sp0rt_king: *terminated.*

"Why did you do that?" Ashlynn looks upset.

"Why did I do what?"

"You so shouldn't have ended that conversation!" She punches the pillow.

"Well, sor*ry*."

"You have no idea how lucky you are." She hugs the pillow to her chest and sticks out her lower lip, pouting.

"Because I have Brett," I say listlessly.

She nods. "Seriously."

"Yeah, maybe, but look what else I'm dealing with."

She rolls her eyes. "A witch and her boyfriend? Oh, big deal."

Oh, please. She just doesn't get it.

"Ashlynn," I begin.

"No, seriously. I'm just going to give up with Brad. If he likes me, then he can come to me. Like the way it should be. See ya."

She leaves my room. But the thing is, she's got a point. And it's a very good point. Even if I do know that Brad is not going to make a move because he doesn't know that she likes him. That really is no reason for him not to do anything, though. I'm going to talk to Sophia later.

Later.

Grey's Anatomy is on.

Trevor

It's almost the end of the day.

Brett and I just finished making up that pop quiz for Señora Lopez. Yeah, I didn't get out of it. But it was easy, and that's good.

Sophia and Miss Halitelli were going at it before English today because Miss Halitelli's big date is tonight! Sophia and Brooke are getting a little too excited over it, in my opinion. But nobody has ever thought of asking me about my opinion.

And lunch is back to normal. Gym, too. In fact, so is everything, now that Jackson and Daphne aren't to be seen.

"Trevor!"

I turn to Brett, who's looking super excited.

"What's up with you?"

Yeah, I can talk to him that way now. We're pretty much best buds.

"I have the best idea!"

Oh, God. I almost don't want to know.

"What?"

"You know how Halitelli's going to the Village or wherever with Lodi Valley?"

I smile. "Yeah. Romero."

"Whatever. We should go to – go to…"

"The Village?" I suggest. "Because I think we both know how much Sophia wanted to go there."

"Oh, please. It doesn't matter if it was only Sophia who didn't want to go. But no, not the Village. We should go to the city tomorrow!"

"The city?" I repeat dubiously. "As in Manhattan?"

"Yeah! Why not?"

He's right. It is a good idea. The four of us…go to Rockefeller Center…see the tree…go shopping a bit…spend some time together…no worries about Daphne and Jackson…miles away from home…No, scratch that.

It's a perfect idea.

Sophia

"Sophia!" Brett calls.

I look up from where I'm kneeling on the floor, putting my books in my bag. I've been dreaming *Mediator* all day. Which isn't so good, considering I've got a lot to worry about. But I do hear Brett. Only question is…where is he?

"Hey," he says breathlessly, appearing out of nowhere and crouching down next to me. "I have the best news."

News? Oh, God. "What?"

"Well, okay, it's not news, but what do you think of going to Manhattan tomorrow?"

Brett

Manhattan. New York City.

I remember going there – a while ago. The last time I was there? I don't even know when it was. Sad, too. We don't live that far away from the city. We're in the same state. And I really want to go with Brooke, Sophia, and Trevor. It would be fun. A good memory. Something I never had before.

That's what happens when I'm an only child, I guess.

Trevor told me that I should be the one planning the trip since I came up with the whole idea. So I have to tell everyone, too. Which really only means I have to tell Brooke now.

Brooke

"New York City?" I repeat. Exciting much?!

I absolutely loved it there the last time I went. It was Ashlynn and me – and our mom, of course. But we shopped for so long and had so much fun there. It was a nice mother-daughter experience, but I had to share it with Ashlynn.

And I would love to go with my friends, now that I've got Brett and Sophia in addition to Trevor. I mean, shopping with Trevor isn't that fun.

No offense meant, obviously. But still.

"Yeah," Brett says. "I figured we all needed to go somewhere – away from Saffrondale – and have some fun. Just the four of us. What do you think?"

That is the best idea ever.

"I think that's absolutely perfect."

Trevor

So here we are. We're standing at the Saffrondale train station (no, I didn't know we had one, either) and I have even better news.

Brett's mom (his family is pretty rich, but then again, a lot of people around these parts are) happens to be distantly related to the girl who's currently playing Meg in *The Phantom of the Opera* on Broadway. And that means she could get us discounted tickets to the Saturday evening show. Orchestra seats, too. Last minute!

Life is good.

Brett

I never thought my plan would work. Even if we had to get up so early this morning to catch a 7:30 train to Manhattan, it was worth it.

Mom even managed to contact her cousin Celeste, whose daughter (my distant second cousin?) Lilia is playing Meg Giry in *The Phantom of the Opera*. And Dad made dinner reservations at B. Smith Restaurant since it's near the play. We're going to Planet Hollywood for lunch.

This is amazing. I can hardly believe it's happening.

Our plan is to take a train into the city (obviously), leave Grand Central Station and walk around and go shopping a little bit in the morning (the girls insist, and I guess I might as well get some Christmas shopping done), have lunch at Planet Hollywood, walk around some more until it gets dark, then go to Rockefeller Center, and have dinner at B. Smith Restaurant, and then go see the play. And then we'll catch another train back to Saffrondale.

Sophia

I can't believe Brett pulled this off. I mean, we're actually off the train, and we're going to have a full day (and part of a night) of fun in the city.

Oh, my God!

I see *the* Macy's store.

And Brooke does too.

We're already up the steps, with the guys following somewhat close behind.

The squad girls are probably just waking up and maybe thinking about hitting the mall for some Christmas shopping, and taking the guys with them.

But oh, no, they can't beat N.Y.C.

Trevor

Well, I'll admit that this shopping is starting to take a toll on me, but I'm still loving the whole trip.

We have Brett to thank for planning this whole thing. It would have been completely pointless without his hard work.

Imagine all those other Saffrondale residents who are either working, sleeping, or doing something equally boring. And here we are in Manhattan, having a fabulous time.

Well.

You've just gotta love high school.

Wow!

We had the most amazing time!

My parents were really nice about the whole trip, surprisingly, and gave me a ton of money to spend. They said that I deserved a reward. I guess that they were happy that the four of us were finally doing something other than cheering and playing basketball. And that's true. We need to have some fun.

Sophia and I each bought a designer bag at Macy's, some

Christmas gifts, plus a bunch of clothes, plus we picked out some stuff for the guys (fun), and we had a great time walking around the city, shopping in SoHo, and everywhere else. It seemed like the day was everlasting. Lunch was great, and so was seeing the tree in Rockefeller Center. I ran out of pictures to take on my camera by the time dinner was over, but that was perfectly fine.

Oh, my God.

The Phantom of the Opera was absolutely incredible! I saw the movie in theaters (Emmy Rossum is a great actress *and* singer) and loved it. I even bought the play's original cast recording afterwards.

Brett's relative Lilia was amazing. She played Meg Giry. And the play itself was unbelievable. Words could never describe it. Those who say that you have to experience the play on Broadway are totally right. Nothing can compare.

I can't believe the day's over. It feels like midnight.

Brett and Trevor are half asleep. I guess Sophia and I tired them out with all that shopping. Plus the play. Trevor about blew a capillary at, like, every single gunshot. It was kind of funny. But then again, I had read the entire libretto beforehand, so I really shouldn't be saying anything…

Sophia taps me on the shoulder. "How fabulous was this?" she asks, struggling to keep a hold on all of her bags.

I smile. "Fabulous. Absolutely fabulous."

Chapter 9:

...Or Not.

<u>Sophia</u>

I can't believe that it's been almost five days since our trip to Manhattan! It feels like it was only yesterday. The memory is that clear.

But no, now it's Wednesday. And we all know what that means. It's game day.

And I have now clue how or why this happened, but somehow they managed to screw up the listings of who's supposed to be playing against who, so now Saffrondale is going to have to play against Lodi Valley. Again.

And the game is in about twenty minutes.

Brooke doesn't seem to care much about it, and I can't say I do, either. I mean, it's just yet another game. Boring. I guess I should be excited, but I'm not. Well, not as excited as usual, anyway. Trevor seems extremely determined to play his best. And believe me, he will. He's just amazing. But so is Brett. Don't get me wrong.

We're hanging around out in the hall, waiting for Coach Sanders to come back from wherever she went and tell us when we're supposed to go into the gym.

So since I'm so bored, I can't help but let my mind stray back to the past. Like what happened this week.

On Monday, Miss Halitelli came to me before English class and told me a fabulous secret: as of Friday night, she and Winston are officially engaged to be married! How sweet is that?!

Trevor and I planned with Brett and Brooke (okay, it was really all done by Brooke and me, but still) to throw a surprise engagement party for her. So on Tuesday we got the cafeteria decorated a little with the help of the rest of our class and Coach Sanders' fourth period class – a.k.a. Brett and Brooke's math class. We had a huge cake and a ton other refreshments (even though it was right before the first lunch period – and that meant we had to clean up super quickly and get out before everyone else came into the cafeteria to eat), and we invited Mr. Romero, and a lot of our school staff. Miss Halitelli and Mr. Romero were so happy. Well, Miss Halitelli looked like she wanted to kill me for telling so many people, but I know she was happy, even if it wasn't exactly showing. They announced that their wedding would most likely be in late June or early July (ah, the gorgeous summer months) and that we were all invited. How totally sweet!

Suddenly Brooke elbows me. "Company."

I glance up and see a couple of girls in blue and white uniforms approaching us.

Lodi Valley cheerleaders.

I recognize one of them as Lynda Tayler, the captain of their squad. She's always thought that she was better than us. Yeah, right. I mean, she goes to Lodi Valley High. That tells anyone everything about her. Okay, so I'm kidding, but her personality is really kind of similar to Daphne Carlisle. I think that if they'd just be introduced, they could be the best of friends.

I straighten up and step up to them. Brooke follows me automatically. I fold my arms across my chest. Lodi Valley students hardly are friends of ours. In fact, the only person I don't mind at Lodi Valley High is Principal Romero. And if you think about it, that's kind of sad. Not to mention weird. But anyway.

"Can I help you?" I ask, trying to sound tough, when all I really am is tired of all of this.

Lynda looks at her friend.

Her friend whose name I've got to know…Kaci Grant. Got it.

Lynda smirks. "Yeah, I think so. We heard you cheering about how you're gonna take our trophy away from us and all that."

"Yeah. It's called an original cheer," Brooke says scornfully, "but I realize that's something you wouldn't know much about."

Kaci snickers. "You're hilarious. But I notice you're new."

Brooke narrows her eyes but says nothing.

"Seems like your squad could use a new captain," I say to her.

Kaci purses her lips. Disapproving. Good.

Lynda, on the other hand, is anything but silenced. "Look, Sophia. All we came here to say is to watch out about what you say. You may think you're so much better, just because your basketball team's been winning a lot lately, but that doesn't make your squad any better."

"I thought the basketball was what mattered in this tournament, Lynda," I respond evenly.

She raises one eyebrow. "In this tournament, yeah. But you're not on the team. You're the captain of the squad. And I'm doing the same thing. Yet not only am I doing the duty of cheering for my team, but I'm also the head of the gymnastics team, which is something your school doesn't have. Beat that."

"You know what? You want me to?"

She doesn't flinch.

I take that to be a 'yes.'

"Well, then I will. But for now? I think you need to get in that gym and watch our team beat yours *yet* again. We *will* take that trophy back."

Brett

Tonight's game was the usual (the way it was before our last game). We won. Lodi Valley sucks. There were no incidents with any unwanted wannabes, thankfully. It was nice. And I'm really tired now.

Sophia and Brooke were talking about how some cheerleaders came up to them before the game, but I was too tired to listen. I guess I'll just have to find out what they were talking about tomorrow.

I don't think I'll really be able to last long enough to sign on to my messenger, and then check if they're online, and then demand an explanation.

Too tired…

Trevor

Now that was a real game.

Real to me, anyway.

That was the first game that I actually played with no distraction. None at all. I barely even paid any attention to the crowd (and believe me, it was even bigger than usual, since a lot of people seemed to want to find out if Lodi Valley could make a miraculous comeback, although that obviously didn't happen – or maybe they wanted to catch the latest Saffrondale High drama… but too bad there wasn't any) or the cheerleaders. Not even Sophia or Brooke. I have no idea what they were saying this time, and I didn't care. I was only focused on playing. And I scored a lot of the points. A proud night for me, let me tell you.

And my parents actually came to the game.

I think Dad's rethought my potential. He even slapped me on the back when I finally got home tonight and told me, "I'm proud of you, son. Congratulations."

And for some reason, that meant more to me than I ever thought it would.

Sophia

Okay. Corinne Carlton is a very nice young girl. Really. But when she gets one of these crazy ideas? Oh, my God, she's just completely uncontrollable.

When Brooke and I walked into the locker room before practice, we found all the girls kneeling and huddled around a bench, whispering like crazy.

"What's up with them?" Brooke whispered to me.

I shrugged. "No clue."

Then I saw Corinne smiling away. And she was saying, "I really think this is a fabulous idea, don't you?" I didn't know who she was talking to. It couldn't have been me. And it couldn't have been Brooke. But then I realized that the girls were poring over a thick book that was open to a page somewhere in the middle.

What was that book? It looked familiar, but I couldn't place it. Where had I seen it before…? And then it hit me all of a sudden. The catalog.

And I know that sounds really random, but, I mean, that's just because you don't really expect a bunch of cheerleaders to be reading a catalog in the locker room before their beloved cheerleading practice – which is definitely something that they do (or should) look forward to daily.

Isn't it?

Brooke

Corinne Carlton really has some nerve. I mean, who died and named her captain of the Saffrondale High varsity cheerleading squad? Last time I checked, no one did. And no one ever will, due to her lack of judgment and her insensitivity and whatever else she could possibly be branded as.

Not that I don't like her as a person, or anything. But she just – ugh. Last night at the game she was totally normal and then, less than twenty-four hours later, she flips completely. That's one totally unpredictable girl.

Okay. First of all, Sophia (the real captain of the cheerleading squad, as if you didn't know that already) and I (her assistant – it's unofficial, but it's practically known by everyone, anyway, so why can't I flaunt it?) weren't even present when Corinne decided to put a totally new idea into the naïve minds of every other girl on the squad.

And get the idea…

Let's just shorten the tank top of our uniform and then we can change the skirt up a bit by making it into even more of a micro-mini! I mean, it only costs so much money to replace a dozen uniforms and then get a few more extras! And besides, we're only shortening it by a few inches – as if the skirt's even a few inches long to begin with – so it shouldn't make that much of a difference, but it will be different, so that's what matters!

Um, hello? That's exactly what we shouldn't do, Corinne.

Apparently she made this whole speech to the girls after getting a sudden inspiration about changing up the uniforms – by shortening them.

Slutty much?

Sophia

Oh, my God. Seriously.

It's almost as if I can't just leave the squad alone for like, five minutes before they all do something drastically stupid and I have to come back again to fix it myself. Oh, yeah, only but this time, it took a while (make that a super long time, actually) to convince all of the girls that it wasn't a good idea for us to try and change the cheerleading uniforms.

All of them were bouncing all over the place, going, "Oh, my God, Sophia, don't you think this is, like, a fabulous idea?"

"Oh, my God, I mean, really?"

"Like, then the guys would so definitely notice and, oh, my God, we'd look so fantastically, incredibly great!"

"Oh, my God!" This one was repeated about ten billion times, let me tell you.

And then there was Corinne. She was standing slightly away from the rest of the girls, with Kellie Hamilton off to the side. And she was going, "Don't you just love the *idea* of it, Sophia?" clearly trying to sound all sophisticated and all 'look at me, I just came up with a better idea than the captain of the squad' – just for show.

God. I could have slapped her for that just then. I really could have. But I wouldn't have. If that makes any sense.

But get this, Corinne: no, I don't love it. Oh, and did I mention…

"No, I don't think so."

This brought forth a chorus of sad responses. Oh, dear. I don't care.

"What's wrong with it? Tell me what's wrong with it."

Yeah, guess who came up with that last one? Three guesses: Corinne, Corinne, Corinne.

But let me remind you of this once again: it's not like I hate her now. But like I've mentioned only so many times before, Corinne Carlton has ways that just tend to tick me off. Her attitude that can get way out of hand, her habit of being such a chatterbox, her lack of a mute button (just kidding), and so much more about her.

But I try to tolerate her, really, I do.

It just isn't easy.

Brooke

"What's wrong with it? Tell me what's wrong with it."

When she said that, I really wanted to walk up to her, look her in the eye, give her a hearty slap across the face, and tell her, "You don't talk to your captain like that." Because seriously? You don't talk to your captain like that. It's just a fact. It's true.

And then Sophia was totally ticked. I know when she's irritated. Believe me. And this time? She was a little beyond ticked off at Corinne.

You know, I never really disliked that girl. She just tends to drive us all a little crazy, is all. Really.

But Sophia went, "First of all, it's not in our budget. And second of all, what's the point of doing that?"

The rest of the girls looked a little sheepish.

"Oh, right, I'm sorry, I forgot. My deepest apologies. You want the boys to notice you're dressed a little more slutty than usual. But allow me to enlighten you: that only makes our sport look bad. And maybe you care more about looking like that, but I will not tolerate a single bit of it, okay?" Sophia turned away to her gym locker and shielded her hands before she started to work the combination lock.

Righteous!

"God, Sophia," one of the girls said.

Corinne added in, "Besides, it would totally help improve our cheering. I mean, we would so have a better range of, like, flexibility, since less uniform would affect our bending back less. I don't see why you won't just accept that."

Sophia swung her locker open and then wheeled around.

"Look, if nobody wants to support me on this issue, then be my guest. Go to Coach Sanders, be stupid, and tell her all about your little idea. You'll see how she won't support you, either."

That's when I stepped in. I mean, what's a girl gotta do in this situation? Support her best friend, all the way, thank you very much. "I'm with you, Sophia."

"Thank you, *Brooke*," Sophia says pointedly, "for your kind show of support of the *right* side." We both looked to Kellie for help, but she stepped away and said, "I'm not in this," before going off to her locker.

Corinne shrugged. "Well, all right, then. Whatever. But you're going to have to explain that to them." She gestured towards the rest of the squad. "Sorry, girls, but I guess it's just tough luck."

"Tough luck?" Sophia repeated angrily. "I'm not doing any explaining. You're the one who put that idea into their heads, so you can do the explaining, Cor*rine*."

Corinne's mouth dropped open. "But I – "

"No buts. I don't want to hear it. Just go get dressed. All of you. Unless, of course, you want to be late to practice."

Sophia

Hmm.

Well, the girls seem to have completely dropped the issue with the uniforms, just as I wanted them to. But I have a feeling that Corinne isn't going to give up so easily. She might be even stupider than I thought, and end up taking this to Coach Sanders. And that would not be pretty for me.

So I guess all I'll have to do now is just go to Coach Sanders later and talk to her about this whole issue. If I remember, of course.

All of this stuff. Seriously. Arguing with one of my subjects (no offense). And so much more than that.

It's enough to drive a girl like me stir crazy.

Unless I already am.

Brooke

I really can no longer deal with this.

I mean, I know Rihanna was totally right when she told one of those magazines, "Let's just say that you find out who your true friends are when you start having success."

And I know that Daphne never was going to be a friend of mine. But wasn't that expected? And shouldn't I be able to go on with something so trivial as cheerleading and not have to worry about being terribly injured, or worse, killed?

I mean, even now I have to take a different route home just in case one of those two tries to jump me or something on my way. I've been doing this for a while now. Since they're suspended (even if it has been six full school days since they were first kicked out, but whatever), and all, they're off school grounds. Which, of course, means that they could be waiting somewhere for any one of the four of us.

How creepy…

And I really hadn't thought about it much for a while. There was so much to think about. We had that incredible weekend. And then Miss Halitelli and Mr. Romero's engagement party on Tuesday (so sweet), plus Sophia lent me the whole *Mediator* series to read, and I was totally occupied with that, schoolwork, and spending time with Sophia, Brett, and Trevor. And last night we had a game against Lodi Valley, along with the snotty Lodi Valley cheerleaders to deal with. But every time I walk home, I spend at least a few seconds worrying that they're going to jump out at me.

It's almost like way back when…Trevor and I used to play hide-and-seek with a few other kids. And they all used to jump out at me and I'd get so scared. I hated that game. And Trevor completely understood, so we never played it again, except when it was completely unavoidable. He was always a good kid.

But I still feel like I'm seeking. It's creeping me out…

Anyway. I still need to stay tuned in to the present.

Sophia finally catches up to me on the slushy sidewalk. She's been calling my name for quite some time now. But I haven't responded.

I don't really think I want to be alone right now. It's just that I'm really getting so sick of this situation.

All of it.

And I'm really starting to hate myself because of it. Which is so not a good thing, I would imagine.

"What's the matter with you?" she asks, studying my face intently.

I take a deep breath.

Why shouldn't she know? I'm going to have to tell her anyway if I end up wanting to quit. And it doesn't make it any more of her problem than it already was.

"Look, Sophia, I don't know about you, but I'm kind of getting sick of this whole cheerleading thing. And the competition. You know?"

She bites her lip for a second, seemingly pondering.

This is so not going anywhere.

I mean, duh.

I just know it by the way she's acting so confused.

"Competition," she repeats. "Competition?"

There ya go.

"Well, yeah. With the cheerleading."

She has a weird look on her face. As if she still doesn't quite understand what I'm getting at. "Brooke, cheerleading is not only about helping our team win. Even if it is part of the point. But we're also supposed to be better than the other team's squad. I mean, duh. You knew that already."

Yeah, I did.

Obviously.

That *was* a 'duh' moment.

But that's so not what I meant.

"Yeah, I knew that. Duh. But I meant the competition with people in our school. People who should be supporting the team as a whole. Like a real team. You know what I mean," I respond.

"*Oh*," she finally says, like she gets what I'm saying. "Brooke, Brooke, Brooke. I know Corinne didn't exactly see eye-to-eye with us on that whole thing about changing the tank for the uniform to be smaller instead of a full-length top. But you've got to let go of it. It seriously doesn't matter."

Okay…

Not what I was thinking…

"Coach Sanders is probably going to agree with me about keeping the uniforms we have the way they are at the moment. Besides, we don't exactly have a budget that would allow us to spend like that, so I doubt it would even have been able to happen, anyway. There is absolutely nothing to worry about, Brooke. Just give it up. That's not going to be a problem at all in the future, I can promise you." She holds up her left hand in the air and waves her pinky around for a bit.

That's supposed to represent a pinky promise, I'm guessing?

Oh, and why should *I* give it up? I wasn't that worked up about it. I don't really care. I guess.

But before she can continue, I interrupt. "Not that."

"And seriously, I really don't think the administrators would have really flown for an idea like that, since all it does is show some more skin, make less of a uniform, cost more money for replacements, and it has absolutely no motive. There's no way it would improve anything, except a few of the girls' chances of getting a guy. But that doesn't even affect Cor, so I don't see why she even bothered trying that.

"I mean, she said that it would improve our cheering since we would have a better range of flexibility by less uniform affecting our bending back. As if that really would have worked anyway. I mean, seriously. It's like she didn't even think before she proposed that to the rest of the squad."

Sophia rolls her eyes super dramatically and waves her hands around some more. A little too much.

"Sophia…?"

She's so not even listening.

Maybe she's got some steam to let off, too.

But it's just too bad she's letting it off on me at what could really be my weakest moment.

"And then all of the girls thought it was a totally great idea. I mean, what's not to love about making the micro-mini's complement micro to match? Plus they get to show off some more skin, especially if we make the micro-mini a little more micro to match! Micro-mini, and a micro tank. What could be better?

"Not like they're trying to be slutty, of course. That's not what they're trying to get across, but what do they want to accomplish by doing that? I seriously don't get it. And it's kind of sad how it was just me and you saying that there was absolutely no point in doing anything like that.

"Even if Kellie was kind of unsure about what she should do in that kind of situation. I guess it was a pretty tough decision. I mean, side with the captain of the squad and her best friend?"

Aww…

I did catch that.

Her best friend.

I have to admit it:

I feel good about that.

And why shouldn't I?

But still.

That's no reason to forget anything else I was thinking before…

Which was about my whole issue with this stupid cheerleading jealousy business that's getting way too out of hand.

Sophia, Sophia.

Can't she pay at least a little attention to me?

I'm the one who was acting all depressed, wasn't I? She asked me what was the matter and now?

She's the one ranting!

"Sophia!"

No response to that.

"Or side with your best friend? Your best friend isn't as super-well-liked as the captain of the squad and her best friend are. I mean, they're only the most popular girls in, like, the entire school.

"She should totally have sided with us, but I guess staying neutral was the best thing to do. I guess that I never really thought of it that way, though. How stupid of me." She smacks the side of her head with her right hand.

I stop short and grab her hand to stop her from slapping herself again.

She stops for a second.

But she totally is going to keep talking anyway. She probably thinks I want to tie my shoe or something. As if. I'm wearing ballet flats.

"But then again, if I hadn't, like, been the mediator of everything, this whole issue might have gone a little further, and that's so not good, you know? Because then Coach Sanders might think that I'm not fit for this position as cheerleading squad captain, since I didn't stop Corinne – not that we'd actually get her in trouble or anything – from poisoning – oh, not literally, of course – the minds of every single girl on the squad with the idea of changing our uniforms not even drastically and then that would *not* be good. Who knows? I mean, she might even think that she needs to replace me."

Yawn, Sophia.

Yawn.

"And I'm sure she'd pick you to be the new captain, but the basketball season's going to be over pretty soon, and then that's it. So there really would be no point in her replacing me. It would just cause more drama, and then my social life would be like, down the drain, and things would be so weird with Corinne and then with Kellie and then all the girls on the squad and then everything great would be over for me, and therefore for you, too. And oh, my God, that would be absolutely terrible. Don't you think?"

She's wriggling her hand around and still waving with the left hand – the one that I don't have a totally secure hold on.

"Sophia!" I say, this time even louder.

She turns back to look at me and completely stops with all of the weird, energetic hand movements.

Finally.

And she thought *I* was getting worked up over it.

"What?"

"That's not what I meant," I answer, speaking slowly so that maybe this time she'll understand.

"Huh?"

Or, then again, maybe not.

"I'm talking about…you know. Our evil nemesis."

"Oh!" Realization really does dawn on her face this time.

It's about time.

"But what about her?"

Sigh.

"Well, him, too. But what my point was…"

"Mmhmm. Go on."

I sigh.

How do I say this?

"Doesn't it all bother you? Just one tiny little bit? I mean, think about it. We can't even do something as simple as *cheerleading* without worrying about Daphne or Jackson or someone trying to hurt us in the process. Doesn't it seem so wrong to you? I mean, you seem to feel so indifferent about it. Doesn't it affect you?"

Pause, pause.

"Well, yeah, I guess so. But what do you think we can do about it? I mean, thinking seriously?"

She has a point.

"I don't know," I admit. "But to me this is so not how I had imagined being on the squad."

"Oh. Oh, really?"

She doesn't sound too thrilled at all.

Or as concerned about my mental health as she was at the beginning of our whole little exchange.

"Well. Then how *did* you imagine it, Brooke?"

"Well, I don't know, but look. Think about gymnastics. It's definitely as competitive as this whole cheerleading thing is here, if not even more competitive, but there's no impact on your actual performance by anyone else."

I glance at Sophia.

She's listening intently. In fact, she's even nodding her head from side to side, in addition to up and down. Like she can't really make up her mind about what she wants to think of this.

I think that whole cheerleading uniform issue really did take a major toll on her nervous system.

Not good.

Better take advantage of her attention while I've still got it.

I quickly continue. "It's all you out there solo. No others helping you – or interfering. People can see your real talent. When you aren't worrying about being hurt while doing something you love."

"Well, then, okay. So?"

"So what?"

"Let's do it then."

"Do what? There's nothing we can do. It's too late, isn't it?"

"Well, maybe you're right and we can't quit cheering, but we can create a new team, can't we?"

"Oh, my God! A gymnastics one?"

"Well, duh, right? But you'd be in charge of it, though, you know?"

"Well, yeah, okay, I guess," I say slowly. "But do you seriously think that would work out?"

"Why wouldn't it work? A gymnastics team has got to be something that would appeal to a lot of girls. Especially if *we're* working on it."

Self-centered (a bit) but totally true.

"Yeah, but is it even allowed?"

I do have my list of doubts, after all.

"Who cares? I mean, I'm assuming that all we've got to do is run it past the administrators. And we're already such good friends with all of them now."

"Yeah, okay."

"Besides, I think there used to be a team, but it just got disbanded because there weren't enough...people. So I think if we can bring it back and make it more popular, then we'll be absolutely fine."

"Okay. Let's go."

We wheel around and walk straight past Brett and Trevor just as they finally catch up to us.

Time to head back to school and catch those educational executives before they leave for home.

"Wait, what just happened?"

"What's with the retreat to school?"

Sorry, boys.

You arrived too late for an answer.

Brett

Hmm.

I can't even think of a reason why Sophia and Brooke would

want to head back to school. Especially after they just had cheerleading practice, which I understand was very tiring for the two of them.

Corinne Carlton came up to Trevor and me right after practice ended, since we happened to be hanging out around her boyfriend, Brandon Sullivan, and told us about some crazy issue with changing up their cheerleading uniforms.

I don't know what the whole change was going to be about, and similarly I have no clue why Sophia and Brooke were so adamant about not changing it. Maybe the budget? Oh, well, not my problem. They obviously have it covered on their own. And they don't need any help from Trevor or me.

But whatever it is that's going on at the moment, Trevor and I have got to play along like we know what's happening. Not that we do, of course.

Even if that does mean returning to school.

Sophia

Wow.

Brooke and I just came up with the most fantastic idea.

And that's why we're returning to Principal Walker's office. Yes, again. But it has been a week, so I think this is a perfectly fine idea. And since she loves us so much (Brooke, Trevor, Brett, and me, I mean), I'm almost positive that she would agree to having a gymnastics team right away.

Brooke seems so excited about it. She's practically flying to school. I guess she really was starting to dislike only doing cheerleading.

But that's why I don't want to mention the possibilities to her.

The possibilities of the all the complications, that is.

Trevor

I'm tired enough. I don't need to end up chasing my friends back to school after a very exhausting basketball practice. Yeah, despite the fact that we had another great victory last night (that makes two in a row, folks, since I've been on team), Coach still calls for practice every day. Sad.

But I really want to know what's so urgent that's forcing us all to return to school. It can't be the uniform thing that Corinne mentioned in front of Brett and me. But then again, maybe it could be.

"Sophia!" I call.

Brooke's too far ahead of us. She's practically hopping. And that only makes me wonder even more about what she's so excited for.

Makes me wonder. Hmm. That's a name of a song.

Anyway.

Sophia slows down just enough so we can catch up to her.

"What?"

"What's going on?"

"Oh. We're going back to meet up with Principal Walker."

"Again?" Brett asks, sounding much more than very disappointed. I guess he was expecting something better. "We went last week."

"Yeah. But this time we've got a different issue to deal with. We want to create a new team."

I can't believe my ears. Maybe that could be because it's so random. A new team? What could she be talking about?

"A new team?" I repeat, completely confused.

She nods. "Yeah."

"And you mean what by that?" Brett asks in a jumble of words.

She raises an eyebrow at him and gives him a weird look.

I do the same, only not on purpose.

"What I *mean* is," she corrects him significantly, "we really want to make a school gymnastics team."

Brett

Bombshell!

Gymnastics team?!

That's definitely something new.

Something no one else in our school would have thought of trying to make. I mean, I'm sure there are a lot of girls that are probably into gymnastics and would love a way to showcase their talents in that area.

But no one has mentioned anything like that.

Trust it to Sophia and Brooke to come up with it.

But that whole idea of going to see Principal Walker? What's with that?

Trevor isn't thinking the same thing, I'm guessing, or he would have asked precious little Sophia about it.

"Brett?"

I must be giving Sophia a weird look.

"Yeah?"

"What's up with you?"

"I don't get why you have to go to see Principal Walker," I admit, hoping that maybe she'll explain.

As was expected…

"Oh. Well, isn't that simple?"

"Not to me...?"

"Well, okay, yeah, but in order to create a new team for Saffrondale High School's sports department, one must go through the administration for approval."

What!?

Why?

"But it's just a gymnastics team!" I say indignantly.

She gives me a withering look.

What did I do!?

"It's not just some insignificant little team, Brett," she explains.

Oh.

Oops.

I didn't mean to dis one of her favorite things.

"Yeah, yeah, yeah, I know. Sorry. Carry on."

No such luck.

I'm not going to be let off so easy.

She rolls her eyes. "You're forgiven, but don't do that again. Basketball isn't the only important sport out there, you know."

"I know. I didn't mean to do that. All I meant was that gymnastics is so, I don't know, innocent. Why would you have to get it approved?"

"Because others might want to create some random type of club or team, and it must be approved by the administrators. I don't know. That's just the way things are, Brett. Accept it and move on."

"I'm moving, I'm moving."

Trevor laughs.

We finally reach the school, where Brooke's been waiting at the main entrance, fidgeting beyond control.

I don't know if I've ever seen her this excited. It's kind of scary. But not necessarily bad, I guess. I'm not used to her being so hyper, is all.

"Going in," Sophia says, and then she turns her head toward Trevor and me. "You guys want to come?"

I throw my hands up in the air in exasperation. "No, Sophia, we don't. We just followed you two halfway home and then back here for no absolute reason. I think we would just love to sit here and wait."

Sophia raises an eyebrow at me and crosses her arms across her chest, obviously thinking, 'You wanna mess with me?'

Brooke giggles.

I appreciate this show of a sense of humor.

Cough.

Brooke, not Sophia.

"Of course we're coming with you!" Trevor exclaims as a translation of what I had been trying to convey.

As if they couldn't figure it out themselves.

Brooke

Miss Warner looks up from her computer screen. "Yes?" There seems to be no warmth in her voice at all.

What a change.

Wonder what happened recently to drop her good mood down the drain…

"We're here to see Principal Walker," Sophia announces.

Miss Warner's eyebrows fly up.

Again.

It's almost like we went into instant replay of the scene that took place the last time we entered this office.

Except that instead of it being instant as in a few seconds ago, that one took place exactly a week ago.

Not much of a difference.

"Again?" Miss Warner asks, as if it's a pain for us to be here.

Not that we drank up that many of the soda cans. It was only four – one for each of us. But then again, it's four missing.

Oops.

I nod. "Yes, Miss Warner, again. We're sorry if it's an inconvenience to you, but it *is* kind of an important matter, you know."

That does it.

Miss Warner about shoots up out of her chair and she hurries over to the glass door to let us into the secretaries' area.

Trevor and Brett smile and elbow each other.

Whatever.

Not attempting to understand their little minds. No offense meant, of course, but they can act so immature sometimes.

Mrs. Carson observes us closely from her desk, where she's eating out of a cup of yogurt. She stares at the four of us, very carefully dropping Reese's Pieces (I think that's what those orange, brown, and yellow little candies are) into her yogurt. Stare she will, but she still says absolutely nothing.

Miss Warner, on the other hand, starts babbling insanely. "Oh, no, no, no, girls, not at all. I'm sorry. It's been a very hectic day, you know."

My heart just melts with sympathy for her.

Hectic?

Please.

Nothing doing.

Trevor

Now that we're finally done explaining that the four of us need to see Principal Walker about a very important and extremely confidential issue (God, that Miss Warner's just a little nosy, not to mention that she thinks that she's so important after having caught Daphne and Jackson traipsing through the halls and sending them off to the deep and depressing wallows of wherever they're going to go now that they've been suspended – but what she doesn't know is that they'll probably go off to the Village or something to spend their time together), we can sit in the waiting area.

Because just our luck, Principal Walker has an appointment that just arrived about three minutes ago.

And now we should be sitting here for quite some time.

Waiting, waiting, waiting.

Sophia, Brooke, why must you do this *now*!?

"Can't this wait?"

Oops.

Sophia

I am beyond hurt.

I mean, seriously, how could Trevor not see eye-to-eye with me? Especially over something like this?

"Trevor! Don't you see how much this means to both of us?"

"Yeah, sorry, I didn't mean it."

Brooke comes to our defense, although I can't exactly say that I admire her methods, no matter how much this gymnastics team may mean to her. "Yeah, well, you *better* not have meant it."

Brett smiles.

But Trevor hurries to prove himself.

"I don't. I mean, I didn't. Really. I'm sorry."

"It's okay." I can't help forgiving him. After all, he really does sound regretful. But besides all that, he's just too cute. "Don't worry about it."

"But Sophia, how can I not?"

I glance up at him, fully prepared to throw him a weird look. It seems that I've been using up my entire supply of them lately. But then again, everyone keeps acting so freakishly.

And then I realize he's just kidding.

My eyebrows shoot up.

The three of them smile.

Ha, ha.

Not funny.

I roll my eyes at them. "Hilarious," I say sarcastically.

Trevor doesn't even flinch. "I know."

I start to shake my head at him, but then we are so very blessed by being joined by Miss Warner.

"Principal Walker is ready to see you now," she tells us.

At last.

Brett

"You wanted to see me?"

No, duh, Principal Walker.

No offense meant, either.

Although that seems to be all Trevor and I can do lately. Make insulting comments to our friends, that is.

But at least now I know to keep my mouth shut. I mean, it's one thing to dis my friends, who I know won't bother to take me seriously, but it's a completely different idea to say something mean to the principal of my high school.

Very, very different.

I mean, look how easily she got those two delinquents (ha, ha) suspended! Let me just tell you that I'm anything but scared. Note the sarcasm.

"Yes, Principal Walker, we did." Sophia has her hands folded on her lap, and her legs crossed. She's looking very professional, except for her general appearance. Let's just say cheerleading practice didn't do much good for her hair. The ends are now a little more droopy than they were before.

And the outfit is a little more wrinkly, but that's probably because it was stuffed up inside her gym locker twice today, and that was definitely done so in a hurry. I wouldn't have noticed anything like that except Sophia's just that type of person who's very touchy about her clothes and her fashion and hair and whatever. I'm sure we all know that only too well from that day Jackson attacked her before school.

Only a week and a half ago (maybe not even) , but now it feels like it was so incredibly *long* ago.

But anyway.

That would make it Brooke's turn to speak up now…

"You see," Brooke begins, her eyes all wide and innocent and it looks like she's trying to earn some pity.

I don't know why.

And besides, it's all fake, fake, fake, but as long as it works, it's all good.

I guess.

"When I first tried out for the cheerleading squad, which was only a few days ago," she continues, "I really wanted to do gymnastics outside of my own home, since performing for myself was getting to be way too boring. And I needed an extracurricular."

"Understandable," Principal Walker murmurs with what she clearly wants to seem like an encouraging smile. And I guess it is, in a way, but whatever. "But go on, dear, go on."

Understandable?

What's *that* supposed to mean?

"So I thought that maybe, just maybe, cheerleading would be like gymnastics, you know?"

Principal Walker nods. "Yes, that's what I would have thought as well." She pauses, too. "Isn't it, though?"

Brooke holds up a hand. "Yeah, see, that's the catch. It is, but only in a way. I mean, cheerleading itself is gymnastics and dance. Kind of. And then you've got the cheering, of course. But after two games' worth of cheering here at Saffrondale High, I realized that there's something else in cheerleading. At least, here at Saffrondale High School, there is. And it's not a good thing."

Principal Walker is now sitting on the edge of her chair, madly interested in what Brooke is saying.

And I am, too.

But what is she talking about?! What else is there…?

Division among the members of the squad? Because I didn't really notice that. It's all in my head.

I think.

"There is just way too much…" Brooke pauses for dramatic effect.

Too much? Too much *what*!?

"Competition."

What!?!?

Trevor

Competition. Hmm. Well, I guess Brooke has got a point. Somewhat.

Competition as in all those girls that showed up to try out for that one tiny opening on the squad. I witnessed that first-hand.

And then Daphne.

And that whole thing that happened at our last game. Not last night's, of course. But the one before that? Definitely a problem.

Okay, so maybe there is a lot of competition.

And if you think about it, that's kind of sad. I mean, high school cheerleading? Get over it.

"Competition?" repeats Principal Walker, sounding kind of confused.

Get with it, Principal Walker.

"Yes," Brooke insists patiently. "You know, like Daphne Carlisle being so competitive with me about the cheerleading squad–"

"And how she took such desperate measures to try and push her way onto the cheerleading squad for so many years," Sophia finishes.

Principal Walker nods. "I still don't see where all of this is going, girls," she says, a crease forming on her forehead. "This is all information I knew already."

"Yes," Sophia begins, "but–"

Principal Walker glances at her watch.

Oh…

Time to get home for dinner?

But it's only half past four.

Not even.

"Okay." Brooke sighs. "All we want is to create a gymnastics team."

Brooke

Am I asking so much of Principal Walker? I mean, really?

Look at this.

I just told her all that we ask of her.

"All right."

Wait.

What!?

Did we seriously just get approval? Just like that?

"What?" Sophia gasps.

Apparently she's just as surprised as I am.

And she can't believe her ears, either.

"I approve. Go ahead. But I'm warning you now: it's up to you to find a coach, find equipment, and get this team started. It's all up to you, girls, but if you can do it, I'll support you all the way through."

Makes no sense to me, but all right, I'll take it.

"Yes! Thank you so much, Principal Walker! I swear that you won't regret this!" Sophia squeals and jumps out of her chair.

Maybe she was more excited than I was.

Trevor and Brett quickly stand up, too, and Sophia and I shake hands with Principal Walker, who looks so happy to see us go (well, look, I don't care at all, as long as we've gotten our approval). Trevor and Brett merely nod their thanks, which is just as well, I guess, considering that they didn't really even need to come with us. It was nice of them to add in their support.

"One more thing," Principal Walker calls, just as we open the door.

"Yes?" I let the door swing shut.

I mean, I totally just caught a glimpse of Mrs. Carson and Miss Warner craning their necks out to try and hear what's going on inside the office. No way am I going to let them hear anything. It's not that I don't like them or anything like that, but I don't want any information about this new team going around the school, as it tends to happen with any other information that these secretaries hear.

Nosy secretaries.

"What kind of gymnastics team is this?"

What kind?

What is she talking about?

And then I realize that she's looking in the direction of Brett and Trevor.

"Oh, no," I stutter, glancing at them, too.

Trevor finally gets what we're hinting here.

"No, we're not involved with this at all," he says. "We just came by with these two for moral support."

Brett offers one of his dazzling smiles.

Enough to melt her heart?

Okay, so maybe not.

But it's definitely enough to melt mine any day.

Sophia

Oh, my God!

I can*not* believe this.

We got the approval.

So easily, too.

It was like, "Oh, hey, uh, Principal Walker, we kind of want to make a gymnastics team," and then, "Oh, okay, honey, sure thing. Whatever you want to do is completely fine by me."

Oh, my God!

How perfect!

Now all we have to do is all that stuff that Principal Walker mentioned.

And let me tell you, it is a lot. I mean, we can't expect to have a team at all if we miss any of these points.

We'll have to spread the word about this new team. All the advertising will be up to us. And then we're going to have to organize tryouts, requirements, and all of that. not to mention find all the equipment that we're going to need.

Oh, and there's that other little thing that might be just a teensy, tiny bit important in a case like this...

We've got to find a coach. Someone who knows about gymnastics. And I guess that would probably be Coach Sanders.

Speaking of Coach Sanders...I've got to tell her about that whole uniform issue. No one mentioned anything about it during practice. There was simply no time for it. We were just way too busy practicing.

Oh, yeah, and another thing that's been bothering me and I just have to get off my back? After those snotty Lodi Valley girls were all, 'You suck, your squad isn't even united, your school sucks,' blah, blah, blah, I can't stand them – plus I've been wanting to do something to make our high school better. I mean, they aren't even that great at cheering. Their routines are clearly off the internet. They're the ones that suck, not us.

And okay, so maybe we *have* got *some* issues, but they're only because of Daphne Carlisle. But that matters not.

Did I mention that they were like, "You don't even have a gymnastics team," too? That's going to change, girls. And we'll beat you in the high school gymnastic team meets. Sorry, Mr. Winston Romero. But even if you and Miss Halitelli are going to be married soon, I think she'll still show spirit for her school. Not as much for yours.

But the gymnastic meets, of course, are something that Saffrondale High School has never participated in.

And now I think it's time we made some kind of difference with that.

Oh, yeah, and by that, I don't mean getting stuffed in a closet and fainting under a bunch of pompoms.

I just can't seem to let go of that, now, can I?

Brett

Well, they got the approval for the new team.

And I've got to say that I'm so proud of them.

Then again, I guess I really don't understand the profundity or profoundness or whatever it is of this whole situation.

But I do know that it's an occasion for us to celebrate.

"Who's up for Giordano's?"

Trevor

Poor, poor Brett.

Apparently he doesn't realize what time it is.

I mean, it's still only a quarter to five.

I mention this to him.

"Yeah, I know that, buddy. I meant, like the garlic bread and mozzarella sticks, or something," he responds smoothly. "But only if you guys want to, obviously."

"Oh."

Smooth.

Brooke is shooting furtive glances at Sophia.

It's been a while since she's looked at me like that. You know. That look that best friends exchange all the time.

Or maybe I'm just so used to it that I haven't noticed it at all anymore.

I like the last choice better.

But I can't help wondering what she's spazzing out in her mind about.

Brooke

I keep thinking that Brett would be grabbing every possible chance he could get to go out. But he was totally cool with everything. I've got to remember that. Even if part of me keeps wishing desperately that he would be on my heels and all that. I don't know why. But I do know that I have to get over this whole 'Oh, Brett, I just can't go out with you' thing. Otherwise, time is going to go so fast that he'll meet some hot girl and my chance will be gone before I know it. I can't let that happen. I just can't. He means too much to me right now. And he will for a while. If not always.

Sophia sighs. "I don't know, Brett. I kind of want to go home."

Trevor nods. "I have a bunch of stuff to do for Telecom. When I signed up for that class, I thought it wouldn't be that bad.

But it's no joke. Sorry, Brett."

Brett nods understandingly. "No, it's cool. So are we off?"

I shake my head. I swear my voice is going to be shaking, but whatever. I can try to sound casual. It's not like I'm asking him out. I'm saving that for the end of the drama. As like a closing for it.

But for the time being…

"Well, I'll go if you want to, Brett."

Brett

Wow.

I didn't think that of all people, *Brooke* would opt for breadsticks at Giordano's with me. Never would I have expected that, but when she wants to, I'll take it.

"Cool."

Trevor says, "I'm going home. 'Bye."

Sophia nods. "Yeah, me, too. See you guys tomorrow."

They separate and go in different directions, leaving me with Brooke.

"Let's go." She starts walking off ahead of me.

I can't think of this as anything more than what it should be. It's not even important. It's no big deal.

But somehow this 'no big deal' equals one very happy Brett.

Sophia

So I really want to plan for this team – Oh, my God! Brett totally distracted me! He had to bring up Giordano's, and then I completely forgot about going to see Coach Sanders!

I whip out my cell phone and start dialing.

Brooke answers right away. "Hey, Sophia, what's up?"

"Brooke, we totally forgot to go see Coach Sanders about the team and the uniforms!"

"Oh, my God!" Brooke squeals. "We *have* to do that. Are you with Trevor?"

"What? No. He went home."

"Oh. Well, Brett and I are, like, not even that far away from the school. Meet back there?"

I hear Brett groan. "Yeah. Tell Brett I'm sorry. He doesn't have to come with us if he doesn't want to."

There's a small rustling sound, and I hear muffled voices. Brooke must be covering up the phone and conveying the new information to Brett.

"No, he said he'll come," she says.

Fine with me. "Okay. Meet you there in a few."

"Yeah. 'Bye."

"'Bye, Brooke."

Time to go. Good thing I can power walk really fast. We wouldn't want to miss Coach Sanders.

Brooke

"Coach Sanders!" My hands are cupped around my mouth to form a megaphone. "Coach Sanders!"

Sophia runs ahead of me.

I stop and give up.

Brett catches up to me. "No luck?"

I shake my head, totally discouraged. No way I'm chasing after Coach.

Coach disappears down the hallway.

But Sophia doesn't give up. She chases in Coach's tracks and disappears, too.

"So much for that."

Brett pats me on the back. "It's okay. You'll find them later."

"I can't just ditch Sophia!"

"I wasn't telling you to."

"Oh." I take out my cell phone, ready to call Sophia.

He extends a hand, like he's going to stop me. "You want to just wait here? Sophia's probably going to come back here looking for us eventually."

I nod. "Yeah. I guess."

We both collapse against the wall and sink down to the floor. Nothing left to do now but wait.

Sophia

Coach Sanders has got to be deaf. I swear. How else would she not be able to hear me screaming her name and tearing down the hallway?

"Coach!" I yell at the top of my lungs. Well, practically.

She finally stops and turns her head a little. Why can't she hear me!? And then I see the ear-buds in her ears. Oh. That's why.

"Oh, Sophia, it's you."

No, duh. Am I not the only human being in sight, Coach? Or do you see somebody else around here?

"Yeah, Coach, it's me."

"Well…then can I help you?" She asks, shifting her heavy (looking) tote bag kind of uncomfortably.

"Uh, yeah, actually, you can. Brooke, too. But first…can I

help you?" I ask, pointing towards her bag.

She stares at me for a second, looking confused. "What?" But before I can explain myself again, realization dawns across her face (hey, when you're actually really good friends with your English teacher, her fine usage of the language tends to rub off on you – even if she does say 'like' or 'totally' once in a while). "Oh. Oh, sure. Thank you so much, Sophia."

So I take the bag from her.

"Wow. That's a lot."

Coach laughs. "I know. You think I should lighten the work load for my pre-calc students?" she asks.

I nod excitedly. "Definitely."

"I'd love to. It lightens the work load a bit for me, too." She pauses. "But sorry. No can do."

I nod. "Yeah, I figured."

"So." She decides to change the subject. "You mentioned that you and Brooke needed my help with something?"

"Yeah," I say, yet again.

"But Brooke isn't here," she says.

"Right." Finally. A different answer. "She fell behind."

Coach nods slowly. "Okay…"

We've gotten to her classroom.

"Here," she says. "I'll take that now, but thank you very much for carrying it for me. I really appreciate it."

What is she talking about…?

Oh. The bag. I'd almost forgotten that it was there this whole time. Although I really don't see how I could have forgotten about it when it's so heavy. But whatever. We all know that I'm a little crazy. At the very least.

"Right." I hand it over.

"How about you go and catch up with Brooke? Then the two of you can come back here within ten minutes and we'll discuss what you wanted to talk about, okay?"

I nod slowly. "Okay."

Wait.

There's a catch.

"Wait, Coach."

She turns to face me again, swinging the door to her classroom open and propping it open with one foot. "Yes?"

"We brought Brett."

She pauses. And then she sighs and smiles.

I let out a sigh of relief, although I really didn't doubt that she wouldn't mind.

"That's perfectly fine."

Brett

Sophia's been gone for at least ten minutes now. And I know it. I've been keeping watch by using my cell phone. And it's been ten minutes. Or maybe a few more. I might have lost track. But it seems like so much longer than ten minutes. Brooke and I have been sitting side by side in complete silence.

I guess it's really been a long day.

Brooke

"Brooke! Brooke! Hurry up!"

Sophia suddenly appears after her voice – completely out of nowhere.

I spring up from where I've been sitting with Brett. So much for going to Giordano's. "You found her?"

Sophia nods. "Yeah. But we have to hurry up. She said to be back within ten minutes. But we have about six left now."

"Cool. Let's go."

We start to head down the hallway, without a single word to Brett.

"Hey!"

Sophia and I wheel around and start walking backwards so that we can keep an eye on Brett.

"Oh, yeah," Sophia says, all casual, "I almost forgot. Coach said that we could bring you along." Clearly she's talking to Brett and not to me.

"Good," he replies. "I thought that you two were going to just leave me here and forget all about me."

Sophia winks at me. Luckily we're too far away from Brett for him to see. "Well," she calls back slowly, "it *was* tempting, but..." She turns to me with an expectant look.

"No, the truth is, Brett, that we would never do something so mean and...Daphne-like," I finish.

What could I say? He might take me seriously if I went along with Sophia, and that would *so* not be good.

Sophia rolls her eyes at me and turns back around so she can walk normally.

I just shrug back at her.

Brett catches up and squeezes between us so that he can put his arms around our shoulders. "Good to know, Brooke."

Of course, Brett.

I smile.

Good to know.

Sophia

"Oh, hello," Coach greets us with a smile as the three of us walk into the room.

"Hi," Brett and Brooke say simultaneously. What a connected couple. Oops. 'My bad.' Couple-to-be.

"Pull up a few chairs, and then tell me what it is that you wanted to talk to me about."

While we're getting our chairs, Brooke shoots me a furtive look. 'Do something!' her eyes are saying.

She's right. What have we got to lose? I mean, the worst thing that could happen would be Coach refusing to help us. And if that does happen, then whatever. We'll get over it eventually.

I sit down. "Coach, we're going to make a gymnastics team for Saffrondale High. Brooke and me, I mean. Not Brett."

Coach pauses and lays down her grade-book seriously. "Well. That's great. Not one of our school's first, but great."

"We want you to be the coach."

Her eyes widen. "Well. That's – I'm honored, girls, but maybe you – there's some things that you probably would like to know."

Brett

"…There's some things that you would probably like to know."

This is when Brooke and Sophia jump to the edges of their chairs. And this is when I lean back in my seat, knowing that this is going to be a long and boring story. But I've got to listen now or be in trouble later.

"When I was in high school – yes, I did go to Saffrondale High, although that was years and years ago, and different rules applied – I felt that the school needed a gymnastics team as well. So I tried to create one, and it didn't succeed. Not many students joined, since I never publicized tryouts properly, and we didn't do well at all in the meets. I was trying to be the teenage coach and captain, and it wasn't working. So we had to disband the team. Everyone in school heard about it, and let's just say I wasn't applauded for my failure."

Okay. Pretty short and sweet.

Brooke and Sophia exchange a glance. They better not be having second thoughts about this team.

"But I'm not trying to discourage you. But I want you to know exactly what it is you're undertaking."

"But Coach, isn't it like the squad? I mean, Sophia's been doing this for ages. She's picked the dates for tryouts, made important decisions, and been the captain of the squad." Brooke looks really worried. Too worried. But then again, maybe I just don't see the importance of the situation. Once again.

Ms. Sanders nods. "Yes, but it's different. I took charge of my team. And I was one of them, so it didn't work the way it would now. I didn't pick a coach. You made the right decision in picking a coach. But the question is…do you still want me to be your coach?"

Brooke looks at Sophia for help.

Sophia shrugs. "This is your team, Captain Dawson. I'm just your assistant."

Brooke smiles. "Definitely, Coach."

Ms. Sanders smiles. "Then absolutely. I'll help you girls out any way I can."

Finally. They got what they needed.

And I'm glad. Maybe now we can leave the building.

"It's a done deal."

Trevor

Apparently I missed a lot yesterday when I went home. Sophia turned back and went to school again because she'd forgotten about talking to Ms. Sanders, and then Brooke and Brett joined her. I was the only one missing.

But the good news is that Ms. Sanders now not only coaches the cheerleading squad, but will soon be coaching the girls on the gymnastics team. And that means now all Brooke (and Sophia) will have to do is find the equipment and other stuff that they need. Plus, they'll have to order uniforms or costumes or whatever. I wouldn't know much about gymnastics other than what Brooke has wasted her time telling me. And that wasn't much, since she spent most of her time related to gymnastics practicing it, not talking about it. Fine by me. I've never been obsessed with gymnastics like she is. And I guess she doesn't like basketball as much as I do. But that's okay. We're still best friends, and that's what matters.

"Trevor!"

"Hey, Brett. What's up?"

"Nothing. I think we can ditch Sophia and Brooke. They're going to look for gymnastics stuff. And Ms. Sanders is going with them. I don't want to go anymore."

I laugh. Ms. Sanders isn't exactly someone Brett has ever wanted to be friends with like Sophia and Brooke. And I'll admit that she's very nice, but he's got a good point. Plus it's not good for your social reputation. I can just hear them saying, "Oh, my God, Brett Evans, Brooke Dawson, Sophia Garrison, and Trevor

Stevenson went shopping with Ms. *Sanders*. I mean, ew!" And that's annoying. Poor Brooke and Sophia. They don't see it. Or maybe they do and they just don't care about hurting their reputations. It is kind of true. I mean, what could happen to them? They're practically the most heroic students – well, to us, anyway.

"Okay." I put my hands in my pockets. "So where to now?"

"Uh, I don't know. No more basketball. Please."

"Of course not. Practice was enough."

"No kidding."

There's nothing to say.

"So. What now?" I ask.

"I don't know. You want to go and see if anyone's hanging around at Giordano's?"

We'll probably run into Corinne Carlton and Brandon Sullivan. They're usually there together. Plus, Kellie comes along as a third wheel sometimes, but it's all cool with everyone. And since today Sophia and Brooke resolved their issue with the uniforms (which I finally found out more about), things won't be awkward with them.

"Sure."

"Cool. Let's go."

Brooke

"Perfect. This is perfect."

We're at the place where I bought most of the stuff in the shed. Gymnastics World. So maybe it doesn't have a unique name, but it's still a great store.

We found the best uniforms just now. We'll need about twelve, I'm guessing. Maybe fifteen. But those Lodi Valley girls are going to faint when they see how great we are. Not that they're the only reason that I want to do this, of course. I've had plans for a while now. And they are no part of it. Well, okay. Maybe they are. But it's a tiny, totally insignificant part. Nothing major, obviously.

"Awesome!" Sophia exclaims with a smile. "Yellow, gold, and white. Just like our uniforms for cheerleading, for the boys' basketball team, and for everything. The best."

Coach Sanders nods. "Absolutely. How many of these do we need?"

"An estimate?" I ask.

She nods again.

"About fifteen?"

I get a slower nod in response. "Okay. That might work. We're going to need a few extras, though, so make that around eighteen."

"Yeah."

The saleswoman says, "Oh, and there is a discount for schools buying in bulk. And since this is our very own Saffrondale High, we'll make the discount slightly more." She smiles. "Is that a good deal?"

Sophia and I nod. "Absolutely."

Sophia

Wow.

I can't believe that we got all of the uniforms just now! And for such a low price! This is totally fabulous!

Now all we need is…all of the equipment. But like that really matters. First we need to form the actual team, and hold tryouts, and all that. Thankfully, it's only the middle of December. We have plenty of time before the real competitions. Plenty of time to practice. Plenty of time to beat out those Lodi Valley girls.

"Oh, my God, Sophia, this is going perfectly!" Brooke squeals in my ear, catching up to me on the sidewalk.

"I know! It's better than I thought it would be. Especially after what Coach was telling us yesterday. I was really worried then, but now I know things are going to be absolutely fabulous." What else can I say? All of this is so totally true.

"Yeah. So…where are we going now? Back to school again, or what?" she asks.

I have no idea where I'm going. But I guess I am heading in the direction of school, so…

"Yeah. Let's go back. Maybe we can go through the supply closets," I suggest. I'm not ready to go home just yet, even though I don't know why.

She raises one eyebrow at me skeptically. "Seriously?"

I nod. "Yeah. Why not?"

"Oh, no, nothing." A kind of sneaky smile spreads across her face. And her eyes are twinkling. Don't I just know she's going to crack some kind of joke or tease me about something now? "I just didn't think you'd still be interested in nosing around inside supply closets after your last experience inside one of them, you know?"

I roll my eyes at her and say nothing.

Now that I look back at the fight I had with Jackson, it was so stupid and kind of funny, but at the moment, it was so not fun for me. Especially when I should have been cheering in the game while I was getting beaten down. Besides, what kind of guy hits a girl? Not that I'm in favor of being a damsel in distress, or anything. I just thought guys were supposed to be – I don't know.

It was just a rule of society. But whatever.

"Unless, of course," she continues, batting her eyelashes insanely, "you en*joy*ed it." She elbows me with a grin.

I punch her on the shoulder. "As if. You know how much I hate that idiot. Besides, you know that I like Trevor."

Brooke smiles. "Yeah, I know. You told me ages ago."

"Hello? It was so last week!"

She laughs. "Whatever. It seems like forever. Or at least way longer than two and a half weeks that we've been friends."

"Yeah," I say with a nod. "That's true."

"Well, obviously."

Suddenly there's a weird rustling ahead of us.

Brooke glances at me quickly. Her eyes have a fearful look in them. I have to admit it…I'm scared, too. I mean, Principal Walker warned us to be careful out of school. She told us to watch out for Jackson and Daphne…to be alert especially when it was just a few of us.

But it can't be them. It just can't. I mean, I would expect them to be enjoying their time off from school, even if it is suspension. I thought they'd be at the Village. Or maybe even go off on vacation for almost a week.

But I will admit that I've been wondering why they never came back to school. I mean, Principal Walker was saying that she would have suspended them for a week, but she couldn't do that. And if all that was true, then how could they have been missing from school for over a week? That doesn't make any sense. Unless, of course, they skipped school for the past few days, but then the school would have taken action. Besides, I'm sure they wouldn't ever want to pass up a chance to torture us. But then why would they have been laying low for so long? I mean, we haven't heard from them in ages.

"Stop. Don't move."

I know that voice only too well.

Brooke

"We just have a few things to say." Daphne steps out from behind a bush (nice hiding place), flanked by Jackson.

A few things to say. Yeah, right. That means that Sophia and I are going to get beaten up.

I wheel around, totally ready to run.

Sophia grabs me by the shoulder and stops me. "No. Wait."

I give her an incredulous look. "What?!" I seriously can't believe my ears. "Why?"

Her eyes are narrowed, and she isn't looking at me. No, she's got her gaze fixed on Daphne and Jackson. "I kind of want to hear them out."

"What?" I'm tempted to ask her why again, but that's going to sound too retarded. I mean, 'What!? Why? What?! Why?' See? "You're kidding," I say instead.

"Just stay, okay?"

What can I say to that?

Daphne's expression doesn't change. Jackson – well, he looks like an idiot as usual. That's the best word I can use that's somewhat wholesome.

Sophia folds her arms across her chest. I take a step behind her and do the same.

"All right. Shoot."

Jackson tilts his head confusedly – that's the first sign of movement that I've seen him exhibit during this whole exchange of about one minute.

God, I'm getting more paranoid every second.

Daphne bites her lip for a second and then tugs on the zipper of her puffy jacket. "Look. I just wanted to tell you that we're transferring."

"What?" I ask, in spite of myself.

Transferring!?

"We're transferring high schools," Jackson explains, looking so happy that he finally knows something that I don't. Wow. And that's what he knows? It's all I can do now to stop myself from laughing at him and his stupidity. That poor guy.

Wait.

Transferring high schools?!

How can this be true? I mean, never would I have dreamed of this. Oh, sure, I've dreamed of them being expelled, falling off a cliff, or getting married and getting kicked out of school because of it, moving away, but I knew only too well that these were too good to be true.

And now? It's coming true? What is the world coming to?

"Transferring?" Sophia repeats. I know that she's got to be surprised beyond description, but she's not showing it at all. I mean, her face is completely expressionless, with the exception of the coolness that's in her voice and attitude. Compared to her, I probably seem like an overexcited little monkey. Ugh. Not what I want to be in front of my mortal enemy.

"Yeah," Daphne says. "To Lodi Valley. We both live on the border of Saffrondale and Lodi Valley, so it's going to work out."

I can tell Sophia is totally shocked. But all she does is raise one eyebrow. "Oh, really?" is all she seems to be able to say.

Daphne nods, brushing a strand of dark hair out of her eyes.

"Yeah. So we won't be seeing you anymore. Except at the games. Which we'll win, of course."

I smirk. "No, I don't think so. Saffrondale High will always be the best, and that's something you can't change, Daphne."

She smiles faintly.

I've never seen her like this. Never. And I can actually say – truthfully – she looks almost...pretty.

Jackson thinks so, too, obviously. He smiles down at her, but she doesn't see him. She's too busy staring at us.

"So." She sighs. "Where are you two headed?"

I exchange a worried glance with Sophia.

A crease forms between Sophia's perfectly arched eyebrows. Now she looks a little surprised. Like she doesn't know if she should answer or not. "School," she finally manages to choke out.

Now it's Daphne's turn to raise her eyebrows. "Oh. Well, okay. Why?"

A small smile curves up the corner of my mouth. I can't help it. Wait till Daphne finds out what we're planning. She's going to faint.

"We're working on something new," I say, trying to sound mysterious.

One eyebrow goes down. "Oh, really? Like what?" Curiosity burns. Darn. She didn't faint.

See, the thing is, this almost doesn't even sound like the Daphne Carlisle that I've known for so long. I can't believe we're actually having a normal conversation together that doesn't involve any or all of the following: sarcasm, fighting, or poking each other's eyes out.

Oh, my good golly gosh.

Am I dreaming?

Sophia takes over. "We're creating a gymnastics team."

Daphne's eyes practically bug out of their sockets. "A gymnastics team? For Saffrondale High? Really?"

Sophia nods, looking only the tiniest bit smug. And why shouldn't she? I mean, it *was* her idea, even if I'm the one who gets, like, all the credit for it.

"So what do you have to get done at school?" Daphne asks.

"The usual," I say. "Searching for any available equipment, digging through the supply closets…"

She nods. "Yeah, I get it."

I notice that although her voice seems nicer, it sounds… strained. And kind of whiny. Annoying, but I'm trying to tolerate it. I mean, it's so much easier than trying to tolerate the old Daphne. Much, much easier.

"So." God, that scared me. I almost forgot Jackson was standing right next to Daphne. I mean, he's been acting like a statue for the past few minutes. "Want any help?" he asks, flashing a smile.

First one from him that I've seen in ages. Ages…I won't see another for ages longer. I can't say I won't miss it a bit. I think I might. I've gotten so used to the craziness, the havoc that Daphne would wreak along with her boyfriend. But what will Saffrondale High be like without that insanity?

I guess I'll find out.

Brett

"Brett! Trevor!" Corinne squealed across Giordano's hangout area when we first walked into the place. "What's up?" She pulled her jacket off the seat next to her and patted it. "Sit down."

"Nothing, just came to hang out," I said. Trevor and I sat down on two of the bar stools (don't worry, they don't serve teens any alcohol) and ordered sodas.

Brandon just came to join us. "Where you been?" he asks. "You used to come here after Friday practice. You didn't stop by last week."

"Yeah, I know," I say. "But I was tired. And so busy."

He pats me on the back. "Yeah. I know. I understand. But what's up with you guys, huh? Where are Sophia and Brooke?"

Trevor shoots me a look. He clearly doesn't know whether or not we're supposed to tell them about the gymnastics team. I don't, either. I shrug at him. And he shakes his head slightly.

"Oh, I don't know," I say lightly, like it seriously doesn't matter to me. "I guess they'll turn up eventually."

Corinne nods between sips of her Sprite. "Yeah. I'm sure they will."

The main door suddenly swings open, and Kellie Hamilton comes hurrying in, brushing snow off her coat and out of her hair.

Snow?

Corinne jumps up. "Kellie! What's that – snow!? It's finally *snowing* again? But I thought that last time a few weeks ago was going to be all."

Kellie bobs her head, smiling and shaking the snow out of her hair. "Yeah!" she says happily. "Finally! And this is even better than last time! Maybe we'll even have a white Christmas!"

A white Christmas! I love the idea. The first white Christmas of Saffrondale in ages. The first white Christmas for the four of us.

Perfect.

Chapter 10:

This Connection of Ours

Sophia

"A peace offering."

I didn't think Daphne Carlisle would ever allow those words to escape from her mouth.

Not ever.

But here she is now, trying to end our battle.

Yeah, folks, that very same one that seemed like it would never, ever end – not even when we graduated from high school and moved on.

But I guess I was wrong. I mean, maybe it's true that Daphne doesn't have a heart (only a piece of it that belongs to Jackson, ha, ha), but apparently she doesn't mind doing this.

"Okay."

One word. That's all I can say. I mean, what else can I say to that?!

Brooke gives me a weird look.

But what am *I* supposed to do? I've always wanted to be the bigger person in all of this, but I never got the chance. I mean, Daphne got there first. Even if I never expected her to do something like that. But whatever. All I know is that it's over. Totally over. I'm completely through with this fighting.

All I want is to see the light at the end of this tunnel.

And that light can totally be Trevor.

Brooke

I totally didn't expect Sophia to do that. I mean, she just accepted Daphne! I don't care if Daphne's leaving Saffrondale High. She might not be. We don't have confirmation of that. I mean, she's the one who told us. And after all of her cattiness, I have every right to suspect her of lying. Every single right.

So now here we are. We've made it back to school without any incidents, but I can't say that I know how long that's going to last.

Okay. I know I'm being pessimistic, and that I'm definitely holding a grudge, but hello? This girl practically plotted to kill me and Sophia! I'm not being stupid here.

But apparently Sophia knows what she's doing. She seems totally calm, and isn't even keeping one eye on the two of them. Nothing's normal, Sophia. It's just weird.

Can we fill the boys in here?

Trevor

Trust Brooke to ruin a perfectly good conversation. Brett and I were talking to Brandon, Corinne, and Kellie, and then Brooke starts texting me insanely.

From: Brooke_D

omg trevor u r not going 2 blieve this...d & j r here.

xoxo ~BROOKE~

Wait. D & J? That's got to be...Daphne and Jackson. That can't be good. Gotta text her back.

To: Brooke_D

what? did they attack u & sophia?

-Trevor

From: Brooke_D

no but they r being rly nice & they r leaving & OMG its so weird. but r u @ giordano's?

xoxo ~BROOKE~

To: Brooke_D

yeah. that doesn't matter though. & i don't get it. whats going on?

-Trevor

From: Brooke_D

they r going 2 help us. gtg meet u there. dont go anywhere.

xoxo ~BROOKE~

Brett nudges me. Apparently there has been a break in the conversation. Corinne and Kellie are extremely busy discussing something with Brandon. Fine with Brett and me, I guess.

"Who is it?" Brett asks.

Simple answer. "Brooke."

He narrows his eyes for a second. "Oh. Well, what's she saying?"

I show him all of her text messages, scrolling through our conversation.

His eyebrows shoot up. "Hmm. That sounds pretty weird. Why would *they* ever be nice to *us*? It makes no sense."

"But they're leaving," I say. Like that makes any more sense to me than why Daphne and Jackson would be nice to us. Wait. Even *that* makes no sense.

"Leaving," he repeats slowly, obviously thinking this over. "What does she mean by that. I mean, leaving?"

"I don't know," I admit. "Want me to ask her?"

He shakes his head. "No. I think she's done with the texting. You have any idea where they're going now?"

Now it's my turn to shake my head. "I don't think so. I'm guessing that they're heading back to school, though. I mean, that was their original plan. So I would expect them to stick with it."

He nods. "Yeah. I guess. But what does she mean? They're going to help Sophia and Brooke? With what?"

All of a sudden, it makes sense. "They went to school to go through the supply closets in and around the gym. At least, they mentioned it. I remember that."

He tilts his head, confused. "Why? For the gymnastics stuff?"

"Yeah. They wanted to check if the school had any old gymnastics equipment or anything like that."

"So you mean that those two are probably going to help?" he finishes.

I nod. "Yeah. As impossible as that sounds, I guess it's true."

He squints into his half-full glass of Coke, absent-mindedly twirling the straw around. "Yeah. I guess. I mean, they had plenty of time to hurt Sophia and Brooke, but if they didn't do anything yet, then I doubt they're going to do anything at all. I guess we can just forget about it for now. Brooke and Sophia will come by here later, when they're done, and tell us everything. As usual." He smiles.

I smile back and nod. "Yeah. At least, that's what we'll hope for."

Sophia

Wasn't I wondering what Brooke was doing with her cell phone? I figured she was texting, but I didn't know who she was talking to. Probably Brett or Trevor, but whatever. I was too busy being on my guard in case Daphne or Jackson tried something quick. I never know what to expect from those two.

And then my phone vibrates once, the way it does when I get a text message. I flip it open and press a few keys to get to my text message inbox.

Uh-oh. It's a message from Brad.

From: Brad_G

OMG sophia i did it!!!!

brad

Wait. What? I have no idea what he's talking about. I mean, seriously. He could have talked to Ashlynn – oh. That's probably it. Gotta check to be sure. I mean, he might have passed his algebra test. And that matters not at all to me.

To: Brad_G

what?

<3 always, Sophia G

"Oh, my God," Brooke starts grumbling next to me.

"What?" I ask her. "Brad just texted me."

Brooke raises one eyebrow, but she's still glaring. "Yeah, well, Ashlynn just texted me."

Realization dawns over both of us, and we exchange a glance

and turn back to our cell phones to check our inboxes.

"Wait," Daphne says. "Who are you talking about?"

"Our little siblings share a, um, connection," Brooke explains.

"Oh."

Jackson puts an arm around Daphne. Ha, ha. That's their connection.

Yes! I have another message from Brad!

From: Brad_G

i asked ashlynn out!!!!

Brad

Oh. My. God.

What!?!? That is so not fair. My little brother gets his dream date before I do!? This is so messed up. But wait. She might not have said yes. Oh, yes. That is so good.

To: Brad_G

well yay 4 u but did she say yes?

<3 always, Sophia G

I'm so mean. But whatever. He should not get praise for that. Well, okay. Maybe he should. It's not his fault Trevor hasn't asked me out yet. God. That is so not cool.

Brooke squeals all of a sudden.

"What?" Daphne and I ask at the same time. We both exchange a glance and then look away. Not cool if we're saying stuff at the same time. I mean, she's still the meanest person I have ever met. Ugh.

"Oh, my God!" Brooke shrieks.

"What did she say?" I ask, trying not to sound too impatient. I can't lose my cool here. Not with Daphne and Jackson around.

"Brad asked her out!" she exclaims, looking both shocked and happy. "Yes! Now she won't be on my case about it! No more, 'Oh, Brooke, please help. I don't know what to do about him.'" She makes a face.

I punch her on the shoulder playfully. "Come on, Brooke. Be nice. She's your sister."

"Yeah, I know. And I still love her. But all I'm trying to say is that she's a little annoying. You would know. You said Brad's been driving you crazy lately."

"Yeah, thanks to your little sister!"

She laughs. "I know. But still. Like I said, you would know."

"I wouldn't," Daphne says all of a sudden, sounding kind of…wistful? "I've always been an only child."

Oh. Ha. That might explain the way she acts like a spoiled brat all the time. She probably *is* one.

"Oh. I'm sorry," Brooke says. Why is she being so nice?

Then again, I've been exactly the same. And it's okay. We're doing the right thing, even if it doesn't feel completely right. That's just because we're so used to being, well, nasty.

How rude.

~ Chapter Ten ~

Brooke

Oh, my God.

I cannot believe that Brad, Sophia Garrison's younger brother, asked *my* little sister, Ashlynn, out on a date. After all this time (okay, so it hasn't been that long, but still – it feels like it), too. How cute.

But the thing that's even better?

"Well? What did she say to him? He hasn't answered my last text."

Trust Sophia to interrupt my monologue (I think that's what it's called).

"She said yes."

"Oh, my God!" Sophia squeals at the top of her lungs. "This is so fabulous!"

I smile. "I know!"

Sophia whips her cell phone back out and starts texting like mad. I catch a glimpse of what she's typing over her shoulder.

To: Brad_G

OMG im SO happy!!!!!

<3 always, Sophia G

My phone plays a little musical sound – the one that always plays every single time I get a text message.

From: Ashlynn_D

now 4 brett & u 2 go out 2nite when brad & i do? i think thatd work better like if we told mom & dad that we r doubl d8ing u kno? plz brooke if not 4 u or brett what abt just 4 me?

<3 ashlynn

I'll admit that I did think of this, too, but Brad is just one of those kids that's totally innocent – at least, that's what he seems to be. Our parents met him already, and believe me, they absolutely love the guy. But it's true that they might not exactly fly with the idea of Ashlynn going out with him, but they'll give in. Believe me. I am so not needed in this situation. But Ashlynn has other plans. I think. I mean, she was so mad when I was talking to her the other night. Of course she's a very smart girl – I mean, she's my sister, duh. She's tricking me into doing something that I wouldn't do on my own. That little sneak. But she knows that she can totally guilt me into doing what she wants. I can just hear her. "But Brooke, I came all this way and you won't help me get what I want? How could you do this to me? I'm your only little sister – and your best sister ever! Even if it is only by default, but still! Please!?"

I don't know what to say. She's so right.

Oh, there's another message.

From: Ashlynn_D

cmon brooke i know u r so thinking that

u dont want 2 but u do PLZ

<3 ashlynn

Okay. Obviously this is something that I've got to do. All right, Ashlynn. This one is so for you. Not me. And I don't lie. Well, okay, maybe I do.

To: Ashlynn_D

ok

xoxo ~BROOKE~

And I immediately get a response.

From: Ashlynn_D

YES THANK U I PROMISE U WONT REGRET IT!

<3 ashlynn

Yeah. Right. So what am I supposed to do now? Ask him out?

Whatever. I'll just wing it when I get the chance.

Brett

I'm sure they'll be fine. Well, Sophia and Brooke, I mean. Like I told Trevor, if Daphne and Jackson haven't tried anything yet, then they probably won't. So we really have nothing to worry about.

Now all that's left to do is wait for them to get here. And listen to Corinne and Kellie arguing with Brandon that we could have a white Christmas.

A dumb subject, but anyway.

"No, seriously," Kellie is saying. "It's possible, Brandon. I mean, come on. Give it up."

"Please, Kellie. Let's think about it reasonably."

Kellie crosses her arms across her chest and gives him a look. "Okay, let's. Got a point?"

She's trying to seem tough, but it's not working. Kellie Hamilton just…isn't.

"Okay. First of all, when was the last time that we had a white Christmas in Saffrondale?" Brandon asks.

Kellie opens and closes her mouth in complete silence.

Brandon wins the battle! Well, Brandon has one point, Kellie has none. But you know what I mean.

Corinne finally decides which side to take: she defends her best friend. "Oh, come on, Brandon. That's just because no one actually remembers the exact years we have white Christmases."

Trevor gives me a weird look. He's probably thinking, 'What planet are these aliens from?' It's kind of true. I mean, who really discusses white Christmases? I mean, this in-depth? No one I – oh, forget that. I know these three a little too well to be saying that no one I know talks about white Christmases.

Plus I can't even get the girl I like to go out with me (even if she supposedly does like me back).

God. What a sad life.

~ Chapter Ten ~

Sophia

Oh, yes! Brad and Ashlynn are officially going out! Well, at least, they're going out on their first date tonight. But Brad probably doesn't want me around. Even if I would, like, die to be there. Besides, it's not like he'll have any issues with convincing Mom and Dad to let him out of the house. He's thirteen. Actually, no, he's soon to be fourteen. He'll be fine on his own. And if he does have even the tiniest problem with our parents, I'll step in and help him out. Besides, he's my little brother and I owe him a lot. The little sweetheart.

Okay, so maybe that's a little too much. But I plan to hang out with Trevor tonight. I mean, I'm sure Brooke will go somewhere with Brett, now that this, uh, 'drama' is all over. Now she has no excuse not to go, so ha. I win.

We're in the school building now, though, and near the gym.

"So," Brooke says. "Divide and conquer, I guess?"

Daphne nods.

I have to admit that I'm a little suspicious, though. Maybe Brooke has a point – maybe these two aren't meant to be trusted. Ever.

"Divide as in…?"

Brooke smiles at Daphne. Fake. But apparently only I can tell. "Daphne. You want to go through the ones on this side of the gym with me?" She waves across the left half of the gym.

Smart. Very smart. She clearly has thought of the fact that Daphne and Jackson could very easily sneak up on us and do something that might be dangerous to our health and safety if we leave them alone somewhere. And she just foiled that. I mean, if Daphne refuses to go with her, then that's obviously giving away that she has something sneaky planned here.

Daphne freezes. Jackson, on the other hand, remains expressionless as usual. Well, except for that dumb look on his face.

"That okay with you?" Brooke asks, sounding a little too smug to be innocent.

A crease forms between Daphne's eyebrows. "Yeah," she says, with her old, whiny, annoying voice that totally belongs to a *witch* (no offense) slowly starting to come back again (Cinderella, the clock's struck midnight, so everything's got to go back to the way it was – hurry and jump into the carriage – no, too late, now it's a pumpkin again), "why wouldn't it be okay?"

Brooke shrugs. "I don't know. Just checking." I can tell that she seems almost a little bit…disappointed? Bad Brooke. She's always looking for the bad in everyone these days. At least, today.

Oh, no, wait. Ew. That means I'm going to get paired up with Jackson. Oh, gee, thanks a lot for that one, Brooke.

"Jackson, you're with me, I guess," is all I can think of to say.

He nods. "Yeah. Come on. Let's go."

We walk over to the right side of the gym in silence. I mean, what is there to say when you're walking to a supply closet with the guy that buried you in pompoms in a supply closet a week and a half ago? Nothing, I would imagine, unless it isn't something very nice. And I can't really say anything nasty right now. First of all, he probably wouldn't understand what I'd be saying, and second of all, what a waste of time. Plus, I don't want to start something else here. I've got calmness (and it isn't just me that's feeling pretty peaceful, but the other three people I'm with – oh, my God, it isn't Trevor, Brett, and Brooke this time…instead it's Brooke, Daphne, and Jackson – are actually acting the same way) and that's what I'm going to keep.

"So."

We're standing outside one of the two main storage rooms. The other one is on the left side of the gym – where Brooke and Daphne are searching.

"Scared to go in?" he jokes, looking a little…nervous? Ha. No way. Not the big, scary Jackson Everett. Yeah. No, that's so not happening.

I shake my head. "No, not really. I'm more prepared this time. I've been practicing my karate moves in case someone like you tries to attack me again. Oh, and I've been learning judo, too, in case I didn't mention that yet," I tell him, trying to sound as serious as possible.

His eyes widen. "No way."

Wow. I should have expected him to think that I wasn't joking, but still. Somehow I'm surprised anyway.

"Yeah," I say. "All the way." It's all I can do now to stop myself from bursting out into laughter. After all…don't want to be making anyone feel bad about themselves for being so stupid. Ha, ha. Just kidding. All I want is a false sense of security. But Jackson doesn't know that it's false, so maybe it isn't. In a sense, in a way, somewhat.

"Wow. That's cool."

"Yeah, I know. Just warning you, you know, because if you, like, try anything, I'll do a demonstration. You'll get a choice of karate or judo, of course, but still. It won't help you much." Okay. So that might have been pushing it a little bit, but I totally couldn't help it. It's so much fun to watch him freak out like this.

"Wow," he says again. "That's scary."

Ha. Don't I just know how scared he is? I mean, he should be. I am a little more prepared, but it really isn't much. I definitely haven't been practicing judo or karate or anything like that. Just what I knew already, but like that was anything in the first place. I mean, it wasn't even karate. It was only kicks and stuff. But that doesn't matter. I doubt he'll even think about trying anything on me now. He's too scared of me.

Ha! Jackson Everett, scared of me, Sophia Garrison. And I thought that'll be the day. But no. It is today.

I'm so proud of myself.

Brooke

Wow. I didn't think we'd find all of this stuff. I mean, I don't even think we're going to need all of this. There's a dusty old balance beam, which we can definitely fix up pretty easily, and Daphne and I (oh, my God, what a shocker – we actually worked together to find this stuff!) also uncovered an extra stack of mats that no one has used. The gym teachers definitely can't say that they need these, because if it was true, then they would have used them already! But that's all we found just now…Daphne just said that maybe Sophia and Jackson found some stuff in the other main supply closet. And considering what we just found, it's actually pretty possible. We're having such great luck.

"You want to try dragging this out into the main area?" Daphne asks.

She and I are still a little stiff, and we so aren't friends. It's more like we're just classmates. Acquaintances. Peers. Whatever.

"Sure." I take another look at the beam and then rethink my

reasoning. "Wait. Do you think we can lift it? This one looks like it might be kind of heavy."

She puts her hands on her hips and gives me a look. The snotty old Daphne look. Something I have never admired about her. Something I never *will* admire about her. "What? Are you too weak? Or are you so scared that you don't want to risk pulling a muscle?"

That just about does it. She has me right where she wants me. At least, right where she thinks she wants me. I'm definitely not weak. Well, okay, maybe I kind of am, but I think I can lift this. With her help, anyway. And I will *not* pull a muscle.

"Oh, please. Come on, let's go."

She and I attempt to lift the balance beam. Attempt. But we don't succeed.

"Okay, weakling, let's give up," I say with a smirk. I can't help being a little catty. We still have our score to settle, even if she and Jackson *did* make a peace offering. It wasn't, like, a super fabulous peace offering, either. I don't know why it's such a big deal. But whatever.

"Fine," she shoots back. And then she tries to calm down. A noticeable change. "So now what? You want to try getting the mats out?"

I think it over and then shake my head. "No, not really. I mean, what's the point? We'll just waste our energy, since we have no team yet, and no one knows about it. Plus we might even get in more trouble" – I give her the once-over that she's given me only about oh, I don't know, maybe ten thousand times – "and you and Jackson really can't afford that."

She narrows her eyes like she's going to say something nasty and then thinks better of it. Instead, she smiles very, very faintly.

But it's still a smile. Wow. I actually can dis her and she'll smile?

Life is so good sometimes.

So very good.

Sophia

Wow, this sucks. I mean, I was expecting to find at least a few things that we could use for the team hidden away in the supply closet. But no. Jackson and I (shriek of horror) dug through every single stack of junk in that whole entire storage room, and guess what we came up with? Absolutely nothing. This is so bad. Brooke and I were totally counting on being able to find some things that we would be able to use for the team. We definitely can't buy all new equipment. That would be way too expensive.

"This sucks," I say aloud to Jackson.

He nods. "Yeah. But think about it this way. You don't have to use old junk."

Helpful, Jackson. So helpful.

"Thanks. Never thought of it that way."

He smiles to himself. And starts humming under his breath. Humming. No kidding. What a weirdo. No offense, but it's true.

We leave the storage room and join Brooke and Daphne.

"So much for that," I grumble to them.

Brooke raises one eyebrow. "Really?" she asks. "I thought you guys would find some stuff. I mean, we found a ton of extra mats and a pretty good balance beam."

"Pretty good?" Daphne repeats. "That's the best you're going to get. Especially for free. And for a school team. Saffrondale High School's gymnastic team, to be exact." She snorts.

"Hey," Brooke says, giving her a dirty look. I guess there's no long lost love between the two of them. "Shut it. Besides, we're going to be so much better than stupid Lodi Valley." She snickers. How many times do I have to think this? Bad Brooke. Bad, bad Brooke. Not like Daphne didn't deserve that one, but still. I guess I do have mixed feelings about these two. Daphne and Jackson. Hmm. That's bittersweet now.

"So," Jackson says. "We done here?"

I nod. "Yeah, I think so. I'm not really in the mood to search anywhere else."

Daphne sighs. "Me, neither. You think we can leave now?"

I nod again. "Yeah, that's the best thing to do, I guess."

Brooke has a mischievous look in her eyes. They're twinkling. I don't want to know what she's going to say next. "Daphne, are your arms too tired from trying to lift that beam? Or did you pull a muscle?"

Daphne squints at her and shakes her head. "Please. Let's get out of here."

The four of us leave the gym in silence. I've never gone through these halls with more than one companion and found the walk so quiet. We pass by the principal's office, and I think of Miss Warner, Mrs. Carson, and our dearly beloved Principal Walker.

Suddenly our peaceful stroll is interrupted. Miss Warner bursts out of the office, squealing at the top of her lungs.

"*You*!" she yells.

Brooke and I exchange a confused glance, and then we look at Daphne and Jackson, who are looking both unconcerned and guilty at the same time, if that's even possible. But you know what I mean.

"It's okay, Miss Warner," I say quickly. "They're just leaving."

She gives us a weird look. Like, 'Why are *you* walking with *them* and not *fighting*?'

I don't really know, Miss Warner. But it's not like I can say that.

"Okay." That's all she says. And then she leaves. Weird or what?

Daphne and Jackson don't say anything for a minute.

"Well," Daphne says slowly. "I guess that – that this is goodbye for now."

"Oh, I doubt it," Brooke says lightly. "I'm sure we'll see you around. I mean, we still live in the same town."

"Yeah," Daphne says. And then she starts smiling. "Of course, I will see you again when I'm cheerleading for Lodi Valley and beating you both in gymnastics. And Jackson will see you when he beats your boys in basketball."

Our boys!?

"Um, okay," I say. "Like that's going to happen."

"We'll always be the best here at Saffrondale High," Brooke adds. But she's smiling, too.

"'Bye," Daphne finally says.

"'Bye," Brooke and I repeat. What else is there to say?

Jackson gives a little wave and then the two of them disappear through the doors to the school.

And just like that, the two of them are gone. And I feel almost as if a tiny, really, really tiny part of me is gone with them. I have no idea why.

Miss Warner pokes her head out of the office door. "What was that all about?" she wants to know.

Brooke shakes her head. "We have no idea, Miss Warner. See you on Monday." And then we walk out of the building for what seems like the millionth time. And maybe it is by now. But the thing is, we've finally walked out of that building changed a little more than usual. And by that, I don't mean our outfits.

Trevor

All right, that's it. I think I've just about had enough of this. How much do these three need to argue about the wonders of whether or not Saffrondale is going to have a white Christmas this year? It feels like it's been years since Kellie Hamilton walked into Giordano's covered in snow. But really, it's only been less than an hour. Time flies when you're having fun. Too bad I'm not having any fun.

Brett looks like he's about to fall asleep.

Suddenly my phone starts ringing. "Hello?"

"Hey, Trevor!" Sophia sings out. How happy am I right now just to hear her voice…? "Did you know it's snowing?"

I groan. "Oh, God, *yes*."

"Sorry. Touchy subject?"

"Well, yeah. Kind of. Sorry about the reaction."

"No problem. You and Brett are still at Giordano's, right? I mean, that's where Brooke said you would be. I just wanted to check if you were still there."

"Oh, we're here. We're being bored out of our minds, but we're here."

Corinne throws me a dirty look. I give her a look of apology right back. Fake apology, but it's still something.

"Oh. Well, that sucks. But the good news is that we'll be there in, like, five minutes."

"Cool. Any bad news?"

There's silence on the other end of the line for a second.

"Sophia?"

"Oh. Oh, no, not really. But we have a lot to tell you. I mean a *lot*. You have no idea how much we have to tell you."

I hear Brooke in the background. "He gets the point, Sophia."

I laugh. "Yeah. I do get the point. But I can't wait to hear all of it. But promise me that it's interesting?"

She laughs, too. "Of course."

"Cool. 'Bye."

"'Bye, Trevor." She hangs up.

Brett's wide awake. "What did she say?"

"They're almost here."

"Oh. Oh, good." And then he goes into hyper mode. "Do I look okay? Is my hair messed up because I had my head on the counter?"

"Come on, Brett, chill." I lower my voice so that Corinne, Kellie, and Brandon can't hear me. "You know that Brooke definitely likes you. So tell me: what are you killing yourself over all of this for?"

He shrugs. "I don't know. Besides, how can you be so sure about it?"

"I know it. And so do you. Come on, man."

He smiles. "Yeah, you're right."

The door swings open and Brooke and Sophia come hurtling in.

"Oh, my God," Brooke bubbles. "We have so much to tell you."

As if I didn't know that already.

Brooke

The story is out. Everywhere. I mean, once Corinne found out about everything, it spread like wildfire.

And now Corinne, Brandon, and Kellie are gone – no doubt to tell everyone what they just found out. The gymnastics stuff, the whole story on Daphne and Jackson's future lives – basically everything.

I nudge Trevor. If he doesn't ask Sophia out now, it's never going to happen.

He nods at me. "Sophia."

She looks up from her hot chocolate. Her expression's kind of dreamy. Gee, I wonder who she's thinking about. "Hmm?" she asks.

"Let's get out of here."

She beams. So sweet. It's, um, a little…ugh. "Okay," she says right away.

They get up and walk towards the door, and as they leave the restaurant, Brett and I watch through the window as Trevor shyly kisses Sophia on the cheek. I can almost hear her giggle. How adorable. They're finally officially together.

Now if only for me and Brett. If only.

"Brett," I suddenly hear myself saying. "You want to go see a movie or something?"

He smiles at me, looking more radiant than I've ever seen him. "Yeah. Definitely."

I think he gets it. That I'm taking back my rejection.

We leave Giordano's and head to the nearby movie theater. Brett goes to the ticket counter, and I go to get the popcorn and drinks. Although I think it's just mostly a formality – not like we're really going to be hungry or anything. Luckily there's a movie starting in a minute or so. And Brett just got a pair of tickets.

We walk into the theater and grab seats in the back. The trailers are already through, and the movie's just starting.

"So," Brett whispers as the beginning credits fly by on the screen to some surprisingly calming music, "everything's, uh, cool with us?"

"Us?" I repeat, smiling to myself.

Oh, my God. *'Us!?'* Ashlynn is definitely going to want to hear about every tiny bit of this. And duh, I'm so going to want to know how her date with Brad goes. Young love. So cute.

"Of course. Why wouldn't it be?" I say, trying to sound all casual, when really my heart is beating so fast I swear it could explode.

He shrugs kind of uncomfortably. And pauses. Like he doesn't exactly know what to say. He runs a hand through his hair. Too cute. "I don't know. Gym. That day. Before class. Well, you know."

Oh. Right. That.

I nod. "Well, yeah. But now that's just…whatever. Everything is just…different now. Everything – and everyone – that ruined our lives for the past few weeks is over. For, like, the first time since the four of us became friends, it's actually all calm. No worries left. It's like a fairy-tale ending. Except the thing is…that it's better than it ever was before."

"Yeah." Brett's smiling to himself.

I glance at Brett out of the corner of my eye.

We've barely said very much to each other, yet somehow I

know that we're glad to have each other's company. Well, more than that, of course.

I see Brett turn to grin at me through the dimmed lights, and seeing him so happy makes me smile, too.

And just when I think I could never be happier to be here in Saffrondale with him, and knowing that my other two best friends are so happy together, Brett leans over and just closes the distance between us without a single word. I could never dream of a more perfect kiss than this one.

And for me?

I think that this is the happiest fairy-tale ending yet.

The End

Printed in the United States
201016BV00005B/5/A